Advance

A Beginner's Guide to Starting Over

"Gabi Coatsworth's debut novel, *A Beginner's Guide to Starting Over*, tenderly explores grief, self-discovery, and reinvention in middle life. Readers will cheer for Molly as she learns that standing on one's own often requires getting comfortable with leaning on others. The heartwarming, hopeful tale is also a gentle reminder that it's possible to fall in love more than once in a lifetime."

> — Jamie Beck, *Wall Street Journal* bestselling author

"To start over, Molly Stevenson, a widow, mother, and owner of a bookstore, must let go. Not an easy task for a 50-year-old woman whose dead husband Simon is speaking to her from the grave—providing business advice and telling her who to date. Anyone who has had to begin again, to strike out on her own, make a new life and new friends, will relate to this debut novel... Gabi has been there and has an inspiring story with a happy ending to tell."

> — Marilyn Simon Rothstein, author of *Crazy to Leave You*

"A warm, engaging novel about love, friendship, and starting over, with a protagonist you will root for from the very first page! Molly is resilient, honest, and complex—in short, everything you could ask for in a protagonist. This is a book about second-chance love and so much more, written by an author who knows how to tell a story. Lovely!"

> — Barbara Josselsohn, author of *The Lilac House* and *The Cranberry Inn*

"Unforgettable and nuanced, Gabi Coatsworth delivers a heart-warming novel about the risks we must take to have a second chance. This is a book begging to be read cozied up in a chair, a fireplace blazing, and a cuppa tea in your hand. Prepare to sit a spell—Molly's stumbling journey to embrace the future will keep you soaring through the pages and by the end, Molly will feel like a much-loved old friend."

— Carla Damron, author of *The Orchid Tattoo* and *The Stone Necklace*

"*A Beginner's Guide to Starting Over* follows the delightful journey of Molly Stevenson and her loyalty to a former love, while confronting the challenge of striking out on her own, and opening her heart to a new relationship. You will fall in love with the characters. A heartfelt read."

— Lita Harris, author of *Christmas in Brookside Falls*

"Gabi Coatsworth absolutely nails the emotional journey of a middle-aged woman faced with losing a love and starting over. Her humorous and uplifting style makes this a delightful read."

— Marie W. Watts, author of *Only a Pawn*

"...Readers will eagerly root for the highly relatable Molly Stevenson as she navigates unchartered waters later in life and allows herself to be open to love again..."

— *BookLife*

A Beginner's Guide to Starting Over

A NOVEL

GABI COATSWORTH

atmosphere press

Published by Atmosphere Press

ISBN 978-1-63988-853-5

Cover design by Felipe Betim

Atmospherepress.com

For Madelyn and Charlotte, who started bragging that
I was a writer while they were in elementary school

CHAPTER ONE

Molly Stevenson looked around the Book Boutique at the end of another long day before switching off the lights and locking the front door. She loved this place, with its smell of paper, its loyal customers, and its solid presence on Brentford's Main Street. Simon's support for her taking it on had been the deciding factor, and the shop had turned out to be a welcome respite from the grief she felt.

But it was still losing money. She hadn't managed to pay herself for the last two months and was living off her savings. The upcoming Christmas season needed to produce its annual increase in sales, or the business would go under, leaving her in debt she had no way of repaying.

And the town would lose its only bookstore, which would be a crime. She wouldn't think about that. She stuffed the day's mail and the letter she still hadn't opened into her messenger bag, and started for home.

Darkness had fallen sometime before she reached her front door. She took out the key and turned it in the lock. Returning to the unlit, empty Victorian often seemed like the most daunting part of losing Simon. It made Molly feel like an actual widow—something she managed to avoid thinking about as she kept busy at the bookshop during the day.

That evening, as if summoned by the rasp of the latchkey, an orange missile came hurtling up the porch steps, and Hemingway stood there, demanding to be let in.

"Hello, you," she murmured. A loud rumble came from somewhere near her feet. As she swung the door open, the cat swaggered into the house ahead of her and made for the kitchen.

She followed him, shrugged off her coat, and threw it onto one of the barstools, where it promptly slid off. She should hang it up in the closet when she came in.

"Come on, Molly—you can do better than this," she said aloud. Was that really her voice? Now and then, she reminded herself of her mother with her relentless—though well-meant—advice.

Mummy would have told her to deal with that bloody letter from her landlord immediately.

Opening the refrigerator door instead, she groaned at the sight of the tired onion, a slightly wrinkled zucchini, and a large eggplant staring back at her from the middle shelf. The idea was that they'd be in her line of vision, so she'd remember to use them, but the plan had failed. She could make ratatouille. She checked the few tomatoes lounging on the island. One of them had a problematic black spot near the stalk, but the other two might be salvageable. Besides, cooking would be soothing.

At least she'd remembered to buy food for the cat, who was now sitting, tail wrapped around his feet, expectant eyes fixed on her. Grateful for his presence, she prepared a dish of Frisky Feast and set it down in the usual place. Hemingway sniffed at it like a Borgia at a banquet with his relatives, and then, apparently deciding it wasn't poisoned, crouched down and started to eat. She wondered how he managed to chew and purr at the same time.

Molly had been making dinner a couple of years before when Hemingway showed up during a late spring thunderstorm, sodden and suspicious. She'd embraced the challenge involved in gaining his confidence, now that, with Simon gone and her daughters away at school, there was no one else around on whom to lavish her affection.

It occurred to her she'd become a cliché—a widow with a cat. Perfect.

Tonight, he'd evidently been waiting for her to return from the Book Boutique.

She would *not* think about the shop—but she couldn't avoid it either. Despite her efforts, sales were only improving at a glacial pace. Her latest bank statement had only confirmed that she would run out of money within months. If something didn't change, and soon, she'd be broke by her next big birthday—a failed businesswoman at fifty. And a lonely widow, too.

The thought of that banished her hunger. Abandoning the idea of cooking for herself, she made a toasted cheese sandwich with the sliced loaf that was beginning to dry out. Having eaten it, she began to write a list of things she needed to do at work. Tidy gift table. Chase incoming orders. Buy British tea bags for the shop.

She knew she was skirting the real issue.

She re-checked the bank statement. Some miracle in the last two hours might show she was inexplicably making a profit. Nope. Nothing had changed.

Now for the letter from Pilgrim Properties. She'd been ignoring it since that morning when the mailman delivered it. Envelopes from landlords only signaled trouble. But she mustn't shirk the task any longer.

She pulled it out of her bag and, picking up the nearest knife, slit it open. A chill ran down her back.

Not even *Dear So-and-So.* Just: *To Whom it may Concern.* How obnoxious. The message only added to her indignation. *Due to circumstances beyond our control, it has become necessary to levy an increase on your rent when the lease is up for renewal, beginning January 1.*

There followed a sum so substantial that they must know she would never be able to pay it.

It has become necessary? Who talked like that? Someone who didn't want to take the blame for putting a lovely bookshop out of business, that's who. Naturally, no one had signed their name to it. *Sincerely, Pilgrim Properties*. Ha.

Buying the bookstore where she'd been an employee had proved a satisfying project to begin with. Just enough of a challenge to occupy her time after Simon died. It was that, for sure. She loved the shop, but its problems haunted her dreams, making her wonder whether she'd got her priorities right. Did she want all the stress of running a business? It would be more fun to get out and see her friends, or travel, maybe.

She couldn't quit. She had to prove to herself that she could succeed as an independent businesswoman. That would bring her the respect and recognition that being a wife and mother never had. And, in theory, money she'd earned herself.

This was all Simon's fault. If he hadn't died, she'd have been content with her part-time job at the Book Boutique, without the responsibility and the headaches of ownership. If only she hadn't allowed herself to be persuaded to take on the store, if she hadn't...if, if, if.

To be fair, Simon hadn't exactly *made* her buy it. Because she'd only owned the shop for ten months. And the love of her life had been dead for thirty-seven months, five weeks, and four days.

"*Cheer up.*" She could hear his reassuring voice in her head. "*This will all be okay in the end, you'll see.*"

She didn't see. Not at all. But these internal conversations with him often helped her work things out.

"I can't imagine how. I should just cut my losses and quit," she said aloud, sounding whiny, she could tell. "Except there's no one who'd want the Book Boutique now. I was the only dimwit who was remotely interested in the business."

She stood and began pacing the kitchen floor. Hemingway gave a quick shudder in his sleep, stretched, and dozed off again. He must be exhausted. She knew how he felt.

"*Molly, honey, I wish you'd let me help you.*" Simon again.

"Don't you think you've done enough already?"

A note of hurt entered his voice. "*It wasn't my fault I had a*

6

heart defect, you know."

He'd been found unconscious on the sidewalk halfway through his morning run. There'd been no time to say goodbye. So, she never had.

"You could have had regular checkups." She'd never mentioned this to him before and knew she was being unjust, since no one in his family had suffered from the same health issue. But his death wasn't fair to her, either.

"Anyway," she rallied, "buying the bookstore was your idea, and now I seem to have made a mess of it. If the shop goes under, I'll have to go out and get a proper paying job—selling kitchen stuff in a hardware store. Or sell the house. Move to an apartment with wonky heating and mice."

She was getting into it now. Almost enjoying the worst-case scenario. Molly adjusted her imaginary mob cap and pulled a fictitious tattered shawl around her against the chill winds of imminent bankruptcy.

Simon's voice brought her back down to earth.

"You're not living in some Dickensian novel, you know. You're a twenty-first-century woman and you have choices."

"Choices? I only have enough money to keep the store going for a few more months, and now there's this rent demand—"

Simon interrupted her. *"You know what? You're more inclined to go down with the ship than to ask for a life preserver."*

Molly racked her brain for an answer to this and came up with nothing. No life preserver would save her.

"You've always taken care of others, yet you won't allow anyone to be there for you in return. People would love to pitch in, sweetheart, because you're a wonderful person and they want you to succeed. But you have to let them know you need help. And you can start with me."

"Start with you? You're not even here."

"That's kinda harsh, don't you think?"

The kitchen fell silent. Only a tiny snuffle emanating from Hemingway's bed broke the stillness.

"Oh, Simon. I didn't mean…"

"*I know, honey. It's the stress talking. So, item one. You need more information.*"

"Like what?"

"*Like the name of a live person at Pilgrim Properties. Someone you can talk to about this. Maybe you can negotiate a smaller increase with a living human instead of a faceless office.*"

He always came up with something.

"Good idea. What's item two?"

"*There is no item two.*"

Okay then.

CHAPTER TWO

Though only early November, most of the leaves, so brilliant a few days before, lay sodden on the sidewalk as Molly headed to work the next morning. The walking formed part of a new regimen that had almost perished at its inception, due to rain and wind, but she persevered. Expecting wet weather, she dug out Simon's old yellow slicker, the only truly waterproof coat she had, and grabbed an umbrella.

At the last minute, she remembered to pack a pair of dry shoes in her bag, in case hers became soggy. But all she encountered was a damp mist, which put her in a more cheerful frame of mind as she unlocked the front door of the store, stepped inside, and inhaled the smell of books. There was nothing else like it.

She'd always found herself drawn to books and couldn't pass a bookshop without going in to browse. To see how the competition arranged its displays. To chat with the owners about successful new releases and disappointing reads. Admire the brightly colored covers. Now she owned this beautiful old-fashioned place.

She switched on the lights and booted up the computer. Checked the cash in the register. She headed into the back to divest herself of the slicker and give herself a last-minute once-over in the mirror. For heaven's sake. Were those gray hairs among the dark blond ones? Too much stress, that was the problem. It didn't help that the cut was growing out unevenly. She swiped her pink lipstick across her mouth before eyeing the boxes of new titles.

She usually enjoyed Tuesdays, when she got to unbox all the latest releases. She'd ordered some of the new Lucinda Parks, of course, and intended to read one herself. She wanted to bring the author to the store one day for a signing—just as soon as she was able to guarantee the sizable audience publishers generally required.

No sign of Luke yet, which wasn't unusual. He wasn't renowned for his timekeeping. As the former owner of the Book Boutique, he'd become accustomed to keeping his own hours—which was why he'd originally hired Molly part-time.

She reached absentmindedly for a mini Snickers bar from the bowl of leftover Halloween treats.

Never mind. She'd have time to call her best friend Amanda to get the name of someone at Pilgrim Properties. Amanda Shaughnessy was a Realtor, with her finger on the pulse of anything to do with the buying, leasing, and renting of property in Brentford and beyond, so if anyone could get the information, she could.

"Hi, sweetie. How are you doing? Any eligible men on the horizon yet?"

Amanda meant well, but Molly sometimes wished she would give it a rest. She'd been commenting on Molly's love life since they were college roommates, and nothing had changed. There was a testy note to her voice when she answered.

"Actually, it's a businessman I have a problem with today."

Amanda's voice lost its teasing tone. "Something I can help with?"

"I hope so." Molly explained about the rent increase. "Do you know anyone at Pilgrim Properties? I can't get hold of a real person when I call their number."

"I don't believe I've had any dealings with them myself. I know they own some of the commercial real estate in town, but they tend to handle their own rentals. Let me ask around."

"Thanks. They're trying to raise my rent, and I need to negotiate some sort of reprieve or I'm in serious trouble here."

"Oh, wow. Look, don't worry, I'll let you know as soon as I can. And if worse comes to worst, maybe I can find you somewhere less expensive."

But I don't want a new place, Molly thought, as she hung up.

The old-fashioned bell above the door rang—it bounced on a spring whenever anyone walked in, and she found the sound reassuring. With any luck, it would be a customer.

A familiar figure blew in like a galleon in full sail and moored in front of the bestseller table. On this chilly day, the woman wore a navy-blue serge overcoat buttoned high under her chin. Molly recognized it as her late-autumn coat. Never a down jacket or a parka for Mrs. Todd.

She nodded at Molly and glanced around, no doubt hoping Luke would appear.

Mrs. Todd formed part of Luke's particular clientele—a group of wealthy older women who actually bought books after they finished browsing. Molly suspected that they cherished romantic notions about Luke. Pointless, naturally, since he never made a secret of the fact that he was gay. Still, they batted their eyelashes at him and placed a hand on his arm as if to anchor him to their side while they discussed what to buy next.

Unable to locate him, Mrs. Todd scanned the volumes before her through her oversized red spectacles, her only nod to a youthful style. She picked up the new Baldacci thriller, without even pretending to glance at it

Where was Luke? This was one of his foremost groupies. Molly smiled at her, and in response, the old lady walked over to the register.

"Where's your top adviser today?"

Molly cleared her throat. "He'll be in soon, but I expect I can help you."

"I'm here, dear." Thank heavens. Luke appeared from the back, well-groomed as always. Today he was sporting the bow tie with pumpkins on it, as a tribute to fall. She reflected, not for the first time, that though he was probably in his sixties, he was still handsome—and capable of being immensely charming when he put his mind to it. No surprise that his female customers were attracted to him.

"Good morning, Mrs. Todd."

"Now, how many times do I have to tell you, Luke? It's Acacia."

Good grief. No wonder he kept it formal. Molly cast about for a way to escape. "I'll go and find your order, shall I? We had some deliveries yesterday."

"I put it behind the register. Let me," said Luke, reaching past her. He pulled out the latest weighty bestseller about climate change and walked around to show it to Mrs. T.

"That's the one." She beamed. "How much do I owe you?"

He glanced at the back cover and rang her up.

"Paper bag?" he inquired, though as a rule, they only offered them if it was raining outside or if people asked.

"No, thanks. Save a tree," she said, giving Luke a coy glance.

Molly rolled her eyes. Did she have any idea that this man would never repay her interest in him? As for the save-a-tree nonsense—she'd just bought a four hundred-page tome, for goodness's sake. Must be at a minimum half a tree, right there. But she kept her thoughts to herself, simply winking at him as she went through to the back to unpack the day's deliveries. When she emerged with a handful of the most recent releases, all she saw was Mrs. Todd's back as the door closed behind her.

Luke took the books out of her hand. "I'll shelve these. Unless another member of my fan club comes in." He gave her a wry smile.

"Do you really want me to save you from flirtatious customers?"

"Well, no. Of course, they can be exhausting." He grinned at her. "They seem to have no clue that, if anything, I might prefer their husbands." A thought appeared to strike him. "Though they're no great shakes, either, from what I've seen."

Molly laughed. "I promise I'll make every effort to head amorous women off at the pass," she said, knowing perfectly well that he rather liked his bunch of devotees.

"Thanks, boss. And after I've put these out, what's first on the list?" Luke teased her about her lists, but they were the only way she could stay organized. Besides, the teasing was always affectionate.

"Well, the back of the counter is a mess, but I'll handle that. How about you start with the other special orders? Someone's waiting for the Margaret Atwood and I told her we'd call when it came in…"

"Okay."

"And keep all the documentation to one side for me to look at. Thanks."

***

"Want anything from next door?" asked Luke. Molly looked at her watch. Two-thirty already.

"Yes, please. I'd love a small cappuccino."

"Sure. Back in a few."

While he was gone, the customer who'd ordered the Atwood walked in.

"I happened to be getting a coffee and bumped into Luke. He told me my book is in."

"You're Jenny Donovan, right? Yes, it is." Molly smiled and turned to the shelf behind her. "I expect you'll find a message from him when you get home. And, if you'd like to leave your cell phone number, we can text you next time. It might be quicker."

Molly knew this customer was the mother of five-year-old

twins—she'd brought them in once or twice. *Start children's storytime*, she wrote on her list, while the woman signed her credit card slip.

"Good idea. By the way, I don't suppose you know of any book clubs around here? I'd love to have someone to talk books with."

The only one Molly knew of was the worthy but specialized Christian reading group at the church. They ordered their books from the Book Boutique, for which she was grateful, but if this young woman liked Margaret Atwood, she might not be the right fit.

"There's the one at St. Michael's," she said. "But I've been thinking of starting one here. Would you like me to take your name and let you know when I do?"

"That would be cool."

Start book club. She'd have to stay in business to do it.

As she walked out the door, Mrs. Donovan almost bumped into Amanda coming in.

Molly raised her eyes from the gift table, where she'd begun sorting through what remained after Halloween. She glanced at the last horrible spider with the flashing green eyes. They'd been an unexpected success with children.

"Hi, there. That was quick. You have a name for me already?"

Amanda shook her head. "Sorry, not yet. But I'm working on it. And I did look around for other locations for a bookstore, but there's nothing available right now." She shrugged. "Oh, well. By the way, I meant to tell you when you called—I think this is yours."

She opened her hand to reveal a pocket mirror. It winked in a stray sunbeam as she placed it on top of the pile of invoices.

"Really?"

"Yes. Or, at least, I think so. I found it after we had coffee at the Java Jive the other day—wedged into the chair you were sitting in."

Molly picked it up, and her face brightened. "You know, this has been missing for a few days. Do you suppose it's been there all this time?"

"Well, it is your favorite spot. In any case, I daresay you're glad to have it back."

Molly gave her an inquiring glance. "Meaning?"

"Oh, nothing. It's just…um…I think you might have lost interest in how you look lately," said Amanda. "Not surprising," she added hastily. "You have a lot on your plate."

They'd known each other for so long that Molly paid attention when her friend commented on her demeanor or looks. She was a true friend, the sort who'd let you know you had spinach in your teeth. Or if she thought you were about to make a terrible mistake. She'd tell you what you needed to know and would take no pleasure in it. She often noticed something going on beneath the surface that Molly hadn't been aware of.

"I didn't know it showed. But you're right. I spotted some gray hairs coming through this morning." She grimaced as she lifted a strand and dropped it again.

"Exactly. That's an easy fix, but you have to take the first step."

Just because Amanda was right, didn't mean Molly had to like what she said. "I don't have time for that stuff. In any case, there's no one to see it."

"If you're saying that Simon won't see it, I get it. But there are other people in the world. Your customers, for a start."

There was such a thing as too much honesty, but Amanda was oblivious.

"You know what? You need to pamper yourself a bit more. Get a haircut and color, and a manicure while you're at it. Pick a day when you're not too busy, and Rosie will be delighted to fix you up."

Rosario Diaz owned Shear Madness, Brentford's premier salon. She'd been cutting Molly's hair for several years and knew just how to do it, so the cut lasted for at least six weeks. Feeling a frisson of guilt, Molly realized that her last visit had been two months ago, if not longer. She'd ask Rosie to squeeze her in soon if she could.

She glanced in the little mirror and smoothed her hair, hoping to improve it. The door pinged again, and a couple of giggling teenage girls came in, putting a stop to the conversation.

"Listen, Amanda, I can't talk about this now. I'm trying to work." She indicated the newcomers with a wave of her hand.

"Oh, kids that age never buy anything, do they? You've got time to spruce yourself up."

Molly raised the mirror and took another, longer, look. Seeing her lipstick worn away to a mere hint of its original color, she winced and replaced the depressing item face down on the counter. Her naturally rosy cheeks looked paper white. It might be the lighting, and pink light bulbs might help. More likely, she'd forgotten to put makeup on that day.

Simon had always paid attention when she made an effort to look especially good. But what was the point if there was no one around to notice? She gave herself a quick mental shake to stop this train of thought and glanced ruefully at Amanda.

"I suppose I am rather disheveled. The advantage and disadvantage of Luke being the guy I spend most of my time with—apart from Hemingway—is that he never notices my appearance."

"Could be he's being tactful." Amanda put an arm around her shoulders and tilted her head toward the girls. "Why don't I keep an eye on your ... um ... customers?" She indicated cynical air quotes. "And you go and freshen up."

"All right, thanks," she said. "Back in a second."

To her astonishment, when she returned to the shop floor a few minutes later, the two girls were standing by the cash register, holding a book each and chatting with Amanda.

"Ah, there you are," she said. "These young ladies would like to purchase something."

"Wonderful." Molly tried not to sound surprised. In truth,

she was amazed. She glanced at the titles. *A Teenager's Guide to Love and Sex*, and *100 Things Your Parents Won't Tell You.* They'd been on the self-help shelf for a while, partly because Luke didn't feel qualified to recommend them. And she'd forgotten they were there. Yet it hadn't taken five minutes for her sophisticated friend to make a sale.

She rang the girls up, and they walked out, chatting animatedly.

"Thanks. I mean it. I'm fine with providing the books if teenagers know what they want, but I haven't read those, so making recommendations is harder."

"I never thought about it that way. Anyway, let's hope those girls find them helpful."

"I'll make a point of at least skimming them in future, so I know what I'm talking about. Times have changed since we were young."

"Which reminds me. Do you have a minute? I want to talk to you about something. I have a suggestion."

Molly had an idea of what was coming and didn't want to discuss it. "Can't it wait?"

Amanda looked around. "You're not precisely swamped with customers. Have you had lunch?"

Molly had only eaten a slice of toast for breakfast and suddenly felt ravenous. And the Java Jive made her favorite sandwich—roasted veggies on a baguette.

"You go ahead, I'll take care of things," Luke said, appearing behind them, holding out a cappuccino. "I can drink this. I put sugar in it by mistake, sorry."

Best to get the conversation with her friend over and done with. "Okay, just ten minutes," she said. Staying resolute wasn't always easy in the face of Amanda's determined "suggestions."

CHAPTER THREE

Having ordered, Amanda and Molly managed to grab a table with two mid-century modern chairs by the window in the Java Jive. While they waited for their lunch to arrive, they chatted about their children (wonderful), the bookstore (not so much), and the real estate business (slow).

But after a few minutes of this, Molly could tell that her old college roommate was about to launch into what her friend claimed was "suggesting" something, and Molly called nagging. Amanda leaned forward and looked her in the eye, keeping her voice low.

"Molly, honey, I understand that you're anxious about the shop, and I will help with that as much as I can. But I'm worried about you—you're neglecting your social life."

Here it came. The reason she was getting grief about her appearance.

Amanda launched right into her previous campaign like a used-car salesperson. "Look, it's been three years since Simon passed. I think it's time you considered road-testing some men," she said.

Molly sighed. Her friend was so predictable. Direct to the point of insensitivity, sometimes. It was all very well for her to go on about finding a man—she didn't need to. She and Jim had been happily married for years and she thought everyone else should be too.

They didn't understand how much she still missed Simon because she rarely talked about him now. People imagined she was "over him," though she didn't think she ever would be. She had no reason to change the status quo. Her friendships were enough. If she began dating, her memories of Simon might disappear—and she wasn't ready for that.

Molly pushed a strand of hair behind one ear and tightened her jaw.

"I've had all the advice I can take about moving on and closure. I don't know what that means, and I doubt anyone who hasn't lost the love of their life does either."

Amanda's eyebrows shot up in surprise. "You still feel that strongly about it?"

Molly was aware that the world expected her to move on. But they had no idea of the butterflies that invaded her insides at the very thought of risking love again. Not pretty little colored ones. Enormous luna moths as big as her hand, bumping into each other inside her chest. They were there now. She breathed in to calm herself and searched for an excuse that would put Amanda off for good, before coming up with a string of them. They sounded a little weak, even to her.

"I'm too old to look for someone new. The bookshop takes up most of my time. And I'm fine as I am, so I don't need a man. In any case, it's not like there's anyone eligible around here," she said, flicking a crumb off her pants. It had been a nice sandwich, though she should probably have chosen a salad, as her friend had. Her current regime of walking to work whenever she could hadn't produced any results yet. She could feel a persistent tightness in her jeans when she tried to zip them up.

She certainly wasn't in any kind of shape to go out on dates, even if she wanted to, which she didn't. Although, truth to tell, she sometimes missed a warm body next to her at night. Not just any body. It was Simon she yearned for.

"Earth to Molly. Come in, Molly."

She blinked.

Amanda was smiling at her. "Are you sure? I know it's been ages, but we're not talking about anything too scary. Just someone for company. A lack of local candidates shouldn't hold you back. Everyone meets people online now." She reached out and put a hand on her friend's knee. "Don't you get lonely? You have to begin to live again, or you'll find yourself stuck without someone to love." Her old college roommate wasn't about to let it go. "You might keep going for another fifty years, you know."

"Perish the thought." She tried to be flippant. But Amanda was right. People lived much longer these days.

"Point is, you don't want to spend those decades alone, do you?"

Molly bristled. "I've got Heather and Jackie—they'll marry someday. And there'll be grandchildren and…" She trailed off. She didn't want to be one of those women whose children were their only interest. And she *was* lonely, even with Simon to "talk" to.

"They've only just gone away to school, so marriage and babies could be a long way off, or not even happen at all. You can't depend on that."

"I know. But I can't handle any more change right now."

"I get that. But it might do you good. You just need to figure out what's holding you back and fix it."

As if putting her back together just required a tube of super glue.

Amanda leaned across the table to deliver the *coup de grace*. "Besides, Heather and Jackie wouldn't want you to be lonely."

It was true that her daughters had hinted—quite strongly, and more than once—that she should make a new life for herself. Molly suspected they'd be less anxious about her if she were trying for a fresh start, rather than just drifting.

Amanda was frowning at her.

"Sorry, what? I lost track."

"I think the girls worry about you being on your own." She paused. "And you know Simon would want you to be happy."

Why did people always think they knew best what Simon wanted? Not even Molly, who'd been married to him for twenty-five years, could say for sure.

"Honey?" Amanda waved a hand in front of her friend's face.

She squeezed her eyes shut, then opened them again and dragged her mind back to the here and now. She picked up her cup and checked the contents. It was empty, but she pretended to sip at it to give herself time to subdue her irritation before replying.

"I know he'd want me to be okay," she said. "And I am. Honestly. I have you and Rosie and my other friends. Plus, my work."

"But that's not everything." Amanda gave her an earnest glance. "You need some fun too."

Amanda and Rosie were her best friends, but neither of them loved the arts as much as she did. They'd sometimes sacrifice themselves on the altar of friendship and accompany her to a production at the local playhouse. Not that they ever complained.

Occasionally, to reciprocate, she would subject herself to a rock concert featuring their favorite, if aging, performers. Though she never learned to appreciate Madonna or the Red Hot Chili Peppers the way they did.

Amanda was still talking. "You ought to check out a couple of online dating sites. People get lucky there all the time. Look at Rosie—she got herself a really cute guy that way."

Molly discounted this last remark. True, Rosie had found her prince, Rocco, but only after kissing a lot of frogs.

"I've sometimes thought that if there was a website that matched women like me with a presentable man who doesn't want sex—"

Amanda laughed. "You'd be dating a gay man."

"No complications. No strings ..." Molly could tell she sounded wistful.

Amanda rolled her eyes. "Meeting a new man doesn't have to be complicated. And no one's asking you to commit for life," she said. "At least, consider it."

"Don't you have a house to show this afternoon or something, instead of worrying about me?"

Amanda glanced at her watch. "I do. And I mustn't be late. House sales are kind of slow these days, so I can't afford to miss any chances. I'll get back to you with a name at Pilgrim Properties ASAP."

With that, she air-kissed Molly's cheek, turned on a scarlet heel, and strode out of the café.

Outside, the town green was leached of color as the November sun struggled to break through an overcast sky. Time to return to work.

CHAPTER FOUR

Luke was ringing up what looked like a large sale when she walked back in. He was scanning a pile of Halloween books for children, now heavily discounted to get them off the shelves. He turned to Molly after the shopper left.

"She's going to donate them to the school library," he said, as if an explanation were required.

"Excellent. They'll have them for next year. Well done."

"What would you like me to do now?" Luke said.

"If you've finished shelving the new arrivals, we ought to get started on the holiday stock."

"You mean the book displays? Isn't it too soon for that? We haven't had Thanksgiving yet."

"We have books featuring Thanksgiving in the kids' section, remember? We should bring those to the front. Plus the cards, those pumpkin fridge magnets, and the make-your-own paper turkey kits. It's only three weeks away."

"I guess you're right, at that." Luke made a face. "This place is becoming more of a gift store every day."

"No reason to sound quite so much like Eeyore," Molly said. "You know those things contribute a decent amount to the bottom line, and people usually purchase a book too. We need all the sales we can make."

Molly knew that deep down Luke believed bookstores should only sell books. He disdained the major chains that now featured cafés, toys, and games.

He harrumphed, and she ignored him.

"Okay. You take the Thanksgiving items and put them out. I'll sort through the other stuff. I'll be in the back if you need me, unpacking the Thanksgiving murder mysteries as well as the Christmas books," she said. "They came in this morning."

"I'll make sure they're up at the front. By the way, I want to ask your advice. I've got a friend who wants to move to Brentford and needs somewhere to live. Any ideas?"

Molly switched mental gears. "The house next door to me is still vacant. You remember. Bert Bowman's place?"

He nodded, though Molly was almost certain he'd never met the man. The Victorian cottage had stood empty since Bert passed away a few years after his wife. They'd been friends, and she still missed him. After Simon died, he'd offered a supportive ear from time to time. Molly would take him dinner or a piece of homemade apple cake, and they'd eat at the scratched but clean pine table in the kitchen, while they reminisced about their lost partners. No point in letting her thoughts stray that way. She must focus on the future.

"Who's your friend? Anyone I know?"

He shook his head. "I don't believe you've met him, no."

"No problem. So, is it just for him, or does he have a family?"

"Nick's unattached, so far as I know. Ever since Sam left him a couple of years ago, he's been avoiding relationships. At any rate, that's my take on it."

It might be interesting to have one of Luke's friends next door. No point in getting ahead of herself though. This was only an inquiry. In any case, he might hate Bert's little house, which could use a facelift.

"Want me to put him in touch with Amanda? She can show him the house. No one's bought it, she says, and so she's persuaded Bert's nephew to rent it out. No takers yet, because it's not that big and needs sprucing up, but if your friend is willing to give it a coat of paint, it may suit him."

Luke shrugged. "I don't think he would mind that. Nick's quite handy. He fixed a running toilet in my house the last time he visited."

Well, that would make him a useful neighbor, even if they never went anywhere together.

At the first party she went to at Luke's, a Cinco de Mayo celebration, Molly had a moment's misgiving when she realized she'd need to talk to so many complete strangers. But Luke never let people languish on the sidelines. After a while, and one or maybe two of his signature grapefruit margaritas, she'd relaxed and learned to enjoy the evening. No one expected her to flirt, which suited her just fine. She'd accepted several more invitations after that. Still, she didn't think she'd ever come across Nick. Or Sam.

"Is he moving up here because of you?" Molly, always a romantic at heart, smiled as she contemplated Luke finding a partner. Everyone looked like part of a couple, or headed that way. Not that she envied them the search for someone new.

He laughed. "Not precisely. He's got a job over at Carnarvon College—biology professor. Quite a coup apparently, since he tells me they hire people with more experience, as a rule. By which he means older, I suspect."

An academic sounded like a serious person. She knew almost nothing about college-level biology. He might not share her thirst for culture at all.

"So how old *is* he?" she asked, "if he's a young professor."

"Somewhere in his forties, I guess. But he's graying at the temples, which adds distinction, I think. Possibly, they thought he *was* older." He smiled. "Anyway, he's a great guy. You'll like him."

Molly was glad that Luke had this to look forward to. He didn't strike her as lonely, but like her, he lived on his own, so perhaps he was, sometimes.

"Well, good for him. I hope the job works out."

"He starts teaching in January but is aiming to move here sooner than that. He says they want him to settle in before the winter break, to prepare for the spring semester."

The college in question was about twenty minutes away, so living in Brentford was a practical choice. Molly had considered taking a few classes there, but running the Book Boutique didn't leave her enough time. At least, that's what she told herself.

"I'm sure he'll find it reassuring to have a ready-made friend. It will make moving to a new place easier."

Luke smiled. "I think mostly he's looking for a short commute."

Molly finished scribbling on a sticky note. "Here's Amanda's email address and phone number, so he can contact her. And I'll mention him next time she and I are in touch."

She moved a pile of literary novels from the table near the door, placed them on the shelves, and let her mind wander. Would Simon have enjoyed Luke's get-togethers? They'd never been invited as a couple. Her late husband was at ease with everyone, but his friends tended to be men he fished or played poker with every so often. They fitted his concept of a "man's man." It occurred to her that you could easily describe Luke as a man's man too, and she stifled a giggle.

She allowed herself a flutter of guilt at the idea that she had more fun at his parties than she would have if Simon had been there. Then she resolved not to worry about it. Simon wouldn't want her to hide away. In fact, he seemed bent on encouraging her to expand her horizons.

If she had a new neighbor who appreciated the things she did, she'd be happy—and maybe that would get her friends off her back.

CHAPTER FIVE

Amanda didn't have enough to do—that was the problem.

She'd stopped by Molly's after work, to ask if she'd take a look at Bert's place with her. She planned to show the cottage to Nick over the weekend.

"It's not my listing, so I've never shown the property. You must know your way around better than I do."

Molly was happy to go. She hadn't been inside the Victorian cottage since Bert was alive. In those days, the cluttered living room was stuffed with mementos of his life with Harriet. Built-in shelves were crammed not only with books, but piles of *National Geographic*, Harriet's collection of china figurines, and the occasional snoozing cat. Bert and his wife had allowed all kinds of strays into their home. Hemingway had probably been one of theirs before adopting Molly. She smiled.

As she followed Amanda into the house, she surveyed the place. Nothing was left of the familiar clutter. Clearly, the interior needed work. Bert hadn't updated anything for a couple of decades at least.

"A coat of paint will bring out the charm." Her friend's voice broke into her thoughts. "They should have done it before, but never mind. If this guy is interested, we can get it painted for him."

Molly squared her shoulders. No good dwelling on the past. "Let's hope he likes the cottage. It would be nice to have a neighbor again."

They returned to her kitchen, and Molly wished she'd cleared all the papers and debris off the surfaces before she left for work that morning. One of the few benefits of living alone was that usually there was no one to see if she didn't tidy up. Only Amanda ever came over without calling first, and she never commented. Still, she could almost hear her mother's voice telling her that one should always be prepared.

As comfortable in this kitchen as her own, Amanda found two glasses in the china cabinet and opened the bottle of rosé she'd brought with her.

Handing Molly a glass, she perched on a barstool by the island, moving aside a bowl of eggs so she could rest her elbows on the edge of the counter.

"It's not as though you'd be the only woman to try online dating."

Molly didn't care if she never heard the word "dating" ever again—online or not.

"I've talked to Rosie, and she's happy to show you. Here or at her place." Amanda eyed Molly and seemingly decided to make the plan as painless as possible. "We could easily come over here—have coffee, walk you through it."

Suddenly, tears threatened to ambush Molly. She wasn't sure whether it was because of Amanda's persistence or because she missed Simon. Either way, she didn't want to cry in front of her friend. That would be pathetic. She wasn't ready for this matchmaking. Amanda meant well, but how could Molly betray Simon's memory by looking for a new man to love?

If you loved a person, they died. There was no escaping that fact. Simon had passed less than a year after her mother, and she still found it hard. Losing them hurt so much—she wasn't prepared to put herself through that again. It was bad enough that someday her dad would be gone too.

Amanda wouldn't understand, because her parents were still here. Or at least, in Florida. She never had any doubts. She remained optimistic in all circumstances, which could become irritating when you wanted to wallow for a while.

Molly paused to breathe in, which made her next sentence sound squeaky. "Don't you get it? I don't want to be walked through anything, least of all internet dating. Anyway, what do *you* know about it? You've never even tried it yourself."

"Oh, honey, listen. I won't make you do anything you don't want to do. I would never…"

"Well, okay, then." Molly blinked and blew her nose energetically into a handy tissue.

"But I've been taking a look at some of those sites."

Molly stopped blowing. "Why, exactly?"

Amanda took another sip of wine and twiddled the stem of the glass between her thumb and forefinger.

"I admit I was curious, but honestly, I wanted to help you," she said.

Molly wasn't completely convinced. "Oh? Gee, that's so kind of you."

Her friend shrugged. "Well, if you must know, I thought it might be a lark to see what all the fuss was about."

In spite of herself, Molly's interest was piqued. Just a tiny bit.

"And was it? A lark?"

Amanda turned to her with a grin that made Molly recall their days in New York, when her sociable friend dated a different man every night, while Molly sat in their apartment watching *Moonlighting*. She wished she knew how to engage in the effortless sexy banter that was the main form of communication between the two stars.

"Definitely. The men I found? They're absolutely extraordinary."

"How do you mean, extraordinary? Extraordinarily fabulous or incredibly weird?"

"Well, the sites are all kind of the same, except the specialty ones like MakinHay.com—that's for farmers. And how about LoveThoseBrits.com? Seriously. It's for meeting people with

British accents who live over here."

"What? People like my parents? Heaven forfend." Her own English accent was faint now, but she still used British expressions that made her friends smile. Still, she had no intention of living on a farm or watching Monty Python for the rest of her life. She'd seen every episode growing up in England. Besides, she'd always loved Simon's voice, with its irresistible American cadence.

Amanda was still talking. "Joking apart, you should see what these guys say about themselves. It's fascinating."

"I'm sure it is," said Molly, gritting her teeth. "But I still don't want to go on a date with some stranger."

Maybe Molly's stubborn tone finally registered, because Amanda backed off somewhat. "Of course not, sweetie. I only thought you might get a kick out of seeing what's available."

"You make the whole thing sound like visiting a used-car place. One careful owner, low mileage, excellent condition…"

Amanda laughed.

"It's not that bad. Still, at our age, better a man with one careful driver than too many, or no driver at all, wouldn't you say? Anyway, some of the guys were all right." She caught Molly's frosty expression and paused. "Fair enough. But any time you want to take a look—"

"Don't hold your breath." Maybe the wine she'd drunk had made it come out sharper than she'd intended.

"Well, pardon me." Amanda sounded miffed. "Don't worry, I'm leaving."

She slid off the stool and gave Molly a quick peck on the cheek before she headed out the door.

Molly shook her head. She should never have had the wine on an empty stomach. Time to eat something. Brie on crackers would have to do.

Yet Amanda had triggered something with her questions earlier—a combination of confusion and grief, with its soupçon of—what? Optimism? Hope?

Absent-mindedly, she topped up her glass, and taking a sip, ran a nervous hand through her hair. Should she try to find someone? Online? The thought made her slightly dizzy. She sipped again.

Her laptop stood on the tiny built-in desk she'd added when they remodeled some years back. No harm in glancing at the websites to see who was listed. Then she could tell Amanda she'd checked them out and didn't want to continue. That would stop her nagging. Molly signed on and, before she could change her mind, did a search for dating sites. She clicked on the first one that came up—YoursTruly.com.

Needing a distraction, she wandered over to the counter and took a gulp of the rosé, as if that might prevent the results from loading. Or, at least, make her feel less guilty.

Butterflies fluttered in her stomach as she set her glass down next to the computer. She breathed out and relaxed her shoulders to steady herself. These sites weren't just for desperate people. Rational, adult women checked them out every day. She was a rational adult. So why did she feel like an anxious teenager?

Whenever she watched TV, commercials advertising happily married couples who'd met each other through these websites interrupted the programming. Always the same three couples, of course. There probably weren't any others. She imagined thousands of sad, abandoned women crying into their martinis over affairs that hadn't worked out.

She inspected her nails, now sporting the pale-pink polish—Babycakes, it was called—that she'd gone back to after Rosie had persuaded her to try the blue. She couldn't even decide on a nail polish color without dithering. How ridiculous.

She was adult enough to deal with this website. She would only take a peek, anyway. She took a deep breath and another generous sip. Shouldn't have attempted both things simultaneously.

Coughing and gasping, Molly hit a button—browse photos.

Within seconds, the screen filled with pictures. She scanned them indifferently, half hoping for someone who might appeal to her. Half hoping no one would.

She knew he couldn't be a man who looked like Simon. That would be too much. So that eliminated men with wavy brown hair tinged with gray at the temples. Those with hazel eyes. Anyone with great teeth except for that one canine a little longer than the other. She made herself flip through the photos without bothering to read what the men said about themselves. Amazing how many pictures were out of focus or taken in a bathroom mirror. What was that about?

She paused and contemplated one man for a moment. He stood on the deck of an impressive yacht and wore a cap that proclaimed him to be the captain. Molly had never met a captain who needed to advertise the fact and was about to pass to the next candidate when a cold breeze ran across the back of her neck. She shrugged and made a note to check the insulation on the back door.

"*You can't go out with him. He's completely unsuitable,*" said a voice she knew. Was it coming from behind her? "*He's seventy if he's a day.*"

She had conversations with Simon regularly—in her head. Yet this was different somehow.

Molly turned slowly and froze as the speaker came into focus. Leaning nonchalantly against the island, arms crossed, was her dear departed Simon, large as life.

CHAPTER SIX

Molly stared. Then she blinked. She was seeing things. She spoke to Simon often, yet he never initiated a conversation. And he'd certainly never appeared before.

"*Hi,*" he said, like someone who'd been outside for a minute and wandered back in.

She gulped. Then she moved her body to try and block his view of the screen. Which made no sense, because this couldn't be happening.

"What…what are you doing here?" She felt her eyes welling up. She must be hallucinating.

"*I've been keeping an eye on you, you know,*" he announced, as though this were an ordinary conversation between husband and wife at the end of a long day.

Molly wanted to stand, to walk toward him, to see if this vision was real. But her legs seemed to have turned to jelly. She took in a breath and held it while she counted to ten. She blinked again. He was still there.

"*Didn't you feel me? Keeping you company?*"

All those conversations she'd had with him in her mind.

"I…I suppose so. I thought—because I loved you so much—that you would always be with me. In my heart, that is, but I never thought I'd actually *see* you…again." A tear began to make its way down her cheek.

"*I know.*" Simon's voice—so familiar, so kind.

Molly looked up through her tears and could make out the look of concern on the face she knew so well.

"*I'm only here because I love you, sweetie.*"

"Yes, but…"

"*Don't you want me here?*" Irritation tinged his words.

"Of *course* I do." Was that true? It had been three years. This was so much to process. This was different. This wasn't only Simon's voice in her head. He was here in person. So to speak.

"Why now?" she asked.

"*Yeah. Well. Nobody tells you this before you go, but you have to pass a kind of test.*"

What the hell was he talking about?

"*Everyone who, um, passes over has to do a final good deed for the one they loved best before they can move on.*"

Molly digested this for a moment. She shook her head. She must be imagining this. Nope. He was still standing there. Half of her wanted to reach out and touch him. The other half didn't want to do anything that might make him disappear.

"What sort of good deed?"

"*It has to be something* they—*in this case,* you—*really need.*"

"So how come you waited this long?" She thought about all the things she'd learned to do without him. "I could have used a hand with all the paperwork after you…went."

"*You know me and desk work.*"

Molly did. Simon moved away from the counter he'd been leaning on to look over her shoulder at the computer.

He indicated the screen. "*So, this might be the thing I could help you with. You might not get around to it otherwise.*"

She didn't bother to block his view of it. It was too late now. In any case, as he straightened up, she was too busy staring to care.

Simon was still good-looking, she had to admit. She felt suddenly shy, conscious that she'd aged more than he had. The frown lines between her brows had deepened, and she lacked the energy she used to have. She shook off these thoughts, sat up straighter, and pulled in her stomach.

In fact, he looked even better than before. He'd been a runner, and he still had his runner's body. She stopped herself. If there was one thing he couldn't possibly have…

Yet he had a tan, and the gray at his temples had vanished from his dark-brown hair. He wore a white suit over a pale-blue T-shirt. When he was alive, he wouldn't have been seen dead in those clothes. She giggled at her inadvertent joke.

"*What's so funny about trying to do something for you?*" demanded her erstwhile spouse, sounding distinctly offended.

"Nothing, darling. Just nerves." Molly made her face a tad more solemn. Then she smiled. "That outfit suits you."

God, it was wonderful to have him back, even if he was only an illusion.

"*Oh, that. It wouldn't have been my first choice, but it's standard issue over here. Obviously, I couldn't wear the clothes I transferred in.*"

"Transferred?" Then she got it.

"*That's what we call it. Remember? I was wearing my sweaty running gear.*"

How could she forget? She'd tried to blank out her shock at the phone call, telling her Simon had been taken to the hospital. He lay in the intensive care unit, having collapsed on his morning run before work. The picture haunted her. Maybe she'd remember him *this* way, now. Handsome, happy. Ironically, full of life. She changed the subject.

"About doing me a good turn. I don't think I need a favor, do I? You provided for us so well. I have the shop, and some money, and the house." She paused as a thought occurred to her. "Although, if you could find someone to do repairs around here, that would be wonderful. There are so many little things that need fixing. Do you think someone from the company might—"

Simon interrupted her. "*It's not that kind of favor. I can't just go and ask someone back at Cavelli Construction to come and change light bulbs for you. They'd have a heart attack if I showed up.*"

"Oh."

"*No. The idea is that I have to help you be happy again.*" He leaned back and waited.

"But I *am*," said Molly, "considering I'm a widow."

"*You could be happier. I appreciate all the grieving, of course, but it's time to wind that up now. So, I thought I might find you a new husband. To take my place,*" he added, in case she hadn't gotten the message.

This was too much. She must be dreaming. Yet she couldn't seem to wake up—and didn't want to.

"*When I saw you checking out the online dating thing, I made up my mind. This is something I can do. I can make sure that these guys are on the level before you go out with them.*"

Molly stared, speechless. Did Simon truly expect to find her someone to replace him? She had to nip this in the bud. "You know no one could replace you, darling. You set a high bar."

She wasn't lying. Simon had been her first and only great love, and the corresponding pain when he died had overwhelmed her. She wouldn't willingly chance that again.

The phone rang a second later, saving her from further discussion. She swiveled her chair to face the desk, and with a shaking hand, picked up the receiver.

"Hi, honey. It's Dad."

"Oh, thank heavens." Hearing his familiar voice, she exhaled in relief. Someone still in this world. The ringing phone had woken her from her reverie, and she was grateful.

She walked through to the front room and made herself comfortable on the sofa. No sign of Simon now, thank goodness. He'd be way too distracting. If he was real. Which he wasn't.

"Molly, what's the matter?"

She and her dad had always been close, but she wasn't ready to tell him about Simon's appearance.

"Nothing, nothing. I thought it might be someone I didn't want to talk to. Amanda's been nagging me about moving on. You know, dating."

"Uh-huh." Her father's voice was non-committal. "And?"

"Ouch."

Hemingway had sashayed into the room and jumped onto her lap, using his front claws to gain a purchase on her thighs.

"Sorry, Dad. Hemingway just joined me." The cat snuggled into her and began purring loudly. She relaxed as she stroked his head.

"Okay." He sounded skeptical. "So, about the dating thing?"

"You know me. I hate change. I like things the way they are."

"I know, but you adapted to a new situation when you came to America."

After her parents moved to the States from Britain when she was eighteen, Molly decided to apply to college in New York. That's where she'd met Amanda. Her parents never went back to live in England, and she stayed on too.

She found the American way of life appealing, though decades later, she still retained some British quirks. Like Tom, she preferred tea to coffee, and she insisted on a genuine imported English breakfast blend to make the strong brew she liked. And the preserve she spread on her toast was Rose's lime marmalade. Delicious.

"I guess you're right. But changing countries wasn't as hard as this. Maybe because I was younger. In any case, I told Amanda I wasn't interested."

"Well, so long as you're okay. How's the bookshop doing?"

To tell him or not? He'd more or less warned her that buying the place would be risky. "If it were going to take twice as long," he'd said, "and cost twice as much, would you still want to do it? If so—go ahead. If you're not sure, though, you might want to do something different."

If she'd listened to her father, instead of Simon's ghostly advice, she might not be in this mess.

"I've had some bad news. The landlord wants to raise the rent, and that's going to put my expenses over the top. If they go through with it, I may not be able to keep going."

Tom said nothing for a minute. Probably thinking, "I told you so."

"I see. That's tough. Still, I know you'll find a way through it."

"I don't see how."

"Have you approached them about it?"

Molly explained. "Amanda's promised to get back to me with a name as soon as she can."

"Sensible strategy. You're on the right track."

A warm glow spread through her, and it wasn't the wine.

"Thanks, Dad. I'll keep you posted. So, were you calling for any special reason?"

"I was wondering what your plans were for Thanksgiving."

"I'm not sure yet, but I expect you'll want to be with your friends, won't you?"

He'd moved into his retirement village, Maple Corners, when her mother died. He found the family home too large for one and too full of memories. Here, a few miles away from Brentford, he didn't need to cook and was never lonely, with plenty to do and people to do it with.

"As it happens, I've been invited to a friend's family. She's visiting her son and asked me to come."

Molly tried not to let her astonishment show in her voice. If there was a special person in his life, he'd given no hint of it. Yet she wasn't flattering him when she maintained that, at seventy-six, he still retained his looks.

"Have I met her?"

"I don't think so. You'd probably remember if you had."

Well. This was a new development, and she was glad. If anyone deserved a romance, he did. Before she could say anything more, Tom spoke again.

"Anyway, I'd love to come over for some of your Scotch-pecan pie after that, later in the day. No one else makes it like you do."

"You mean they don't make it with alcohol where you are, right?" She laughed. Her father enjoyed a small glass of Glenlivet with his dessert "in case there's not enough in the pie." A familiar joke, which made her smile.

"Exactly."

"We'd love it if you came. I'll send one of the girls to pick you up."

"Smashing." Only Tom ever said "smashing" in that British way.

"Listen, Dad, talking of dinner, I haven't eaten mine yet."

"Your mother would be horrified."

Molly heard the smile in his voice. "We wouldn't want that, would we? Love you, Dad."

Would he say it back? Old British habits died hard.

"Me too."

She'd take it.

CHAPTER SEVEN

Amanda's number came up on her phone a couple of days later, while Molly was adding titles to the Thanksgiving window display. With any luck, she was calling with the landlord's name. Hastily putting the books down, Molly answered.

"Do you have any news?"

"Good morning to you too. Yes, I do. You'll never guess."

How she hated guessing games. "Just spit it out, for heaven's sake."

"No need to get cranky." Amanda paused, presumably for effect. "The person at Pilgrim Properties? It's Channing Madison."

Molly's heart sank.

A moment's silence hung in the air, while the man took form in her mind's eye. She'd been introduced to him at social events for the Wentworth Library, where he was a trustee. She had little difficulty in picturing his bowling ball of a head, with its bland, round face and pale appraising eyes. He might have been quite good-looking in his youth, though she hadn't known him then. In middle age, he'd acquired more pounds and pomposity than he needed.

"You've met him, right? Through the library?"

"I have, a while ago, but I can't say we had an instant rapport. He's not very…approachable."

"He sounds rather intimidating, but you're going to have to

give it a shot, sweetie. Looks like he's your only hope."

If true, she was doomed. Get a grip, she told herself. Look on the bright side.

"You never know—he might be in a charitable frame of mind. 'Tis the season, and all that."

"That's the spirit."

"Thanks, Amanda. I don't know what I'd do without you."

"Don't leave it too long to call. It's usually best to get scary things over with."

"You're right," said Molly, though she couldn't muster any enthusiasm. Just thinking of begging Channing Madison for mercy was enough to make her break out in a sweat.

***

How had she missed his name when she studied Pilgrim Properties' website? She returned to it and scanned the pages. No one could accuse them of making the information obvious. Ah. Here it was, hidden away in gray type against a black background at the bottom of the page, as though they didn't want anyone to know who was running the company. She recalled her stress when she'd checked before. Probably why she'd given up too soon. Thank goodness Amanda hadn't.

She googled him. The results indicated he was single, with teenage daughters, if the photos were anything to go by. They had that in common, at least. Luckily for his girls, they didn't resemble him. They must take after their mother, who appeared in the archive of the local paper, the *Brentford Bee*, in her capacity as a sponsor of various charitable events. Hopefully, some of the philanthropic impulses had rubbed off on Channing.

No time to waste. Molly dialed the landlord's number and got the automated answering system. When asked, she spoke his name into thin air.

"Please hold while we connect you to his voicemail," came the disembodied voice.

"This is Channing Madison. I am out of my office until Monday, November twelfth. Please call back then."

She had no chance to say anything, because the system cut her off. Unbelievable. Not even the courtesy of allowing her to leave a message. What kind of a way was that to run a company? She made a note to phone again after the weekend. Another five days—and nights—of worry.

***

To distract herself, she spent the rest of the day coming up with content for her new website. Her after-school employee, Bradford Fitch III, better known as Trey, had designed it. She enjoyed reviewing the latest titles, but that was as far as she'd gotten.

When he walked through the door just after three, he'd come up with an idea. "What about a blog?"

"Good thought. I could feature a book of the month. Or an interview with an author."

As they brainstormed together, Molly began to feel a lot more optimistic. She could do this. At the end of the afternoon, she took thirty dollars from the till and paid Trey.

"Same time next week?" he asked, as he pulled on his black leather moto jacket.

She nodded. "Thanks. I think this is going to be excellent."

Molly watched him walk out of the store. She enjoyed having a young person around. Her thoughts went to her daughters. It seemed like ages since they'd been home. They'd be back for Thanksgiving soon. Something to look forward to.

CHAPTER EIGHT

Miss Elaine Johansen stopped in later, carrying half a dozen eggs. Molly knew what that meant. Elaine wanted something new to read. The barter system had been established long ago—before Luke owned the store, and no one had the heart to change it. They were delicious, and even though the price of a book far exceeded that of the eggs, Molly wasn't about to haggle. Besides, some of the chickens laid colored ones—almost translucent jade, some with the merest hint of sky. They were beautiful.

The lady in question, who must be approaching ninety, put the carton on the counter and gazed hopefully at Molly. Her hair was an unlikely shade of red, perhaps a throwback to her youth, if her pale skin and faded blue eyes were anything to go by. Today she was sporting a short fake fur jacket, a black leather miniskirt, and her Pippi Longstocking tights in stripes of scarlet and black.

Molly picked up the carton, opened it to admire the contents, and placed it under the counter. "Thanks so much, Miss J. They're lovely. Don't want them getting knocked off by accident," she explained.

"You're standing in ladies' lingerie, you know."

"Sorry?"

"This used to be the Ladies' Lingerie department when I worked here. Next to Cosmetics."

She must be talking about the original shop on this site—before Molly's time.

"When was that?"

"Oh, after the war," Elaine said vaguely. Her eyes had lost focus as she stared into some past only she could see.

Time to get her back on track. "How's your sister, Elaine?"

"Slightly improved, she says." She gave a shake of her head, as if to contradict what she was saying. "So, we're looking for something interesting, if you know what I mean."

The younger sister read to the elder, who'd been bedridden for the last few months. They managed with no other help, and Elaine ran all the errands. By now, Brentford residents knew better than to get too close to the battered yellow Toyota that weaved uncertainly along the streets. Its diminutive driver, peering over the steering wheel, did not inspire confidence. Every so often the local police officer would wait for her to pull over somewhere and suggest she stop driving. To no avail.

"I've got just the thing. How about the newest Lucinda Parks? It came in the other day." These sisters loved romances, and though they sometimes contained what they called "naughty bits," never returned anything she'd chosen for them.

The aquamarine eyes twinkled.

***

At home that evening, Molly rinsed her eggy hands under the kitchen tap. She had never mastered the art of cracking eggs with one hand without getting covered in yolk, but she continued to try. The egg mixture was standing on the counter, and she stared at it, uninspired. She intended to make an omelet, but Hemingway was circling in and out of her legs, demanding to be fed.

She'd make something else after she gave him his dinner and checked her messages. She found her phone in the pocket of the yellow slicker. A text from Heather. A voicemail from

Jackie. Funny, both her daughters getting in touch the same day, but they often did that. They'd once given her the identical birthday card—without consulting the other. This would be about Thanksgiving. She read Heather's message first.

Hi Mom. Sorry Can't make it home for T-giving Tons of snow here and more to come Plus no ride and bus takes so long Hope OK w/you See u Xmas. Call me later Love U Heart Heart H

As the meaning of the words sunk in, disappointment settled over her like a heavy, gray blanket. Was snow the real problem? Heather had mentioned a new boyfriend the last time they'd spoken. If he was the reason for this decision, she hated him.

Though it probably had nothing to do with this young man she'd never met. The five-hour drive from Maine was a lot to ask for so little time in Brentford.

With a sinking feeling, she jabbed the screen and held the phone to her ear to listen to Jackie's message. Her daughter sounded upbeat, as she usually did.

"Hi, Mom! Listen, my friend Ingrid has asked me to her home for Turkey Day. I told her I'd check with you first, but she lives in Constantia, which is only thirty minutes away from here. On Oneida Lake, you know? And there might be skiing some-where nearby, and her parents said they'll pick us up and—" Her voice faltered. "That is, if you don't mind, of course. Can you and Heather go to Amanda's? You know I'll come home if you want me to, but whatever, let me know. Love you."

Molly bit her lip to discourage the tears that were pricking the back of her eyes. She found a tissue and blew her nose before checking her face briefly in the bathroom mirror.

No point in wallowing. She left voicemails and wandered back into the kitchen to finish making her omelet, only to stare at the empty bowl that had contained two broken eggs only a short while ago. Hemingway disappeared under the table—a clear admission of guilt, if ever she'd seen one.

"Oh, you," she said, at a loss for how to reprimand him. Never mind. She might find something in the fridge. Some split-pea soup looked promising, but when she lifted the lid on the container, the sour smell sent her straight to the sink to pour it away. An aging chunk of English farmhouse cheddar, her favorite, lurked at the back of the middle shelf. Starting to dry out, but it would do. So, a grilled cheese sandwich again.

She was making it when her younger daughter called back. "Hi, Mom," said Jackie. "Your message sounded kinda…" Her voice trailed off as though she was reluctant to say what she meant.

"I was, kinda."

Jackie laughed. "So, what do you think? Will you be okay if I go stay with Ingrid?"

Her voice expressed both hope and anxiety. No point in Molly showing her disappointment. Jackie needed to make new friends at school. With luck and care, some would last her a lifetime. And, frankly, skiing at Constantia did sound like more fun than spending the holiday with her mother.

"Sure, honey. It sounds like a good plan."

Since Simon's death, she'd suffered through two difficult Thanksgivings—the first with Amanda and her family, who, without meaning to, made her feel the lack of him more than ever, and one at a restaurant. So last year, she and the girls had celebrated at home.

They'd done what they could to make it like the old days. But the turkey was way too big and noticeably underdone. Heather came up with the bright idea of mashing the potatoes with a beater, which turned them into soup. They'd made the best of it, and the pie, which Molly baked on autopilot after so many years, proved successful. Her dad, Tom, enjoyed a slice when he came over after dinner that evening.

But she understood why her daughters were ready to move on.

**

The smell of smoke told her that she'd singed the grilled cheese sandwich, but she ate it anyway.

Life sucked.

She made herself a comforting mug of cocoa and curled up on the sofa to read. The mystery novel about a young woman living with a ghost in her bookstore ought to have been intriguing, but Molly's brain refused to follow the sentences. A cold draft was coming from somewhere. Setting the book aside, she glanced up to see Simon standing by the window, silent.

Was she conjuring him up again, or did he just show up whenever he felt like it? Or was it that he arrived when she was stressed?

"I heard from Jackie and Heather about Thanksgiving."

He turned and smiled. *"Great. I'm looking forward to seeing them again. They must be…"*

"Nineteen and twenty-one, now," Molly finished the sentence, knowing that he always had trouble tracking birthdays, even those of his daughters.

"So, yeah, it'll be a treat to see them again, even if they won't see me."

He wasn't making it easy for her to tell him.

She reached over to pick up the mug from the coffee table and tried a sip.

Still too hot to drink. Setting it back down, she said, "Darling, I meant to tell you. They won't be here until Christmas."

"Why the heck not?" Interesting. He'd uttered an unusually mild curse for a man who used to employ an impressive vocabulary. Maybe they frowned on swearing in the afterlife.

"Well, I don't know if you recall, but Heather's at school in Maine, and Jackie's a freshman at Syracuse. It's too long a trip for them just for a day or two."

"I guess it is, at that. I remember how it was when I drove Heather up there to look at colleges—we had to stay overnight. I'm glad I did that, but I wish I'd been able to take Jackie when it was her turn."

He'd forgotten that they visited more than one place. Evidently didn't know that the girls had managed to come home for the last two years. She didn't want to tell him that, this year, they'd found other options more alluring. He might think his daughters were less than perfect.

"She loved that trip."

"*Me too. You must feel disappointed, though,*" said Simon. "*And I was looking forward to being around them too. They look so grown-up in their pictures.*" He strolled over to the upright piano, where a range of photos in white frames jostled along the top. He lifted one and studied it.

"*Look at this. I hardly recognize them. I remember teaching them how to play ball when they were what—six? Seven?*" A nostalgic note overlaid his words.

"You were a great dad."

"*Now Jackie, she's changed so much. Since, you know. No more braces.*" He pointed at a second picture. "*And Heather's lovely too.*" He leaned forward for a closer look. "*If I'm not mistaken, she's thinned out in the last three years.*"

"Heather's the only one among her friends who actually lost the freshman fifteen."

"*The what?*"

"You know, the weight people gain in the first year of college."

Simon smiled as he turned back to Molly. "*That's my girl. So, what will you do about the holiday?*"

"Well, I expect Amanda will ask me over again."

He'd always been swift to recognize the feelings in her voice. "*But..?*"

"There's no 'but.' Except, I don't feel like being outnumbered in a happy family where everyone else has a husband and some kids."

He gave a rueful smile. "*I didn't mean to die, you know.*"

"I know."

"*Well, you could always go and see your dad, couldn't you? He'd be delighted.*"

"He's been doing the pie run over here for the last few

years, like he always did. But when I called, he told me he's going to someone's family this time. She's his new girlfriend, if I'm reading the situation right."

Simon said nothing for a moment. "*Well, good for Tom. If he's meeting this woman's family, it sounds like it might be serious.*"

Molly stood and went over to light the gas fire she'd installed a couple of years before.

"I guess it must be. Well, I'm happy for him. He likes her, I can tell. I suppose I'll have to ask them both over here sometime."

"*Good idea.*" Simon inspected the fireplace, as if noticing it for the first time. "*Is that new?*"

She flushed. "I found it so difficult to keep up with ordering the wood and stacking it and carrying it inside," she explained. "And this is so much cleaner…"

He gave a small shake of the shoulders. "*Of course. Much more practical. Though it will never smell the same.*"

"Well, no." Seeking to distract him, she returned to something she'd been pondering. "I can't quite figure out why I only ever see you downstairs. How come?"

"*I'm not sure. This whole thing is a mystery to me. But I like it down here. I get to talk to you.*"

"I imagine I'm not much of a conversationalist while I'm asleep." Molly grinned ruefully.

"*Exactly. And listening to you snore was never—*" He broke off as she threw a pillow at him. Or rather, through him. It hit the side of the piano and landed on the floor. Simon looked disconcerted for a moment, then he laughed.

She found herself laughing too. When they fell silent, he smiled at her. "*I'm guessing you're ready for bed.*"

She stretched her arms out to her sides. "I am."

"*I'll let you get some sleep. But I want to say—about the holiday. I'm sure something will turn up. You don't have to decide anything until you're invited someplace. You never know—you might feel different as it gets closer.*"

"I might." Molly wasn't convinced. Maybe he was right. Being on her own held little appeal. Though it would be better than feeling like an outsider among other people. She could volunteer at the church, which provided a free turkey dinner for the lonely older folks who lived on their own. But what if they thought she was one of them?

"It'll work out—you'll see."

She couldn't imagine how, as she picked up her cocoa and began to climb the stairs.

She'd altered nothing in the bedroom since Simon was alive. She hadn't had the heart to change anything, though the king-size bed was too wide and its mattress too hard. Not that it mattered, really. No one ever saw it, unless one of the girls wanted to borrow something from her closet, and *they* seemed to want everything in the house to stay the way it was.

Molly went over to the large bay window to draw the curtains. A car stood in the driveway and a light gleamed from one of the windows in the cottage next door. Several lights, in fact. Perhaps someone was showing it to a prospective renter. Nick, maybe?

Pulling the curtains closed, she turned back to the room. She considered a different color on the walls—like her favorite shade of periwinkle blue.

Almost out of habit, she spoke aloud. "Would you mind, darling, if I changed the wall color?"

No answer, but she did feel a warm glow inside. Was that a message from him? Or, god forbid, a hot flash? Surely, those were over, weren't they?

CHAPTER NINE

Luke stood outside the front window of the Book Boutique, gesticulating and mouthing something. "I'm done. Come take a look."

She'd left him organizing a Thanksgiving table while she updated the window displays, so she was facing the street. She'd just put her head into the bay window to remove the current offerings, and, reversing too fast, banged her head on the side of the frame.

She swore under her breath and rubbed at her forehead before straightening up, more carefully this time.

Even though he deplored the non-literary stock, Luke had, as always, displayed the items in as elegant a way as could be achieved with magnets, turkey key rings, and the like.

Turning, she saw him standing behind her.

"Something up?"

She winced. "Apart from nearly knocking myself out on the window frame, you mean?"

"Do you need an aspirin or something?"

"I'm okay." She knew she sounded ungracious.

If only people wouldn't be sympathetic. She wanted to remain cross. Concern or kindness often made her tear up. There was no logic to it, but she found her defenses pierced when it happened. She sometimes wondered whether these minor but painful accidents occurred when she needed to cry about something else, like missing Simon, or feeling lonely without her daughters.

"It's just...the girls won't be coming home for the holiday," she said, her voice low.

"How fortunate."

She looked up, confused. He could be sarcastic, but never unsympathetic.

Luke took out a large white handkerchief and was busy breathing on his glasses. He began polishing them vigorously as he spoke.

"I'm planning a small gathering for Thanksgiving and wondered if you'd like to come too. I've invited a few friends over."

Luke lived on his own, but his social gatherings were legendary. He never referred to Molly's possible loneliness, but she suspected he invited her because he wanted to do his bit to help. Behind his gruff façade, he was a kind man.

Overcome with remorse at her grumpy attitude and his unexpected solicitude, she felt her eyes misting up and pulled a tissue from the sleeve of her sweater to blow her nose.

"Gosh, Luke, you have no idea how much I'd like to join you. I love Amanda, but the family thing, with the kids and all, it can be overwhelming."

"That's settled then," said Luke, turning back to the desk. "Oh, you can bring some of those cookies of yours, if you want to contribute."

"Of *course* I will." She smiled. "And thank you."

He meant the salty, chunky, dark-chocolate and walnut cookies that Molly only baked for friends. Simon had loved them. He nicknamed them "forest floor cookies," because the knobby treats in varying shades of brown reminded him of the leaf-strewn ground in the woods of Hart's Hill. They were a universal favorite, and though she'd shared the recipe and others had tried to bake them too, Molly's just tasted better, for some reason.

That Luke had asked her to bring some to his home she

considered an honor, since he liked to do all the cooking and baking without help when he entertained. He prided himself on being an excellent chef, and an adventurous one. It was quite possible that his guests would be eating something more exotic than turkey with all the trimmings, if his previous parties were anything to go by. Her spirits started to lift. This might not be such a dismal Thanksgiving after all.

"By the way, I asked Nick, if he's around."

"Has he decided to take the cottage next to me?"

"I think so. At least, he told me he'd be moving into a new place in a couple of weeks."

"That will be nice for you. Me too, I expect, if he ends up next door."

Luke smiled benevolently. "It's about time he caught a break."

A loud harrumph broke into their conversation. "Have you got the latest Jack Reacher?"

Mr. Schlegel often turned up just before closing time, to leaf through a number of histories, biographies, or thrillers. Then he'd make a note and replace them on the shelves. This evening, he'd walked straight past Lee Child's book, on display with the new releases. Molly swore under her breath. Those books were cheaper online, of course, and she doubted he would purchase this one from her. "Here you are," she said through gritted teeth. "I'll be happy to ring you up when you're ready."

Fat chance.

CHAPTER TEN

Remembering Amanda's comments about her hair, Molly rang Shear Madness to make an appointment.

"Hi, sweetie," said Rosie, when she realized who it was. Molly could hear the smile in her warm familiar voice with its faint Puerto Rican accent. "Your timing is perfect. I've just had a cancellation for this evening. Can you make it at six?"

Turning this chance down might mean waiting a week or two.

Rosie was still talking. "Otherwise, it might have to be after Thanksgiving, because I'm all booked up."

That settled it. "Six would be ideal, Rosie. Thanks."

"Must run. I have someone on the other line. See you later."

***

Rosie claimed she was her father's daughter through and through. He'd moved his wife and family from Puerto Rico to Brooklyn long before that borough was hip, to open a barbershop that continued to do a brisk business, even in an age of beards and longer hair. She'd inherited his tenaciousness as well as his talent with clippers.

Molly always allowed Rosie to ramble on about her love life while Molly sat, draped in a purple cape, the scissors snapping around her head—especially since it meant she didn't have to discuss her own status.

In her early forties, Rosie had been divorced for five years. She and her preppy first husband had been a mismatched couple from the start, she explained when they split up. But she added that if it weren't for him, she wouldn't have her teenage son, Kyle, nor be here in Brentford, with a flourishing business. And she and her ex remained on good terms.

Seemingly undaunted by the failure of her marriage, she began meeting men. She had plenty of outrageous stories to tell. Molly submitted to the unwritten law of beauty salons: Thou shalt sit quietly while getting a haircut or face the consequences. And: Thou shalt not object to thy stylist's conversation.

"So, Amanda tells me you might be ready to check out a few dating sites?"

Molly jumped, eliciting a mild "*Acho, no,*" from the hairdresser. "Sit still, *chica*, or you will be missing a chunk of your hair."

Until now, Molly had always put her friends off when the subject of online dating came up—making excuses about not having any idea how to go about it—too polite to say that the stories she'd heard in the salon chair would scare anyone away from internet matchmaking. Some of Rosie's experiences had been hair-raising, to say the least. Perhaps that explained the short black cut she sported, which flipped out on both sides as though she'd just had some sort of electric shock.

Rosie's fizzy personality masked a firm resolve. "I'll be over Sunday to get you started online, okay? How's three o'clock?" she said, as she ran Molly's credit card through the machine.

Was there no escape? Apparently not.

"Sure. Thank you." Molly shrugged on her jacket, ready to leave. Maybe it wouldn't be too bad. After all, Rocco, Rosie's current—and by all accounts steady—boyfriend suited her perfectly. She might find someone too.

***

In the shop the next morning, Molly picked up a stack of Christmas romance novels and scanned the titles. She might put *Sizzling Holiday* somewhere near the bottom. The guy in the Santa hat on the cover had startling abs that caused her to blink. He didn't appear to be wearing much else, though his position, standing behind a pile of gifts, made it hard to tell. She didn't remember ordering that. Then she read the blurb. A steamy gay romance. She smiled. She'd leave it where Luke could find it. Which reminded her.

"Luke?"

"Over here." He was tidying the books at a small round table in the corner. A floor-length crushed-velvet cloth hid the stacks of extra copies they used to restock the most popular titles.

"I have a question for you. Are you doing anything on Sunday afternoon? We need to begin staffing our holiday hours, but I have someone coming over to the house." Molly felt herself blush, hoping he wouldn't ask who. Or worse, why. She didn't want to admit that Rosie was planning to sign her up for an online dating site.

"I was waiting for you to mention the new schedule. I can do this Sunday, but not next. We should work out a timetable and get Trey in to help. With any luck, we'll be needing him."

"Thanks, Luke, you're a star."

***

After a couple of hours in the bookshop early Sunday afternoon, Molly left Luke to deal with the slow but steady stream of customers who were coming in for gift-giving advice.

Satisfied that she had done what she could, she returned home to bake and put a pot of coffee on. Rosie's visit gave her an excuse to fill the kitchen with the aromas of warm butter, sugar, and chocolate—something she avoided unless she was expecting a visitor. The forest-floor cookies were too much of a temptation.

It was kind of her friend to forfeit her Sunday afternoon at such short notice—the only day on which they were both free. Molly wasn't exactly thrilled by the reason for the visit, but she appreciated the company.

***

"Okay, let's take a peek at some of these guys." Rosie, her olive complexion still summer golden with the help of a tanning bed, sat at the little desk in Molly's kitchen, clicking away at the keyboard of her laptop. Her hands, nails glistening and fingers be-ringed, flashed across the keys with a speed Molly envied.

Molly sat on the other side of the room, about as far away from the computer and its threatening websites as she could. On her lap, a reluctant Hemingway allowed himself to be stroked, but eventually could bear it no longer and jumped down.

In spite of the blustery weather outside, Molly found herself thinking longingly of a hike through the nature preserve close to her house.

"Come on, sweetie. They won't bite," said the expert. "We're just doing the research so I can explain these so-called gentlemen to you."

"They shouldn't need explaining, should they? Amanda told me they write down a description of themselves, and if you spot somebody you like, you tell them you're interested."

Amanda had made it sound simple. Yet Rosie was the one who'd met dozens of men on Yourstruly.com, so she must know what she was talking about. Being several years younger than Molly, she had a carefree attitude toward men and sex that Molly could only admire, in a fascinated kind of way. She could never be as relaxed about romance.

"Ah, well, here's the thing. You have to read between the lines." Rosie gave her a look from her shrewd, maple-syrup eyes. "Come on. Grab your mug and sit here next to me. I'm using my account, so you don't have to commit to anything.

This is only an exploratory session."

She signed in and began to run through photos of the prospective dates. Molly edged a few paces closer to the computer screen, but instead of sitting, remained a step removed, looking over Rosie's shoulder. Transfixed, she found herself leaning in to assess the men in the pictures, who seemed to range in age from around forty to north of seventy. Hadn't they asked for people no older than sixty? She mentioned this, and her friend turned to grin up at her.

"Well, that's the first thing they lie about, of course. As do most women. You should always add at least five to ten years to whatever they put here."

Even Simon had known this.

Rosie turned back to the laptop and indicated one of the photos. "Take this guy, for instance."

She clicked on a man who appeared to be in his mid-sixties. "Total loser. He says he's fifty. Not a chance. And you see the guitar?"

Molly saw. "That might be interesting—someone musical."

Rosie snorted. A ladylike snort but a snort, nonetheless. "Forget any guy with a musical instrument," she said. "All they want is an adoring audience—whether they actually know how to play the thing or not."

Molly had been right to think this was a dicey idea. Yet some little spark of interest still flickered.

"What about *him*, Rosie?" Molly indicated a man in a suit, standing in a brand-new apartment.

"Nope." She didn't even pause to consider this one.

"Why not? He looks nice, and the place is lovely." If she were in the market for a new home, that man might be a candidate.

Rosie sighed, as if to let Molly know that she despaired of her naiveté.

"See the background?" She pointed. "It's blank. Empty. Not a thing in it. *Nada*."

"So, what are you saying?"

"It's not his, that's for sure. He's taken a photo there because it's got a fireplace and big windows, with a lovely view. But do you see a stick of furniture? No. Anything on the walls? Ditto."

Such a harsh assessment. Rosie did tend to make snap decisions, and they weren't always right.

"Well, maybe he's about to move in. What does he say?"

"No, honey." The voice was firm, like a kindergarten teacher repeating something to a particularly inattentive pupil. "He says he's divorced, and if this photo *is* his apartment, the wife has obviously cleaned him out. He's not a good bet. Plus, divorce makes them hate women for a while."

The number of possible suitors appeared to be dwindling fast. The next turned out to be someone Rosie met only once before ditching him. Smelled kind of strange was all she said. They kept going.

"That one looks okay," Molly ventured, trying to enter into the spirit of it.

Rosie scrolled down to the notes.

"Oh, my god, not that one. He says he's into adventures."

Molly frowned, confused.

"But you and Amanda are always telling me I need to be more adventurous, try a new activity."

"Not this, you don't." She leaned back to glance at her friend. "Adventurous is code for…you know—weird sex," she whispered, as if someone might hear.

Molly gasped, and her eyebrows shot up. "Oh, come on."

Rosie shrugged. "Trust me on this one. I know."

"Okay. *Okay.* I get the picture." Molly held up a hand to forestall the revelation of any more details. They could quit now.

She attempted to convey disappointment by dropping her shoulders and sighing. "Well, I guess we've tried. There's no one here for me." She straightened and stretched. She needed to clear her head. Breathe some fresh air. "It's still daylight. Want to go for a walk?"

Rosie waggled her foot, clad in a kitten-heeled navy pump. "I don't think so, sweetie. Why don't you go out for a while, and I'll keep at it."

Well, at least Molly wouldn't have to watch.

CHAPTER ELEVEN

Molly walked along the woodland trail, breathing in the smell of dead leaves and loam—the familiar scents of late autumn. The snow would coat this scene in white as the holidays approached, but for now, somewhere beyond the preserve, smoke from a log fire wafted through the bare tree branches. The wind had died down, leaving a clear, powder-blue sky with a few fluffy clouds scudding across it. A new sense of energy rose in her, and she smiled.

She was lucky to live so close to a protected woodland. Nature always soothed her when her mind was conflicted or sad. She wasn't sure what her feelings were right now. Since she'd escaped from Rosie's kind attempts to help, this exhilaration likely stemmed from relief.

A squirrel ran across the path in front of her, dropping an acorn as it did so. Molly laughed. The next moment, she lay sprawled on the ground. The second she felt her sneaker catch, she knew that an unseen tree root was to blame. With no way to prevent the fall, she watched herself, as if in slow motion, land with a thud. She did a quick mental scan of her limbs—nothing broken, luckily. Her right palm stung as she scrambled unsteadily to her feet. She turned her hand up to assess the damage and, without warning, found herself sobbing.

It was always the little things that exposed her vulnerability. The small hurts that revealed the intractable ache of Simon's death. And every so often, the pain escaped her careful efforts at control.

She fished in the pocket of her quilted jacket for a tissue and discovered one that had been there for a while, judging by its crumpled appearance. She unfolded it carefully and dabbed at her eyes. She never used to fall like this. But then she and Simon always held hands as they strolled between the trees. This line of thought only made it harder to stop the tears.

Her mother's voice sounded in her head: "Blow your nose, sweetie, you'll feel better." Molly did as directed, and soon the tears trickled to a halt. She brushed her cheek with the back of her hand. The palms were still covered with earth, so she rubbed them cautiously against the front of her jeans. In a while, the trail crossed a small stream—she might be able to rinse her hands in it.

As she dipped her fingers into the water, the numbing effect of the icy brook helped her breathe easier. She stood and shook the drops off her hands. Stuffing them into her pockets, she turned for home, eyes down to make sure she didn't miss anything that might cause her to stumble again.

Her mother, who hadn't always been wrong, would have reminded her to think about something to be grateful for. The notion cheered her. Counting her blessings generally chased away the blues. So—she was thankful for her mother's advice and relieved she hadn't broken any bones.

She headed for home, glad it wasn't too far away. She washed her hands in the kitchen sink and applied a swipe of ointment to the scrape. Meanwhile, Rosie filled a couple of glasses with the remains of a bottle of rosé she'd come across in the fridge and handed one to Molly.

"I've been busy while you were gone."

Rosie had found her a possible date. Someone calling himself Starman97. "I'd rate him a six as far as looks go. He's a bit younger than you, he says, but he's probably older. Likes walks on the beach—"

Molly stopped her in mid-sentence. "The nearest beach is twenty miles away." Her hand still stung. Walking by the sea held no attraction right now.

"Don't quibble. He's romantic. That's what he's trying to say. And he's a reader. Perfect for a person who works in a bookshop. Here." She nodded toward the profile section.

The man on the screen was nothing like Simon—a point in his favor. The photo had been underexposed, which made his features difficult to make out, but he looked harmless, at least. He had graying hair in a conservative cut and darkish eyes. His smile revealed a mouthful of even teeth. Too even? Presumably, the trees in the background were intended to show he liked the outdoors.

Right now, the best thing she could say about him was that he sounded non-threatening. The pit of her stomach churned at the idea of someone new. Before she could change her mind, she said, "Okay, what do I do now?"

"That's the spirit," said Rosie. "Let's sign you up. First, you need an online ID for the site."

She gazed expectantly at Molly.

"Why can't I use my name?"

Rosie raised a perfectly plucked eyebrow. "You can, if you want all the trolls on the internet to track you down. It has to be kind of anonymous. Like Bookgirl or Flirtyfun."

Rosie tapped away, rapidly filling out a form on the computer.

"Oh. In that case, I guess Bookwoman might be more accurate."

"Oops—there are already a bunch of those, so we'll need to add a number or symbol." Rosie's fingers flew over the keyboard. Unnecessarily fast. "Okay. You're a woman, looking to meet a man." Rosie appeared to be thinking aloud as she filled out the form. "You'd like a man of what, say forty-five to fifty-five? With a view to friendship and possible romance? That should get you guys from fifty-five to sixty-five."

Molly experienced the sensation of having inadvertently stepped onto a moving walkway that had accelerated without warning, knocking her off balance.

"We're still just doing research, right?"

"Sure," said Rosie, though she sounded a touch absent-minded.

Molly sat in a daze as Rosie asked her for her credit card—to try the site for a month, she explained—and then checked Molly's photo files for pictures she could add to her profile.

Rosie skimmed through the thumbnails. "Don't you have any photos of you on your own? So many with the girls, or with…" Her voice trailed off as she realized where the sentence would end. "Let me check my phone," she went on. "I've taken some of you after doing your hair, and I took one that time we hiked to the top of Hart's Hill. That'll show you're a fun person, physically fit."

Rosie completed a description, including Molly's musical preferences, her love of reading and baking—well, she did enjoy making cakes and cookies for her friends, occasionally—and a hint about her political views. She balked at this, but Rosie insisted.

"Hey, you wouldn't want to spend time with someone you didn't agree with. This guy says he's an independent, which should be okay."

"Can you say I'm a moderate?"

"Don't see why not."

She typed it in, added some entirely fictitious exercise habits, and leaned back with a satisfied smile.

"Okay, you're good to go," she said. "I'm just going to…" She typed something else.

"What's that?" A sudden suspicion had come over Molly.

"Ah. I just sent Starman here a message to say you might be interested in coffee. Nothing to worry about. He might not bother to reply. Most people don't."

She seemed to register the alarm on Molly's face. "I'm sure he won't," she added hastily. "In any case, you can always say no."

CHAPTER TWELVE

Starman apparently decided to ignore the feelers that Rosie put out on her behalf. Molly was relieved. Other more important issues needed her attention. Specifically, she had to speak to Channing Madison, before she lost her nerve completely. She'd already mislaid her courage a couple of times in the past week, as she waited for him to return from wherever he'd been.

Meanwhile, she debated whether it would be better to call him from home before leaving for work or to risk someone overhearing in the store. Finally, on the day his voicemail system had told her he'd be back, she compromised by taking half an hour off "to run an errand" and returned home to do it. Luke looked puzzled, but said nothing.

Pacing the living room carpet, she dialed the landlord's number. A ray of sunlight penetrated the front window, and dust motes hung in the air. She needed to vacuum. Her thoughts were interrupted by a voice.

"Thank you for calling Pilgrim Properties."

Molly was about to say something when she realized she'd got the machine again. *"To speak to one of our team, listen for the instructions. If you know your party's extension, you may dial it now."*

How should anyone be expected to know that? They kept the names of their so-called team a secret.

"Otherwise, say the name of the person you wish to speak to, followed by the pound key."

Aha. She tried not to clench her teeth as she said Channing's name.

After hearing some clicks on the line, she reached the man himself. No going back now. She plumped down on the sofa, and fumbled in her pocket for the envelope with her notes.

"Madison," he said, like a man not wanting to commit himself too much.

"Good morning. This is Molly Stevenson."

Silence.

"From the Book Boutique?" She didn't mean it to be a question, but that's how it came out. She picked at a loose thread in the mohair throw lying next to her.

"What can I do for you, Miss Stevenson? Is this about the Wentworth Library?"

"What?" Molly felt as though she'd suddenly fallen off a narrow plank over deep water. She must get her thoughts in order.

"The Library, of which I am a trustee, as you surely know, buys books from you every year when we have author events. I assume it has to do with that."

The Wentworth bought around forty books for the few author talks they held each year. Those were mostly by local authors, and their contribution to her bottom line was minimal.

"No. Not at all. It has to do with the fact that you're my landlord." And to begin with, you could refrain from trying to bankrupt me.

She didn't say the last part aloud—she wasn't reckless. "I'm calling about a letter we received from your company the other day."

"Ah."

"Yes. Ah. Mr. Madison, I'm sure you're aware that retail has been having a difficult time of it lately."

"Things have been tough everywhere." His reply came so fast—he hadn't even paused to consider his answer. She decided to ignore him. She'd never get to the point if she didn't.

"I took over the Book Boutique nine months ago, and my business plan was predicated on the income and expenses of that time."

"Could you be more concise, Miss Stevenson?"

"*Mrs.*," interrupted Molly. He ignored this, not giving her time to reply before continuing.

"We can't be responsible for changes in the retail arena. We have to take into account our shareholders."

Our shareholders? She'd done her research now. They were all members of the substantial Madison family. Which meant it was all about the Madisons getting richer.

Molly gritted her teeth. "Be that as it may, should I agree to pay your suggested rent increase, the bookshop has every likelihood of going under." If pomposity appealed to him, she could be as pompous as he could. Her bravado was replaced immediately by a sinking feeling. Admitting that the store was in such bad shape, to someone like this, put her in his power.

"I have a proposal to make." The confidence in her voice was entirely manufactured. This was more of a begging request, if she were honest.

"I'm listening."

Well, that was something. He hadn't cut her off yet. She closed her eyes and visualized a positive outcome.

"As you can imagine, the holiday season is our busiest time of year, the period when we normally make most of our profits. I won't know how we've done until February or so. I'd like an abatement on the higher rent until March, to give me time to budget for the fiscal year ahead." She let out a breath, conscious of the fact that she'd been speaking faster than usual in an effort to get it out before he interrupted again. Simon had used the word "abatement" and she'd looked it up to make sure she got the meaning right.

"You mean you won't pay the new rent before March? Absolutely out of the question. We are not a not-for-profit, Miss Stevenson."

She heard him chuckling at this witticism. No indeed. They

were all about the profit. She glanced at the notes she'd made before calling. Time to make her fallback offer.

"In which case, would you consider a smaller increase?"

"That would be inappropriate. Were I to grant you a reduction, everybody else would want one too."

So, it was about wielding power too. Using the word "grant" gave him away. He wanted to lord it over his puny little empire. She didn't care if he heard her gnashing her teeth.

"Listen, Brentford needs the Book Boutique. It serves people of all ages, and some customers come from out of town to buy from us, which brings more business to Brentford."

She pictured Mrs. Todd and Miss Johansen, Trey, kids of all ages, and the young mothers. Not to mention the tourists who wanted postcards and local history books when they showed up to take photos of the town. She cherished this place and wasn't about to let it down if she could possibly help it.

"I'm sorry, Miss Stevenson."

His tone made it clear—he couldn't care less.

"Mrs.," she said, her thoughts elsewhere.

"Quite. But the rent increase, the current one, will go into effect on January 1, as stated in our communication. Should you be unable to pay it, there are other people who will. Good day."

He hung up, leaving Molly staring at her phone in bewilderment and fury.

***

That night she dreamed in black and white, of a young and beautiful maiden with tearful eyes shrinking before a villainous man with a huge black mustache and a top hat. As the victim's kohl-rimmed eyes beseeched him, she raised her arm to her forehead and kept pleading, "I can't pay the rent!" The wicked landlord leaned forward each time, twirling his mustache ominously and repeating, "You must pay the rent!"

Molly woke herself up. She wasn't going to be a victim. Kohl didn't suit her.

CHAPTER THIRTEEN

"I didn't realize I'd been so long. Any problems while I was out?"

"Nope," said Luke. "We sold three Nancy Drews to Mrs. Petrillo, for her granddaughters. And I had a couple of phone orders."

"That's great." She sounded flat, even to herself.

Luke glanced at her. "How did things go?"

"How did what go?" Did he know about her phone call?

He raised an eyebrow. "Your errand, of course."

Oh, right. She'd mentioned an errand. "I needed to order something," she improvised. Catching his expression, she added, "It's a surprise."

And not necessarily a nice one. Especially if the big reveal turned out to be that the Book Boutique would have to close.

She mustn't think about that now. If they worked hard over the holidays, they might make enough to cover the increased rent. At least for a while.

Thank god she didn't have to worry about the online dating situation. No one had contacted her, including Starman97.

A few days passed, and she began to relax about the whole enterprise. Then, as she was pouring herself a glass of rose one evening, Rosie called.

"How's it going? Made any connections yet?"

If Amanda was the mastermind behind this find-a-man-for-Molly scheme, Rosie had been the perp. She'd been the one who identified Starman97, after all, and set up the online account, gliding over the fact that Molly was about to be fifty, and a widow too. "Single sounds sexier," she assured her, and she should know.

"For heaven's sake. I don't have time for this. I have too much on my mind—the holidays coming up. You know what it's like."

"Well sure. I'm practically booked at the salon through Christmas Eve. But didn't you ever hear back from that Starman guy?"

"Not a peep."

"Hmmm. You are checking the app, aren't you?"

"What?"

Rosie raised her eyes heavenward with all the patience of a saint. "We set you up with the new identity, remember? Just for this."

"I'd forgotten. I don't know how to access it."

"Don't be such a dunce, Molly. You're perfectly capable if you put your mind to it. Want me to come over and show you?"

"No. No," she said hastily. "That won't be necessary. I'll check for messages this evening."

"Promise?"

"I swear. There's probably nothing there, anyway."

"Well, call me if you need a hand with anything."

She would die rather than ask for help with this. "Sure," she said.

Reluctantly, she logged on to YoursTruly. Best to get it done with. Rosie had made her pick an easy password and suggested Romeo123. Horrified, Molly stared at the screen. Nineteen messages confronted her. And there sat one from Starman97.

He'd only sent it a day ago, so he hadn't been waiting too long for a reply. He sounded somewhat stodgy, but innocuous enough. A couple of appropriate comments about how pleased he would be to get acquainted. A suggestion that they meet for dinner and a movie.

She'd have to ask for advice now. Was this a foolish idea? After speaking to Rosie, she turned the dinner down and suggested a daytime rendezvous a few days later, at a café some way away, so it needn't be a long-drawn-out event if they didn't click. And there'd be no local witnesses.

A flurry of cool air announced Simon's appearance in the kitchen the day after Molly had agreed to the date. Apparently, he'd come prepared to share a skeptical opinion.

"He's not the one I'd choose. But if you must go out with him, I guess you could think of him as a starter guy." Molly thought she detected a note of irritability in his voice. *"I don't suppose you'll come to any harm, even if he turns out to be a mistake."*

"How do you mean?" Alarm bells sounded in her ears.

"Well, he looks okay on paper, but you can never tell."

Molly, all too aware of this, had fought her recurring anxiety ever since she'd arranged to meet Starman97. Now it was back. With a vengeance.

Simon hadn't finished. *"At least you're not seeing him at night. You can tell me how it went when you come back."*

Well, that was something. He wouldn't be going with her. But was she now obliged to report back to him? Did *he* have to approve of her choice? And why was he grinning? Wasn't he supposed to be helping?

"And don't go to too much trouble for this guy. It's only coffee."

***

"Good for you, setting up a date," said Amanda when she stopped by the store the following day. Naturally, her friends had weaseled the truth out of her almost immediately.

"At this moment, all I feel is slightly nauseous at the thought."

"No need to worry. Dating is like riding a bike. You don't forget."

"That's what's making me feel sick. Thinking back to Adam Rankin in high school. He broke my heart."

"And look how well it mended," said her friend briskly. "You just need something to boost your confidence. Want me to come over and help you choose the right thing to wear?"

"It's only coffee," she began, but she needn't have bothered.

Amanda, who despaired of Molly's sense of style, showed up later in the day with a pair of fashionable leggings with a discreet diagonal pattern. "I found these in my drawer. Never worn them. Here you are—for luck."

***

Early Friday morning, she and Rosie texted her with last-minute reminders.

Got perfume? Men love it. X. Amanda.

Want me to give you a blow-dry before you go? On the house. Rosie

And now both were no doubt waiting impatiently for every detail of her first date with this man, whose real name, it turned out, was Charlie. If men loved scent, Molly wouldn't use any. Besides, she wasn't sure the bottle of Chanel Allure that Simon had given her just before he died was still usable. Didn't perfume go stale after a while? Like three years? She refused Rosie's offer too. She wouldn't waste time on a trip to the salon. She didn't need help doing her hair, and if the guy didn't like it, too bad.

She gave herself one last glance in the hall mirror and headed into the garage. As she fired up the engine of her trusty Volvo station wagon, she checked the fuel gauge. Crap. Practically empty. Oh well. If she didn't have enough gas to get to her rendezvous, then she wasn't meant to be there, right?

CHAPTER FOURTEEN

Molly arrived at the agreed-upon Starbucks early. Regrettably, everything had conspired to get to her destination on time. The traffic hadn't been as bad as usual, and she'd even found a parking spot nearby. She suppressed the butterflies in her stomach as she dug in her purse for enough small change to allow herself an hour's parking. Then she thought better of it and stuffed a couple more quarters in the meter. The last thing she needed to worry about was getting a ticket.

As she walked toward the rendezvous, Molly wished she'd worn warmer boots. Her black knee-high pair were good-looking, but the soles were thin. The cold rising from the frigid sidewalk penetrated her toes. With any luck, she'd warm up once she was indoors.

A blast of hot air hit her as she entered. Her nose twitched at the smell of coffee. At least that would be something she'd be able to enjoy without anxiety. She would order a decaf, though. The butterflies hadn't quite subsided yet, and she'd always been unable to taste the difference in a cappuccino, with all that steamed milk.

She stared nervously at the other patrons. Had Starman97 arrived early too? She couldn't see anyone who resembled him. She would find a place to settle and wait. All the comfy chairs were occupied. Still, better not to get too comfortable, and to have a table between them. One never knew.

Molly spotted a small table against the wall, where two customers were getting up to leave. She chose the seat facing the room, so she could keep an eye on people walking in. She'd picked up the idea from a thriller she'd read, where the hero always expects some assassin or other to show up and doesn't want to be ambushed unawares from behind.

At this time of day, late morning patrons kept the baristas busy, and the hubbub of orders and conversation made the place much noisier than the Java Jive.

The chatter, underlaid by some cheerful reggae music, bounced off the walls. Should this man turn out to be deaf, she'd have to shout, and that would be awkward. Unlikely, surely, given that he was a couple of years younger than her. She tried to concentrate on the calming breathing technique she'd learned in yoga classes years ago. In, out. Inhale, exhale. She took out her phone when it pinged to alert her to new text messages. One from Amanda: *Send me a selfie.* Another from Rosie: *Did you remember your eyeliner?*

For crying out loud. She glanced at the wall clock. A minute past eleven. If he didn't arrive in the next five minutes, she would leave. The thought steadied her, so she checked the time again, and began the countdown.

She continued scanning the caffeine junkies who walked in, but so far, she hadn't identified anyone who resembled the man on YoursTruly.com. Her spirits rose. One more minute, and she'd be off the hook.

Just before eleven oh-six, a lone man finally entered through the swing door, and she nearly missed his arrival. If he hadn't stopped to check out the room, she might not have recognized him from his photos. This man was almost bald, for one thing, and chunkier than she'd expected.

And yet, there was something familiar about him. OMG. What the hell was Channing Madison doing here? She hadn't seen him in a while, but there was no mistaking the self-satisfied smirk that greeted her whenever she walked into the lobby of the Wentworth Library, where his photo hung alongside those of the other trustees. She shrank back in her chair, hoping he was here to buy coffee to go and wouldn't notice her. If he were to witness her meeting someone here, she'd be mortified.

But as he scanned the room, his eyes fell on her and he smiled. Of all the dumb luck.

She tried to make herself inconspicuous. Too late. He made a beeline for her through the tables, barging past the other customers en route. His obliviousness as he brushed the back of various patrons' heads with his overcoat, set her teeth on edge.

She fixed a tight-lipped smile on her face.

"Good morning." She couldn't bring herself to say anything else to her nemesis.

He indicated that she should sit down again. Almost as though he was her…

What the…? No. No. This couldn't possibly be her date. He looked nothing like the man online, the one called Charlie.

"Hello there, Mrs. Stevenson," he said, with a heavy emphasis on the *Mrs.*, as if to demonstrate that he'd bothered to remember the appellation she preferred.

"Mr. Madison." She paused. "I didn't expect to see you here."

His hand felt chilly and slightly clammy to the touch, and Molly added this to the reasons she disliked him.

"I'm meeting someone else," she said. That should take care of things. He'd have to leave her alone now.

A fleeting grimace of embarrassment crossed his features before he laughed.

"But I expected *you*, I confess. I'm Charlie." He probably thought that his accompanying expression was a winning one.

"Charlie?"

"Your date. I have to travel under a pseudonym. I don't want women contacting me because they know who I am."

No. This couldn't be happening. The butterfly or two that had taken up residence inside her chest had suddenly become a universe of moths. She'd stopped breathing. Must start again. In. Out.

His smug voice grated on. "I recognized you from your on-line photo, and thought this might be fun." He bared his teeth in a smile—oh, those too-perfect teeth—and threw his coat over the back of a chair.

In any other circumstances, she would have left immediately. But she had to survive this encounter first, because if there was one person she couldn't afford to alienate, it was this man. She would kill Rosie later, for setting this up.

He asked her what she'd like to drink and went off to order their coffees. Molly watched him as he stood at the counter.

Best to keep the accidental rendezvous businesslike, and as short as possible. But what on earth would they talk about? The only thing she wanted from him was a rent reduction. She had no idea what *he* wanted. So, though it galled her to do so, she would treat this as a strictly social meeting.

She needed to find something positive to focus on. He might not be so bad, really, and, if he knew her, would possibly be inclined to help save the bookshop. They might discuss books as a way of breaking the ice. He must read, or he wouldn't be a trustee at the Wentworth.

He returned carrying two steaming lattes. Molly was about to remind him that she'd asked for a cappuccino when he walked off again and came back with two huge brownies on a plate, which he placed on the table between them.

"I didn't expect anything to eat," she said. "I don't have much of an appetite right now."

Still, at least he'd offered her something. He picked up one of the brownies.

"No problem." A mouthful of chocolate crumbs was no hindrance to conversation, apparently. "I'm hungry enough for both of us." He chuckled, revealing teeth filled with brownie dough.

Molly glanced away. Any trace of hunger had disappeared

completely. She couldn't face talking to him while he continued to chew, even if she could come up with a safe topic. As an opening gambit, she wanted to ask him how come his profile picture showed him to be at least thirty pounds lighter, with luxuriant locks. Though the answer to that was obvious, if he consumed all this with a latte. The spotlight above him gleamed through his thinning hair.

Yet she had to give him the benefit of the doubt. Looks weren't everything. And if he got to know her better, he might think again about increasing the rent.

"So, how long have you been online?" he asked.

She hadn't expected this. "Not long. This is my first appointment."

"No need to make it sound like a visit to the dentist."

She faked a smile. "My friends…" How to put this? Encouraged her? Forced her? "Persuaded me it was time."

"I've been on there quite a while. My mother said I should try it, and I thought, why not? Usually, I don't go out with local people. Too incestuous. But I thought you might have potential."

Molly bristled inwardly. He made her sound like one of his investments.

"I do. At least my bookshop does."

"Now, now. No business talk. We're here as friends."

She had no idea what had given him *that* impression. She tried a safer topic.

"So, you like to read?" He'd mentioned this on his profile.

"Yesh," he responded, impeded by a mouthful of crumbs. Mopping his mouth with a paper napkin, he swallowed. "I imagine you're interested in that, since it's your job."

"If you mean that my livelihood depends on people reading, you're right, of course."

"I said we wouldn't discuss business."

"You brought it up. I was simply trying to converse."

"Hmm. Well, if you must know, I like thrillers and history

books. World War II and so on." He took another bite.

"Have you read the latest title? About a spy working in the Polish resistance? I have some in stock. I'll save one for you if you like."

Channing frowned. "I'm more fascinated by the roots of the conflict, if you know what I mean."

She didn't, and wasn't sure she wanted to.

"The rise of Hitler, the economic situation in Germany. That sort of thing."

"I can order you a copy of *Mein Kampf*, if you like. I hear it's required reading for serious students of the period."

If he heard the irony in her voice, he ignored it. "I've read that a couple of times," he said. "Very interesting."

This conversational thread would lead to disaster, she predicted, and changed tack.

"Where do you walk?"

"What?"

"You said you liked walking on the beach."

His eyes cut away and back to her. "Well, it's not the season now, obviously."

By the look of his paunch, it never had been the season.

"I meant, when the weather's good."

"Oh, anywhere along the coastline," he said vaguely. "Near the yacht club."

Finally—a less contentious subject. "Do you sail?"

"Lord, no. My father was the last sailor of the family. Nicknamed the Commodore. He owned a forty-foot racing yacht."

And he was off.

Molly tried to look attentive, but she needn't have bothered. The man was unstoppable. Talking about his perfect father, growing up with a family history of maritime pursuits, and on and on. He barely paused for breath, so all she needed to do was nod from time to time. He could have won gold if there'd been an Olympic boring team—for putting the judges to sleep. A giggle escaped her as she visualized it.

"That struck you as amusing?" His outraged tone let her know that she had blundered.

"Of course not." What had he been saying?

"The death of my great-grandfather William Channing, who fell overboard at the America's Cup in 1881, was a tragic event."

"Of course." She should be sympathetic. "So, he was a competitive sailor?"

"He drowned in the harbor, if you must know. The Pilgrim was moored there. Since it was late at night and he couldn't swim…"

Oh, dear. *Not* funny. She must not laugh. "Goodness. What a shock for the family."

Somewhat mollified, he replied, "Indeed. We named the company after the yacht, in his memory."

"Is that why you don't sail?"

"No. I just don't like boats."

A moment of intuition flashed in her mind. "Seasick, eh?"

His brow furrowed in annoyance. "I prefer duck hunting as a sport."

He would. He embodied everything she disliked in a person.

Her phone pinged with another text message from Amanda: *How's it going? If you need to bail, tell him someone's sick or something.*

Relief coursed through her. Thank god for her friend. Molly had forgotten that her daughters sometimes used this method as a backup on a first date with someone new. Never mind. Rescue was at hand.

She tried to look distressed. "I'm so sorry, but something has come up and I have to leave."

Channing looked confused rather than concerned. "What is it? Can't it wait?"

She crossed her fingers behind her back and stood.

"No. My father isn't well. They need me to come over right away."

"Can we continue this another time?" Channing's voice was hopeful.

"I'm sure we can," said Molly. When hell freezes over, she added silently.

CHAPTER FIFTEEN

Without pausing to check her phone, Molly drove back to Brentford on autopilot, stopping only to get gas, which she did in a kind of irate daze. This was the problem with online dating. People *lied*. Blatantly. The man hadn't even apologized for calling himself Charlie. And as for the photograph he'd used on his profile—there was no excuse for that. Except no one would date him if they saw what he actually looked like now.

Part of her was furious with her friends and Simon for pushing her to do this. Yet a small voice kept telling her it was her own fault. She could have refused. Then she wouldn't have had to ditch Channing at Starbucks.

What if she'd dashed her chances of him ever being cooperative? Her hands felt clammy. She could only hope he was too thick-skinned to feel slighted, since she couldn't afford to risk his ill will. She'd surely have to deal with him again. With any luck, he'd find someone else to pursue.

She tapped her fingers on the steering wheel and slowed to swerve around a runner. She must stop focusing on Madison. The thought of him would only make her more livid.

This whole day was a disaster. And—she glanced at the dashboard clock—still only eleven thirty.

Well, one thing was certain. She would never go on a blind date again. Her mind buzzed with a swarm of unanswerable questions. Was that a typical first meeting? How did Rosie stand it? How on earth had she managed to find someone as lovely as her current guy, Rocco?

As Molly swung onto Main Street, the sight of the bookstore soothed her spirits. Her shoulders relaxed when she walked into the safety of the Book Boutique. No matter what happened with Channing, she would keep the bookshop going as long as she was able.

Luke peered into the back room with a mildly curious expression on his face. He'd started wearing his coral pink and orange vests, a sure sign winter was on its way. Today's was a deep rust, complemented by a pumpkin-colored bow tie. "So, how did it go? You're back earlier than I expected."

She wished she hadn't mentioned where she was going. Just said it was a meeting.

"Horrible," she said eventually. "I don't want to talk about it."

Luke simply nodded. "Fair enough."

He would wait for her to confide in him, for which she was grateful. Unlike Amanda and Rosie, who had buzzed around her like gnats before she went and let her know they'd be expecting a complete rundown of her first date. She would not think about them. It only raised her blood pressure when she did.

"But since you ask," Molly found herself saying, "it turned out to be Channing Madison."

"How do you mean? Didn't you know who you were meeting beforehand?"

Oops. She hadn't told him what kind of an appointment this was.

"It's a long story." She felt a blush rising and wished once again that she weren't so fair-skinned. "It was sort of a blind date."

Luke nodded, then took off his glasses and began polishing them with a pocket handkerchief. Perhaps this was too much information for him.

"Anyway, I was expecting someone different, and I got so mad at him that I walked out of the café."

"Good for you." It appeared he had decided to be support-ive. "I've never known how Acacia puts up with him. Pompous jackass."

"Acacia? Mrs. Todd?"

"Oh yes. Didn't you know? She's his mother."

Molly was having trouble taking this in. "But his last name is Madison."

"I know, but she's been widowed twice. She never says any-thing about her first husband. Just that her second, Mr. Todd, was a lovely man."

The situation was getting worse every minute. Molly had just rejected not just her landlord, but the son of one of their most regular customers. In public. The store really couldn't af-ford to lose any business. Luke ought to have mentioned this before.

"You do know who he is, don't you?"

"I just told you. Acacia's son."

"Sure. But he's also the CEO of Pilgrim Properties."

Luke's eyebrows shot up. She'd got his attention now. "He took over from the old guy?"

"That's right. And they want to raise our rent, which is go-ing to make life difficult, to say the least."

His stricken face let her know he'd had no idea.

"So you see, walking out on him in Starbucks probably wasn't ideal."

"I guess not." He kept his voice level, but Molly read the anxiety in his eyes and hastened to reassure him.

"We don't need to worry about that yet. If we can make our holiday sales targets, we might be okay."

"Targets?"

"Yes, remember? We talked about trying to sell one extra item each time someone comes in to buy something. A gift, or another book. Every additional sale will help."

Luke nodded vigorously. Clearly, he hadn't listened the last time she mentioned it. But the real danger the shop faced might spur him on.

"The least I can do is persuade Mrs. T. to purchase more," he said.

"Right. Though I doubt even that can make up for her son's deficiencies."

***

The next few hours flew by. Almost as if her supporters had heard her, a constant stream of customers came through the doors, and Molly noticed Luke pointing out some of the despised gift merchandise to each one. About half of them bought an extra item, which cheered her up.

During a lull, she made herself a cup of tea and was standing behind the desk, sipping it, when Luke strolled up to deposit a pile of elegant volumes on the counter. Red leather embossed in gold, with transparent covers for protection, she guessed.

"Sorry. I was miles away. Did you just ask me something?"

"I did." He paused. "I've been unpacking new titles for the big display. I'd love to add these. They're the luxury edition of *A Christmas Carol*, and they always sell well."

"Sure. They'll look great next to the abridged versions for children. We could use them to segue from kids to adult holiday books."

Luke handed one over, and as she leafed through it, he said, "By the way, those candles named after famous authors? We only have a few Louisa May Alcott ones left. Do you think we ought to order some more?" He kept his tone airy, but Molly realized it must have cost him a lot to say that. It was tantamount to admitting he'd been mistaken about her ideas for seasonal gift stock. She gave his arm a squeeze.

"Good idea. I'm not sure we can get them in time, but I'll try." She caught something in his expression. "Something else you wanted to say? We've got plenty of wrap, and—"

Luke cleared his throat. "I wondered if you'd seen Nick around."

"Who? Oh, your friend. I haven't met him. So, is he the man who took the house next door?"

Molly hadn't asked Amanda whether the house was rented, and Amanda hadn't volunteered the information. Too busy trying to launch Molly into the dating swamp, obviously.

"He is. I only brought it up because he's coming to my Thanksgiving dinner."

"That will be nice," said Molly, her thoughts elsewhere. The seasonal cards would need more space. They came from a local artist, and people loved them, attracted by the watercolors of Brentford buildings covered in snow, with bright wreaths hanging on the doors.

"I think you'll like him."

"I'm sure I will. Any friend of yours…"

CHAPTER SIXTEEN

Cheese was protein, wasn't it? That's what Molly told herself when she settled into an armchair with a glass of pinot grigio and a bowl of cheese popcorn that had somehow made its way onto the coffee table. A favorite episode of *Find It and Flog It*, a British import on PBS, would distract her from the day's events.

Damn. The phone. She should have turned off the ringer. Molly glanced at the screen. Two names on the caller ID. Really? Amanda and Rosie were planning to interrogate her via conference call? Knowing they wouldn't give up, she gritted her teeth and pushed the green button.

Before she had time to say anything, "So? How'd it go?" and "What did you think?" her friends chorused.

"One at a time," pleaded Molly, adding, "If you really want to know, I'm thinking I'd like to wring both your necks."

A pause as they seemed to be digesting this response.

"So, not a hundred percent successful?" asked Rosie.

"You might say that."

"Why *me*?" Amanda sounded aggrieved. Another pause. "I did text you. At least I gave you an out."

Molly started to thaw. "I must admit, I am grateful for that. I couldn't think of how to get away."

"That bad, eh? Well, I'm glad I was able to help."

"As for you, Rosie, how you ever came across someone online as perfect for you as Rocco, I can't imagine." Not that

Rocco was Molly's type. He was sweet, but his puppy-dog energy and love of a good time would drive Molly crazy.

The act of expressing her exasperation was surprisingly satisfying, but almost immediately, a sense of remorse drowned out the feeling. "I guess you meant well," she conceded. "But the road to hell, you know—"

"Honestly, now, was he as bad as that?" Rosie sounded chastened. "Want to tell us about it?"

"Yes, he was. And no, I'm not going to share anything about it," said Molly. "The whole thing was a catastrophe."

Amanda wanted details. "Come on. You're exaggerating, aren't you? What was wrong with him?"

Molly relented. She may as well tell them. With any luck, they'd quit this project if she explained how badly the date had gone. "Where to start? First off, he looked nothing at all like his profile picture, and he obviously lied about his age. A midlife crisis frog comes to mind. And the sight of him with a mouthful of—"

"Flies?" interrupted Rosie.

Molly couldn't help laughing. "No—that might have been better. Messy brownies. Crumbs all down his front. You get the idea."

An awed silence greeted this description.

"Which might not have mattered, but then he only talked about himself. A lot more than I cared to know. All about his hunting, and sailing, and the Third Reich."

"The Third Reich? What the…?"

"More like WTF to be precise. His bedside reading is *Mein Kampf.*"

She waited for this to sink in.

"Wow," said Rosie. "Sounds like you had a narrow escape there."

"There's one more thing. Amanda, you'll appreciate this. His name was Channing Madison."

She heard Amanda gasp. "No!"

Rosie's response came out more plaintive. "Who?"

Amanda explained. "He's Molly's landlord. Not one of her favorite people. How come you didn't recognize him from his photo?"

"Rosie warned me that you couldn't rely on photos, but I had no idea how devious people could be. Channing's profile picture was several years old at least, and he's bald now." A fit of conscience made her add, "Well, almost. If I'd known it was him, I'd never have gone."

"But you kept things polite, right?" Rosie, generally willing to confront any injustice, had apparently decided to take the high road.

"I tried. I used Amanda's text as an excuse to leave. Told him my father had fallen ill."

Silence greeted this.

"Oh, dear." This was mild, coming from Amanda. "Do you think he believed you?"

"That's beside the point now. He wants to raise my rent, Rosie, which I can't afford. Then he had the nerve to approach me online so he could take me out. So obnoxious."

"Well, now he's dated you." Rosie's deadpan delivery caused a laugh to bubble up in Molly's throat. But this was serious.

If he were obtuse enough to call for another date and she turned him down, it might not only affect her chances of a cooperative relationship with Pilgrim Properties, but with the Wentworth Library as well. Damn Channing. She would have to avoid him at all costs from now on.

***

The popcorn had lost its appeal. She needed something to soothe and warm her bruised spirit this evening. So, she headed into the kitchen to reheat some of the delicious pumpkin bisque from Jackson's Pantry, the freshly made food market further down Main Street.

As she poured some of the sunny soup into a bowl and placed it in the microwave, she shivered, sensing a sudden coolness in the room, and turned around.

"Did you hear that?" she demanded as Simon materialized nearby. This time, he was sitting on the counter, swinging his legs like a four-year-old and grinning at her.

"*Not everything. You should have let me help—with the manhunt,*" he clarified. "*I would never have picked a jackass like him. I know what you like.*"

His expression was wistful as he spoke.

Did he miss her as much as she missed him? The pang this caused passed in a second. "You encouraged me! Did you hear the part about the date being Channing Madison?"

"*Yup. Not a good idea to mix business with pleasure, you know.*"

God, he could be obtuse sometimes. "I didn't know it would be him. In any case, that's not the most important takeaway."

"*How do you mean?*"

"The point is, I as good as dumped him, and I don't think he likes that sort of thing. Although it's possible he didn't realize that's what I'd done. Doubtless, it's happened to him a lot—with his social skills."

"*Didn't he pretty much blow you off when you called him about the rent?*"

"He did. And he wouldn't give me any leeway over that, yet apparently had no scruples about dating me."

"*Very unprofessional.*"

"I know. But do you think I should have gone along with him—tried to win him over, I mean?"

Simon made a gagging sound. "*Absolutely not. Using his business to prey on women is despicable. You'll have to come up with another solution to the rent issue. In the meantime, don't give up on men. They can't all be bad. There must be a few that are okay.*"

Not exactly encouraging. Perhaps he was having second thoughts about his project, which would be fine with her.

Molly grimaced. "I know you have your project, darling, but

I'd rather have your professional advice than your matchmaking ideas."

"*Listen. I'm supposed to help you out, so how about I try to find you someone who's, you know, not quite as wonderful as me, but—um—suitable.*" He grinned at her.

Molly realized her jaw had dropped and shut it firmly.

"Suitable?" she wasn't sure what to say.

Simon pointed at himself and laughed. "*Yeah. You know—good-natured, supportive, sociable, easygoing—*"

"So, I should get a dog and be done with it?" she interrupted him, with a touch of asperity.

Simon's face turned serious. "*Only not too...exciting.*"

What? Molly could hardly frame the thought. Was he talking about—sex? She felt the blush on her cheeks. Must be the wine. Time to nip this topic in the bud. "I don't need any more excitement in my life." Or in any potential date. If he was supposed to find her a second-rate husband... She rolled her eyes. Well, he'd already succeeded with the second-rate part.

"*That's settled, then. You'll check with me before you agree to meet a new guy?*"

How had he derailed the conversation about her money problems? And how had she let him?

"Sure," she said, but she wasn't at all certain. Time to concentrate on the bookstore. Forget even *thinking* about men. When she turned to look at him, Simon had gone.

She opened the microwave door. She'd forgotten to turn the damn thing on. The pumpkin bisque was still stone cold.

CHAPTER SEVENTEEN

Thanksgiving was approaching at something like lightning speed, and business was picking up at the store, much to Molly's relief. She worked long hours, re-ordering unexpected bestsellers, making sure they were in the right place to catch a customer's attention. She chose some children's books relevant to the season and placed them at a child's eye level to encourage sales. Like candy displays at the supermarket, but a lot less harmful to the kids' health. In fact, positively beneficial.

As she went through the cooking section, choosing appropriate books to display up front, she found herself leafing through some of them, admiring the beautiful photography. Customers bought new cookbooks around Thanksgiving. Before she owned the bookshop, she used to do the same herself, only to find that she reverted to the tried-and-true recipes she'd learned from her mother.

Reluctantly, she closed the last copy of *Fifty Foolproof Cookies* and set it back on the table. If Luke wanted her to contribute her forest-floor cookies for his holiday dinner, she'd bake those.

So much activity didn't allow her time to wonder about her new neighbor, who'd moved in the previous weekend. Since she returned from work after nightfall, the only glimpses she'd had of the occupants were of a large, bouncy golden retriever rushing around the yard next door, barking when its owner let it out early in the morning.

She walked over with a plate of home-baked cookies to introduce herself, but the professor was out, and she didn't want to leave them on the doorstep. His enthusiastic dog might get to them before he did.

Occasionally, she caught sight of the man's outline, but their houses were sufficiently far apart that it didn't tell her much. Oh, well, she'd meet him at Luke's.

***

She decided to close the store a couple of hours early the day before the holiday. Luke would be taking that Wednesday off to handle his preparations, and after four o'clock it was rare to see a customer that day. She could use the time herself, to locate the Christmas decorations to be hung before the weekend was over. Other stores had started featuring red and green décor by now. The bakery over the way had painted laughing gingerbread men dancing across the top of its windows. The real ones were already displayed in tempting rows below.

Gingerbread men. Men. Luke's party. She must stop woolgathering.

She'd forgotten to ask how many people would be coming, so she made two dozen cookies early on the day itself. Just to be on the safe side.

There was no point in plating them—Luke was fussy, and any plate she chose would be wrong. So, she loaded them carefully into a decorative cardboard box, placing a sheet of wax paper between the layers. Then she tied the package up with a rust-and-gold ribbon and put it on the seat of the car, so as not to forget it.

Just after four that afternoon, she pulled up by Luke's converted farmhouse, not far out of Brentford. It stood near the road, as all the old dwellings in town tended to. Molly aimed to arrive early enough to give her host a hand, but even so, a few cars were parked outside the barn Luke used as a garage.

Carrying her contribution to the feast, she walked through the front door, which he'd left unlocked.

Inside, she surveyed the familiar space and took a breath. Across the room, she could make out several of Luke's friends whom she'd met before, standing chatting to each other, drinks in hand.

The previous owner of the house had knocked out a couple of walls to blend the dining and living rooms, leaving a large open area where people could mingle comfortably. Molly always admired the oak beams and relatively low ceilings that made it cozy. The mixture of antique armchairs and the unexpectedly comfortable 1950s sofas looked enticing after a morning spent on her feet, baking. Brightly colored rugs added to the festive ambiance as the setting sun streamed in.

She spotted Luke's sister and her husband standing by the wide stone fireplace, where logs crackled as the flames roared up the chimney. They had drinks in their hands, and she gave them a wave on her way through to the kitchen, where she expected to find her host.

Unlike the original part of the house, the kitchen was built to accommodate the most demanding of chefs. Luke enjoyed cooking for his friends, and, not wanting to get in his way, Molly hesitated before walking over to deposit the cookies on one of the few spaces left on the counter.

The heat from two wall ovens made the place distinctly warm. She sniffed appreciatively. The seasonal smell of a roasting turkey made her mouth water. How lovely. It would be a traditional meal, after all.

"Not there, Molly," came the instruction from behind her. Luke, pink in the face, waved at her with the dangerous-looking carving knife he held in one hand. He wore a scarlet apron over his yellow-striped shirt—one of the few people she knew who could pull off such a contradictory look without appearing ridiculous. She smiled.

"Could you put them on that platter?" He pointed with the

knife. "And they can go on the table behind the sofa. We'll have them with coffee after," he said.

"Of course. Let me know when you need a hand. And— Happy Thanksgiving." She kissed him lightly on the cheek and left him to it.

Back in the main room, she set the platter down and walked across to check out the dining table. How beautiful—more gorgeous than anything she'd ever managed to prepare. The mahogany surface gleamed, and a hint of beeswax polish hung in the air.

The centerpiece, which ran down the middle of the long table, boasted small pumpkins, fat candles, and colorful chili peppers interspersed with pine cones and greenery. Every place had been laid with antique china printed with hunting scenes, crystal goblets, and silverware that sparkled. Linen napkins lay encircled with silver rings, with a few heads of wheat peeking out between the folds.

And in front of each setting stood a handwritten menu, detailing the delights to come.

"It's lovely enough to be in *Town and Country*, isn't it?" came a voice behind her.

Molly spun around to find herself looking up at a rangy man, informally dressed in dark jeans, a white T-shirt, and a navy blazer. His expression made him seem rather forbidding, and she took a step back, bumping into one of the chairs.

"It definitely is," she managed. "Luke's a man of many talents. I'm Molly Stevenson, by the way."

"I know. Our host pointed you out. I believe we're neighbors. Nick Hokkanen."

Molly took a moment to assess him. His nose was too beaky for him to be called handsome, and the heavy horn-rimmed glasses didn't allow her to read the eyes behind them, but when he smiled, his face became transformed. A faint dusting of gray highlighted his curly auburn hair. She could see why Luke might find him attractive, though he was a decade or more younger.

Around forty-five, she guessed.

"That's right." Realizing her reply might sound lukewarm, she added, "I think I've seen your dog. He's quite a character, isn't he?"

"Hadley? Yes, she is. I'm sorry about the way she barks—it's the excitement of being in a new place and having a yard. We didn't have one in the city, of course."

"Hadley?" She smiled.

"Yes. After Hemingway's—"

"First wife," they finished together and laughed.

"Funny, my cat is called Hemingway. Let's hope they have a more harmonious relationship than their namesakes."

"I second that. Hadley's pretty easygoing."

"I have no idea about my cat's attitude to dogs. He may be a bit leery."

"I'm sure they'll work it out," said Nick, with an easy grin.

"I imagine it's been quite a change for both of you, coming out here from the city," said Molly. "New beginnings can be hard, can't they?"

He cocked his head to one side, as if trying to decide whether her words had some hidden meaning in them. Evidently choosing to take her at face value, he nodded.

"True. But we're settling in now and aim to be good neighbors. Hadley is already barking less, don't you think?"

Before she could answer, Luke summoned her, and, making her excuses, she headed off to help in the kitchen. Nick seemed harmless. And it might be nice to have a man next door again.

***

"Have you tried these cookies? They're delicious," Nick said as he pushed a stray crumb into his mouth. "Though I have no idea how I managed to make room for one after that meal."

Molly felt her cheeks flush with pleasure. "I made them," she said.

"I'm impressed. They're fantastic."

"Thank you. But your pumpkin pie? Just yummy."

Nick colored slightly. "Don't tell anyone, but I bought it from a bakery near the college."

She laughed. She'd known the minute she saw the immaculate crust in the foil pie pan. "Your secret's safe with me."

Luke had placed Nick and Molly side-by-side for dinner, so she'd taken the opportunity to learn a little more about her new neighbor. He told her about his position at the college as head of the biology department.

"It's a small place, but they say they'll be happy to support my research, which is a bonus."

"What does that mean, exactly?"

"There's no money involved, but they'll help find sponsors and grants for trips I make to study butterflies."

"That's your specialty? I've never met a—what is it you're called? Lepi-something?"

"A lepidopterist." In response to the interest in her face, he added, "Butterflies aren't just beautiful, they're important. They act as an early warning system for environmental problems."

"Of course. So why do you need to travel? We have butterflies right here."

"Unfortunately, the best place to see endangered species is in their native habitats—in Brazil and Costa Rica, for example."

"I remember. We saw tons of them when we went to Costa Rica on vacation once. My late husband and I." She shook off a passing shadow. "Have you been? It's simply stunning. So much unspoiled nature."

They talked about places they had traveled, though Molly didn't want to ask whether Sam had been part of the trips. In fact, she didn't ask about Nick's ex at all, feeling it might still be too painful for him. Apart from that self-imposed restriction, their conversation flowed, and she found herself relaxing as she told him about Jackie and Heather, and why they weren't around.

She discovered that Hadley, a beautiful golden retriever, had been a rescue, and was too big to live comfortably in New York. Coming to Brentford gave her plenty of room to play.

"The change might be challenging at first, but we're a friendly lot around here, and I hope you'll come to love it as much as Hadley seems to."

Nick smiled. "I'm sure I will."

**

Amanda called later that evening to ask how the holiday had been.

"I had a surprisingly good time," said Molly. "I met my new neighbor, among other things. You know, the one you never mentioned to me."

"Oh, that's right. I'd forgotten he's one of Luke's friends."

"Didn't you meet him when he rented the house?"

"I was supposed to, but in the end, I had someone else show it. That's why the whole thing slipped my mind. Nick, isn't it? I heard he was friendly. And cute, too."

Cute? Not exactly. Molly would say he was more attractive than cute. If she were going to describe him at all.

"Well, I guess I wouldn't object to being seen with him, if that's what you mean. And him being a friend of Luke's is a plus—there's no pressure to flirt."

Amanda laughed. "Sounds like you've found your perfect guy. Did you manage to discover if he likes all those cultural things you do?"

Molly was surprised to realize that she and Nick hadn't discussed culture at all.

"Not really. But I'll keep my fingers crossed."

CHAPTER EIGHTEEN

The warm glow of a Thanksgiving with friends had worn off by the next morning. Molly woke to the steady thrum of rain lashing against the roof, something she normally found soothing. Today, the downpour, heavy and insistent, reminded her of all the things that weren't working in her life. Specifically, she was in the awkward position of having to hold Channing's advances at bay, while making sure she didn't offend him. Dating was the pits.

She lay in bed, reluctant to start her day. Her choices were limited. In a nutshell, she'd have to make a success of the bookshop by herself, or go under. Even the few books she sold via the Wentworth Library would be threatened if Channing decided to play hardball. And a rainy Black Friday wouldn't help sales.

Time to get up. Brush her teeth and make the bed. Eat breakfast today. She knew going through these rituals would put her in a more positive frame of mind.

She sounded like her mother. Had she always done that?

By the time she swallowed the last piece of toast, spread with her favorite lime marmalade, the world gave off a more cheerful air. Yet not quite welcoming enough to walk to work in the rain.

She parked behind the Book Boutique and let herself in. The gray skies above were reflected inside, as though they'd seeped through the walls. She flipped on the lights and surveyed the shop.

The Chamber of Commerce had decided to make Black Friday a town-wide event. As the store's contribution, she and Luke had dug out some stock and priced it to sell fast. Classics were reliable sellers. Jane Austen fans always bought them when a new film or TV version came out. Mark Twain came and went, depending on the political climate.

She had a couple of clients who simply purchased books in matching editions because they liked to have complete sets of things. So, she guessed, unlikely companions jostled against each other on their home bookshelves. She smiled as she pictured *Dracula* hanging out with *The Three Musketeers* and *Anna Karenina*, who was wearing a *Scarlet Letter*. Quite a party.

She pulled out some discounted books that hadn't sold, and small gift books of humor or golfing tips. The plan had been to display them outside on a rolling bookshelf, but the rain had put paid to that idea. It was supposed to clear up later. She doubted that her customers were waiting for reductions on books, but she wanted to show she was willing.

She placed the bookshelf just inside the front door and arranged the books by subject. A couple of days before, she'd printed out a simple banner reading "Black Friday Specials" and taped it to the window, facing out. Standing back to look at it, she felt her optimism trickling away, like the rain on the roof.

No one was going to come in today. Why would they? The weather was foul, and who needed to buy books anyway? They were a luxury, not an essential. Why bother trying?

Self-pity brought her close to tears, but crying was for the weak, of course, so she refused to let them fall. Echoes of her English mother's voice in her head again. *How you're feeling is nobody else's concern. They only use it to take advantage of you.* So British.

Molly learned that lesson early on, and only Simon had ever been able to break down her defenses. Which had left her even more vulnerable when he died. They'd assumed they grow old together. He had no business dying without warning at the tender age of forty-nine. The damn running was supposed to keep him fit, not kill him.

Despite her efforts to resist, a tear ran down her cheek. So much for not crying.

The sound of the bell penetrated the cloud of self-pity hovering around her. A customer. She mustn't be seen like this. She reached for a tissue and dabbed at her cheeks before turning to see who it was.

Of course. Acacia. Her reliable shopper. Since Luke wasn't in today, Molly would have to deal with her.

"Good morning, dear. How was your Thanksgiving?" The old lady smiled across the counter.

"Very nice, thank you." She was aware that her reply lacked something. A hint of animation would have improved it. "I went to Luke's."

"That must have been special," continued Acacia with interest.

The last thing Molly wanted to do was talk. But there was no avoiding it.

"It was quite...festive."

Her voice came out raspy, and Mrs. T looked at her with fresh intensity.

"Is everything all right, dear?"

Her sympathy was too much for Molly. Because no, everything was not all right. The bookshop was about to fold, and Simon might disappear if she dated someone new. And to top it off, Acacia's obnoxious son featured in both depressing scenarios. His last words to her had been "continue this another time," which could only mean that he wanted to date her while he put her out of business.

"There, there," said Acacia, and steered her toward the back, where the antique loveseat stood between the self-help books and the travel section. "Come and sit down for a minute."

"But the store...there might be customers..."

"Well, I'm one of them, and I need you to take a break." She handed Molly the box of tissues from the counter and sat back. "Why don't you tell me all about it? I'm a widow too, you know. Twice over. I think I can understand some of what you're going through."

So long as they only talked about Simon, the conversation might not be too hazardous. But if she *mentioned* Channing, Molly couldn't trust herself not to alienate a loyal customer.

"It's been three years since Simon—my husband—died. I should be over it. You'd think I'd be able to manage life on my own now."

"No one stands on their own two feet without help, dear. At least to begin with. It took me a while to learn that after Mr. Madison passed."

"Did your friends keep suggesting you find a new man? Mine want me to."

"Well, no. I wasn't looking when I met Archie Todd. I was lucky. He was the salt of the earth. Different from Channing's father. Though I didn't have him for long."

Molly recognized the sadness in the older woman's voice and covered Acacia's hand with her own. She'd always thought of this woman as something of a battle-ax, determined to get her own way all the time. Now she saw a more vulnerable side to her. Was it possible she was lonely?

"I'm so sorry."

"No regrets, now. Things were lovely while they lasted."

Molly found herself suddenly expressing a thought that had been lurking just beyond her grasp.

"I worry I might forget Simon if I start seeing someone else."

Acacia put a hand on her arm. "Oh, my dear. That will never happen. Those we've loved stay with us always. They needn't prevent us from loving again."

"That's what Simon always says."

"Sorry? I don't think I heard you correctly."

"Slip of the tongue. I meant, he used to say so."

"I understand. Funny how they keep talking to you. In your head." She nodded as if reinforcing the last comment. "Sounds like he was a lovely man."

Molly needed to end this soul-baring tête-a-tête. Acacia had proved so easy to talk to, that she'd lowered her guard. Talking about her feelings didn't come naturally, especially with people she didn't know very well. Because once she allowed herself to cry, she might never stop.

She looked around for a distraction. But nothing disturbed the peace of the bookstore. If she turned the conversation to focus on this unexpected ally, it might be safer.

"So how did you cope? After you were widowed the first time?"

Acacia's eyes took on a faraway look, as though she were traveling into the past. "He'd taken care of everything, and at first, I was at a loss. So, I did what you must learn to do. I asked for help."

"I have help. Luke is terrific. So is Trey." In answer to Acacia's frown, she said, "My teenage tech whiz."

Acacia tilted her head to one side, as if to appraise Molly. "They're wonderful, I'm sure, when we're talking about the day-to-day operation of the store. But Luke, bless him, isn't a great manager when it comes to business. You need someone else for that."

"I know," Molly said. "I have been trying to solve my problems on my own."

"And I don't suppose your love life is top of the list at the moment, is it?"

What did she mean by that? Had Channing told her about their date? The clang of warning bells drowned out thought.

"Try dealing with one thing at a time," the old lady went on. "If this place is important to you, tackle that first."

"It definitely is," said Molly. "The rest can wait until I have the business sorted out."

Acacia beamed at her. "That's the spirit! What can I do to help?"

Without meaning to, Molly started to explain her difficulty with the rent and the danger of the Book Boutique closing forever.

"We can't have that. Brentford *needs* the Book Boutique." Her voice was as vehement as Molly had ever heard it. "Would you like me to talk to my son and tell him to get his act together?"

Now what? Should she agree, and have Channing tell his mother about their dismal date at Starbucks? Or confess all, and see whether Acacia would still be willing to give her a hand?

"I'm not convinced that's a good idea," she began tentatively. "He's not exactly happy with me at the moment."

A pair of painted eyebrows rose behind Acacia's red spectacle frames.

"Nonsense. I'm sure he'd like you very much if he met you. He'd want to do right by you, I know."

No escape now. She'd have to throw herself on this woman's mercy.

"The thing is, I accidentally went on a date with him last week."

"An *accidental date*?" Acacia had every right to be puzzled.

Molly felt the color rise in her cheeks. "Only for coffee, you know. But I wasn't expecting it to be Channing. He'd misled me on the dating site after refusing to reduce my rent. I felt so stupid, not recognizing him from his photo…" She trailed off and raised her eyes to meet Acacia's gaze.

There was a moment's silence. Not surprising really. No mother wants to hear unpalatable truths about her child.

Finally, Acacia spoke. "Well, if that isn't just typical. No wonder he's finding it so hard to meet someone."

Molly's astonishment must have registered on her face, because Mrs. T elaborated. "He's always been something of a know-it-all, I'm afraid. Like his father. He doesn't want to listen to anybody. But I think I can persuade him to give you some sort of delay. At least long enough so you can come up with another plan. After all, I *am* a shareholder."

"You are? You would? Really—you would do that?"

"I would do that," she said, smiling.

"Mrs. Todd—Acacia—thank you so much. All I need is a little breathing space."

"Glad to help." She paused to take in the gift tables.

Impulsively, Molly kissed her new confidante on her faded powdery cheek.

"Thank you," she said with feeling. "A pep talk was just what I needed, and since my mother's been gone—"

"Don't say another word. I'm happy to be of use. Only let me know how things are going." She reached into her handbag and drew out her wallet. "Now, I must pay for this book. Every purchase adds to the bottom line, right? And when you see Luke, tell him I was asking after him."

CHAPTER NINETEEN

Later that day, Molly leaned into the window display and added one more book to the pile of Christmas murder mysteries. It proved to be the last straw, and they toppled over, just as Channing phoned. She wanted him to tell her that he'd talked to his mother and she'd persuaded him to view her situation more positively. He turned out to have other things on his mind.

"How would you like to have dinner with me some evening this week?"

"Do you mean to talk about the bookshop? Because we could do that by phone."

"We don't have anything to discuss regarding the business, do we? I've explained my position. I simply thought you might like to spend some time getting to know me."

So very Channing. She should get to know *him*, not the other way around? And the Book Boutique wasn't even a consideration.

She didn't hesitate. "It's out of the question."

"What?"

No point in beating around the bush. "There is no way I would consider going out with a man who's trying to make sure my business fails. I have no idea why you have me in your sights, but I'm not going to become one of your victims." Truth to tell, she didn't know whether he had any other victims, either professional or social, but she'd be willing to bet he did.

"Well. If that's the way you feel—"

"It certainly is. Good day, Mr. Madison."

***

Only when she saw her father's headlights pulling into her driveway that evening did she sense some relief. He always made her feel safe. She stepped onto the porch to greet him. Damn, the porch light was out.

"Mind your step, Dad. The bulb has gone."

He made his way up the steps, the glow from the doorway sufficient to light his way. She reached out a hand in case he needed help, but he ignored it.

"Hello, Dad," she said, giving him a hug. "Come inside. I've lit the fire, so you'll soon warm up." Even bundled up in a winter jacket with a ski hat, he still looked chilled.

He settled in front of the fireplace, where Hemingway sought him out within minutes. He stood purring loudly by Tom's feet, waiting to be picked up and placed on his lap. Molly was delighted that her cat and her dad got along. Hemingway was very selective when it came to bestowing his affections.

She went to fetch some pie and two glasses. Her father would appreciate a tot of Glenlivet. Not too much, since he would be driving and was conscientious about it. She must remember to order more—the bottle was almost empty. She walked back into the room a few minutes later with a tray, and seeing him firmly anchored to the chair by Hemingway, poured the whisky.

She handed him a slice of pie on a plate. He cut a piece with his fork and raised it to his lips. Then he shut his eyes and gave a low hum. "Delicious as ever." He swallowed. "How was Thanksgiving?"

"It wasn't the same without the girls, of course, but they phoned, and we chatted. They send their love." No point in dwelling on their absence.

"You went to Luke's?"

Molly felt relieved to have something cheerful to talk about. She described the party, with its elaborate meal, and told him about her new neighbor.

"I'm glad," he said. "You've missed having Bert around, haven't you?"

"I have. But this guy seems nice, and the other plus is, I think he's gay." That sounded odd. Her father's following words confirmed it.

"Sorry? I don't get it."

"I don't need to have someone attractive *and* eligible living next door."

That wasn't much of an improvement. Almost like she was assuming she'd have to fend off the advances of any unattached man. "I mean, I won't need to worry about him flirting or anything." Oh, dear. She was getting more entangled by the minute. "Tell me how you got on with your friend's family," she managed, hoping a change of topic would prove less awkward.

"Her name's Bonnie. I thought I'd mentioned it. Anyway, let's just say she's the best of them. I don't think her son took to me."

Molly grimaced, already disliking the man. "That just shows he has terrible judgment."

"They live in one of those huge houses on the other side of New Haven. No taste, but plenty of money. He probably thinks I like Bonnie because of her rich relatives. Fact is, I'd be happy if I never had to see them again."

"Well, why should you? She's just one of your many lady friends, isn't she?"

Tom shrugged. "There's not much competition here from other guys—so if you're still breathing, a lot of women are interested."

"I'm sure it's not just lack of choice. You're a catch because you've got all your marbles. You're good-looking. And fun."

She wasn't flattering him when she told him that he'd retained his looks. For one thing, he still had enough pure white hair not to have to do a comb-over—enough to make him appear younger than his seventy-four years. He'd recently added a well-trimmed beard, which brought to mind an older actor, whose name she couldn't recall. She smiled at him affectionately.

It was reassuring to know he had a circle of friends. She lived only twenty minutes away, should he need her, but her dad valued his independence. He was determined not to be a burden.

Her father, who always shied away from a compliment, coughed and blushed. "How was business today? Isn't it supposed to be a high sales day?"

"Actually, Dad, it started off slow, and I thought no one would come because it was raining, but then one of my customers arrived and cheered me up and things began to improve."

"Oh? Who was that?"

"Acacia Todd. A widow. About your age. Very sympathetic, and smart too. You'd like her."

Tom laughed. "The last thing I need is one more woman to deal with."

"Understood. But I still think you'd get on with her. Anyway, she told me I have to ask for help when I feel overwhelmed."

"Ah. You're like your mother that way. Always wanting to do it by yourself. You were like that when you were little. Remember the time you climbed the apple tree in the back garden and couldn't get down? But you didn't want any help."

"Well, I did manage to get myself down eventually, didn't I?"

"Not before you'd scared your mother and me half to death. I stood there hoping I'd be able to catch you if you fell. I'm too old for that now. So asking for help before you get stuck is good advice."

Molly remembered the dizziness that had almost overwhelmed her as she looked down at the ground so long ago. "Maybe that's why I'm frightened of heights now. Thanks for being ready to catch me then, Dad. I love you."

"Me too, honey." He raised his glass, where the last drops of Glenlivet shimmered in the light of the fire. "Cheers."

"Cheers to you, Dad." The warm glow of whisky seeped into her veins. Her father always made things right.

CHAPTER TWENTY

At least there was one thing she'd managed to fix without any help. Molly had succeeded in changing the bulb on the porch by standing on a chair and trying not to look down. A sigh of relief escaped her lips when she reached terra firma again, and a glow of accomplishment spread through her. Success.

But a few days before Thanksgiving, the light at the top of the stairwell blew. It was located where the stairs turned a corner and impossible for her to reach on her own. It required a ladder and someone who, unlike her, didn't feel queasy on one. She at least needed a person to hold it, and she'd intended to ask the girls to give her a hand over the holiday, but they hadn't come home. In the past, she'd have asked Simon.

He had worked for a large local construction company, which was ironic since he had no idea how to fix anything around the house. He was the VP of operations and was a genius when it came to organizing building materials and planning and executing projects. Although he recognized a hammer when he saw one, changing a light bulb marked the limits of his talent when it came to other domestic jobs.

She'd been putting off dealing with the stairwell light, but she could wait no longer. After the holiday, stumbling up the stairs in the dark with a pile of clean sheets in her arms, Molly had tripped over her mother's tall vase, which stood on the landing halfway up. Her misstep sent it rolling to the bottom, where it landed in the hall with a dramatic crash and broke into shards.

Damn. She'd never liked the thing—heavy and somber with wilting lilies painted down one side. She'd intended to palm it off on one of her daughters someday. They might describe the vase as "retro" instead of plain ugly. Still, this had been a timely reminder that she absolutely must find someone to replace the bulb.

The next morning, as she often had recently, she woke to the sound of Hadley barking. This didn't last long, because, she supposed, Nick was trying to keep the noise down. Still, she opened her eyes, and swinging her legs over the side of the bed, wandered over to draw the curtains. She glanced down and smiled. It took a dog to enjoy the simple pleasure of chasing her tail out on the frosty grass.

As she watched, Hadley spotted a squirrel, which had had the temerity to scamper across the lawn and was now disappearing through the hedge into Molly's yard. The retriever stiffened for a second and then gave chase, flattening herself down to wriggle through the tight gap in pursuit of this animal who might threaten her master.

Where was Nick? He should be sorting this out. The dog might escape altogether, since Molly's yard had no fence on the other side.

She ran down the stairs and rummaged in the hall closet for a warm jacket. Stepping outside, she shouted for Hadley, who stopped, puzzled at this interruption, and ran over, her tongue hanging out and what looked suspiciously like a smile on her face.

"Good girl." She leaned down to ruffle the fur on the dog's head, before slipping two fingers under Hadley's blue leather collar and walking her next door.

Molly rang the bell, and when Nick opened the front door, she let go of Hadley, who bounded inside. Only as she straightened up did the amused expression on his face remind her that she was still in her pajamas. She clutched her jacket tighter around her.

He looked different, too, without his glasses, and with his hair still tousled. She registered his eyes clearly now as he blinked in the morning light. They were a deep sea-green color, and the laugh lines around them told her he was a man with a sense of humor.

"Thanks for bringing her back," said Nick. "I hope she didn't do any damage to your garden."

Molly shook her head. "She didn't stay long enough for that. She was much too intent on the squirrel. But you might want to do something about that gap in the hedge. I don't have a fence on the other side of my yard."

She moved from foot to foot as the cold air chilled her ankles.

"Thank you for letting me know. I'll get some chicken wire and plug the hole up. I'm grateful you caught her. I don't know how I'd have found her if she'd disappeared. Can I repay you in some way?"

Molly shook her head. "I'm glad to do it. Good neighbors and all that."

Then a thought struck her. "Actually, I do have a light bulb that needs replacing. It's in a spot I can't reach."

"Not a problem. Just let me know when's a good time to come over."

***

Nick knocked at her back door on Sunday morning, wearing his spectacles and carrying a stepladder. He took off his black bomber jacket and she hung it in the utility room. The irresistible smell of home baking was beginning to permeate the air, since Molly had just slid a tray of cookies into the oven, intending to take them into the Book Boutique later.

She followed him as he carried the ladder upstairs and set

it up, bracing its legs against the wall. At six feet tall and wide in the shoulders, he filled the space on the small landing. She stifled a twinge of anxiety at the prospect of him falling, but he appeared to have no such qualms.

In an effort to avert a possible disaster, she positioned herself on the stair below to break his fall—if he had one. As she stood looking up at his rather attractive behind, she wondered whether she'd chosen the best vantage point. She was definitely well placed for admiring his physique, but if he should, in fact, fall, she'd be crushed beneath his weight.

She shouldn't be thinking like this at all. He was easy on the eye, in a purely objective way. But being a friend of Luke's ruled him out of any further type of interest. And that was a good thing.

His voice broke into her thoughts. "Do you want to check that it's working?" He handed the old bulb down to her.

"You'll be okay if I let go of the ladder?"

Nick smiled. "Sure."

Molly headed down to the hall and flipped the switch on and off again. "Fantastic," she said. "I nearly missed my footing in the dark the other day, and I—I'm scared of heights," she confessed.

She expected him to laugh at her, but he just kept smiling. "Well, I'm not. On the other hand, I'm not certain I'd want to stay up here all day."

What was she thinking? Of *course* he needed to come down from his perch. The aroma of baking cookies floated out of the kitchen.

"Can you wait a minute? I need to take something out of the oven. I'll be right back to hold the ladder for you to get down."

She got to the cookies just in time and was soon back. Nick was taking his last step down to the floor, having descended without any help. Naturally. He was likely fitter than she was, and he must know what he was doing.

She smiled at him. "Thanks. That was a big help."

"No problem." He smiled back as he folded the ladder up with neat, precise movements. "It's the least I could do."

He picked up the stepladder as if it weighed nothing and slung it over his shoulder. Molly started down the stairs, then turned back.

"Would you like a cup of coffee?"

"I'd love some."

CHAPTER TWENTY-ONE

Nick set the ladder by the kitchen door. "Something smells delicious."

Molly, in the middle of transferring the warm cookies onto a cooling rack, smiled at him.

"I put these in the oven a few minutes before you came. I enjoy baking—I find it relaxing. I take them into the store for customers." She must stop babbling.

"Are those the same kind you brought to Luke's?"

She nodded. "Would you like one with your coffee?"

"Sure. That would be a treat. Is there someplace I can wash my hands first?" he said.

Molly, now busy with the coffee maker, turned away from the sink. She pointed with her chin toward the mudroom. "Help yourself."

It felt odd having a man around the house. Even an off-limits guy. But that kept it casual. No pressure.

She busied herself with filling the percolator she and Simon had bought in Venice, before taking two mugs out of the cabinet.

Nick walked back in and perched on a stool at the counter. She offered him the plate of cookies, and he took one.

"So, you'll take them to work tomorrow?" He bit into it and closed his eyes. "Good as ever."

"These are for today. We have Sunday hours now, from

noon to five, because of the season, so…"

He glanced at his watch. "I promise not to stay too long."

"Don't worry. I have time before I have to get going."

Molly poured him a mug of coffee, and they sat in companionable silence for a while. She handed Nick a small pitcher of half-and-half, and he lowered his eyes as he added some to his mug, giving her a chance to size him up.

It didn't matter if she gazed at him, she supposed. It was a bit like admiring something in a museum. Pretty to look at, but not something you could form a romantic attachment to. Which was fine, since she wasn't in the market for romance.

She watched him wolf down another cookie. Was he really hungry? Should she have offered him a sandwich? Oh, well. Too late now.

As if feeling her gaze on him, he raised his eyes. "Sorry. I didn't mean to pig out, but they are delicious."

A memory of Simon came to her. He used to call them more-ish—an English expression he'd picked up from Tom. Eating one always made him want to eat more. This wasn't the time to think about him, though. As if sensing another presence in the room, the conversation stalled. Nick broke the silence.

"Boy, these are great," he said, licking a stray crumb from his lips. "So good, I might become a customer myself, just to have another."

"You should. Have you ever been in? When Luke owned it?"

"I don't think so. I usually visited when he wasn't working, so there was no reason to."

"I've expanded the range of offerings since I took it over. You'll probably find something you'd enjoy reading. And we have other things too. Gifts, mostly."

She ought to quit talking shop.

"Luke tells me you like music," said Nick. "Do you sell any?"

"We used to stock some CDs, but there's not much call for

them now, I'm afraid. Not with online streaming. But to answer your question, yes, I love music. Mainly classical and jazz. That's what we play in the store."

"I was asking because—and I know this is kind of sudden." He seemed to be struggling to string his words together. "So, don't feel obliged to say yes, but would you like to come to a concert next week? I have tickets for the New Haven Symphony on Thursday."

Molly wondered who the second ticket had been intended for. Luke maybe?

"I was going with someone from the college, but they had to cancel," Nick said, as if reading her thoughts. Thursday was a few days away, and Molly found herself tempted. He'd proposed the exact scenario she'd wanted—a companion for cultural activities. She mustn't get ahead of herself. This might turn out to be just a one-off. Still…

"It's been so long since I've heard the Symphony live. None of my friends are all that interested."

Something of an understatement. Amanda would go to a Lady Gaga concert at the drop of a hat, but assumed a pained frown at the mention of classical music. And Rosie would always rather dance than sit still for an hour or two. It hadn't been Simon's thing either. He'd preferred the movies or an evening at the theater.

"They're doing Prokofiev and Liszt."

"Sounds lovely." She remembered that Nick was waiting for an answer. "And I'd love to," she said. "You'd be kind of a relief, after Starman97."

"Sorry. What?"

Molly hadn't realized she'd spoken aloud. She blushed, and wished she were better at telling lies. "Oh. Well. It's just that my friends Rosie and Amanda pretty much *made* me go on a horrible blind date. Internet, you know? I didn't want to go in the first place, and he turned out to be a complete waste of time." There was no need to identify Starman97 by name.

Biting into his third cookie, Nick made a sound Molly interpreted as encouraging.

"You could make a living selling these instead of books, I'd bet." Catching her expression, he continued. "I interrupted—you were saying?"

"The date I went on. I mean, he had no hair, and was quite overweight."

Nick's eyes twinkled. "But surely you'd seen his photo. On his profile."

"Well, of course. But it must have been taken decades ago. Plus, he had no manners, and ate all the brownies and hunts ducks…"

He was making an odd gurgling sound. "Are you okay?" she asked.

He sounded like he was choking. His eyes were closed as he pounded his chest with a fist.

"Nick?" Molly was about to get up and check on him when she realized he was laughing. "It wasn't funny," she said. But another glance at his watering eyes and pink face, displaying a mixture of mirth and apology, suddenly made her realize the ridiculousness of the situation. "Well, I suppose it's a little bit funny."

He stirred his coffee. "So, have you given it another try?"

"Not a chance. My girlfriends think I should, but I'm not interested."

"Understandable." He took a sip. A silence fell.

He rose to his feet. "I'd better be going," he said. "You have things to do."

"Thanks again," Molly said.

"Any time," said Nick. "By the way, the concert starts at seven. So, I'll pick you up Thursday evening at, say, six?"

No dinner, just the Symphony.

"Perfect." She wrapped some cookies in waxed paper and handed them to him.

"Are you sure? You'll have enough for the Book Boutique?"

"I expect so. Anyway, I can make more."

***

Molly looked forward to telling Amanda and Rosie that she'd finally found an appropriate escort. They might be disappointed that the man she was doing something fun with was only her neighbor, but they would have to stop saying that she needed a man. Possibly, they might envy her. A companion with no strings. And no benefits. She smiled.

CHAPTER TWENTY-TWO

Molly stopped by Rosie's after work on Tuesday. She had no real reason to be nervous about going out with Nick, but she needed reassurance that she'd look appropriate. Rosie suggested she bring over a few possible outfits from her closet, and she'd help her choose.

Now Molly stood in her friend's guest bedroom, the clothes she'd brought with her strewn over the bed. She tried to be decisive, but couldn't make up her mind. As she contemplated her choices, she caught sight of herself in the full-length mirror hanging on one wall. "Do you think I've let myself go?"

"You need to relax. This is just a date," said Rosie, ignoring the question. "Look, if you're too stressed, have a massage or some reflexology. The Chinese place on Hart's Hill is really good and not too expensive."

"It's not a date. Just a concert with a new friend. So I'm not sure why I feel anxious." Molly fell silent. She knew why she wanted Nick to like her. Because if he did, she would have an attractive but harmless person to hang out with. Which would save her from meeting another strange man off the internet.

"What do you think—about a massage?" Rosie prodded.

"I guess that might help." Unconsciously, Molly rubbed her lower back with one hand. "Standing in the shop all day is murder sometimes."

"*Ay, Dios mío*. Take some aspirin for a bad back, but get a massage just for the sense of someone touching you again."

That would be another kind of letting go entirely. Her thoughts drifted back to the cruise she and Simon had taken for their twentieth wedding anniversary. He had booked them a couple's massage.

She felt uncomfortable at first. Having to take off all her clothes in the women's changing room—all air-conditioned marble, hard and cold. The relief when she wrapped a warm terrycloth robe around her. Her husband's appreciative glance as he sneaked a peek at Molly's behind when they lay down on the tables scented with lavender and frangipani oils.

Her massage was firm but not painful, and had it not been for the continuous awareness of Simon next to her, Molly might have dozed off.

Rosie said something and Molly dragged her mind back to the present.

"Why don't you try this on? It's a wraparound, so it should work." Her friend handed her a dark-blue dress.

"I doubt it. We're not the same height."

"Give it a shot anyway. I never wear it, because it's too long for me, but I think we're roughly the same size. In any case, you can tie it looser or tighter to fit."

Molly held the garment out in front of her. She ran her fingers across the fine wool fabric, a rich blue—almost violet—and soft to the touch. After some maneuvering, she tied the belt around her waist and studied her reflection in the mirror.

"There. It's perfect for you. Kind of classic, right?"

"I guess it sort of is, at that. Disguises a few minor flaws." She loved her endlessly enthusiastic friend. "But I'm surprised you went for something that's not quite like your usual…"

"Like my usual taste? Well, no. An unfortunate mistake—for me, at any rate. I've never worn it, so you're welcome to keep it."

"Oh, I couldn't," Molly protested, already knowing she would take the dress home. "Or, at least, let me pay you for it."

She lifted the skirt to find the price tag.

"You see? I got it on sale. Amanda insisted on coming with me, and you know how that goes."

Molly did. Shopping together could be fun, when Amanda was looking for something for herself. All too often, though, Molly would return with some unintended purchase her friend had persuaded her to buy. Usually, Amanda's choices were right on the money. She'd made a mistake with this item for Rosie, but hey, one man's meat and all that.

"Okay. Deal." She slipped out of the dress and hung it back up. "And thank you so much."

Now, she only needed to start walking again, every day, and she'd be fine. Not by Thursday. But eventually. In any case, she reminded herself, you couldn't call this a date. At least not a romantic one. Nick didn't seem like the kind of guy to pay any attention to what she wore.

***

Molly drove them into New Haven. "It might be quicker this way, because I'm more familiar with the city than you, and I know where to park."

Nick settled into the passenger seat. "Okay, then. Thanks."

After, she couldn't have said what they talked about. He told her about the book he was working on—one about butterflies, designed for the general public, rather than an academic textbook. Long ago, Molly considered attracting more of those gorgeous creatures into her garden, but never did anything about it.

"Have you heard of Pollinator Pathways?"

Molly was curious. "I haven't. What are they?"

"The idea is to encourage people with yards to grow more plants for butterflies and other beneficial insects. So, after a year or two, there'll be a whole series of connected flower gardens and parks across the country and they can thrive."

"I like the sound of that."

"I can help you with some ideas if you're interested—next spring might be a good time."

Next spring. She might have a *lot* more time for gardening if the shop failed. A vision of the perfect English cottage garden she would plant, perhaps featured in a magazine, ran through her mind. Even at its best, this summer's blooms had revealed that what she had now was a mess of disorganized perennials, and would require a ton of work. Better to focus on making the bookshop successful. That way, she might be able to afford a gardener.

***

It had been too long since she'd sat in Woolsey Hall and let herself succumb to the music she loved. She could kick herself for not coming on her own before now. After all, nothing was stopping her.

The opening strains of *Romeo and Juliet* began, and Molly felt her heart respond in time to Prokofiev's seductive pounding rhythm—the power, the drama, the drive. Did Nick feel it too? She stole a look at his profile. With his eyes shut, he appeared entranced. Or might he be asleep? That seemed unlikely, since the century-old wooden seats must have been specially designed to keep college students awake.

At that moment, he turned his head toward her. "Okay?" he mouthed.

She nodded and gave him a thumbs-up. He closed his eyes again. He had a firm jaw, and she wondered if his nose had ever been broken. She must stop wondering about things like that. Concentrate on Prokofiev.

The intermission provided an opportunity to stretch their legs, and they wandered out of the auditorium.

Nick studied the rotunda of the building before turning to her. "Would you like a drink?"

"Ah. I'd forgotten that you don't know this place. There's no bar—those who are so inclined run outside to one of the little places nearby for a glass of wine."

"Would you like to do that?"

"We'd probably be too rushed. Perhaps another time? In any case, it will be cold out there now, and we left our coats on our seats."

He didn't pick up on the suggestion of another time. A shame, because she was enjoying herself.

"Talking of the seats, they're kinda hard on the—" He paused, as if trying to find the right word.

"Glutes?" she offered with a smile.

"Exactly."

Molly, who was feeling like a local guide, confessed. "It's been a while since I was here, or I would have remembered to bring us each a stadium cushion."

"Well, we'll know if we come again."

If. Not when. Oh, well.

***

"So, how did it go?" These were Amanda's first words when she stopped by the bookstore on Friday morning. "Spill."

"Nothing to tell." Molly laughed. "I enjoyed myself, and I think Nick did, too."

"Did you wear the blue dress?"

"Wait. How did you know about the… Amanda, did you buy that for *me*?"

Amanda looked like a child caught doing something she shouldn't.

"Well, we were pretty sure you wouldn't go shopping just for this date," she began.

"Not a date," was Molly's instinctive reaction.

"Whatever. I happened to be at the mall with Rosie, and we came across it, and we both agreed it'd be perfect for you."

No choice but to forgive them. They knew what they were doing. Wearing something comfortable that made her feel attractive started the evening on the right foot. "You'll be pleased to know Nick complimented me on it."

"A man with sound judgment, obviously. So, who paid for what?" Ever practical.

"He wouldn't let me pay for the tickets, so I'll get them next time." If there was one.

"Next time, huh? I'm happy for you. You've got a nice escort to tide you over. And who knows? You might meet someone you really could go for when you least expect it."

Molly saw no point in arguing. Though they drove her crazy sometimes, she was grateful for her friends. They'd gotten her this far. She gave Amanda a big hug. "Thanks for everything."

She hummed the melody from *Romeo and Juliet* as she returned to shelving books.

CHAPTER TWENTY-THREE

An unfamiliar receptionist sat on duty at the front desk at Maple Corners when Molly arrived to see her father. Festoons of fall leaves made from brightly colored paper hung above the receptionist's head, and a dish full of candy stood temptingly on the counter. Molly explained she was there to see Tom Beresford and headed through to the lounge.

Someone had attempted to decorate for the Thanksgiving holiday the week before. Turkeys, pilgrims, and wheat sheaves still clung to the windows. Garlands of pumpkin-shaped lights festooned the normally tasteful, but bland, sage-green walls.

She spotted her father as he walked toward her—his twinkling eyes and big hug indicated his pleasure at seeing her again so soon. It had only been a week since he'd come over for pie. He led her over to a corner, where they settled into two adjacent armchairs. On the low table stood a tray with a coffee pot, cups, and all the fixings for two. "I was going to make you some in my flat, but I thought this would be easier."

"Whatever works for you, Dad."

"I ordered it a few minutes ago. I know you're always punctual, so it should still be hot." He poured a cup for each of them. "Sorry, sweetheart. It's decaf. No caffeine here after two o'clock. They don't think we could stand the excitement." He smiled wryly.

She sipped at it. "No need to apologize. It's not bad, considering."

"Speaking of becoming overexcited, the social scene around here starts to heat up about now, with the holidays coming."

She waved a hand at the decorations. "I guess they'll be taking these down and replacing them with the Christmas and Hanukkah ones soon, won't they?"

"Those should have come down a few days ago, but our janitor had a week's leave, so everything's behind. Still, our next event is the Christmas Bazaar. Can you come?"

"I will if I can. It's always fun."

He beamed at her. "That's wonderful. I'll be able to show you off to all my friends."

Molly had met some of Tom's neighbors in passing and enjoyed talking to them. Several were already customers of hers. But she'd never been introduced to this new friend, so far as she knew.

"So, you'll introduce me to your latest conquest?" She gave him an inquiring glance.

Her father coughed and blushed. "I hope you'll like her. Though you might find her a little eccentric."

A picture of an aging hippie with a penchant for smoking cigarillos flashed into her mind. In an old photo that had stood on the piano when she was a child, her father had been a vision in a psychedelic shirt, bell-bottoms, and shoulder-length hair. Practically a hippie himself.

He was still talking. "She dressed as a fairy godmother for Halloween."

Molly, making a quick mental leap, imagined a sparkly character sitting on the other side of the lounge in a silver cloak, a tiara over her silver hair, waving a wand with an oversized silver star at the end of it. She smiled.

"I expect she looked lovely. Is she around?"

"To tell you the truth, I asked her to come down to say hello in…" He glanced at his watch. "About ten minutes."

"So, she's special," Molly said.

"She is, but I feel a bit conflicted about her—or anyone.

After your mother."

"Not surprising, Dad. Mum was a force to be reckoned with."

They considered this. "But I think she always had your best interests at heart."

At that moment, someone entered the lounge and waved at them. Her father stood and took a step toward the new arrival.

"Let me introduce you to Bonnie."

A sprightly woman of comfortable proportions, with a pretty face, was smiling at Tom. Molly realized she'd been entirely wrong in imagining a silver-hued fairy. This woman wore a neat fuchsia two-piece trouser suit, with some chunky orange beads. Her most striking feature was her pixie-cut hair—an unlikely shade of pink. It suited her perfectly.

Bonnie proved to be easy to talk to. Even more important, she had a sense of humor. Molly hadn't seen her dad laugh as much for a long time, and she detected a particular twinkle in his eye whenever he looked at his—what? Girlfriend, companion, squeeze, inamorata? None of those seemed appropriate.

A pang of something surfaced in Molly's chest when her father reached out for Bonnie's hand. No doubt, he meant it to be a surreptitious move, and she pulled away quickly, with an apologetic glance at his daughter. Still, they clearly made each other happy, which was what counted, after all.

Maybe *she* could be happy again too?

CHAPTER TWENTY-FOUR

There'd been no sign of Acacia for several days, and Molly began to doubt that she'd managed to talk to Channing. Every time the doorbell rang, she had to stifle her expectations on seeing it was a different customer. Still, at least people were showing up. Not all of them bought something. The Book Boutique was just one of many bookshops suffering from the window-shopping syndrome—where customers ended up buying online.

Other people were more supportive. They were beginning to buy gifts for Christmas, which bumped up the store's November income. Molly paid the rent on December 1 and forced herself to ignore January. This season would make or break her finances.

When Acacia showed up, at last, Molly almost wished she hadn't.

"I'm sorry I haven't been in, dear," she said. "I've been out of circulation with the worst cold I've had in years."

"Vitamin C," murmured Molly automatically. Her prescription for all her sick friends. Mrs. T ignored this.

"I finally talked with Channing."

Molly could detect no clue in Acacia's tone as to the outcome. Her mouth felt dry, and she was finding it difficult to catch her breath. "Any luck?"

"I'm afraid..." Acacia hesitated. "I tried hard to persuade

him, but he insisted it wasn't a wise business decision. I'm sorry, dear."

Her expression reinforced her words. Behind the scarlet spectacles, her eyes were full of concern. "I explained how important the bookshop is to this town. But he said his duty was to—"

"The shareholders. I know." Had he bothered to consult them? She doubted it. He was not a man to ask when he could get away without doing so. He must have been a very annoying child.

"I feel bad about this." Acacia spoke with regret. "I'm one of them, and *I* would have voted for you. I believe in you and the Book Boutique."

Molly raised her eyes to the old woman's face. "Thank you, Acacia. That means a lot. But I need a long-term plan which will show Pilgrim Properties I'm worth supporting."

"Is there anything you could cut back on? To economize?"

She gave it some thought.

"I've done what I can in that regard. I try not to order more than I can sell. It's hard because looking through the catalogs is like putting a kid in charge of a candy store. I always want more."

"I'm sure you've been thinking of ways to sell more books."

"I'm selling audiobooks now—the kind you download to your phone and listen to on the go. And more eBooks. Those are things we'd never tried, but they're not enough to pay the extra rent. So, I'll just have to figure something else out. I'm not quitting yet."

Before she left, Mrs. T bought half a dozen books she probably wouldn't read, but Molly didn't question her. This was likely her contribution to the bottom line, and every dollar helped.

***

To Molly's surprise, Trey, who came in daily after school, had become the Book Boutique's gift-wrapping expert. Molly hated this job, yet it was a service people expected. So, she was grateful for the detail-oriented computer whiz with a talent for this too. Today, she installed him at a table with instructions to pre-wrap some of the bestsellers, and headed next door for a cup of coffee.

It occurred to her that Renzo might have received the same rent demand from their landlord. If so, what did he plan to do about it? Perhaps the Java Jive was doing so well that it made no difference to him. No point in speculating. She would ask.

She didn't know much about his private life. He'd come from Brazil originally, and his dark good looks made him almost exotic in this old New England town. She'd always found his trace of an accent charming.

He might be in his forties—his clothing gave nothing away. He wore pressed indigo jeans and a crisp white shirt, open at the neck, practically every day.

His short sable-colored hair showed narrow streaks of steel at the temples. Laughter lines near his eyes attested to a sense of humor. Yet although undeniably attractive, she'd seen no signs of a love interest.

He'd made some subtle changes when he took over the Java Jive. Instead of the pine-green walls and white trim, fashionable twenty years before, he'd repainted the place in an elegant shade of pale mocha. Vintage travel posters of his homeland and Colombia hung on the walls—and a 1930s one for Indochina, since he served Vietnamese coffee too.

"A lucky find, that one. Perfect for this spot," he'd told her when she admired it. "Also, it's gorgeous, no?"

When she walked in, Renzo greeted her cheerfully from behind the counter, where he was stacking cups. "The usual?"

"Please."

"Coming right up."

"How's business today?" She turned her head to check out

132

the room. It was almost empty.

"We've been busy as ever, but this is the slowdown before we close. It gives me a few minutes to breathe."

"I'm sure you need it. It gets packed in here sometimes."

"Definitely. During rush hour, I could certainly use more space." He handed her a cappuccino. "Do you have a minute?"

Glad of the chance to catch her breath before she began discussing finances, she said, "Sure. I'm okay for a little while."

"Let's sit." He led her over to a couple of chairs and surveyed her as she took her first sip. She smiled at him.

He grinned back and indicated a small line of foam on her upper lip by pointing at his own neat pencil mustache and handing her a paper napkin.

"I have been…"

"Renzo, I want to know…"

They'd spoken simultaneously. He held his hand out, palm up. "You first."

"Thank you. May I ask you something? You don't need to answer, if you'd rather not."

He frowned, but she plowed ahead. "I got this demand for a rent increase from Pilgrim Properties. They're your landlords too, aren't they?"

He gave a single nod of his head.

"So, I wondered whether you'd received the same letter. Did you?"

His face cleared. "I did."

She waited for him to say more, but he remained silent as he fiddled with another paper napkin.

"What did you think?"

"It's steep."

This was like pulling his perfect white teeth. She'd have to share her issue with him to provoke a reaction. She glanced around to make sure they weren't being overheard. The only remaining customers were a couple holding hands as they sat gazing into each other's eyes.

Molly's anxiety came pouring out in a whisper. "I can't afford it. If they make me pay, I may go under. I requested a postponement or a reduction, and they refused everything. I'm getting to the point where I'm running out of ideas. Even if Christmas is successful—and it's shaping up to be decent—it's going to be a problem going forward." She ran out of steam and leaned back in her chair.

She'd shared too much. Renzo's eyes were sympathetic, but otherwise hard to read, as he listened.

"I know something of your problems."

She looked up, surprised.

"Luke mentioned…"

Had he hesitated over Luke's name? Had his voice taken on a different timbre? Or only a hint of Rio de Janeiro? No time to worry about that.

"But also, I contacted them about this."

"And what did they say?"

He waved his hands in a "what can you do?" kind of gesture and shrugged. "I got the same reply. From the man Madison."

Molly must have made a face, because he laughed.

"You do not like him?"

"That's putting it mildly. Not even his mother could make him change his mind."

"His mother?"

"Mrs. Todd. You know, the older lady with the scarlet specs."

"Ah, yes. The decaf cappuccino with cocoa powder on top."

"The thing is, we have to do something. Do you have any suggestions?" A sudden misgiving struck her. "You're not going to quit and leave Brentford, are you? We need you here. Yours is the best coffee for miles around."

"Thank you for saying this." He smiled. "I like to think so. Business is doing well, but to pay the extra rent, it has to be better. As it is, people come here from out of town, which I'm not complaining about at all. But I don't always have room to seat everyone. I'm losing customers, I'm sure."

"So, you need somewhere bigger?"

Renzo nodded. "Yes. I've been considering…" He paused again, and his cheeks reddened slightly. He cleared his throat. "I can't afford to lose customers for lack of space. We both have a problem with the rent. I am thinking you might consider a merger, or some sort of arrangement, anyway."

She stared at him. "How do you mean, a merger?"

Renzo glanced away, as if doubting himself. Then he straightened and returned her gaze.

"I thought it might be possible to make a combined book-shop and café. Like the one in New Haven. The Book Boutique has places where people can sit and read, doesn't it?"

Molly pictured the two rockers and the old velvet loveseat in the shop. "We do."

"And they are not always full?"

"Well, no."

This wasn't what she'd anticipated at all. Though she had arrived without a plan, so she couldn't complain. His idea sounded ridiculous, yet she owed it to Renzo to hear him out. "What do you have in mind? Like, people could bring their hot drinks over and consume them there?"

"Not exactly. Look, we could break through the wall here," he pointed to a spot behind her head. His voice took on a more enthusiastic note. "We could carry some books here—cookery and home décor ones, for example. Or some biographies. My customers could drink coffee in the bookstore as well as here, which would increase traffic for you."

Molly lost track right after "break through the wall." What was he talking about? They couldn't possibly do that. Pilgrim Properties would never allow it. Even if they did, there'd be liquids spilled on books, people disturbing the quiet, cleaning up to do. The whole idea was a nightmare.

"I don't know what to say." She groped for a reason to re-fuse him and came up with the obvious one. "We'd need money, and I don't have any, do you?"

"No. Which is why I haven't mentioned it before. Still, if we could get a loan…" He gazed at Molly hopefully.

This was ridiculous. The man sounded like Simon, with his ideas for simply conjuring cash out of thin air.

"I must have time to think about the basic concept. When I walked in here for coffee, I had no idea where this conversation would end up. So, I'm just not sure."

Judging by his expression, he only heard her say she would think about it.

"Thank you, Molly. This means so much to me."

She drained her cup and rose to go. To her surprise, Renzo came around to her side of the table and hugged her. Nice aftershave.

CHAPTER TWENTY-FIVE

Simon proved a welcome distraction when he showed up that evening. Molly was sitting at the kitchen counter, wearing an extra sweater as the December chill seemed to seep into the house. She sipped at a glass of wine as she covered a writing pad with notes. She'd drawn two columns for the pros and cons of a merger. So far, the minuses were winning.

"Hi, sweetheart. What are you up to?" Simon said.

Molly put down her pen and looked up. She blinked a couple of times to bring him into focus.

"Oh, hello, darling. I'm figuring out if Renzo's idea would work."

She was about to explain when Simon interrupted, his expression irritated.

"Renzo? Who the heck's that?"

"I'd forgotten you wouldn't know him. He's the guy who opened the café, Java Jive. Remember where the bicycle repair place used to be? He's in there."

This didn't appear to be sufficient explanation for Simon, who was now staring moodily out into the gloom of the garden. At nothing much, in reality, because the sun had set a while ago.

"How come you haven't mentioned him before?" He turned back to face her.

Molly would have to be patient. "It never came up. The point is, he's got this proposition—"

"So, is he handsome? How old is he? Any sign of a wife?"

Might he be jealous? Where had her friendly "let-me-find-a-replacement-husband-for-you" Simon gone?

"You dimwit. He *is* very good-looking. Around my age, I'd guess. Not married, as far as I'm aware," she teased. "And I'm pretty sure he's not in the market for a partner—or," she added, "at any rate, not the kind you're thinking of."

Simon turned toward her, eyebrows raised. *"Oh, sure."*

Molly felt a niggle of exasperation.

"For your information, his main interest right now is in doing a merger with me."

"I'll bet it is."

Seeing the scowl on Simon's face, she explained. "A business partnership, silly. We both had this rent demand from Pilgrim Properties."

"So?"

"Actually, you might approve of this. Renzo says the best way to handle it would be to expand."

"He wants to buy the bookshop?" Simon appeared to consider the idea. *"It would solve your problem, I guess. But you love the place so much."*

"That's not it." She tried not to let her impatience show. "I don't want to sell. That would be quitting. No. He's suggesting we join forces. Break through the wall between the two shops, and turn it into a bookstore café."

Simon cocked his head to one side. *"So, it would be like Aristotle's in New Haven?"*

"That's what I had in mind. People would be able to find something to read, and drink coffee in the same place. What do you think?"

Simon's expression was now more interested than aggravated. *"Not a bad concept. So, apart from money, what's holding you back?"*

Molly wasn't sure she could put her reservations into words. She hunted in the cabinet for something to nibble. Mustn't drink on an empty stomach. She sat down again with a handful of almonds on a napkin and took a sip of wine. "You know me. I love the Book Boutique, and I've always believed I should be capable of succeeding on my own."

She popped a nut into her mouth.

"*Aha.*"

"What?" God, he could be aggravating.

"*Still don't want to take the help that's offered, eh? It's not a sign of weakness, darling.*"

She stared miserably at the lists in front of her. "I need so much help. It's discouraging."

"*Look. All successful businesses need a hand to get them off the ground. Don't you like this guy? Or is he a terrible businessman?*"

"He's a lovely man, and I'd guess the café is doing well. Better than the Book Boutique." This was only making her feel worse. Molly crunched down on another smoke-flavored nut—a guilty pleasure. She allowed herself one small can a month and tried to make the contents last.

She raised her eyes to Simon's face.

"*The fact that he wants to merge should tell you something. He clearly believes in you,*" he said.

"Do you really think so?"

"*Sure. Come on, Molly. You can do this. It might be easier if you look at what's involved, before making a decision.*"

A faint glimmer of hope pierced her negativity. "Come to think of it, this is something where your input would genuinely be welcome."

Simon laughed. "*Asking for help now? See how easy that was? And* of course *I'll do it. Happy to.*"

"He's suggesting we knock the wall down and turn the stores into one, which is a great notion. But I have no clue how mergers get done in the real world, and I doubt Renzo does either. There would be all kinds of contracts, planning permissions, and such to deal with. Selling the idea to the landlords. Decisions to make about the alterations. That kind of thing."

She glanced up to find Simon grinning at her. "*You know*

more than you think you do. I guess you paid attention when I used to come home and tell you how work was going," he said.

"I suppose I did. So, help me come up with something."

"I'm an expert when it comes to business plans, and I've had tons of experience with getting permits and dealing with construction issues too. I can be a sounding board—I'd like to get my hands dirty again."

Molly checked out his strong tanned hands and smiled. She'd loved walking along the street with him, her hand in his, as they went about their weekend errands. Though it had to be said—Simon had worked in construction for twenty years without ever building anything himself.

But he knew the business side of things. With his advice, she'd be able to consider something more concrete than just a vague concept. She'd have answers to her questions and objections. She felt a rush of gratitude and relief.

"That would be terrific. Are you sure you don't mind?"

He chuckled. *"It's not as though I have much else on my calendar."*

She slid her notes across the counter to him and settled in with her notepad, ready to write the proposal.

An hour later, she was looking at a rough outline of a project that might succeed. It would take an awful lot of work. Money too, probably. At any rate, she had something she could show to Renzo. All she needed to do was type it up. She turned to thank Simon, but he'd vanished.

She slept like a baby that night.

CHAPTER TWENTY-SIX

The days leading up to Christmas were beginning to blur. Although there were still three shopping weeks left, Molly knew how quickly time would fly. Already sales of pre-wrapped books were increasing, and the gift items were selling too.

Acacia was delighted to discover Trey wrapping books. "Those of us with arthritis, you know, find wrapping fiddly things difficult," she said.

Molly sourced some almost-clear bags with white snowflakes on them, and she and Luke bagged a few small gifts whenever there was a lull in customers. While engaged in this simple task, she worried about her daughters and the holidays. For as long as she could remember, Christmas had been a special time, a highlight of their family's year.

Simon swearing under his breath as he wrestled with the tree before finally getting it upright in its stand. Him kissing her beneath the mistletoe.

Jackie singing a carol by the fireplace on Christmas Eve—an antidote to Heather's rendition of *Silent Night* on the violin. She'd abandoned the instrument by the time she was ten, thank goodness. The day itself was always spent at home. Walking to church while a huge turkey roasted in the oven, providing a welcoming aroma when they returned. The girls stirring the cranberry sauce.

These memories were lovely, if tinged with sadness, but

she must find a new way to celebrate the holidays. She could organize a quiet Christmas, as she had over the last three years. Though now that her daughters were grown, they might prefer something more interesting. If she had to compete with skiing and boyfriends, she'd need to come up with something special, even if it meant dipping into savings.

Amanda and Rosie had insisted she join them for their annual seasonal get-together one evening at the Black Horse Inn. It overlooked Main Street at the edge of town and had been welcoming visitors, as a sign above the door announced, for over two centuries. The low oak-beamed ceilings and wide-planked oak floors did indeed convey a cozy sense that diners would be in good hands.

Now, dressed in its holiday finery, it sported an especially festive air. Molly had planned to plead too much work, but her friends overrode her.

"You absolutely need a break," said Amanda. "Besides, it's our tradition."

"That's right," chimed in Rosie. "You don't want to let us down, do you? It won't be as much fun if you're not there. Plus, I reserved a table overlooking the garden a while ago—for three—so you have to come."

The yard, with lanterns hanging from the trees, would be particularly pretty. Laughing, Molly agreed, glad they'd insisted.

As they sipped at the popular Winter Fizz cocktail that the inn offered every year—prosecco with cranberry juice and a touch of Cointreau—Amanda exuded an air of palpable excitement. In the background, jazzy holiday standards were playing over the sound system, just loud enough to add atmosphere without drowning conversation.

Rosie gave Amanda an inquiring look. "You've obviously got something exciting to look forward to."

"I have my sister and her family coming to stay for a few days," said Amanda, and seemed to be suppressing a giggle.

Hardly earth-shattering. Was this really her first glass of the evening?

Amanda straightened her face and carried on. "Remember her, Molly? She used to visit when we lived in New York. She's in Maryland now, and she loves it. Married with four children."

Molly nodded. "That'll be fun for you. Quite a full house."

Amanda's house could sleep more people than Molly's, but with her two sons and six guests, it would likely be creaking at the seams.

"Sure. It's rather last-minute. But it's been a while, and three nights won't hurt."

There was still something Amanda wasn't saying. Before Molly could ask another question, Rosie changed the subject.

"I'm going to the City to see my family. They've invited Rocco too."

"That's a big step, right? So, I'll drink to that," said Amanda. "Speaking of which, cheers, ladies. Now let's order."

While they shared a Caesar salad as a starter, Molly took her turn to update them on her own holiday plans.

"I haven't had time to think about it in depth, but I'd like to do something different. Like, go away for a long weekend. New York, say. We could go to the theater, see the lights."

"Good idea," said Rosie. "I'm sure the girls would like that. I would, myself." She speared an anchovy and popped it into her mouth.

Amanda put down her fork. "They might enjoy the City. But don't you think they'd prefer someplace new?" Her eyes sparkled. "Like a nice inn in the Berkshires, for example?"

Rosie clapped her hands together. "*Perfecto*! If you take them somewhere like Stockbridge, you won't even have to buy them a Christmas gift—that'll be it."

"I can only take a couple of days off, you know. Three nights max. The store won't take care of itself." Molly looked at her friends, their faces lit up on her behalf. The idea was ridiculous, surely. "You're not thinking straight," she said, determined to rein in these flights of fancy. "It's way too late to book now. Places like that sell out years in advance."

Amanda's face resembled a conjuror's about to pull a rabbit out of a hat.

"It would be, normally. But…"

Was she waiting for a drum roll?

"Oh, Amanda, you want to make us crazy? Tell us." Rosie waved her hands.

"Well. As you know, my sister will be here for the holiday. Originally, though, they planned to go to the Berkshires and then come to us for New Year's."

"And?" Rosie, never the most patient of people, lifted her fork from her venison stew and pointed it at her friend.

Amanda leaned back a little. "Hold your horses, sweetie. So, her youngest broke her ankle and is still on crutches, and they decided that adding an extra two hours to the drive would be just too much. They can't cancel their reservations." Amanda paused. Then she smiled at Molly. "So, *you* can have the rooms instead." She sat back in her seat, evidently satisfied with her friends' stupefied expressions.

Molly's head was reeling. She'd never visited the Berkshires in the winter. Thoughts of Norman Rockwell's painting of Stockbridge's Main Street flashed through her mind. A picture-perfect New England Christmas.

"*Querida*, that sounds ideal," said Rosie.

"Plus, she's booked an appointment at the hotel spa, and she'd love you to take it." Amanda interrupted Molly's reverie.

Molly's back, as if to urge her to accept, gave a small twinge. She'd been on her feet all day and the thought of a massage was enticing.

No doubt such a trip would be lovely, but she couldn't possibly afford this now. Not to mention the fact that someone would have to man the shop.

"But—"

"No buts," said Amanda firmly. "We'll figure something out."

***

Simon did nothing but encourage her.

"*I think it's great,*" he said. "*You and the girls don't often have a chance to hang out together. They're always off visiting friends and such when they're home.*"

"True. But isn't that like running away from my responsibilities?"

"*Not at all. You need a break. Why not switch off completely for a few days?*"

She had to admit that having someone else taking care of things would make a wonderful change.

"But the money—I can't afford it."

In fact, Amanda had told her she needn't pay for the trip immediately. Her sister would be only too grateful to know that they'd get the money back at some point, rather than losing it all.

"*Business is going well right now, isn't it?*"

"I'm cautiously optimistic, as they say. But I doubt it will make enough to cover a vacation. And let's not forget that little thing called a rent increase. I may have mentioned it."

"*Consider it a medical necessity,*" said Simon breezily. "*If you're not in top form, the bookstore will suffer.*"

The man was incorrigible. God, she missed him.

Her father was all for it too. She told him about her doubts, and he remained silent for a moment.

"Listen, honey. I was planning to give you and Heather and Jackie a check each for Christmas. You know how bad I am at choosing presents for you. How about I contribute something to your vacation instead?"

"Oh, Dad, you don't have to do that. Actually, I'd rather you didn't."

"Nonsense. It won't cover the whole cost by any means, but I want you to go and enjoy yourselves. I'm sure the girls won't mind." She could hear the smile in his voice.

The trip was on. But first, the business proposal.

CHAPTER TWENTY-SEVEN

Writing up the first draft of the proposal took longer than Molly expected, but ten days before Christmas, she was ready to show it to Renzo. She'd been skeptical when he first suggested the idea, but after talking things over with Simon, everything seemed more real and more possible, somehow. Typing the *hows* and *whys* into a coherent document had made the concept more tangible.

Although—the number of dollars Simon thought they needed sounded dauntingly large. She wondered whether Renzo had considered the costs at all.

She printed out two copies of the proposal and stashed them in her messenger bag before she walked to work. On her way, she stopped in at the Java Jive for her daily cappuccino. The café was looking festive, with swags of greenery above the windows, and two oversized nutcrackers standing guard at the door. The scent of cinnamon, ginger, and nutmeg permeated the air.

Renzo was walking out from the back with a tray of baked goods, which he placed on the shelf beneath the display cases. They were running low, and he'd evidently intended to refill them, but he paused to acknowledge Molly. His two baristas were dealing efficiently with the line of customers, but Renzo wouldn't have time to talk to her now. She should have waited until the rush was over.

"Hi, Renzo. I don't mean to disturb you, so we can get together later if you like."

"Good morning. No, no. Now would be fine. Have you given my suggestion any thought?" He walked around the counter. "Would this be easier if we talked in the Book Boutique?"

A flash of worry illuminated his face. Perhaps he expected to be rejected. Not surprising, after her initial reaction. Molly smiled. "This won't take long. I've drafted a rough project description, because we're going to need one if we take it any further. Here's your copy."

The anxiety in his expressive eyes turned to relief. "Thanks." He eyed the document. "I don't have time to read it right now. Can I stop by this afternoon to discuss it?"

Luke wasn't scheduled to be in the shop today, so she nodded. "How about after work?"

The line of customers was growing, and Renzo had no time to pay attention. "Sure. I'll call you."

As she was about to go, he said, "Wait. It's Thursday."

She must have looked blank. "Your croissant. On the house."

Molly cherished a not-so-secret passion for the Java Jive's almond croissant, which she allowed herself once a week. If she didn't claim one by nine-thirty every Thursday, they would set one aside for her, knowing she'd stop in for it.

She added free baked goods to her mental list of advantages to merging with the Java Jive.

After they'd both closed up for the day, Renzo drove her to the Black Horse. Looking around through the atmospheric lighting, she registered someone who gave her a tentative wave from across the room. She recognized Rosie's son, Kyle—he appeared to be busing tables. She waved back. That boy worked hard—how lucky Rosie was to have him.

They made themselves comfortable on two tweed-covered barrel chairs in a corner of the lounge and talked. An hour—and a glass of wine—later, they'd decided on the details of the proposal. Renzo held out a hand, and she shook it.

"Partners."

"Partners," she echoed.

"So, what now? Do you want to have your lawyer look at it?"

"I don't think so. My…" How should she refer to Simon? "My consultant has already vetted the concept, but I'll have him take a look at the wording. He recommends we take the plan to Pilgrim Properties first. We need their okay to do anything."

Renzo nodded. "This makes sense. Will you approach Mr. Madison?"

Would she hell. She wanted a positive result, not humiliation.

"I think it would get a better reception, coming from a man," she said. Or a more pliable woman than me, she added silently.

"Very well. If you are sure."

"I'm sure. You really are our best chance. I'll make the changes we discussed and drop some copies off to you tomorrow."

All she could do now was focus on work and pray.

***

Molly was so busy in the days that followed that she barely had time to think about Renzo's meeting with Channing. Picking up her morning coffee, she would catch his eye and he'd simply shrug in a "Who knows?" kind of way. A week later, though, his expression indicated something different. He called her out of the line and led her into the back of the coffee shop.

"Did you hear from him?" Molly asked, as soon as the sound of the café faded away.

"I did."

She only had to look at his face to know the news wasn't good. "Not successful, huh?"

"It depends on how you look at it." Renzo glanced down at the floor.

"Meaning?"

"He gave us an extra two weeks to pay the January rent, so now it's due on the fifteenth."

"Better than nothing, I guess. At least we'll have an idea of our end-of-year financials. But what about the proposal?"

Renzo shrugged in a resigned sort of way. "He barely looked at it. Said he would study it over the holiday break and let us know when he gets back."

"One thing, though. I will be away in Brazil over Christmas. Will it be okay if we put this on hold until I return? It's a lot of pressure. I will do what I can before I go, of course."

"That makes perfect sense. The end of the year is so busy." She looked at Renzo. "So how come you're going now? Not that it's any of my business."

"It's not a secret. My father is not well, and this may be the last time we can celebrate this holiday together."

"Renzo, I'm so sorry. You know that if there's anything I can do to help here, you have only to call or text me."

"Thank you, my friend. I wish you a very happy season."

As she considered him, Molly felt her courage rising again. If he could persevere through his father's illness and the problems with their landlord, so could she.

CHAPTER TWENTY-EIGHT

With her holiday plans settled and the pressure to deal with Pilgrim Properties temporarily on hold, only one problem remained. There was never an ideal time for a bookstore owner to take a vacation. Someone always needed to be at the helm. Normally, Luke would be top of her list, but he planned to be out of town too, visiting friends on Cape Cod. Trey was too young, and anyway, he'd earned a break.

This mini vacation would require a responsible person to take over for the two days after Christmas. If she couldn't find anyone, she would have to close the Book Boutique, which essentially meant that she'd have to cancel the trip. She racked her brain for a solution and came up with nothing. The next time she headed over to the Java Jive with Amanda, she picked a quiet corner where they could brainstorm the problem. After all, the vacation had been her idea in the first place.

She explained her staffing issue.

"Hmm. I don't think you should turn down this chance, but I hear you." Amanda looked thoughtful. "Can't you think of anyone who might take your place for those two days?"

Molly shook her head. "No. The thing is, no one knows the business like I do." This fact only occurred to her as they were discussing the logistics.

"True. But how much would a temp need to know, when you think about it? Anyone can put titles in alphabetical order and work the till."

"You'd think so, wouldn't you? But you'd be amazed at the number of mistakes a person can make. I did when I first began working there."

Amanda nibbled at her chocolate biscotti before answering.

"I'd offer to help, but with family coming, I'll be up to here." She waved a hand somewhere in the vicinity of her eyebrows.

"Of *course* you will. I didn't expect you to do it."

"Which reminds me—what will you do about Hemingway?"

"I was hoping Trey might keep an eye on him."

"No need. I can send one of my boys over to feed him. Which takes care of one problem."

"Wonderful, thanks. Now all I have to find is someone to man the shop."

"How about what's her name—the one who was looking for a book club? She's sensible."

"Jenny Donovan. There's no chance. She has twins, for heavens' sake. Anyone who does this needs to be free over the Christmas weekend. That rules out everyone I can think of."

They lapsed into silence. Amanda broke it, almost jumping out of her seat.

"Got it. It's perfect. He should be around, and he's fully conversant with the alphabet for sure."

"Stop. Wait. What? Who are you talking about?"

Amanda could hardly get the words out. She squirmed in her chair, practically fizzing with delight. "Nick," she announced.

"My next-door neighbor? You mean he might suggest a student or something?" Molly didn't understand Amanda's enthusiasm.

"No, don't you see? Nick hasn't started his new job yet, and professors can always use some extra money, I'm guessing. Plus, he's a friend of Luke's, so obviously, he's trustworthy. I'm sure he'll agree when you ask him."

"Me? Ask him?" Molly squeaked. "I couldn't possibly. He's a professor—this is way below his pay grade."

"Oh, come on. He can only say no. But I'll bet, if you ask him, he'll agree, and you'll be all set. After all, he obviously likes you."

Molly was speechless, partly because she'd taken in a breath and forgotten to breathe out. She and Nick were friends, true, but still. She considered Amanda's suggestion from all possible angles, and in the end, sat back, defeated. If she wanted to take a few days off, which she did, she needed to find someone, and Nick might be her only option.

"Okay," she said, at last. "I'll ask him."

"Sooner the better."

"What if he's away, or says no?" Molly's voice betrayed her apprehension.

"Cross that one when you come to it."

If only she had Amanda's self-confidence.

***

Molly spent the rest of the afternoon trying not to think about the impending conversation with Nick. Finally, in a quiet moment, she sneaked into the back of the store, grabbed her phone, and texted him. *Hi. Are you home tonight? I want to ask you something. M*

First, she would invite him to go to the Christmas tree lighting on the town green with her. Everyone went. Maybe he'd enjoy the *Messiah* at the local church too. After the invitations, she would mention the bookstore.

He answered a while later. *Sure. Want to do takeout?*

She hadn't bargained on this. No problem if he said yes to her request—distinctly awkward if he didn't. But she had no choice. She typed in: *Okay, so long as it's my treat.* No, no. He might think she wanted to bribe him. She deleted her original message and tried again: *Fine. See you around 7?* Then she waited for his answer, which came in the form of a thumbs-up.

***

They finished the food they'd ordered from the Golden Pagoda and were sitting companionably at Nick's kitchen table. Molly had almost forgotten why she'd come.

"Let me help with the dishes," she said.

"The dishwasher doesn't work, so I've been washing them by hand. I don't use many plates. If you like, we can both do them. Wash or dry?"

Molly offered to dry. Nick handed her a tea towel before rolling up his sleeves and sinking his arms into a sink full of soapy water. How heartening to know a man who seemed so comfortable doing chores. Simon would offer to load the dishwasher, but he always did it wrong, so she had to redo it.

Molly had figured out his stratagem, eventually. "You do this the wrong way so I'll stop asking you, don't you?"

"Busted," he used to say with a grin.

She smiled at the memory.

Nick passed her a clean wet plate. "So, what did you want to ask me?"

No more procrastinating. She should start with a simple question first.

"There's a performance of the *Messiah* at St. Michael's this weekend. Would you like to go? They're not professionals, but they're a lot better than you might expect."

She put the plate on the counter and reached for another one. Nick pulled the sink plug, allowing the dishwater to drain out, and dried his hands on a towel.

"Which church? I can't say I know my way around the religious establishments in town."

"It's the white Episcopalian one on the green—it has the tall spire. Supposed to be based on Salisbury Cathedral in England."

Molly rarely attended a service, but when she did, she preferred to go there. The building wasn't as gloomy as some of the others.

"Opposite the town hall? I know the place you mean. I

might be able to make it. What day is it? I'm busy on Saturday."

"It's Sunday at four—if you'd like to go. And the Christmas tree lighting on the common is right after."

"Sounds good." Nick closed the cabinet door where he'd finished stacking the clean china. "Would you like some tea? Coffee?"

"Tea, please." If he weren't facing her, she might pluck up the courage to ask him about standing in for her at the Book Boutique. He turned back to the sink to fill the kettle. Molly took a breath.

"Do you have plans for the holidays?" she asked. It occurred to her that he might be away too.

"I'm around. Going to friends in the City for Christmas Day."

She wondered briefly if he was planning to see Sam. None of her business.

"Nice. You'll be able to get there in record time. And it's lovely to be with friends."

"Yup. How about you?"

Molly folded the tea towel and, not knowing what to do with it, placed it over the back of a chair. "As it happens, I want to take the girls to the Berkshires over the holiday."

"I think you mentioned you were considering it. That's great. I haven't met your daughters yet, but I'm sure they'll enjoy it." Nick unfolded the towel and hung it on a hook on the back of the door.

"It was a last-minute thing, and I'd love to take them, but I have a problem."

Nick poured hot water over the chamomile tea bags. He made a sound that might have been a question mark. He turned toward her with two steaming mugs in his hand. "Honey?" he said.

Had he just called her *honey*?

He set the mugs on the table and reached into the cabinet for a jar of amber liquid. Of course. What had she been thinking? The heat in the kitchen ratcheted up suddenly.

"Just one spoonful, please."

Nick gave her a teaspoon and the honey and watched as she stirred it into the tea.

"What were you saying, before I distracted you?"

What *had* she been talking about? Oh, yes. "It's the shop. Luke's away too, so there are two days—right after Christmas—when I have no one working there."

"Hmm. I get how that might be difficult."

Difficult barely covered it. "I knew you'd understand." Molly's next words came out in a rush. "I've been racking my brains to think of someone to fill in for me, but people are already committed. Though it's not as if there'd be a lot to do." She glanced over at him to find out whether he was registering this.

So far, his face gave nothing away. "Right. I see your predicament."

Oh, well. Nothing ventured, nothing gained. "So…I was wondering, hoping…you might consider doing it. Being in the store. Just for two days. Thursday and Friday. I'll be home Friday night."

The second the words were out, she realized what an idiot she'd been. He wouldn't want to work in a bookshop, even if he were free. She should never have asked. She'd offended him. She listened to the wall clock ticking. Almost nine o'clock. The minute hand twitched over, and still, he said nothing.

Well, what could he say, after all? He'd only just moved, and was probably busy preparing for his first semester in a new place. He might be going away—to visit relatives, or abroad to look for butterflies. In any case, this wasn't appropriate work for someone as overqualified as Nick. She ought to have kept her mouth shut.

"Actually, forget I asked. I was just thinking out loud. I can easily close for two or three days. It's not the end of the world."

She breathed out, surprised to find she believed it. Things would be fine, no matter what.

Without a word, Nick raised his eyes to look at her. Molly

couldn't fathom what he was thinking. Why wasn't he saying anything? Had she ruined their friendship by asking?

He spoke. "It's been decades since I worked in a bookstore—long before automated systems became commonplace."

He had work experience! Molly held her breath but didn't answer.

"I enjoyed it, in a way, but I'm not sure I'd be able to handle a job like that nowadays—the way things have changed."

"I understand." She did, but part of her still clung to a tiny sliver of hope. Oh, well.

"Do you really think I could replace you? Be honest now."

"Of course. Anyone with half a brain…" She registered his expression. "That came out wrong. It's simply—there's not much damage you could do. No, no, that's not right. I'm trying to say it's fairly straightforward for someone who knows computers."

"Okay."

Had he agreed? "Oh, Nick. You mean it?"

"Why not? I have nothing better to do. Might be fun."

"Are you sure? What about—"

"Don't come up with objections, now." He laughed. "I do have one condition, though."

Molly felt a small flutter of apprehension inside. Let the issue not be too onerous.

"Don't make me handle any gift wrapping. I'm a disaster where that's concerned."

What a relief. "I promise. It's after the holiday, so that's one thing people won't be needing." Fingers crossed that was true. There were always the belated gift-givers. And the returns. Well, they'd have to wait until she got back.

"I don't know what I've let myself in for, but I think we ought to drop the subject for now, in case I change my mind," said Nick.

"You've saved my—our—Christmas. Thank you. The girls will be so happy. I don't know how I'll ever repay you."

"You just go and have a good time."

He was a sweetheart. This outcome was so much more positive than she'd expected.

"Nick, I owe you."

"You sure do. And I'll definitely collect, at some point."

Molly tried to imagine how she might return the favor and failed. "I'll do anything—really. Within, you know, reason."

CHAPTER TWENTY-NINE

Molly and Nick stopped on the Common on their way to St. Michael's that Sunday to admire the town Christmas tree. Sitting next to him in the church, Molly let her mind wander as the music filled the space with the joyful sounds of the season. A wall of scarlet and white poinsettias arced around the floor, the colors echoed in the greenery that decorated the ends of the pews.

As the next performer wheeled herself in front of the altar, Molly recognized, with surprise, the high school math teacher who'd taught her daughters. When she opened her mouth to sing, the audience gave an audible gasp of appreciation as the rich contralto soared up to the heavens. If it had been appropriate to clap, the singer would have brought the house down. As it was, more than one person surreptitiously dabbed at their eyes with a tissue.

Molly wasn't religious, but the voice transported her to another place. For the first time in a long while, she welcomed the peace and pure happiness that had been eluding her.

Emerging into the crisp evening air, they watched the town Christmas tree being lit and joined in a chorus or two of *Rudolph the Red-nosed Reindeer* and *White Christmas* before sauntering homeward. They lapsed into a companionable silence. He was a restful man to be with. No subtext. No conversational quagmires she needed to avoid. No sexual tension.

What had put that thought into her head? She glanced at Nick, to find him looking at her at the same moment. He crinkled up his eyes in a smile and she returned it, feeling a warming glow spread through her, despite the evening chill.

***

At three o'clock on Christmas Eve, Molly took a last look at the bookshop and prepared to close for the holiday. The twilight outside promised a clear frosty night and a starlit sky. She'd tallied the sales figures for December so far, gratified with the way things were going. Empty spaces on some of the shelves gave her a sense of satisfaction. Books had sold well. Not many seasonal items remained on the tables.

Nick had come in a couple of days before to learn how to ring up sales and how to check the wholesaler's website for any titles people wanted to order. He'd looked distinctly dazed by the end of his visit, but had grinned manfully and told her it would all be fine.

She'd given Trey two graphic novels he'd had his eye on. And even managed to pay him a small bonus, since he'd worked steadily and without complaint for the last few weeks. In fact, he stayed late some nights to make sure there was nothing more for him to do. She dimmed the lights and turned the key in the lock.

She'd already packed for the trip to the Berkshires and had left Jackie and Heather that morning with instructions to be ready to leave by three. At ten minutes past, she pulled up before the house. To her amazement, she spotted their suitcases by the front door. A Christmas miracle.

***

Light snow started falling as the main highway morphed into the scenic road that would take them to their destination.

"It's going to be a real Christmas," said Jackie.

Molly squashed a momentary pang at the thought of a "real" Christmas without Simon. Her daughter's almost child-like pleasure was a sign that she was healing, and that could only be good.

Stockbridge's Main Street was awash in the gleam of lights strung from every visible building. A huge tree, also illuminated, twinkled in front of the inn. As they drew up next to it, a young man in a navy parka opened the car door for Molly and arranged to carry their bags in.

Brightly lit miniature fir trees stood in crimson pots at intervals along the porch, which spanned the whole facade. Shaker-style rocking chairs were strategically placed behind them. It would be a brave person who chose to sit out there at this time of year. Molly shivered. When they entered the warmth of the lobby, she inhaled the fragrance of another large tree, elegantly decorated with cinnamon sticks and cranberry garlands.

"You've arrived just in time. The carolers are assembling in the lounge, if you'd like to join them." The doorman indicated a group of men and women in Dickensian garb, who were walking through the doorway into an oak-paneled room on the left.

"Well, I'm not sure…" began Molly, but she was drowned out by her daughters.

"Oh, yes, Mom, let's."

"It'll remind you of your childhood, with the Victorian costumes and all."

Hilarious. She would have been happy to put up her feet and relax. Still, she found their enthusiasm infectious. People were already singing, and she was content to sing her favorite carols, as well as some of the more popular holiday songs.

As she absorbed the spirit of the season, Heather thrust a glass of something bubbly into her hand. "Merry Christmas," she whispered.

"Thanks, darling. You too."

Heather raised her champagne. "Here's to us."

***

The concierge showed them to their rooms at the top of the building. As they entered theirs, she heard the girls let out a breath of satisfaction.

"Look, Mom, sloping ceilings." Jackie pointed up at them.

"And those beds look comfortable," Heather chimed in.

The depth of the mattresses suggested she was right. The doorman pulled the floral curtains closed.

Her room was smaller, but just as enticing. A velvet-covered ottoman stood under the window, which overlooked the gardens. A soft terry robe hung behind the door. She patted the bed. A down comforter. She'd sleep well tonight.

***

Molly woke to a shaft of sunlight sneaking through the gap in the curtains. They went down to breakfast at ten, and she gave the girls a bracelet each with a tiny silver Christmas tree charm. Jackie and Heather presented her with a long silk scarf printed with Norman Rockwell's painting of Stockbridge Main Street at Christmas. The subdued blues and grays would go beautifully with her winter coat.

"It's beautiful. Thank you so much." She'd never forget this.

Heather smiled at her. "You deserve it, Mom. We wanted you to have a souvenir of this holiday."

"That's right. We love you, Mom, and we'll always remember this," Jackie added. "We think you're amazing to have brought us here."

No one expressed the thought that it would have been even better if Simon had been with them, but Molly sensed that they were all thinking it. In time, the girls would learn to make their own new traditions and would miss their father less.

For herself, though, this Christmas holiday, while different, still conjured the empty space that used to be Simon's. Tears rose behind her eyelids, but she blinked them away. She made a show of tying the scarf around her neck. "I shall treasure it, girls. And Merry Christmas, my sweets."

"We need to do something outdoors today, Mom," said Heather. "Especially if we're planning to eat Christmas dinner with all those delicious calories. I asked the person at the desk, and she told me they have an ice rink in the field behind the hotel. You can rent skates and everything."

Molly hadn't skated for years and planned to sit out this event. She'd spotted a couple of huts next to the frozen pond, one where you could collect your rentals, the other where you could warm yourself with cocoa. But the girls insisted she give skating a try.

"It's like riding a bike—you don't forget," said Jackie.

"What if I fall? I'll feel like such an idiot if I break something."

"Come on, Mom. They have someone on the ice all the time to give you a hand."

"You'll be great. And if you're really scared, you can push yourself around using one of those walker things they have for old people."

Jackie and Heather dissolved into giggles. Molly tried to look severe. "A little more respect for your elders and betters, if you don't mind. I'll have you know I used to be pretty good. Oh, well, nothing ventured."

They pulled her to her feet and took her to find skates. Soon, she found herself tottering onto the rink, hoping she wouldn't disgrace herself. Within minutes, the girls were twirling and laughing, their cheeks flushed with their exertion and the cold. After a few false starts, Molly too was sailing around the ice, feeling the cooling bite of the wind on her face. She'd not felt this exhilarated for years.

***

When the girls returned from cross-country skiing on their last day, they all ate lunch at a café in town and wandered the street window-shopping.

"What are you going to get for Nick?" asked Jackie, taking Molly by surprise.

"Nick?"

"As a thank-you. He's the reason we're here, isn't he? I mean, if he hadn't—"

"You're absolutely right. But I've no idea. If you see something, let me know."

Heather had stopped in front of a window filled with brightly colored leather gloves.

"What do you think, Mom?"

"I'm not sure they're quite his style..." Although one never knew. He might consider them original.

"Not for him, silly. For your friends."

"I knew that, of course." She'd planned to give Amanda and Rosie a book each, but these gloves were lovely.

While she was paying, her gaze was drawn to a display of long woolen scarves like the one Luke wore. She turned the price tag over. Wow. Well, no surprise, really. Cashmere was bound to be expensive, and this was a beautiful, soft scarf, with a designer name discreetly woven along one edge. And so many colors to choose from. She wondered about getting a scarlet one for Nick, but she'd never seen him wear red, so she chose a color that would go with his sea-green eyes. Perfect.

Apparently, this was to be the year of the scarf.

CHAPTER THIRTY

Driving back to Brentford along the quiet streets and highways, no one talked much. They played some favorite songs but were content to remain mostly silent. The girls wanted to stay as late as they could, to squeeze every second out of their holiday, so they finally pulled up in front of the house around ten o'clock. It had been a long day, and Molly had dozed on and off while Heather drove home. The old Victorian lay serene in the starlight, mantled with a deep layer of snow.

"I guess it's been a white Christmas here too," said Molly, glad to see that someone had shoveled the driveway and a path to the back door.

"Yup. And more coming overnight. We timed this just right." Jackie was consulting her phone.

"It's good to be back," said Heather sleepily, as they hauled their luggage into the house.

Molly let Hemingway sleep on her bed that night, as an apology for having been away. He graciously agreed to forgive her, though he made sure he slept smack in the middle, forcing her over to one side.

***

The next morning, Molly stood in the kitchen making what she referred to as a proper cup of tea, and sat at the counter to enjoy the quiet before the girls were up. A new flurry of flakes drifted past the window, leaving her cocooned in the silence of the white world outside.

She'd need to get to the bookshop soon, to see how things had gone, but since it was Sunday, it wasn't due to open until noon.

Revived by the tea, she wandered up to her bedroom, where her suitcase lay half-unpacked on the rug, a pile of washing next to it. Hemingway was stamping up and down on the dirty clothes as if determined to make himself another bed. Molly shooed him away, and he sauntered off to sit upright on the rug, the end of his tail flicking in annoyance as he pointedly kept his back to her.

Kneeling by her case to finish unpacking, she heard a small thud of something landing on the floor near her bathroom door. Shaking her head, she told herself she'd imagined the sound.

Splat. There it was again. She turned just in time to see a heavy drop of water joining a growing pool on the carpet. Scrambling to her feet, she went to check it out. When she patted the rug, her hand sank into it with a squelch. This couldn't be good. She glanced up and gasped as she took in the ominous bulge in the ceiling.

She found the number of her builder, Dave. His phone kept ringing as she paced the room, one eye on the leak, until he answered.

"Hello? Dave?" The only response was a message.

"*I'll be away through January 2. Please call back then. Happy holidays!*"

She had no time to vent. She needed something to catch the trickle of water, and fast. She ran downstairs to the mudroom. Damn. Someone had moved the bucket. Why did people move things and not put them back?

"*Behind the door.*" Simon was leaning against the counter, pointing. Oh crap. She didn't have time for him now.

"Darling, I can't stop to chat right now. There's some kind of leak in the bedroom."

"*Need a plumber?*" Simon asked.

"I don't think it's pipe. I have a feeling it's coming through the roof, so I called Dave, but he's on vacation. Got to go."

She grabbed the pail and headed up the stairs, conscious of Simon's eyes on her retreating back.

"*Welcome home,*" came a plaintive voice behind her.

The ceiling was still holding, thank god. She stood the bucket beneath the bulge and said a silent prayer before calling Amanda.

"Wow, sweetie. I don't know. Let me think. I normally use Dave for jobs like this. But I'll call a few of my real estate people and see if they can recommend someone. I'll get right back to you."

Molly's eyes were fixed on the bubble again when a sudden movement in the yard next door caught her eye. Hadley was bounding around, delighted with the snowballs Nick threw for her to fetch. Another plop of water brought Molly's thoughts back to the room.

Her phone pinged with a text from Amanda. *Sorry, hon. The people who answered had nothing to suggest.*

Could Nick do anything? This was hardly as simple as changing a light bulb. But he had repaired a toilet for Luke. That was in the realm of plumbing, though.

She ran along the landing and knocked at Heather's door.

"Honey, I need you. I've got a water crisis happening here."

A moment later, her older daughter appeared in the doorway, bleary-eyed but more or less awake.

"Can you stay in my room and keep an eye on things?" Molly said. "There's a leak."

Heather snatched up her robe and followed her mother down the corridor. She surveyed the floor, the drips, and the bulging ceiling. "Wow."

"I'm going over to Nick's to see if he can help," said Molly.

"The builder's away."

"Okay. I'll hang here."

***

Molly returned with Nick about twenty minutes later. He wore heavy boots and a bright yellow slicker.

"Hi there," said Heather, now clad in a pair of Molly's sweatpants and one of her sweatshirts. Evidently, she'd stayed in Molly's room and borrowed some of her clothes. "I'm Heather. I don't think we've met."

Molly made a mental note never to wear sweats again. Even Heather couldn't make them look anything but dowdy.

Nick answered Heather's greeting in a rather distracted manner, all the while staring up. He let out a low whistle.

"What do you think?" Molly's anxious frown cleared as he turned to her.

"Well, the first thing is to burst that bubble and allow the water to drain. D'you have some scissors, or better yet, a sharp kitchen knife?"

"I'll get one," volunteered Jackie, who'd emerged from her room in her red pajamas with the cheerful moose on the front.

By the time Jackie returned, the floor of the bedroom was covered with old towels. Nick stood on a stool, balancing the bucket on his left hand, like a waiter with a tray of drinks. He reached out for the fish-filleting knife and grasped it firmly.

"Stand back, ladies."

They took up positions a couple of paces away, and Molly held her breath as he gingerly poked at the plaster above his head.

An almost inaudible curse escaped his lips. The women glanced at each other and struggled not to laugh.

"Okay. Going to have to stab this. So, watch out in case it sprays all over."

He thrust the knife into the bubble, and wobbled slightly as he tried to hold the pail under it. Molly stepped closer to grab the stepladder. Too late. Although most of the water ended up in the bucket, several pints fell on his head. He stood there blinking as Jackie removed the bucket from his hand, careful to avoid any more spills.

"Oh, dear, Nick." Molly eyed his sopping hair. "I'm so sorry. You're soaked. Here, let me find you a fresh towel." She ran a hand over her head, which had caught some of the deluge. It would be fine, but her neighbor was drenched.

He stepped down from the chair, and his booted foot squelched as it landed. Molly handed him a towel and gazed at him as he rubbed at his hair.

"I'd better get dried off." Nick's voice broke into her musings. "And the rug needs to dry out too. I can carry it down to the garage if you like."

"Thanks so much," said Molly. A totally inadequate word. "I'm truly grateful. Not sure what I'd have done without you."

He'd saved that rug. She and Simon had bought it at an auction in Vermont one summer, and it remained one of her favorites. That had been such a lovely vacation.

Nick was saying something. "I think it's ice above here that's causing it. We had almost a foot of snow while you were away, then some warm weather that melted it, then another freeze. So, I guess I'll have to get up there and brush some of it off before it gets any worse. I don't think you'll find anyone else to do it this week."

"I couldn't ask you to do that. You've done enough already—keeping the shop open, and now this…"

"You didn't ask. I offered. I'll be right back."

Suddenly a cashmere scarf seemed a totally inadequate gift.

CHAPTER THIRTY-ONE

The girls had left to visit friends by the time Nick knocked on the front door, carrying a snow shovel and a long extension ladder. His hair was still damp where it peeked out from a woolen ski hat, but his expression was cheerful enough. He set the ladder against the wall at the side of the house and climbed up, the shovel in one hand.

"Don't stand there watching me. I'll be fine. And it's cold out here."

She glanced up at the overcast sky—a snow sky, Simon used to call it, and he knew his skies. Molly wasn't dressed for the outdoors.

"I'll make you some hot chocolate," she offered—the least she could do on a day threatening dire weather.

From the kitchen, the sound of a steady push and sweep reached her from somewhere overhead, and when she emerged on the porch, clutching a large mug, fluffy white piles of snow were visible where they'd slid off the roof. But she could make out no sign of him.

"Nick?" she said.

"Up here." He stood directly above her bedroom. She felt a little queasy as she craned her neck to look up. She'd never intended this. Hadn't realized just how high he'd be.

"Don't worry. I grew up in Vermont, so I've done this before. It won't take long, and I'll come down for the chocolate when I'm finished."

Molly couldn't take her eyes off him. He seemed so vulnerable up there.

"Really," he said, "why don't you wait inside?"

She hesitated, but as he lifted the shovel and swung it back, she reluctantly started toward the front door. Then a single "fuck" interrupted the scraping sound.

"Nick?" she shouted, running back to where she'd seen him. She stared upward. He had disappeared. Only an ominous silence greeted her as she rounded the corner of the house, where the ladder stood, abandoned.

He must be there somewhere. But Molly's sight line was obscured by the tall mounds of snow that he'd swept off the roof. The shrubs below them made them even higher. She called his name again.

"Here," came a subdued voice. She could see him sprawled on top of one of the piles, wincing as he attempted to raise his leg. The azalea bush, flattened beneath him, would never look the same again.

"Don't move. You might have broken something."

"That's exactly why I *am* moving. To check that everything's working." He sounded irritable, and she could tell that he was in no mood to be bossed around.

"Oh, my god. Are you sure you're okay?"

"I'll live." He spoke through gritted teeth. "I think I can stand if you'll give me a hand."

He took off a glove so she could grasp him more securely. Molly extended her hand and seized his icy one. He might be in shock. Nick took a deep breath and began to lever himself up using his other hand to gain momentum. Suddenly, though, he collapsed with a gasp of pain and a stream of impressive curses. She suppressed an illogical urge to laugh. This wasn't funny. He'd clearly injured his foot, perhaps seriously.

"I'm calling an ambulance," she said, ignoring his protests. His injuries might turn out to be worse than he realized. "I'll get you a blanket. Be right back."

She ran inside to find a cushion for his head and a throw from the living room.

Simon was lounging in his favorite armchair. "*See what you get for employing inferior workmen?*"

"Be quiet," she snapped. "He needs help now." She walked out of the room, a pillow under her arm, being careful not to trip on the long fringes of the throw.

Outside, Nick lay silent, his eyes closed. He opened one at her approach, squinting slightly into the sun.

"Angel of mercy, eh?"

She admired his attempt to lighten the mood. "Hardly."

Molly tried to smile reassuringly as she knelt to place the cushion under his head and covered him up. She stayed next to him, her knees beginning to freeze where the damp penetrated her jeans. His back must be icy too. He needed help and fast.

It took only ten minutes for an ambulance and a fire truck to pull up in the driveway, though it felt much longer. The sound of their sirens coming down the road reassured her.

"They're here." She rested a hand on his arm. "They'll soon sort you out."

"Hadley," he murmured, his voice sounding sleepy.

"What?"

"Take care of her."

Right. The dog.

"Of *course* I will. You mustn't fret about that."

"Food in the kitchen, leash by the door."

Molly nodded. " You don't need to worry about Hadley. She'll be fine."

"Okay, ma'am. If you wouldn't mind moving so we can take a look at your husband." A huge first responder in a dazzling yellow jacket and enormous boots with crampons loomed over her.

"He's not my…" She started to say, but it wasn't worth getting into now. She stood back while the medic and two of his colleagues took the patient's vitals and asked him a series of questions to which she couldn't hear the answers. Apparently satisfied, they lifted him onto a portable chair and carried him to the ambulance.

"I'll see to Hadley and then I'll come and find you in the hospital," she promised him.

Nick didn't answer.

CHAPTER THIRTY-TWO

Hadley scrambled to her feet when Molly walked into Nick's kitchen. She gave a yelp, but evidently recognized that this human wasn't hostile and ambled over to sniff at her jacket.

"Looking for Nick, eh, girl?" She petted the top of the golden's head and glanced around for her feeding dish. She spotted it behind the door, noting that it contained some kibble. Not hungry yet, she supposed.

"Do you need to go out, girl?" Hadley gave some small yips of delight and began to bounce at this suggestion. Taking the leash from the peg close by, Molly fastened it to the retriever's collar and opened the back door. She could do with a walk too. They stepped outside into the pale sunshine.

An hour later, having walked Hadley and replenished her food and water, Molly parked in front of the hospital and entered. The lobby had no discernible smell—unlike the hospitals of her childhood—but that made no difference to her memories.

The subdued lighting in the entrance and hallways, the hand sanitizer dispensers that stood guard at every door, the silent bustle of nurses and the occasional doctor—all of it forced her to recall the terrible two days she'd spent there after Simon's heart attack.

Back then, she'd moved through the halls and corridors as if in a trance, on her way to the ICU. She gazed at him, lying ashen and motionless, while she searched his face for any sign of life. And she waited, incapable of coherent thought, for Jackie and Heather to arrive.

Everything came rushing back as she walked through the emergency room doors.

It mattered little that conditions outside were different this time. Winter, not summer. Not her husband, just a neighbor. Well, she admitted, a close neighbor—a friend, even. But still, not Simon. Not fighting for his life. And hers.

***

"They tell me it's a sprained ankle. Nothing serious." Nick lay resting on the bed, his left foot raised on some pillows, the color back in his cheeks. He gave her a wry grin. "They told me it's lucky the snow and those shrubs cushioned my fall—and the cold probably helped keep the swelling down."

The way he managed to look on the bright side of a disaster like this was something she envied. She couldn't do it. Well, for someone else, she might.

"Never mind my plants. It's your foot that's important." She eyed the bandaged foot doubtfully. "I imagine the damage might have been a lot worse. It looks enormous from here."

"Oh, that's just the bandage. They never know when to stop, do they?"

Nick's voice was light, but shadows ringed his eyes. He looked vulnerable in his hospital gown, and as if reading her mind, he strained to raise himself a few inches higher. The effort caused him to wince.

"Can I help? Do you need a nurse?"

"No, no. I'm fine. Actually, quite comfortable, if I don't do too much. They were going to bring me a painkiller, but it hasn't shown up yet."

Molly took a step nearer the door. "I'll find someone to give it to you."

"Don't worry about it. The ankle only hurts if I move it. But you should sit."

Seeing no seat in his room, she stuck her head into the corridor and, spotting an empty chair against a wall, brought it back. Perching on the edge of it, she leaned forward.

"I'm so sorry this happened. You've been doing all these favors for me, and now you've been rewarded with this."

"Stop looking so worried. This is minor, they tell me."

Molly tried not to let her incredulity show on her face. "So, what's the prognosis?"

Nick winced momentarily. "Normally, sprains heal relatively fast. But as it turns out, I've cracked a bone in my foot, too." In response to her look of alarm, he hastened to reassure her. "It's not bad, honestly. Not broken, only a small fracture."

Her shoulders relaxed. Thank god, it wasn't disastrous. She immediately tensed up again. This was all her fault.

"That still sounds painful. So, what's the treatment? How long will you be here?"

He frowned. "I've told them I'm fine. But they want to keep me in overnight to make sure I'm not concussed."

To look at his face, no one would guess there was anything wrong. But one could never tell.

"Would you like me to call someone for you? Family? Luke, for instance?"

Nick raised an eyebrow. "Luke? No reason to do that."

"Of course not. I just thought, being as how he's a friend—"

"Well, sure. I don't mind if he knows, but I don't feel like speaking to anyone right now."

"No one in New York?"

He stared at her, clearly puzzled. "New York?"

Molly hesitated. "Sam?"

The silence went on and on.

"I don't think she'll be interested." His voice expressed no emotion at all, positive or negative.

What? Sam was a woman? How had she not realized that?

She assumed an air of detachment at odds with her feelings. "You don't talk about her really, and I don't like to pry. But I thought…"

"I don't discuss her because she's not part of my life anymore."

His face was turned away from her so she couldn't read his eyes. Oh, dear. Had she poked at an old wound? She'd only meant well.

"Of course. Sorry." That sounded so inadequate.

As the silence became more and more uncomfortable, she felt obliged to say something.

"How long will it be before you can walk?"

"As soon as they give me some crutches, I think." He was looking at her now, and the frown on his forehead was smoothing out.

Molly relaxed back into the chair, glad he'd be taken care of, at least tonight.

This had all happened because of the stupid roof leaking into her bedroom. Because of her running to Nick for help. And now she'd put her foot in it about Sam.

"I'm so sorry—about everything."

"Don't be. I'm the one who insisted on going up there. I should have been more careful. I discovered ice under that snow. I guess it's melting and causing the leak."

He was ignoring the reference to his ex. She breathed out in relief.

"Don't worry about that now. It's down to the occasional drip, so you must have done something right. And the builder will be back from his vacation in a couple of days. In the meantime, let me know when you can leave, and I'll pick you up and take you home. I'm sure Luke won't mind covering for me."

"Thanks. That'd be ideal. I don't feel like another ride in an ambulance."

"No problem. I want to help."

"Well, in that case, I accept. And I'm grateful. Which reminds me, I'll need some clothes. They cut off my pants, so I don't have any."

A fleeting picture of this attractive man without any trousers flashed through her mind. Focus, Molly.

"I'll be happy to bring your things for you. Where will I find them?"

"I left clean clothes in the dryer in the utility room—there should be enough to get me home. If you could bring me some sweatpants, they might be easier to handle."

Molly began a list on the back of a bookmark that she found floating around in her purse. "Is there anything else I can bring for you?"

"I don't have my phone, come to think of it. It should be in the kitchen."

At that moment, a young nurse came in, pulling a rolling blood pressure unit behind her.

"Sorry you've had to wait. We're short-staffed due to the holiday." She smiled in a distracted way and consulted his chart. "I need to check your vitals…Nick."

Molly stood to give the nurse some space. He held out his arm, and they waited as the cuff expanded and deflated.

"So far, so good." She studied the patient. "How's your pain level on a scale of one to ten? One means negligible, ten is unbearable."

"About a five, unless I move my leg," Nick said. "So, I'm trying to lie still."

"Excellent. Here's the medication you were promised." She handed him a tablet and a small cup of water. "That should take care of it."

Molly felt superfluous as she stood by the wall. There seemed to be nothing she could contribute. Then something occurred to her. She watched the nurse leave and turned to Nick. "Have you had anything to eat?"

"Not really. They brought me some crackers and some Jell-O, but I'm not supposed to have anything more substantial for another hour or two. In case I have a concussion."

"Well, I know the food here is okay, but would you prefer some takeout when they say it's allowed?"

Nick's face brightened. "That would be great. So long as it doesn't mean you'll be asking me to take over at the bookshop again."

She looked up, embarrassed, but met his eyes, which were laughing at her, and relaxed.

"Never again, I promise." She smiled at him. Finally, she could do something useful.

"Speaking of work, at least I'm not missing any. I have a couple more weeks before I need to be back at school."

He knew how to see the glass as half full, for sure.

CHAPTER THIRTY-THREE

Molly walked through her front door with Hadley trailing behind her, sniffing the unfamiliar air. Hemingway, sauntering into the hall, stopped dead, hissed, and raced upstairs. Hadley stood, looking longingly after him, but retired behind the sofa, hackles slightly raised, the minute Simon materialized.

"*Why have you brought the dog over? Is Nick okay?*"

"He will be, but he'll be on crutches for a while." Molly sank into an armchair and unzipped her boots.

She started, as footsteps on the stairs indicated one of the girls was on her way down.

"What got into Hemingway? He's under my bed, refusing to come out. And who are you talking to, Mom?" said Jackie, putting her head around the door.

"Um…Hadley." Seeing her puzzlement, Molly explained, "Nick's dog. Hemingway didn't think much of my bringing her home."

Simon was nowhere to be seen now, thank heavens. Hearing her name, Hadley emerged from behind the sofa.

Jackie's face cleared. "Hello, girl." She crouched on the floor and reached out a hand to the dog. The dog sniffed cautiously before she gave it a lick and contentedly succumbed to having the back of her silky ears scratched. "She's lovely, Mom." After a moment, she added, "So, how *is* Nick?"

"He's sprained his ankle and cracked a bone in his foot,

but I think he's in good spirits, considering. They might let him come home tomorrow."

"Wow, what a shame. The injuries, I mean. Does he have anyone to help him until his ankle's better?" Her daughters always had sympathy to spare.

"I suppose *I* will," said Molly. "After all, he was helping *me* when he fell."

"In that case, I guess it's the least you can do."

Her mother nodded. "I agree. Not to mention that it happened right after he stood in for me at the Book Boutique so we could go away for Christmas."

"Speaking of the bookshop, how will you manage if you're taking care of Nick?"

"I'm hoping Luke might be available to take over, if he's back. I can't recall how long he was supposed to be away."

"Well, if push comes to shove, Heather and I could give you a hand for a day or two."

"That would be great. I don't think I'll have to be at Nick's all day."

"Whenever you need someone to fill in, let us know. I worked there at Christmas last year, before you bought it, remember?"

Help seemed to be all around if she was willing to accept it. "Thanks," she said.

"No problem, Mom. Come on, Hadley, you can help me put a load of laundry in the dryer." The dog began to follow her through the hall toward the utility room.

"Listen, sweetie," said Molly, and Jackie turned back. "Why don't we eat out tonight? I really don't have the energy to cook. We could leave Hadley here while we're gone—I'm sure she'd be all right for an hour or two. She's often alone there at Nick's when he's teaching, I think."

"Okay, Mom. I'll tell Heather. She's been on the phone with that boyfriend of hers, but it's time she got herself organized too."

***

Molly walked in through Nick's back door and began searching for the dog's bed. She couldn't see it on the floor in the kitchen, so she went through to the main room. It struck her that she hadn't been anywhere else in the house since her visit with Amanda. It had been somewhat gloomy then, but now a fresh coat of white paint brightened the place considerably.

Textbooks and novels, some of them literary, lined the bookcases. A collection of classical-music vinyl records was piled next to a player. Molly approved.

She wandered across the room propelled by simple curiosity, Hadley's bed forgotten. On the desk stood only three photographs—one of a couple she took to be his parents, judging by the resemblance and the dated clothes they were wearing. Another showed Nick in a group of people—at a barbecue, it looked like. She picked up the photo and studied it. She smiled at a shot of a laughing man with his arm around Nick's shoulders, waving a bottle of beer at the camera. Nick was grinning. They were obviously close.

And—she paused. The last frame held a snapshot of a younger Nick with a boy of seven, or thereabouts, on his knee. Who was that? Clearly, someone important, or he wouldn't keep the picture on his desk.

Remembering her mission, she put the photo back and moved into the dining room.

When it came right down to it, Molly didn't know much about Nick. He'd told her about his work at the college, the students he taught, and some of the other faculty. But he rarely offered anything about his family.

What kind of friends were they, really? When she knew so little about his past? She'd not paid enough attention as she talked to him about herself and her concerns.

She decided she would be more supportive when he came back from the hospital. She walked upstairs, still looking for

Hadley's dog bed, and found it at the foot of Nick's neatly made queen-sized one.

She gave a small grunt as she wrangled the dark-blue cushion downstairs. It wasn't particularly heavy, just awkward. Hadley, a large beast, required appropriately big sleeping quarters. Molly wanted her to be comfortable that night, so she struggled on.

She almost forgot to find clean clothes for Nick. She came across an empty basket on top of the washing machine and emptied the dryer, before folding a Rolling Stones T-shirt and placing it on the washer. It had been a long while since she'd folded a man's laundry. She stopped folding a pair of jeans to consider that. It should have reminded her of the past, shouldn't it? Yet it felt okay.

She left the rest of the clothes in a messy pile and walked into the kitchen to find Nick's phone and a charger on the counter, as he'd told her.

When she picked up the phone, it came to life momentarily, showing her the screensaver—a smiling young man. He might be in his late twenties or early thirties. Another mystery. The screen went dark again.

Now she needed something to carry everything in. Spotting some fabric shopping totes on a peg, she took one. Naturally, he'd have reusable bags. Doing his bit for the environment.

She put his stuff in her car and went back for the dog bed, glad that someone had scattered salt on the driveway, so she didn't slip.

Molly spotted Heather standing in the kitchen and called out to her. Within seconds, her daughter arrived to help heave the dog's bed into the house.

"Jackie said she'd have Hadley in her bedroom overnight, but this will be such a pain to get upstairs," Heather said. "Plus, Hemingway's still hiding under her bed. And isn't Nick coming back tomorrow?"

"I managed to wrestle it down the stairs in his house, but I expect you're right. Okay. Since Hadley seems to like being near the sofa, let's put it down there, at one end."

That way, the dog would be able to hide from Simon if he showed up again.

***

When she walked back into Nick's hospital room a short while later, the brown paper bag in her hands allowed a delicate but alluring aroma of Chinese cuisine to escape.

"Perfect timing," said Nick, with an exaggerated sniff. "I'm ravenous. And five minutes ago, they finally gave me permission to eat."

She unloaded the bags onto his tray and opened the tote full of his stuff.

"Do you want to change your clothes first? I brought some for you. And your phone."

"Thanks. Is there a T-shirt in there? I'd like to get out of this hospital gear."

Molly pulled out a plain white shirt from the bag. "Long or short sleeves? I have both."

"Short will be fine. They keep it kinda warm here."

She did, indeed, feel quite warm as Nick unbuttoned the shoulder of his gown and began taking it off. He was in pretty good shape for a man of his…

"Back in a moment," she said and beat a hasty retreat. A few minutes later, she headed back in, a little more composed.

She studied his face. "You do look more like yourself. Though I should have remembered to bring you a comb."

"No problem. I'm sure there's one in that kit they left for me. The one with the toothbrush. So, what do we have here?" Nick peered into the takeout bag. "Fantastic. Want some?"

"Nope. It's all for you." She helped him organize the meal on his hospital tray table before she said, "The girls and I are eating out this evening. We haven't decided where, yet. They can choose."

"Sounds like the right solution after a long day. Well, in that case, double thanks—for bringing my dinner in first."

She watched him open some of the containers. Fried noodles, spare ribs, and stir-fried vegetables.

"Perfect." He picked up a rib and chewed one end. Swallowing the morsel with a contented sigh, he turned to her again. "The doctor's confirmed I can go home tomorrow if nothing changes overnight."

"That's great," said Molly. "The girls are going to take over at the store when you need a lift."

"Glad you mentioned that. You don't have to drive me. The hospital insists on taking me home because of the snow and ice around. They don't want me falling again on the way into the house."

"I'll put some more salt on your front path to make it safer. But I have to agree, an ambulance might be a better way to go."

"And how's Hadley? Is she okay? I've been worrying about her."

"She's no trouble at all. Although Hemingway isn't exactly thrilled."

Nick was frowning.

"My cat, remember? He's gone into hiding upstairs," she said. "Anyway, I've brought Hadley's bed into our house. I thought she'd be less anxious about being away from you if she stayed with us. Is that all right?"

"Of course. Thank you."

"Do you think she'll be upset if I leave her on her own when I take the girls out for dinner tonight?"

"She'll be fine. She stays in when I go out in the evenings. Might want to make sure Hemingway's somewhere safe, though."

"I'm not worried about him. He's as tough as his namesake, and we won't be late. Is there anything else you need before I go?"

"I'm all set, thanks. Enjoy your dinner."

CHAPTER THIRTY-FOUR

Before he came home, Molly rearranged Nick's kitchen for him so everything would be within reach. The sink and the fridge stood fairly close together, which helped.

She plugged the toaster and coffee machine into the wall by the refrigerator. Then she moved the table closer to the countertop, so it would be easier for him to put down a hot drink. She came across some cereal in the cabinet and bought him a loaf of sliced bread so he could make toast.

"You'll require some help with things," she told him when he was settled in. Seeing him frown, she added, "Only to begin with. I'll come over to see if I can do anything for you before I go to work—and on my lunch break."

"Listen, I can reach everything I need. And I can get up and down the stairs on my butt until I figure out how to do it more elegantly."

"Lucky your butt wasn't injured when you fell." She glanced at him to see how he was taking this. His grin reassured her. "But Hadley will have to be let out. I can at least do that. Take her for a walk at lunchtime. And if I'm coming over anyway, I may as well bring you something to eat."

***

Molly walked into Nick's kitchen the evening after his homecoming with a dish of pasta carbonara she'd made. As the door opened, an unwelcome smell stopped her in her tracks. Was something burning? She almost tripped over Nick, sitting on the floor looking dejected. On the stove, wisps of blue smoke rose from a frying pan. Pausing only to put the pasta on the table, she stepped around him, whipped the pan off the heat, and found a lid to cover it.

She turned to look at her patient.

"Nick, what happened? Are you hurt? How's your ankle?"

"I'm okay." He looked up at her. "I've only been down here a few minutes. On the floor, I mean."

She took a step toward him, but he shook his head. "I can manage. More important, how's the frying pan?"

He was worrying about kitchen equipment? Perhaps he was looking for reasons to avoid the real problem.

"It'll be just fine." She relented. "You can easily buy a new one online. Can I help you up?"

Nick's tired face showed a couple of days' stubble. Mainly gray, but it suited him. She felt rather than saw the inward struggle between wanting to be independent and requiring help.

"Thanks." The clenched jaw appeared to be hindering his speech. "Why don't you start by bringing that chair a bit closer, so I can reach it. I'd like to try to get up on my own, in case you're not here the next time I find myself lounging around on the floor." He gave her a crooked smile.

Molly walked across the room and picked up the bright red kitchen chair, placing it next to Nick. Pulling it nearer, he braced himself against it as he struggled onto his right knee. She wanted to give him a hand, but knew she shouldn't. He had to feel in control of this. Giving a grunt, he pushed himself off the seat and straightened up. Only now, his crutches were out of reach. She handed them to him without a word.

"Thanks."

"Nick, what in heaven's name were you thinking?"

"I hate feeling helpless. I figured I could at least make some scrambled eggs. But after I put the butter on to heat, I turned around to reach for the eggs—" He indicated the table. "And Hadley bounced up and knocked my damn crutch out from under me."

Molly, who'd been wondering where the dog had gotten to, spotted her hiding in the utility room. She came sliding out on her belly as if trying to apologize. Nick held out a hand to her, and, cautiously, she came over and licked it.

It hadn't occurred to Molly that Hadley might be a liability in this situation. She'd imagined Nick would enjoy the dog's company while he convalesced.

"Would you like me to take her back for a few days?"

"No, I don't think so. She might be lonely when you're at work." He petted Hadley's head. "And I would miss her, too. Plus, I'll be doing a lot better in a day or two."

Nick's determination to get well fast did him credit. But Molly's imagination ran riot. What might have happened if she hadn't come through the door at exactly the right moment? His whole kitchen might have gone up in flames. The whole house, actually.

"How about you leave her in the utility room if you're cooking? Or better yet, don't cook."

"I guess you have a point."

She looked at him. He must feel like an idiot for ending up on the floor with his home about to catch fire. He probably needed more encouragement than advice.

"It'll only be a week or so before you'll be walking without crutches," she said. Nick told her he planned to drive as soon as he came off the painkillers he was taking for the broken bone in his foot.

"So, until then, why not let me help around here?"

A thought appeared to strike him. "You know, I'm kind of hungry. How about you? Would you like some scrambled eggs?"

Molly, who'd eaten an egg salad sandwich for lunch, demurred. "I think we can do better than that. I brought over some pasta carbonara, and there should be some lettuce and avocado in the fridge, unless you ate them earlier."

Nick shook his head. "Too complicated."

"Excellent. Oh, and I have a bottle of chilled bubbly at home. I'll run and fetch it."

Nick looked up. "Champagne?"

"Yup. Tonight is New Year's Eve. And we ought to drink to a better year next year, don't you think?"

"What about your girls? Don't you want to see the New Year in with them?"

"They're out partying with their friends. Heaven knows when they'll be back. So it's you and me, Nick." That sounded odd, yet okay, somehow.

Sometime later, but long before midnight, they moved into the living room. He sank into the sofa and rested his foot on the coffee table while Molly opened the champagne with a satisfying pop. "No point in hanging on for the clock. You look like you could use an early night."

They toasted each other to greater luck, starting the next day.

"No more falling off roofs," said Molly as they clinked glasses.

"Some people might conclude that damaging my ankle had something to do with not moving forward with my life."

She stared at him. This was the first time he'd confided anything personal.

"What do *you* think?"

"I guess if the thought crossed my mind, there might be something in it. I thought starting at Carnarvon and coming to live out here would give me a new way of looking at things."

Molly sipped at her champagne and leaned toward him. "Taking the next step in life is hard, I know. But it's one little step at a time. And a step back sometimes."

Nick's gaze seemed to see right into her. "I get that." He laughed. "Though I could have done without stepping back off a roof."

* * *

The next ten days set Molly's life off-kilter. Three years had passed with no man to take care of, and she found it both familiar and time-consuming.

She checked on him every morning, on her way to the bookstore. She let Hadley out, put on a pot of coffee, stood a mug nearby, and made sure he had fresh milk in the fridge. At noon, she, or one of the girls, would bring him a sandwich from the Java Jive or Marino's, the local supermarket. His current favorite appeared to be the seasonal sub—turkey with cranberry sauce and stuffing, and for the first few days, he ate one daily. When she was alone in the shop, the girls handled the lunchtime shift.

"He's nice, isn't he, Mom?" said Jackie one day. "Easy to talk to."

Molly nodded. She hoped Jackie's chatter wasn't tiring him.

"I wouldn't mind him as a professor," volunteered Heather.

"Shame you're not studying biology, then. In any case, he's going to teach Mom all about butterfly gardens, so hands off," her sister teased, grinning.

Molly felt her cheeks flame and fanned her face with a hand. "Hot flash," she murmured. The girls winked at each other. Right, then.

* * *

Over the next two weeks, she watched as Nick gradually returned to his former excellent health. As soon as he graduated from crutches to a cane, he started to walk—gingerly—and even to drive himself to the physical therapist's office. Though Molly noticed he had to tie his sneaker loosely because his foot still showed some swelling.

The girls went back to school, and he went back to teaching when the semester began, staying late each day. "It's difficult for me to carry a lot of stuff the way I usually do when I'm bringing back homework for grading and textbooks. I find it easier to deal with at school. But they're letting me take Hadley in with me, which solves one problem."

Nick had never taken her visits for granted, but the fact that she no longer felt obliged to visit him every day came as something of a relief. On the weekends, he and Molly would take a short, slow walk with Hadley in the neighborhood while his ankle healed. Pretty soon, he could get around as if he'd never been injured at all.

And Molly was able to turn her attention back to the issues at the bookstore and the challenges of dealing with Mr. Channing "Big Shot" Madison.

CHAPTER THIRTY-FIVE

When Renzo finally returned from Brazil, he walked like an older man, lacking his previous energy. They met in the café when the day was over, and Molly looked at the faded tan and the new lines across his forehead.

"How did it go?" Her voice was tentative, not wanting to tread on unfamiliar turf, but to let him know she was there for him.

"My father? He still lives, but I couldn't stay for the end." His eyes grew bright and he turned his head away.

"Oh, Renzo, I'm so sorry." She couldn't imagine anything worse than being far away when someone you loved was dying.

He gave a small shake of his head, as if to clear it. "I have a letter from the landlord. I will give it to you, and we will talk later, yes?"

"Of course. Whenever you're ready."

If a change of subject was what he wanted, she would go along. After all, she'd been waiting for Channing's reply for days now. Renzo disappeared for a moment and emerged from the back office with an envelope.

She took it from him with a sinking feeling. "I'll come over after we close."

***

Restless, she couldn't wait for six o'clock and sought him out when she judged there'd be few customers left.

"Did you read this?" She waved the letter in front of his chest.

Renzo shook his head.

"He wants to invest in the project."

"I don't understand. Who wants to invest in what?" He stopped whatever he was doing behind the counter, came round to her side, and took the paper from her. He scanned it. Then read it again.

Molly, trying to curb her impatience, waited for him to finish before she spoke. "Madison. He likes our idea. He's offering to give us most of the money we need in exchange for sixty percent of the business. Otherwise, he won't agree to our plan."

Shock was visible on Renzo's face.

"Are you okay? You look pale," she said, concerned. No mean feat for someone with his tanned complexion.

He took a deep breath. "That pig," he hissed. "We have a word for this type of person in Brazil. But I will not say it in front of you."

She didn't intend to, but she smiled. Yet the seriousness of the situation soon broke through again.

"I don't think we should react too fast. Let's take a little time to decide what to do."

"You are right, I know. But I hate to have my choices taken away from me."

Understandable, naturally. She agreed with him. They needed to stall for time while they came up with an answer.

"Renzo, do you have enough to pay the rent on the fifteenth?"

"I think so, but it will not be easy. And you?"

Molly had enough, but paying Pilgrim would leave her working with almost no leeway for any unforeseen expenses.

"I'm in the same boat. We need to come up with a solution, because I don't want to give this up now. After everything we've put into the shop. And the café, of course."

They fell silent for a moment.

"Molly, can you ask your consultant what we should do next?"

What was he talking about? Consultant? Oh, right. Simon.

"I will find out, but I'm pretty sure the answer will either be a different plan or more negotiation. Like persuading Madison to accept a smaller stake. Less than fifty percent. There's no way we can have him running our business."

Renzo raised his eyes. "Absolutely not. But we will still need his permission to break through the wall."

"Maybe. But I believe Luke made changes when he took over the place. I'll find out if he needed approval from anyone."

"Agreed. And I will examine my lease and check out what it says about making alterations."

***

When Luke arrived for work the next morning, Molly took him aside before they did anything else, to tell him the latest news. That seemed only fair, and he might have something useful to contribute, though she couldn't think what. She was almost certain that she could predict his reaction. He'd be horrified at the idea of merging the bookstore with the café. But surely, once he understood their sink-or-swim situation, he would view things differently.

So she was astonished to hear him say, "Turning the two shops into one space could work."

She goggled at him. "Really?"

"Well, stands to reason that if the rents go up by such a large margin, you need to do something drastic."

Had she mentioned the rent to him before today? She couldn't remember. And how was he managing to retain his composure?

Luke pretended to straighten his pine-green bow tie, the

one with the snowflakes. She could tell he was pretending, because it was already perfect.

"Have you asked Pilgrim about what would be involved in merging the two shops?"

Her feeling of optimism, buoyed by his reaction, faded. "That man…" She would not utter his name. "… says he'll let us go ahead if he can invest."

"That's good, isn't it?"

"He's demanding sixty percent of the joint business in exchange."

Luke remained surprisingly unmoved by this. All he said was, "Then we'll have to figure out a different solution, won't we?"

We. So, he was on her side after all.

"Like what? If you have any suggestions, I'd love to hear them. I'm racking my brains, but so far can't come up with anything."

"You have a business plan, right? And you're looking for money to carry it out."

"Uh-huh. We also need an okay from Pilgrim to knock down the wall between the two stores."

Luke frowned. "When I made alterations to the bookshop ten years ago, I didn't ask for permission. Of course, the changes weren't structural. Unless you call the new partition at the back, to create a bigger office, structural."

"I think," Molly chose her words carefully, "that building something like that might be considered structural. So, how come you never mentioned it to me?"

"To be honest, I forgot. Plus, the topic never came up, either with the landlords or you. At the time, I always figured I could make good when I sold the business, if I had to."

"That's all very well, but I think making a huge hole in the dividing wall is probably a step too far. Anyway, Renzo and I have to figure out the funding before we get carried away."

Luke didn't appear to be paying attention. His eyes were

fixed on the tin-paneled ceiling, his head tilted to one side.

"Luke? Are you listening?"

"Yes. Sorry. I've just had a thought. But I need to do some research to be sure."

As he spoke, Miss Johansen tottered in, wearing black patent boots with chunky heels and a pair of burgundy cord knickerbockers. She deposited a half-dozen speckled eggs on the counter. "We finished the Lucinda Parks," she announced. "Do you have any more by her?"

There'd be no time to finish the discussion with Luke now, but Miss Johansen's hopeful expression dispelled Molly's annoyance.

"Of course," she said. "Come this way."

CHAPTER THIRTY-SIX

As with learning to crack an egg with one hand, Molly persevered on the dating site, mainly to satisfy her girlfriends but also to prove to herself that she could manage her own dating life. Amanda urged her on, as a way of "switching off from business," while Simon hung over her as she sat in front of her laptop, providing a running commentary.

"Man's got no muscle tone at all."

This one did have rather narrow shoulders.

"Self-obsessed. No one should spend so much time at the gym. And this one's neck has disappeared into his enormous shoulder muscles."

"Too nerdy." Because of the horn rims? Nick had horn-rimmed glasses and he looked pretty good in them.

"Too conservative." That too-short haircut was somewhat off-putting, she had to admit. She preferred men's hair a little longer. Like Nick's.

For a man who claimed he wanted to help her find someone new, he was being remarkably unhelpful.

***

Ignoring his advice, for the most part, she went on a few weekend dates with men who were either too dull, too talkative, or cripplingly shy. She was almost relieved when she met BigPeter, despite his online moniker.

Simon approved of him too. "*He looks solid. Go for it.*"

BigPeter, as his name suggested, was tall and wide. In good shape, although not handsome, he displayed a relaxed demeanor that reassured her she had nothing to fear in his company. His sense of humor wasn't immediately apparent, which was disconcerting, since for Molly, being able to share a joke was an essential part of attraction. Perhaps he just needed to cotton to her British ideas of what was funny.

Their dates progressed from coffee, to lunch, to dinner with no obvious drawbacks. They were halfway through their third date before the cracks in his facade started to show.

She'd asked him about the books he read. Apparently, they liked some of the same authors.

"I don't tell everyone this, but I'm partial to the occasional romance novel." BigPeter almost whispered this, as if concerned they might be overheard.

Molly thought this confession was endearing, not as startling as he'd obviously expected. "Me too. I love Lucinda Parks."

"I don't think I know her. But you're not surprised?"

"Each to his own," she said, smiling in response to his admission that he enjoyed the cowboy romances she found tedious. "You're not the only man to read them. They usually claim they're buying for their wife, even if they're not married. I think it's sweet."

"Sweet, huh?"

Molly laughed. He didn't.

She concentrated on the shrimp *a la puttanesca*, but it tasted a little too salty now. BigPeter's eyes never left her face until she gave up trying to finish the pasta and put her fork down.

"I have a question to ask you," he remarked as the waiter placed their desserts in front of them with a flourish.

"Shoot." Molly, who'd sipped her way through a couple of glasses of wine, was feeling quite relaxed. She scooped a teaspoonful of smooth chocolate gelato and popped it into her mouth. She followed up with a nibble at one of the rolled wafer cookies they served alongside it.

"Do you ever wear high-heeled sandals?"

What? Surprising herself, she giggled. The temperature outside had sunk into the twenties, so she was wearing her black knee-high boots, though she would have preferred her unsexy but practical fur-lined winter ones.

"I'm serious," he persisted. "I like to see a lady's foot in a sandal. Especially with gold nail polish." He twirled one of the long, tube-like cookies and began sucking on one end of it.

Something in his tone, and the way his eyes were boring into her, caused her to stop laughing. The evening had taken a very odd turn. She dropped her cookie and shifted in her chair, uncertain as to why she felt uncomfortable. She must try to get the conversation back on a regular footing. *Footing.* The thought made her giggle again. She tried to compose herself.

"Well, I doubt you'll be setting eyes on any feet in sandals for several months. Not around here." She toyed with the ice cream, no longer hungry.

His eyes bulged as he stared at her. "But I'm partial to feet—particularly small ones, like yours."

That was lame. *Lame.* Molly coughed to hide her mirth and pushed her seductive limbs under her seat. "What?"

Actually, she didn't want him to clarify.

"You know, toes. As a prelude to something more interesting." His eyes, which, until that moment, she'd thought of as chocolate-colored, now looked muddy as they bored intently into hers.

A prickle of unease ran across the back of her neck. She wanted to leave. "I'm not comfortable with this conversation," she said, putting down her spoon, leaving half the gelato melting in the dish. He didn't even pause for breath.

"But I think you owe it to me to listen, don't you?"

Really? Owed what to him? She'd told the truth on Yours Truly, unlike him. He'd advertised himself as tall, easygoing, and charming.

Now he'd turned into wide, uptight, and distinctly unattractive.

Her eyes widened. "Owe you?"

"Yes, you owe me. You could have given me the bad news before I bought you dinner."

Sober now, Molly said, "The bad news? You mean the information that I don't wear sandals in winter?"

"Not exactly. But you sure as hell don't seem interested in letting me see...your feet."

"And because of that, you resent buying me dinner? It's the money that's bothering you?"

"I didn't say that." BigPeter continued digging himself in deeper. "But when a man spends big bucks on a meal for two, he's entitled to a little something in return."

A flush rose from her throat to her cheeks then to her scalp. This was not a hot flash. This was a rising tide of anger.

She took a deep yoga breath in and exhaled slowly for a count of ten. Then she told him precisely why they wouldn't be meeting again.

"Any man who thinks pasta and a glass of Ruffino at a cheap Italian diner buys him any kind of bizarre sexual favors is not a person I plan to see again." She apologized silently to the owner of the delightful trattoria and their delicious menu. "Furthermore, I'd need to know someone a lot better before the question of my feet, or any other part of me, enters the conversation."

BigPeter's mouth still hung open when she rose to her feet, trying not to draw attention to them. As she walked to the door, she called a cab, confident she'd handled things pretty well. She smiled at herself in the rococo mirror near the exit. And left BigPeter to foot the bill.

***

Simon snorted when she recounted the story of the debacle. They were sitting in the living room, unchanged since his death, apart from the lack of his thrillers. She'd given those to her dad for the library at his retirement village.

"*I guess you went toe-to-toe with him, eh?*"

Molly laughed and unzipped her boots. She rubbed a foot to restore the circulation to her extremities.

"It was kind of funny, now that you mention it. Still, I hated his whole attitude—so entitled."

"*Well, if you'd listened to me…I said he looked shifty.*"

There was no point in reminding Simon that this was the guy he'd endorsed as almost ideal.

CHAPTER THIRTY-SEVEN

More convinced every day that online dating was no way to search for love, Molly buckled down to work, determined to find a means of financing the merger. Ever-present distractions claimed her attention, though. As she sat behind the cash desk one afternoon, racking her brains for things to post on social media, Acacia walked in, smiling as if she hadn't a care in the world.

She waved at Molly before noticing Luke, who was sitting at one of the small tables, occupied in writing staff recommendation cards for the biography section.

"Luke," she called, and he looked up, his expression wary.

Molly saw them conversing and returned to Facebook. She was uploading a photo of a pile of new books, when the two of them popped up beside her. She lifted one hand.

"Just a second." She finished writing a few words and hit "post." "That'll do for today."

"Acacia wants to talk to you about something," said Luke. "I think you ought to listen to her."

"Of course." Why would he think she wouldn't?

Acacia looked around the store. Apparently satisfied they wouldn't be overheard, she leaned closer. "You probably know that Luke phoned me to ask when Pilgrim Properties originally purchased the building. He said it had something to do with the lease. I didn't really want any more information at that point, frankly. I thought I should stay out of it."

Luke put in his two cents' worth. "Tell Molly what happened next."

"I was coming to that. Channing called me, which he sometimes does. Mainly when he wants something. He told me about your ingenious idea of merging the stores. He'd like to invest in it, you know."

Molly was reminded of the disadvantages of living in a small town. No chance of keeping a secret. "So he said. But why call you about it?"

Acacia shook her head, confusing Molly.

"He asked me to approach you to get you to agree."

Molly gritted her teeth. How unfair to ask Acacia to intervene. Then it occurred to her she'd done the identical thing. "I'm so sorry he put you in that position," she said.

"No need to apologize. My first response was to support the proposal. It sounds like a fabulous combination. But this morning Luke explained that my son wants more than half the company in exchange."

"It's true." Molly searched for what to say next. She'd have to be diplomatic. "The thing is, Renzo and I want to be in control of our business. Only we don't have the money to do it."

"Not yet," added Luke. "Still, Molly has plans for getting financing, don't you?"

"Sure," Molly lied. "So, you can go back and tell him you tried to persuade us, but we've found financing from another source."

Acacia looked crestfallen. "What a shame. I was looking forward to being part of the shop."

Luke hastened to reassure her. "While we're in business, you'll always be one of our favorite people, won't she?" He glanced at Molly for confirmation.

"Of *course* you will," she agreed, without any idea of how long they might survive.

"You might have investors lined up, but you can never be

sure until every last document is signed," said Acacia. "I'd like to help, and, if you want, I'll check with my friends to see if anyone's interested."

"That's very kind of you." Molly caught Luke's eye as he frowned at her and tilted his head in the direction of the café. "Though I need to run your offer by Renzo, naturally."

Luke gave her a discreet thumbs-up behind Acacia's back.

"I understand. This project was his idea, wasn't it? So Channing told me."

"That's right. But we do appreciate your support. Don't we Luke?"

"Indeed, we do." Luke paused, his brow furrowed. "How about I take Acacia round to the Java Jive for coffee, to thank her?"

The old lady smiled at him. "That sounds delightful." She turned to Molly. "I'll be back to buy a book or two afterward."

Combining the two places would make that little trip so much easier, especially now that a light snow had begun to fall. Renzo and she must get on with their loan applications.

***

At home that night, Molly sat at her computer, checking out bank loans. Every so often, Hemingway, supposedly sleeping on the desk next to her, would stretch out a paw and hit the keyboard.

"*Decided to take my advice, eh?*"

Simon's voice made her jump and Hemingway typed an accidental row of x's in the search box.

"We need to raise a hundred and twenty thousand dollars to put the plan into action. So, I'm looking at the options."

"*You could use the house as collateral for a loan,*" he offered. "*You ought to be able to find at least fifty thousand that way.*"

"You think so? Sounds risky."

"*Business is risky. But if you do it, you'll make enough so you can*

203

pay it off."

"I suppose so. Only I hate filling out all the forms. There's so much paperwork."

"You're making excuses now. So, call Amanda. She must know people who deal with mortgages."

"I seem to do nothing but ask people for help these days." That still felt like a failure on her part. She ought to be able to handle things herself. She shooed Hemingway off the desk and watched him saunter over to his dish, ignoring Simon. Apparently, he'd decided this apparition was harmless.

"Excellent." Simon sounded pleased.

Her eyebrows shot up. "What do you mean?"

"You've never allowed anyone to help you, and it's high time you did. Don't you get it? People like to feel they've contributed to your well-being, the same way you contribute to theirs."

"It feels weird, though."

Simon brushed this aside. *"Get used to it. It takes a village, as they say. Which reminds me. Have you talked this over with Tom?"*

"Well, I've mentioned it to Dad, of course, but not given him any details. Why?"

"He was in business, so he might have something to suggest. Besides, he likes to be involved in your life, doesn't he?"

A worm of guilt wiggled inside her stomach. "Well, yes. I haven't seen him since Heather and Jackie were home."

"So, get in touch and explain the situation. I'd bet he'd like to know."

"I will. And I'll give him a copy of the proposal. Thanks for the reminder."

"By the way, made any progress with getting permission to do this?"

"That's the other problem. We need Channing to okay the changes, because, as the landlord, he has to put in the application. And so far, he's refused."

"Creep."

"Well, yes. I have no idea how much of his attitude has to do with that dreadful date we went on, and how much is…well, just him. You know, it's not that he doesn't like the concept. In fact, he's so enthused that he wants to trade a cash infusion for almost two-thirds of the equity."

"*I like how you're using the financial jargon.*" Simon grinned. Then his expression hardened. "*You clearly can't allow that. He'll turn your shop into something different. He has no idea of what this place means to you and everyone else in town.*"

"I can't think about that now. I'm trying to figure out how to raise the money for all of this. I can't stand the thought of being put out of business by that man."

Simon was silent for a while. She expected him to disappear at any moment, as he did when their conversations ended—then he spoke up. "*Something's nagging at my memory,*" he said. "*I have a feeling Cavelli Construction did some work for Pilgrim Properties. Before my time, but they would mention it when they pitched other jobs.*"

"Interesting, I suppose, but I can't see how it helps us."

He frowned. "*I vaguely recall it concerned turning the old department store that was there before into two shops. Yours, and the bicycle repair place that used to be next door. The café, I mean,*" he explained, seeing her incomprehension.

"So?"

"*I don't know. Might be worth looking into.*"

Molly couldn't see why, but she made a note to tell Luke. He might be able to dig something up while he was making inquiries.

***

Nick walked into the Book Boutique the next afternoon. "Good morning. And how are things at the best bookstore in Brentford?"

He smiled at her and she felt cheered by his interest. "Plodding along. Still working on financing."

"You'll get there. I only wish I could help. A professor's salary doesn't really allow for investments."

"I wasn't expecting…I mean, I would never dream of asking…" Molly could feel the warmth rising in her cheeks. "Were you looking for something?"

"A couple of things, in fact. The first is a textbook, so you'll likely have to order it for me."

He gave her the details. This would be a profitable sale. Textbooks cost a fortune. So kind of him to buy it from her, when he could probably purchase it cheaper via the college. "I'll give you a discount. Twenty percent okay?"

"You don't need to."

"I want to. It's the least I can do. I owe you for all the favors you've done me."

"In that case, thank you. Want me to ring it up?"

She stared at him and then noticed the twinkle in his eye. He was teasing her.

"No, thank you. It's my turn to run the shop, and yours to be the customer."

They laughed. Things hadn't changed in the last ten minutes, but she suddenly felt that her prospects looked better than they had for a while.

CHAPTER THIRTY-EIGHT

Molly sat near the cash register at the Book Boutique, going through invoices on the computer, a task she'd been putting off all week. When Rosie rang her, Molly was relieved to have an excuse to abandon it. She walked through to the back to make herself a cup of tea while they talked.

"What's up?" Molly said, pouring boiling water into the Edgar Allan Poe mug and poking at the tea bag with a spoon.

"Nothing too urgent, honey, but I think I may have found someone."

A couple of reactions flitted through Molly's head. This was unexpected, to say the least.

"What do you mean? What happened to Rocco? I thought you guys were solid." So much for successful online relationships. Molly poured a little milk into the tea and stirred.

Rosie laughed. "Not for *me*, Molly. How could I give Rocco up? I love him. No. This one's for you."

This must be what white-tailed deer felt like when they emerged into a clearing to discover that they were right in the line of fire.

"Come on, Rosie. You know I'm not looking." But curiosity got the better of her. "Is it someone you know?"

"I found him online." Rosie paused, but before Molly could respond, she said, "No, honest. He sounds great."

"But didn't you cancel your account?"

After a beat, Rosie answered. "Ah, well…I checked into yours, just to take a look on your behalf. But before you say anything, listen to this."

She should never have let Rosie open an account for her. Rosie had set up the password, so of course, she could access it whenever she wanted, and Molly's subscription had another month or two to run. She must remember to cancel it.

"Absolutely not going to listen, Rosie. You've gone too far this time. And I've got a customer. Got to go," she lied, watching as a shopper walked past the store. And she hung up.

She gave a small sigh and then, deciding to procrastinate a while longer, checked her messages. She was about to delete one from YoursTruly without reading it, when something made her pause. Idly, she clicked to open it, to be rewarded with a short message, different from the others she'd seen.

> *From: AndyYachtsman*
> *Hi there*
> *I liked your photo and wondered if we might have something in common. I'm a widower with three grown children. Self-employed, and as you can see by my moniker, I love to sail. Favorite authors: Hemingway and Roth.*
> *If you'd be interested in a drink sometime, let me know. I think it might be fun.*

She reread the message. He read literary novels. He enjoyed sailing, so he probably lived far enough away that she'd be able to avoid him if things didn't work out. She had to admit, he sounded interesting. Oh, what the hell.

She hit reply.

***

A few days later, she and Andy were sitting in Aristotle's, the bookstore café in New Haven, introducing themselves.

"Sorry I'm late," Molly said. "I'd forgotten how hard it is to park around here."

"Don't you come here often?" He looked at her and laughed. "Well, that came out stupid, but you know what I mean."

"As a matter of fact, I come here, to Aristotle's, whenever I'm in New Haven," said Molly. "I think the café has something to do with it."

"I guess it does, at that."

He looked at her and she realized, for the first time in her dating history, that this man actually looked like his photo. His fair hair had probably once been brighter and was fading closer to platinum these days because of the gray, but it suited him. His complexion, somewhat pinker than in the picture, didn't put her off. His weather-beaten cheeks resulted from the time he spent sailing, she supposed.

And his eyes were an interesting color, somewhere between green and brown. The laughter lines around them showed he had a sense of humor, and he looked to be in pretty good shape. Not athletic, but about right. She stopped her mental assessment when she found him appraising her, too, and wriggled self-consciously, tugging at the pencil skirt she'd squeezed herself into that morning. It was riding up, leaving her lower thighs exposed. Oh, well. Either he noticed or he didn't. Too late now to change into something longer.

"Penny for them," said Andy.

"I was wondering…" What could she say? If her first question concerned the yacht pictured on his profile, she might come across as a gold digger. And if she asked about his work, that, too, might sound as though she was checking on his financial status. Children—that was a safe subject.

"Tell me about your children," she said. "Your profile says they're grown."

Andy nodded. "I have two sons and a daughter. The boys are out of college, living on the West Coast, working in computer sciences. My daughter's still in school—UNC."

"North Carolina? That must be nice. Do you visit her down there?"

Andy looked momentarily surprised, as if Molly had asked about him visiting the moon.

"Well, no. She comes up here when she has vacation, sometimes. But she's twenty, and you know what kids that age are like. I mean, you probably know, don't you?"

"I'm familiar. My girls are twenty-one and nineteen," said Molly. "They came home from school for the holidays."

"Lucky you."

Molly nodded. A moment of silence followed as she sipped at her cappuccino.

Andy put down his cup. "So, tell me about your work. Do you like your job?"

He proved to be a sympathetic listener. Molly found herself explaining how Simon's death had precipitated her buying the Book Boutique. Only when the waitress came over for the third time to clear their coffee cups away, did Molly realize she and Andy had been there over an hour.

"I guess we'd better get going," he said, looking at his watch. "Let me walk you to your car."

"Thanks," she said and allowed him to open the door for her as they headed out into a surprisingly mild day.

"Can I call you?" he asked when they finally found the place.

"Sure," said Molly.

"Okay. Why don't you call me right now, and we'll have each other's number. That's what the kids do these days, or so my sons tell me."

She punched in the number he gave her, and startled, hearing *Hey, Big Spender* issuing from his phone. He smiled as he answered it and immediately hung up. "There you go. You have mine, and I have yours."

Apparently, her face had alerted him to her unspoken question. "One of the boys put that song on there for me as a kind of joke," he explained. "And I just got used to it."

"Well, at least you'll never mistake your phone for anyone else's." Molly smiled. "Thanks, again. This was nice."

Andy leaned forward and kissed her cheek. The light touch of his lips felt comfortable. This might turn out well, after all.

***

Molly had barely locked up the store that evening when her phone rang again. Andy. Already. An almost forgotten shiver of anticipation, tempered by anxiety, coursed through her.

"Hi, again." Then, perhaps feeling he sounded presumptuous, "It's me, Andy."

"I know. I have you in my phone." She laughed, liking his mellow voice. When he asked her to see a play at a small experimental theater near Hartford, she accepted, delighted he liked culture too. They arranged to meet there.

To Molly's surprise, the director announced, before the performance, that it had been approved for mature audiences only. She hadn't seen any information or reviews so was unprepared when, toward the end of the first act, the three main characters took off all their clothes and sat around discussing their intentions, completely naked. When it became clear that they were about to engage in some extremely "mature" activity, she could only be grateful when the lights came up for the intermission.

Andy turned to her, his eyes innocent. "So, what do you think?"

Molly *thought* she wanted to go home, but she didn't want to appear unsophisticated. "I can't say it's what I expected," she began. "Were you aware it would be like this?"

"Well, no. Of course not."

Molly tried to read his expression. Was he telling the truth?

"But I'm familiar with this playwright," Andy said, "and he's always been avant-garde."

"Right. Avant-garde. I suppose one has to keep up with the times." Did she sound as ridiculous as she felt? She had no personal interest in the risqué plays that passed for art nowadays. But it took all sorts. And evidently, some of these people genuinely thought they had merit.

"Let me get you a drink," Andy said. "What'll you have?"

Oh, Lord. They were going to stay until the final curtain. In which case, a little alcohol might take the edge off the play.

"A cosmo for me, please." She would try to make it last till the bitter end.

By shutting her eyes at certain moments and indulging in a low hum designed to drown out some of the dialogue, Molly managed to get through the rest of the performance. The cosmo helped. But she resolved to make sure she researched precisely what was playing before accepting another such invitation.

Only a few vehicles remained in the parking lot when Andy walked her back to her car. He took her hand, and his fingers closed around hers, setting off a current between them. She wanted to pull away, but gave herself a pep talk. She needed to live in the present, not the past.

When he took her in his arms and kissed her, she surrendered to the moment. His lips were warm and soft, yet firm at the same time. She found herself responding effortlessly, with a corresponding thrill of excitement in her belly that she hadn't experienced since she'd been widowed. Wow. Her breath turned to mist in the frosty air as they stepped apart.

She thanked the gods of love and war that Simon hadn't been able to see Andy yet. She wanted to keep him to herself.

"I really enjoyed this evening," he said, before saying goodbye.

* * *

"*Who was that on the phone?*" asked Simon, making Molly jump. Reluctantly, she put down the page-turner she'd just picked up.

"Must you sneak up on me that way?" She was annoyed at

herself for feeling guilty. She'd done nothing wrong. "If you insist on knowing, he's called Andy. He seems okay. More than okay, actually."

Simon's forehead creased in a frown. *"Seems? How do you mean, seems? I don't think your intuition about men is reliable. Except when it came to me, of course."*

She bristled at this. "Oh, really? Amanda and Rosie came up with those other guys for me—it wasn't *my* fault they were failures."

"Point is, didn't Rosie find you this, what's his name, Andy?"

"Well, yes. But he honestly does appear to be on the up and up." Why was she still justifying herself to Simon? It was time she made him see that she could handle dating on her own. "As it happens, Andy is a regular guy. Like you."

Unaccountably, she found herself welling up.

"Oh, honey. I didn't mean it," Simon said. *"Come on now. It's okay. I should give him the benefit of the doubt."* He pointed at a box of tissues.

She took one and blew her nose.

Simon kept speaking. *"He can't be exactly like me, obviously."* He heaved a dramatic sigh. *"After all, he's alive, right?"*

Molly couldn't decide whether to laugh or cry. She managed a watery giggle. "Let's wait and see, shall we? He might have terrible table manners or eat with his mouth open, and you know how I hate that."

"Quite right. Those are absolute dealbreakers." His voice was solemn, but she detected a twinkle in his eye.

***

The next time Andy called, Molly was sitting in front of the television in the den, watching a program about redecorating houses while working her way through a bowl of trail mix. She hadn't had the energy to cook that evening and told herself that nuts and fruit were a healthy meal. She finished chewing a stray almond and swallowed, almost choking in her haste to answer the phone, where Andy's number glowed like a beacon.

"Hello?"

"Are you okay? Your voice sounds kind of…"

"Hi, Andy. I'm fine. Just a frog in my throat. How are you?" she said, before he could ask for details.

"I'm terrific. Wondering if you'd like to have dinner one evening. Friday?"

She nodded, then realizing he couldn't hear that, said, "I've no other plans that night."

"Great. I'll book a table. You want to text me your address, so I can pick you up?" He laughed.

"I'll do it as soon as we hang up."

She had hardly opened the texting app when Simon, accompanied by a faint gust of cold air, registered in her line of sight, his face expressing interest. Molly placed her phone on the table, screen down.

"*Excellent. I'll be able to check him out,*" he said. "*See if he's appropriate for you.*"

"What?"

"*Well, I never got to see the other guys. I only have your word for it that they were hopeless. Though I must say, the one who wanted you for your feet—*" He stopped when she grimaced in annoyance. "*Anyway…*" his voice trailed off.

Molly was thoughtful. She wasn't at all certain that Simon ought to be vetting these men before they were anything serious. Come to think of it, he shouldn't have any kind of opinion.

And she shouldn't be giving out her home address, either.

She made a decision. "I have to work late on Friday, so I'll meet him at the restaurant, I think." Noticing his reaction, she added, "You can see him another time." Sometimes it was like dealing with a toddler.

***

She and Andy were to dine at a small Greek place with discreet lighting. The maître d' greeted Andy as though he were an old friend and seated them at a table by the window. While the waiter went to fill their drinks order, Andy reached across and lifted her hand, rubbing his thumb gently over her knuckles.

"Molly, I want to say something."

She remained silent, unsure of what was coming.

"I like you. More than anyone I've gotten to know in a long time."

She waited, but evidently, this was all he wanted to tell her. Eventually, she could stand it no longer. She had to say *something*. "I like you too, Andy. I'm glad we met." She looked up from under her lashes and found him smiling at her.

"I'd like you to meet some of my friends soon."

Whoa. Molly wasn't expecting that. Being presented to his circle at this stage would be awkward.

Andy was looking at her, a question in his eyes. She'd hesitated too long before replying.

"That would be lovely, at some point," she said. "Maybe in a month or so? When we know each other better?"

Did she imagine it, or did a momentary flicker of annoyance flash across his face? It had been replaced by that disarming smile so fast.

"Of course," he said, and picked up the menu. "What strikes your fancy this evening?"

She ordered the shrimp in preserved lemon sauce over rainbow quinoa, and as she sipped at a glass of sauvignon blanc, she began to relax again.

"I have to see a man about a dog," Andy said. "Back in a minute."

Funny. Simon would say that when he excused himself to go to the bathroom. He'd heard the phrase on a trip to England and liked it so much he'd used it from then on. She must ask Andy about his foreign travel.

Something on Andy's phone pinged. He'd left it faceup on

the white tablecloth. She stretched out a hand to pick it up. It might be urgent. No, just a text. From someone called Bluebird. None of her business. She would ignore it. She was about to do that when the complete message appeared on the screen.

How's it hanging, you sexy thing? Got her lined up yet? Can't wait to meet her. Send photo so can get good and ready. This was followed by two lipstick-kiss emojis and by what looked oddly like a picture of an eggplant.

Molly dropped the phone as if it were red hot. A flush of embarrassment rose from her breasts to her face, as though she were the one who'd betrayed Andy, not the other way around.

He looked at her with concern as he sat down.

"Feeling okay?" he asked. "Wine getting to you? Or is it the heat in here?"

Molly pushed the phone across the table. "You got a message." She kept any emotion out of her voice. The air seemed less bright than it had only minutes ago. Even the outdoor lights had stopped twinkling.

He glanced at the phone. Then his eyes widened, and Molly could have sworn that he'd muttered the words "stupid bitch" before he looked up at her. His expression had suddenly gone from friendly to blank. "Did you read it?"

She considered denying it, but she was hopeless at lying. Her face always gave her away. She nodded.

"I wasn't planning to bring this up yet," he said. "But since it's on the table, so to speak, what do you think?"

"About what?"

"About joining us for a relaxed evening of fun. Nothing kinky, you know. Just—oh for Chrissake."

Molly had shot out of her chair so quickly that a glass of water tipped over and now dripped steadily into Andy's lap.

"Perhaps that will cool you down," she said, as a rush of anger welled up. "It's not so much the threesome, though that's not my thing. I would have simply refused. But you were getting me lined up? Like the next one on a conveyor belt?" She inhaled. "As for this Bluebird person, whoever she is…"

"As it happens, it was her idea, to begin with." He paused before delivering the final nail in his own coffin. "She's my wife."

He had the grace to look a little ashamed as he admitted this, but Molly wasn't buying it. His pretending to be a widower made her feel queasy.

"Then you two deserve each other."

She collected her things and, head high, stalked out of the restaurant. She was becoming an expert at that.

CHAPTER THIRTY-NINE

Molly no longer had time to contemplate a social life, never mind meeting bizarre men with weird propositions. Pilgrim Properties would be expecting the February rent soon. December's earnings would allow her to pay it for a few more months, but after that... The only proposals she'd listen to now would be offers of financing for the business.

She and Renzo had filled out loan applications and were waiting for replies from two banks and a mortgage broker. She couldn't count on them, or at least not for all the money, so she would need to find the rest somewhere else.

Taking out a notepad, she tried to think of anyone who might help. She stared at the page, with no idea whether any of her friends might be in a position to invest or not. And she wasn't on familiar enough terms with any of the wealthier people in town to feel comfortable approaching them.

She sat in the café after work one evening with Luke and Renzo, who'd produced a bottle of *cachaça*, three glasses, and a lime.

"We need something to cheer us up," he announced. "I will make a *caipirinha* for everyone."

To her surprise, Luke stood and disappeared into the kitchen at the back, reappearing with a bowl of sugar and three teaspoons. He seemed surprisingly familiar with the place.

Renzo smiled at him. "You also know how to make this?"

Luke's cheeks turned a deeper shade of ruddy. "This cocktail from Brazil? It's always been one of my favorite drinks."

Molly stared at him. She'd never been offered one at his house. The two men were smiling at each other.

Oh. So that's how it was. How had she missed the clues? Too wrapped up in her own woes, that's how.

Good for them. This needn't affect the business relationship she and Renzo had.

Luke handed her a glass. She'd never been offered a *caipirinha* before, so she accepted the drink cautiously and sipped. "Delicious."

Renzo held up his drink. "*Saude!*"

"Cheers." Luke raised his glass in reply. Then he brought them back down to earth. "How's the financing coming along?"

"I heard from my bank this morning, and they will only lend me twenty-three thousand," said Renzo.

Molly tried to sound upbeat. "It's a start." Though at this rate, it would take forever to get what they needed. "I should hear from mine soon. They required so much backup paperwork, and I'm not sure that I can show enough income to cover a loan for the whole amount."

"What about the mortgage company?" Renzo wanted to know. She had told him she was trying to refinance her house.

"I've filled in a bunch of forms, but they've asked for more. The application just drags on and on."

"So they haven't said no yet?" Luke said.

"No, but they say things are difficult right now. Not very encouraging. We're going to have to come up with more ideas."

"I have a suggestion."

Molly hadn't expected this. Luke was one of the least business-like people she knew.

"I sold you the business for a reasonable sum a year ago. I feel I must help keep it going. So, I'm prepared to put in twenty-five thousand dollars."

She could barely take this in. Almost a quarter of what they had to find. Renzo's face gave nothing away. Would he agree to this?

"Do you mean it?" She'd never known Luke to joke about money matters before.

"Yes. We'll keep things on a professional basis, naturally. You'll give me a small share of the new business in exchange."

Renzo turned to Molly. "An excellent idea, no?"

She smiled. "An excellent idea, yes."

Then his gaze returned to Luke. "We shall accept, I think."

Unused to having a decisive business partner, she could only concur.

***

Her father stopped by the store later in the week, with Bonnie on his arm. Her bright pink parka stood out against the slushy gray palette outside.

He scanned the displays with interest. "Getting ready for Valentine's, sweetheart?"

A month before, Luke had put Valentine's Day cards out on the racks, and they'd been selling well. Molly designed a display of appropriate children's books and added some romance novels and classic love stories.

Tom asked her how things were going with the business. Two other customers were exploring the stacks. One had ventured upstairs. Not that there was much to find up there.

Luke never made use of the second floor of the bookstore when he owned it, and Molly couldn't afford to do much with the space. If she had, she'd have expanded the shelving, moved different books up there, and redecorated to create more room downstairs.

"Not bad. Christmas was successful, which is keeping us afloat. But raising funding for the new enterprise is taking a while."

"Have you got a minute to talk?"

"What, now?" She glanced around. It wasn't too crowded. "Luke, can you hold down the fort for about fifteen minutes if I go for coffee with Dad?"

"Sure."

"I'd like Bonnie to come too," said Tom.

She'd looked forward to chatting with her father, but if he wanted to include his girlfriend—so be it.

***

When they entered the Java Jive, Molly introduced them to Renzo, who found them a table with three seats and left them to it.

Bonnie's presence made the conversation stilted at first. Molly inquired politely as to how they were doing and about their activities at Maple Corners.

"We haven't been hanging out much with the others, actually." Bonnie smiled at Tom. "We've been going out to galleries and gardens. Just the two of us. Little trips."

Her dad? Going to art museums? Molly gazed at Bonnie, awed. If she could expand her father's horizons this way, she was a keeper.

"But that's not what we wanted to talk to you about." Tom was determined to keep them on track, apparently. "We read your business plan."

We? She said nothing except, "And?"

"And we can see you've got a tough task on your hands." He paused, and Bonnie kept her eyes on him, as if to urge him to continue.

"We'd like to help."

"Thanks, Dad. I know you would, and I'm open to any suggestions."

"I'm not making myself clear. Bonnie and I have talked about this and we'd like to contribute ten thousand."

Molly stared from one to the other, stunned. We? Contribute? What did this mean?

"We both want you to do well, dear. Your father and I are friends, and when he told me about your plan, I thought it sounded like a winner." Bonnie beamed. "So, I wanted in."

Molly looked from one to the other. Their kind gaze, no, the love in their eyes, was almost too much for her. Love was an amazing thing. Tears were welling up, and she brushed them away.

"I love you for thinking of it, but I can't possibly accept." She searched for a tissue to blow her nose, and Bonnie silently handed her one.

"We've already decided, and would be extremely disappointed if you didn't take it." Her father's tone suggested a particularly stern school principal. She raised her eyes to his and saw a twinkle that belied his words. "Seriously, honey, we want to be part of this brave new enterprise."

***

Amanda checked in by phone a day later, and when Molly gave her the update, immediately offered ten thousand dollars.

"It's a purely business transaction," she insisted. "This town needs both of you—the bookstore *and* the café. You're an irreplaceable asset, and I, for one, am not going to watch you fail. No matter how hard that man Madison tries to make it happen."

Rosie, snipping at Molly's hair the following week, wanted to support her too. "I can't do much, but if two thousand would help, you can have it. As Brentford's premier salon owner, I can't afford to let a landlord put anyone out of business."

Molly's bank came through with a loan of thirty-five thousand. All they needed now was the last fifteen thousand dollars. And permission to go ahead.

CHAPTER FORTY

Luke took a bite of the home-baked, heart-shaped cookie Molly had just offered him. She'd brought a plateful of them into work that morning. "Hmm. Not bad. I think I'll save one for later too." Wrapping a cookie in a paper towel, he hid it below the desk. "Some people say Valentine's Day is overrated, but I enjoy it." He was honoring the day with his bow tie with the pink hearts.

"I agree it's too commercialized," Molly said. "People in clothes with hearts on them, for instance." She feigned an innocent smile.

Luke frowned. "Too much, you think?" He touched his tie.

"No, of course not. At least it's more restrained than the one with the cupids you wore the other day." She smiled at him. "It may be all hype, but it's fun too. And you have to admit it's what drives sales in February."

"It does. Though we sell plenty of romance novels year-round, don't we?" He shrugged. "I guess love is always in fashion."

"Everyone can use a little love. Look at Tom and Bonnie and the effect love had on them. Plus, that genre has a huge audience. All kinds of people." She gave him a look but read nothing in his face.

Luke smiled. "So, you're a hopeless romantic, eh? Doubtless, you like those gewgaws you sell along with the books."

"Gewgaws?" Molly laughed. "You and your medieval vocabulary. And I do like them. They're corny, but people buy them. Surely even you can't resist this one, can you?"

She picked up a small teddy bear wearing glasses and reading a tiny book. "All he needs is a bow tie like yours, and he'd be a perfect addition to your mantelpiece," she teased.

Luke looked appalled. "Are you nuts? I would never… a stuffed bear in my living room? So tasteless."

Molly tried to keep a straight face, but failed spectacularly and began laughing.

"You should see your expression. It was worth suggesting just for that!"

As she tidied the display, the van from Sarah's Flowers and Gifts pulled up in front of the store. She didn't recognize the driver—probably hired by Sarah for the day to help handle the orders. He sported the name of the flower shop on his dark-blue jacket and walked in carrying a vase with a dozen yellow roses in it, tied up with matching ribbon.

"Delivery for Stevenson," he announced.

Her first reaction was delight. Quickly followed by bewilderment. "That's me, I guess." Molly was doubtful. "Who are they from?"

"I don't know, ma'am. You'll have to check the note. Got a bunch of deliveries today. Bunch. Get it?" He gave her a wink and headed for the door.

The envelope tucked into the flowers had her name on it. Sarah would never have made a mistake. Molly hesitated before opening the little heart-shaped card.

Inside, the only message said: "From an admirer," and someone had typed it.

An anonymous valentine? She bent her head and sniffed the bouquet. She could definitely detect the faint scent of roses. How lovely.

"Are those for me?" said Luke, appearing from the back room, where he'd been unpacking a box of new novels. He grinned at her. "Guess not, huh? Since you're reading the card. So, who's your fan?"

She shrugged. "There's no clue on the card." How could she find out who they were from? Perhaps better not to know. It surely wasn't anyone she'd dated recently. All those relationships ended with Molly giving them a piece of her mind.

Luke's voice broke into her thoughts. "What about calling Sarah—the florist?" he prompted.

"What? Oh, right. Good thought." She checked the card again and punched in the number on her phone.

A woman, sounding slightly harassed, answered. "Sarah's Flowers and Gifts. Happy Valentine's Day."

Sarah didn't sound like *she* was enjoying today much. Molly supposed that being the biggest day of the year for cut flowers—or was that Mother's Day—she was extra busy. No, Mother's Day meant chocolates, didn't it?

"Is there something I can do for you?" Sarah sounded as though the last thing she wanted was one more order to deal with. In the past, Molly might have apologized and hung up, but today she needed to know.

"Sarah, it's me, Molly."

"Oh. Hi, there. You don't need flowers, do you? I've practically nothing left. Just some gladiolus and a few daffodils."

"No, not right now, thanks. Anyway, your guy delivered some beautiful yellow roses to me at the Book Boutique, and I wondered who sent them. Can you tell me?"

"Just a second. Let me check my records."

Molly heard her put down the phone and the tapping of keys on a computer before Sarah picked up again.

"I can't, I'm sorry. The purchaser ordered them online and insisted on remaining anonymous. Why, is there anything wrong?"

"No, not at all. I'd like to thank the sender."

"It's romantic, don't you think? Look, I hate to cut you short, but the other line is ringing. So, if there's nothing else…"

Molly hung up. She should just enjoy the roses. They'd brighten her living room if she stood them on the little table by the window.

As she backed into the house that evening, holding the vase carefully, so as not to spill the water, she could hear Simon's voice, fainter than usual, calling her name. She carried the arrangement into the front room and gingerly lowered it to the table before turning to reply.

"Hi there."

"Roses, eh? Where are they from? Or should I say who?"

"I believe you *ought* to say whom. To answer your question, I've no idea. But apparently, I have an admirer. That's what the card says."

"Of course you do," said Simon. *"I might have sent them. I want you to have something nice for Valentine's Day."*

"What? After all this time?" Momentarily confused, she could see by his grin that he was teasing her. "Oh, as *if*. First, when you were alive, I had to book the restaurant, or we'd never have gone out for dinner. And as for flowers…" She paused and took a breath. "Anyway, I'm not precisely clear about the rules of your current gig, but I'm convinced they don't include using the phone. Not to mention the fact that you don't have any way to pay."

Simon's mouth turned down in a comical grimace. *"Busted,"* he said.

Molly relented. "But it's sweet that you *wanted* to get me something. Still, I have no idea who these are from."

"No clue from the handwriting?"

"Nope. The message was dictated—the order came in by phone."

Simon glanced at the bouquet. *"Well, they're okay, I guess. But they look like they're starting to droop to me."*

She was beginning to wish the roses had never arrived. "No, they aren't. What do you mean by—" She hesitated. "You're not jealous, are you? Simon? Simon."

But her erstwhile husband had dematerialized.

Her phone indicated that her dad had called. As she made a mental note to call him back, it dawned on her—Tom must have sent the flowers. He used to send her Valentine's cards for years—always signed the traditional British way, "from an admirer."

She was conscious of an unworthy niggle of disappointment. Never mind. She'd phone to thank him. Just as soon as she brought in the shopping.

She thought about him and Bonnie as she went outside to fetch the bags of groceries. On the top of one of them sat the small box of chocolates that called to her as she wandered the aisles in Jackson's Pantry. She'd stopped to pick up a portion of their homemade lasagna—the vegetarian one that might save a few calories. She'd ended up with more items than she intended because she'd rashly shopped while hungry.

As she slammed the car door shut, her arms full of purchases, Nick's Volvo pulled up in his driveway.

"Hi. Need a hand?"

"That would be great, Nick. If you could just grab this bag. It's not too heavy." She handed him the groceries, and he followed her through the front door and into her kitchen.

"Could you leave them right there? Thanks. How are things?"

"The ankle's holding up. The students are their usual selves—all of them distracted today, with Valentine's and all."

"Did you get any cards?"

Nick laughed. "Not from anyone at the college, thank god. It would be way too embarrassing if I did."

So, had he received something from someone outside school? How intriguing. He hesitated for a beat before saying, "How about you?"

"I had a delivery of yellow roses." She walked into the living room to show him. "From an admirer."

"Very nice. Whoever it is must really like you."

"I'm pretty sure he does. Has done for years." Molly couldn't help smiling at the confusion on his face. "They're from my dad."

"Oh?" Nick seemed at a loss. Then he went on. "How thoughtful of him."

"Oh, yes. And much better than getting them from a person I might not like."

"I guess so. Well, Happy Valentine's Day."

"You too, Nick."

CHAPTER FORTY-ONE

Renzo reached into the baked-goods case and withdrew Molly's almond croissant. "No charge for my partner." He smiled as he wrapped it and handed it over.

She opened the bag and inhaled the aroma of ground almonds, her spirits rising. She liked having company perks.

"Delicious. How kind of you Renzo. Thanks."

She blinked when he said, "Thank *you*, Molly. You are wonderful."

Her attention was diverted by a quick flash of blue that made her turn toward the window. Was that Nick's car? It slowed and stopped across the road. As she watched, a slim, booted leg emerged from the passenger seat, followed by the rest of an attractive female.

So, he had a girlfriend. Molly couldn't quell the sense of disappointment. All of a sudden, the day had become gray. She didn't want to deal with this now, so she glanced at her watch and sighed. "Must go, or I'll be late," she announced, assuming a fake carelessness that belied her internal agitation.

"You realize it is still seven minutes until nine o'clock?"

"I like to be there early on a Tuesday. It's the day when new books are published. Mind if I go out the back? It's quicker."

He nodded. She grabbed her cappuccino and the croissant before threading past the restrooms on her way out. Both the shops backed onto a small courtyard, where delivery trucks

229

pulled up and Luke parked each morning.

As she checked her bag and pockets for the back-door key, Molly frowned. Damn. She must have left it inside the store last night. No sign of Luke yet. Damn again. She had the key to the front door, so now she had no choice but to walk to the end of the row of stores and turn into the street to get in. Honestly, life would be so much simpler if she didn't care what Nick was doing. She did not want to meet his girlfriend. Not now, anyway.

She made her way to Main Street and peered around the corner to see if Nick's car was still there. It was. Triple damn.

Thankful for the bay windows of the Book Boutique, which obscured its doorway, Molly sprinted toward it, and, heart hammering, let herself in.

For heaven's sake. Adults didn't behave this way. *Grow up, Molly*, she murmured under her breath as she leaned against the inside of the shop door—now shut again. She wouldn't turn the "closed" sign over to "open" until she was sure Nick wouldn't be coming in.

She switched on the computer, checked there was money in the cash drawer, and opened a box of books delivered the day before, searching for the special orders. More of them would be arriving later. Normally, she looked forward to this, but today her mind was distracted.

***

Luke arrived an hour after his usual time. He'd left a message, telling her he needed to do some research, and when he walked in, was as animated as Molly had seen him for quite a while. This morning, he wore the bright blue tie with jaunty yellow rubber ducks printed on it. The one he donned when the outlook was positive.

After hanging up his jacket, he asked her to sit down.

"Is this going to be bad news? If so, I'd rather remain upright, if that's okay."

"No problem—it's nothing terrible." He stood in front of her and placed his thumbs inside the royal-blue suspenders that matched the bow tie. "I think I've found something."

"What?" Molly ran through the possibilities in her mind. A new author? Some antique fire irons?

"Remember what you told me about getting permission to make changes here? It got me thinking. So did the ceiling."

"The *ceiling*?" She wasn't able to follow this at all.

"Yes. Look at this."

He walked her over to the wall that adjoined the café and pointed upward.

"See where the tiles and molding are?"

"Uh-huh." They needed a paint job. Was that what he meant?

Luke carried on. "There's no molding along the dividing wall."

She peered up, and sure enough, the tin tiles ended abruptly at the place where wall and ceiling came together.

"I never noticed. What about it?"

"I took a look in the coffee shop."

He was evidently warming to his subject. His cheeks were turning pink. Molly became more confused than ever.

"What are you getting at?"

"The café has the identical feature on the same wall. Which means..." His eyes took on a sparkle of exhilaration. "Means that once upon a time, these two spaces were one."

Molly, geared up for a major announcement, felt hope leaking out of her again.

Luke, who'd been studying her face, spoke. "Wait—that's not all. I talked to Bill Hawley at the *Brentford Bee* and asked him whether he knew anything about building permits in town. He's been around forever, as you know, and when I mentioned the Book Boutique, it struck a chord."

Would he ever get to the point? This was nerve-racking. She should have sat down when he asked her to.

"He suggested I go through the back issues, but there are so many of them, I gave up."

Molly, becoming more impatient as she waited for the good news, started to tap her foot. "And?"

"So, I called Acacia, to ask if she could remember when Pilgrim bought the property, and she went through her papers and told me—May 1993."

"Luke—you're driving me crazy here. Can we cut to the chase?"

His crestfallen grimace conveyed this had been a faux pas. He prided himself on being a raconteur and didn't relish interruption once in full flow.

"I'm sorry. Do go on. I'm just hoping for something encouraging. I promise not to interrupt again."

"Very well." He took a deep breath and launched into the tale again. "So, I headed over to the Town Hall to research property transfers. And I found the evidence. Pilgrim Properties purchased the premises in 1993. But here's the thing. They bought one shop. So, of course, I wondered which one. And guess what?"

She raised her hands, palm upwards, in an I-have-no-idea gesture, but remained silent. A promise was a promise.

"They acquired both." He gazed at her with a satisfied smile. "Don't you get it? The Book Boutique and the Java Jive were one big unit back then—a small department store. The owner's wife died, and he sold the building to the Madisons. *They* closed it down and built a dividing wall to turn it into two retail spaces."

"Okay." She still couldn't see how this benefited them at all.

"Here's the kicker—I couldn't find any sign of a construction permit for them to build that wall."

"How is that possible?" Molly remembered Simon complaining about how difficult it was to get building permits in Brentford.

"This happened before I bought the bookshop," Luke went

on. "Bill Hawley told me there was a scandal involving kick-backs on the zoning board, and the guy got some jail time. He got away with it for quite a while."

He stopped, satisfied he'd recounted the story well and impressed his audience of one.

The light began to dawn. "You mean…"

"Right. If we take it down, we won't be violating any regulations. In fact, we'd be putting things back the way they were before." Luke subsided as he came to the end of his speech.

Molly plumped down in the armchair, the breath knocked out of her, to be replaced by a tingle of excitement and hope.

"Luke, you're a star. An absolute treasure." She jumped up again and threw her arms around his neck. "This makes all the difference."

He extricated himself and stepped away, blushing.

"Yes, well, you're welcome. And this gives us some leverage. He won't want this to come out, even if it happened before he began working for Pilgrim Properties."

"Fantastic. And this puts us in the clear as far as permission goes, don't you think?"

He nodded. "You want to tell Renzo? Or shall I?"

"Let me do it. I'm too excited not to share this."

Even the thought that they still needed to raise the rest of the money couldn't suppress the spring in her step as she headed out to announce the news to her prospective partner.

***

She succeeded in shortening Luke's presentation considerably when explaining it to Renzo, but he grasped the gist immediately.

"*Optimó*," he said, and though she didn't speak Portuguese, she could tell he was as pleased as she. "So, Luke discovered this?"

"He did. Isn't that amazing?"

"Indeed." He hesitated. "So, all we need is fifteen thousand dollars and we can go ahead?"

Molly fought the sense of being a balloon that had just sustained a tiny pinprick and was slowly losing air.

***

Back in the shop, she found Acacia talking to Luke as if it had been weeks since they'd seen each other, instead of only days. He waved a hand in Molly's direction, but she couldn't make out whether his gesture meant she should join them or not. She'd become fond of Acacia, but her relationship to Channing Madison made it complicated to enlist her help. How she had managed to produce a son like him was a mystery.

The old lady was frowning, not something she usually did when talking with Luke. As though feeling Molly's gaze on her, Acacia raised her eyes and turned to stare back. Oh, no. Her face reflected a mixture of embarrassment and chagrin. What on earth had he been saying to her? She ought to rescue them from this mess, no matter what had caused it.

"Hello, Acacia. Everything all right?"

"Good morning, dear. And to answer your question, it doesn't seem to me that everything *is* okay. Luke here tells me Pilgrim Properties made some unauthorized alterations to the building."

"Come and make yourself comfortable over here." Molly pointed at the two armchairs and took a seat herself. "We believe that's true, yes."

Mrs. T thought for a minute. "So, what does this information mean for your project? How does it affect the future of the bookshop?"

"As a matter of fact, it works in our favor, but I don't think your son will be happy about it." She tried to sound apologetic, but the thought of Channing Madison getting his comeuppance was balm to her soul. Though Acacia, a shareholder in the family firm, might be affected too.

"He doesn't deserve to be. I didn't bring him up to be so ruthless. I'm afraid he's his father all over again." She sighed. "But this is encouraging news, isn't it? I daresay you don't need permits to put something back the way it was. So, when can you begin? Knocking down the wall, I mean."

Molly and Luke looked at each other.

"As soon as we have the last fifteen thousand dollars. We could take a chance on raising that after the building work is underway, but Renzo and I would rather be safe than sorry."

"Still," said Luke, "we're going to start getting estimates, aren't we?"

"I expect so. So long as we can pay our rent and keep ticking over while we wait."

Acacia rose to her feet. "Well, I'm sure you can raise it. You're a determined young woman, and I think Renzo must be resolute too. I have to go, but you've given me plenty to think about."

CHAPTER FORTY-TWO

Molly mulled over the day's developments as she walked slowly up Main Street on her way home.

How dreadful to be the mother of a son like Channing. Acacia was so lovely—he clearly didn't take after her. Molly could just picture him as a little boy, modeling himself on his no-doubt-entitled father, treating his mother as a source of food and hugs, but giving her no consideration. What was that quote? The son is father to the man, that was it.

It just went to show that no matter what a parent did, a child's character was something they were born with. Molly thought about her own two daughters, how independent they'd grown up to be, how kind. And she felt grateful.

Channing. She and Renzo ought to tell him they were planning to knock down the wall as soon as possible. Her first instinct was to ask her partner to approach the landlord, though he hadn't been any more successful in getting results than she had. They should probably go together. And they'd better get their story straight.

Molly agreed to meet Renzo for dinner at the Black Horse Inn on the outskirts of town two nights later.

The maître d' greeted them with a smile. "Good evening Mr. Perreira. Good to see you again."

He dined here often enough to be known by name. Interesting. She wondered how much time he spent here with Luke.

"Hello, George. Do you think you can find us a quiet table?"

"No problem." The maître d' placed them at a table for two near a window. Molly wished he'd chosen one closer to the middle of the room. The inn was old, and not all the windows were double-glazed. She threw her outdoor jacket around her shoulders—after eating something, she'd feel warmer.

When George returned to take their drink orders and hand them the menu, he smiled benevolently at them. If he thought they were a couple, he was sorely mistaken. Although, one could do worse than be seen with someone as handsome as Renzo. Her trance was interrupted by the man himself.

"Molly, before we go into details, we must decide what we want from a meeting with him."

Right. She placed the starched napkin on her lap as the waiter set down a bowl of carrot-and-ginger soup in front of her. Two Parmesan crisps lay alongside it. The very sight of the deep orange soup, a thread of steam rising from the surface, made her hungry. She picked up her spoon. This would warm her up.

"So, Molly, if we could have anything we wanted, what would we ask for?"

"Well…a rent reduction would be wonderful. In fact, if we become one store, he ought to charge us no more than we were paying before he tried to raise the rent."

"Agreed. That's our priority. I think we should approach it this way. Because he turned the building into two stores without permission, the town will make him take it down when they realize."

"So it's in his best interest to put it right before they find out."

"He's a good businessman, so he will see that immediately."

"He won't like it."

"Of course not. But I would not be surprised if he is paying taxes on only one property. If they make him change it back, he will be responsible for the expense, and worse, there will be a fine, I'm sure, and a scandal. I don't think Madison wants that."

Renzo had certainly thought this through. If a little gentle blackmail could solve their problem, she was all for it. Not blackmail. No. Leverage.

Renzo's eyes glowed with an enthusiastic brilliance in the atmospheric light of the restaurant. "Also, if we managed to negotiate whatever we want, we would like him to pay for the construction, wouldn't we?"

Molly had to rein him in. "That's crazy. He'd never agree. Why should he?"

"I think he must."

"Come on, Renzo. It's enough that he allows us to make these changes."

"His standing in this town means a lot to him, no? He cannot afford the disgrace of this." He forked up a helping of Moroccan lamb stew and chewed steadily, giving her time to formulate her reply.

He'd nailed Channing's character perfectly. "That would be an amazing outcome, for sure." Something still bothered her. "But you don't think it smacks of, you know, blackmail?"

A flash of surprise ran over Renzo's features—then he laughed. "Of course not. We just remind him of his civic duties. Whether he chooses to do the right thing is up to him. Even if he doesn't, I suspect we can still go ahead."

Could they? Molly didn't think she'd be able to say any of this to Channing with confidence. The memory of his smug self-satisfaction when they'd met for coffee, and the way he'd taken no interest in anything she had to say still rankled. She took an empowering breath in through her nose. It was time he took her seriously as a businesswoman.

They spent some time discussing the approach they would take when they next saw their landlord.

"I suggest we ask him to visit *us* so we can show him what we are talking about."

She swallowed a mouthful of tilapia Provençale before replying. "Do you think he would come?"

"We will tell him, quite truthfully, that we've considered his offer and have a response for him."

True. But still. Channing's ability to do the right thing without being prodded had proved limited. She nodded.

As they were enjoying a cup of coffee after dinner, Renzo, looking past her shoulder at something on the other side of the restaurant, frowned.

"Isn't that your neighbor over there? The guy who ran the shop over Christmas?" he asked. Apparently, the question had been rhetorical, because he smiled at whomever it was. She tried to look without making her curiosity obvious, but failed. Nick didn't spot her, but the attractive woman with him did. Molly saw her scarlet lips move and then Nick turned his head in their direction. Caught off guard, she waved at him before turning back to Renzo.

"Yes, that's him."

"I thought so. He looks as though he's enjoying her company."

Nick's love life was none of her business. She wasn't envious. Or upset. Only, something unidentifiable was giving her indigestion. The fish? Or the espresso. She should have had decaf.

**

Channing arrived at the Java Jive dressed in head-to-toe Brooks Brothers, and draped himself over one of the corner armchairs. Or he would have, except that mid-century modern didn't really lend itself to sprawling. Neither did his physique. Which all helped in cutting him down to size in her head. Impossible to be afraid of the man behind the Wizard of Oz.

He stood when Molly approached him, which meant nothing. Just years of breeding and a belief that manners made the man. Which they didn't. Respect and loyalty—they counted. Without those, all bets were off.

Channing clearly imagined he had the upper hand here. He expressed surprise to find they had no documents for him.

"I thought you planned to present a counteroffer. Or possibly some new ideas. I need to see anything like that in writing before I can give it my consideration."

Renzo and Molly glanced at each other. She gave an almost imperceptible nod.

"We would like to discuss the options with you before we come up with a final plan." Renzo, in spite of having worked a full day surrounded by coffeemakers and baked goods, looked amazingly fresh. He was wearing a pressed shirt, open at the neck, and gave a much more relaxed impression than their landlord. Madison's cravat was giving up the will to live. Who wore a cravat these days, anyway?

The man made a big show of looking at his watch.

"'I'm sorry to keep you from your evening engagements." Molly could dole out sarcasm as easily as anyone. "So, let's get straight to the point."

In great detail, she and Renzo told him about the information they'd unearthed, and how it might affect the future not only of their shops, but of Pilgrim Properties as a whole, and Channing in particular.

Despite some facetious interjections from their landlord when they began, he gradually fell silent. His face had gone from a rosy pink to a livid cherry, possibly due to the volcano of emotions that must be seething below the surface. If he reacted badly to what they'd said, he'd end up knee-deep in lava.

The volcano gave up the struggle. "You have a colossal nerve." He gazed at Molly. "People like you, trying to take me on?"

His tone suggested that they were beneath contempt. Renzo's face remained impassive. Molly felt the heat rising and forced herself to unclench her fingers, which had formed themselves into fists.

"Let me make certain I have this right." Channing went on.

"If I don't take down the wall and pay for it all, you'll make sure the zoning commission knows about it."

"Obviously, there will be no need to mention any of this to the town if the work is carried out before it all becomes an issue." Renzo kept his voice light—not a threatening word escaped his lips.

Channing appeared to be struggling with himself—and losing.

"We're not done here. You'll be hearing from my lawyers." As he rose, Molly was sure she heard his knee joints creak.

CHAPTER FORTY-THREE

With the ball in Channing's court, they could only kick back and wait for a response. So, Molly focused on the bookshop and started a list of additional improvements she wanted to make if he agreed to pay up. Because if he did, they would have enough cash to renovate the whole place, hire some extra staff, and organize more events.

This gave her plenty to think about as she stood in line at Jackson's waiting to pay for the soup she'd chosen for dinner.

She'd expand the most popular sections—romance, mysteries, and psychological thrillers—and design a children's department with space for storytime and other activities. A couple of weeks before, she'd ordered a few more gay romances to test the response, and they'd disappeared from the shelves. Luke must have either sold them or kept them for himself. They needed a separate LGBTQ section.

She imagined Lucinda Parks, one of her favorite authors, standing in front of a packed room, with the audience sitting at tables, enjoying a cup of tea or coffee, while they listened to her talk about her latest novel. In her imagination, Renzo and she stood surveying the scene, both delighted at the increase in business.

Her shoe caught on a stray twig lying in her path, but she managed to straighten up before she tripped. She reminded herself to pay attention—she couldn't afford to break an ankle.

No convenient neighbor would take care of her, if she did.

Feeling stupid because of her misstep, she glanced around to check that no one had seen her. Damn. On the other side of the town green, Nick was walking in the opposite direction. He picked up his pace and kept his gaze fixed straight ahead. With any luck, he hadn't spotted her. A blush suffused her cheeks as she continued homeward.

Her thoughts strayed to that evening at the Black Horse. Nothing stayed a secret in a town this small. Since she was able to see his house from her bedroom window, she found it difficult to ignore the occasional sight of the same woman disappearing through Nick's front door, on her way in or out.

Not that she paid attention or anything. After all, he had a right to be with whomever he wanted. It was nothing to do with her.

She continued down Main Street, endeavoring to look as composed as if she hadn't tripped at all.

***

The gravel crunched beneath Molly's tires when she pulled into her driveway the following day. Her windshield wipers needed replacing—they had barely dealt with the steady rain that accompanied her trip home. Nick's car was parked next door.

They were still friends, weren't they? His dating someone didn't change anything. So why did she feel so weird about dropping in for a casual chat? Molly shivered as the Volvo cooled. She would ask him where they stood. Just in passing.

She approached his front door and rang the bell. Inside, she heard Hadley barking to alert her master to a visitor. Moments later, footsteps crossed the hall. He opened the door and, seeing her, smiled.

"Molly, hi. What brings you here?"

Good question. What kind of a visit was this? "Just checking in."

"Come on in. It's miserable out there."

Molly edged past him into the living room, so familiar to her when old Bert was alive, and now bearing Nick's tasteful stamp.

"Have a seat. I was about to have a drink. Would you like something? Malbec?"

"Thanks." She experienced the sensation of falling down the rabbit hole. What *was* she doing here? She scanned the room for evidence of the other woman's presence, but apart from the unusually messy desk, nothing stood out.

Nick handed her a glass of something red. "I didn't expect you to be at the Black Horse the other night."

Wait, hadn't *she* been about to say that? She sought for a neutral answer. "I was there with Renzo."

"And why not? He's a good-looking guy. Nice too."

Hardly the point. "We were discussing business."

"I assumed you were."

Why would he jump to that conclusion?

"I *might* have been on a date."

He stared at her. "Okay." There wasn't a shred of conviction in his voice. "But that isn't likely, is it?"

"What do you mean? You and I have been out together."

"Well, yes. Though not on a date—just as friends, right? That's what you wanted."

She nodded. "I liked it when I thought you weren't interested in women. It made everything safer."

Oh, god. Had she actually said the words aloud?

"Safer?" Nick sat down abruptly. He frowned. Then he burst out laughing.

She glared at him, piqued.

"Why on earth would you think that?"

A sinking sensation told her that she'd blundered. Big time. But she had no idea how to retreat, so she forged ahead. "Well, you're Luke's friend. You'd been in a relationship with someone called Sam, so I thought—" She could almost hear her mother's voice, warning her against wading into mud, and changed tack. "I never worried about you making a pass at me." Oh, no. Too much information. Where had her discretion gone?

She knew she ought to turn back before things went too far.

"What did you say?" But he'd caught it. "I never made a pass at you? Why would I? You're completely uninterested in men."

Molly, face aflame, remained silent.

"Not that I blame you," he went on, as if he'd registered her thoughts. "You've been out with some jerks."

She wasn't certain what hackles were, but was pretty sure hers were rising. "I told you about them because I thought you were a friend. I wouldn't have, if..."

If what?

"But we *are* friends, aren't we? How does this change things?"

She wished he weren't being quite so reasonable. "Friends are honest with each other," she said, realizing too late that he hadn't been dishonest. Her self-absorption had prevented her from paying attention to who he really was.

Nick's hands were clenched now. "Well, they sure as hell don't lie to themselves."

Molly attempted to convey nothing but indifference. "What exactly do you mean?"

"You're not interested in men because you're still married. Anyone can see that."

She stood frozen, stunned into silence. A succession of emotions ran through her. First came anger. What right did he have to say such things to her? He couldn't be more wrong. She had made a life of her own now.

A shiver of apprehension was succeeded by a sudden pricking behind the eyes. She mustn't cry. Not now. Not in front of him. He would only think he was right. And he wasn't. Not at all.

Almost immediately, a cold finger snaked its way up her spine. He'd accused her of deceiving herself. Could that be true? And if it were, did it matter?

Of *course* she would always love Simon. One person didn't just stop loving another because he'd been so thoughtless as to die.

Yet Simon had told her he would help find her someone new—just not as good as him. So that they could both move on. And she'd allowed him to try. Odd that Nick hadn't been on Simon's list of possibilities.

But she'd given dating a shot, so no one could say she was still married. No one. Taking a breath, she turned away, the icy finger lodged in her throat.

Tears threatened to overwhelm her.

"I've got to go…thanks for the wine," she said and made her escape. Hadley let out a sad whine when Molly closed the front door behind her and emerged into the cold, dark evening.

***

Back in her own chilly living room, Molly threw herself onto the sofa, embraced a pillow, clinging to it like a life preserver, and started to sob. Not small, elegant sobs, but noisy, breathtaking ones that left her exhausted.

She didn't know how long she'd been lying curled up when she opened her eyes again. The cushion under her head was damp with tears, and she couldn't summon the will to move. Her limbs were weighed down with burdens too heavy to carry. What a mess she'd made of everything. She shivered.

"*Feeling better?*" came Simon's sympathetic voice. Molly blinked, attempting to make him out. Her weeping must have done something to her eyes, because he wasn't quite in focus, so she closed them again before answering.

"I guess so." Knowing he was around always comforted her when she felt overwhelmed.

"*Something's upset you,*" he said, unnecessarily. "*What happened?*"

Molly had no idea how to answer the question, or even whether she should. Did she still think of herself as a wife, not a widow? If she let Simon go, she might never see him again. At least not in this world.

"I had a row with Nick." She struggled to sit up, trying to restore her dignity. She didn't want to talk to Simon while collapsed on the couch.

He raised his eyebrows. "*Nick? Why? From what you've told me, he sounds like a reasonable guy.*"

"Well, he's not." She came across as infantile. Next, she'd be claiming Nick started it. Her eyes welled up again.

He frowned. "*So, what's his problem? And who the heck does he think he is, to make you cry?*"

She detected animosity in his voice, and the last thing she wanted to deal with was an irate husband.

Late husband. Surely not a jealous one?

No. This was *her* issue, not his. She found a crumpled tissue in the pocket of her skirt. Smoothing it out as best she could, she blew her nose.

"He's dating some woman." She sniffed and tucked the tissue into the sleeve of her sweater, where it lay, slightly damp, against her skin. "Which he's totally allowed to do, of course."

"*So, what's the problem?*"

"We used to go out together, platonically, you know. Now we won't be—not after this. I knew he wasn't interested in me, since he wasn't interested in anyone, so far as I could see. Turns out he just didn't find me attractive." Because she was still married to the man in front of her.

Simon paced the room, his face thoughtful. He stopped and his eyes met hers. They must be swollen from crying, because he still appeared blurry.

"*Oh, honey. That's not enough to make you lose it like this. So, what's the real reason?*"

Molly took the soggy tissue out of her sleeve. Useless. Instead of blowing her nose, she sniffed. She expected a "not very ladylike" from her mother, but apparently, she was offline.

What *was* the source of these emotions? How to explain them? She felt curiously reluctant to tell Simon why Nick's remark about her still being married had upset her. Simon and she had been together so long that she'd learned to predict how he'd react to things. Even so, she hadn't encountered a situation like this before, and she didn't know how she wanted him to respond. Or if. Would he be flattered if someone thought she was acting like his wife? Or annoyed?

She took a risk. "He says I'm still married to you."

"*What? Is this guy for real?*" Was that a tinge of smugness in Simon's words?

"I'm not, am I? I can't be, because you're…" Molly couldn't bring herself to say the word. Not with Simon's hazy figure standing in front of her.

Her late husband said nothing for some minutes. Then he spoke. "*Whether he's right or not, I don't think you should hang around with people who make you cry.*" His voice remained level, giving nothing away.

She lifted her head and faced him, her jaw set. "Don't worry about *that*," she said with some force. "I don't care if I never see him again."

Her head in her hands, she burst into tears once more. She sensed that Simon had disappeared even before she opened her eyes.

CHAPTER FORTY-FOUR

Molly tried to ignore the tumult of feelings that kept waking her in the middle of the nights that followed. The movies in her dreams never stopped. Visions of the shop, its windows boarded over while she watched, helpless, from the sidewalk. Channing standing smirking next to her, telling Nick, who seemed to be there too, that if he'd known Molly was married, he might not have...the picture faded. All she could do was shout at them both, trying to explain, but when she tried to speak, nothing came out.

She woke, her mouth dry, unable to get back to sleep until four or sometimes five in the morning. She awakened groaning when the alarm went off. All she wanted was to roll over and try to fall asleep again, but she forced herself to swing her legs out of bed.

She must get up—work beckoned. Admittedly, the bookshop offered less distraction nowadays. The thought that Channing might take them to court weighed on her, making her shoulders ache.

Why did she find sleep so much harder these days than when she first lost Simon? It made no sense. She didn't want to discuss this with her girlfriends. They wouldn't understand the way grief could catch her unawares so long after Simon's death.

But, as if to force her back into the world again, Rosie called to tell her she was overdue for a haircut. At first, Molly searched for an excuse, but her friend would have none of it.

"You'll feel better if you take a little time for yourself—you know you will. I think you have too much on your mind. This will give you a chance to relax. And Luke will look after the store."

***

As Molly sat in Shear Madness a few days later, Rosie regarded her appraisingly. She'd just finished blow-drying her hair, which gleamed under the bright lights of the salon.

"Seems to me, honey, you could use a makeover. I fixed your hair, so it's fine now, but you look like you haven't slept in a while. Which is never good for a woman of our age."

Molly studied herself in the mirror. It was true. There were dark shadows around her eyes, and her skin appeared pale and dry, despite her attempts to disguise it with makeup.

"I do my best, but nothing works." Even the little she did do was an effort.

Rosie clucked sympathetically. "Let me help. Stay here." She walked off and came back with a box of beauty products. Picking up a bottle of moisturizing cleanser, she began to swab at Molly's face with cotton pads, tossing each into the bin as she went. Molly kept her eyes closed, pretty sure that without any makeup at all, she looked worse. The warm spicy fragrance of Rosie's perfume was comfortingly familiar.

"You're right about the lack of sleep. I'm in bed around ten and drift off with no trouble. But I wake up in the wee hours and can't fall back asleep," she clarified.

"Have you tried chamomile tea?"

Molly grimaced. "Yes, though I detest it. Tastes like grass, doesn't it?"

Rosie dabbed something around Molly's eyes, stroking it in with a finger. She shook her head. "I happen to like it, but that's not the point. Did it help?"

"I don't think herbal tea works, at least not on me," said Molly, when she was free to speak again. Rosie had outlined her lips with a pencil before applying color with a brush. Molly checked her reflection again. She did look better.

Rosie said nothing for a while, her expression thoughtful as she scanned her friend's face.

"You need someone to talk to, if life is worrying you so much."

Molly couldn't explain how she discussed things with Simon. In any case, she didn't share everything with him. And she didn't seem able to summon him either. As far as she could figure, he showed up at his whim, not hers.

"You know Amanda and I are always here for you," Rosie went on.

Molly glanced up at her friend and found herself staring at a gigantic eyebrow pencil. Or rather, two of them. Hoping she hadn't just crossed her eyes, she closed them quickly to let Rosie draw lines over her brows.

"I'm grateful, truly. I can't imagine what I'd do without you two. But this is something I must work out for myself."

"Look up," said Rosie.

What now? Molly started to fidget. She'd been in this chair too long.

"Just a touch of mascara." Rosie worked the wand for a few moments. "There. Now, take a peek."

Obediently, Molly looked at herself in the mirror. Staring back at her she saw a younger version of herself. The way she'd been before Simon died. The foundation had taken away the wan aspect of her skin. The lipstick warmed her face. The one she usually wore didn't do that. Her eyes appeared bigger, and her gleaming hair was the icing on the cake. She smiled.

"Wow, Rosie. Thanks. It's been ages since I've had anyone do my makeup. I feel like one of those women on television. You know, an ugly duckling turned into a swan."

"You'll never be ugly. But everyone can improve on nature.

I'm so glad you let me do it. You seem a lot more cheerful."

"I'll buy the lipstick and foundation, please. And I'll take the mascara too. Mine is so old it must have dried up by now." She'd given up wearing it because she cried so much back then that it was always running down her cheeks.

"That's the spirit."

Molly stood and went to pay the bill. "Just seeing myself like this gives me a lift. You're an angel."

Rosie blushed beneath her tan. "What are friends for? Speaking of which, don't forget we're having a girls' night out on Wednesday. That should help boost your spirits too," she said, placing the new makeup in a small pink paper bag.

"Thanks for reminding me. I almost forgot. What are we doing, again?"

"I know you have a lot on your mind," Rosie said tolerantly. "But this will be fun. We're invited to an art show opening in New Haven. Some little gallery. It's owned by a friend of Amanda's. Drinks, nibbles—and art," she added as an afterthought. "And then we plan on having something to eat at a new place on Chapel Street."

"Oh, right."

Rosie's frown told her that her reaction hadn't been enthusiastic enough. She tried again. "That will be fabulous."

Rosie brightened. "Yeah. Who knows? You might meet the man of your dreams there."

The man of her dreams? What dreams?

***

"You look good this morning," Renzo said the next day, when she stopped by for her cappuccino. "Been to see Rosie? She's a genius, don't you think?"

"She is. Worrying about Channing has kept me awake at night, and she managed to disguise the damage."

"You know, I believe that if he was going to call in his lawyers, he would have already. What do you think? Should we make plans for the construction and send them to him? Then he can start the work."

Molly stared at him. This was a bold suggestion, for sure. On the other hand, why not?

"We might ask Jim Shaughnessy to draw them," she said. "He's good, and he'll charge a fair price."

"Who is he?"

"Amanda's husband. Architect. You must know him. He comes in here sometimes. Everyone does," she ended, with a smile.

"I've probably seen him, and if you think he's the right guy, we ought to talk to him."

"Great. I'll call him and start the ball rolling."

Amanda was delighted that Jim would be helping to move their project forward. "And if you need any ideas for revamping the new space, I'd love to offer some suggestions."

"If Channing pays for the building work, we might be able to make other improvements." Better not count her chickens. Their friends might want their money back. "And you'll be the first person I come to, as soon as I know what kind of a budget we have."

"You know, I think Channing Madison might cave. That man is so concerned about his social standing, he won't want any scandal attached to his name."

"Fingers crossed." Things were looking up.

CHAPTER FORTY-FIVE

Molly refused to look out of her bedroom window these days, except when she heard Hadley barking in the garden. One time she saw her chase Hemingway up a tree. Fine. If that was how her neighbors were going to behave, up a sturdy maple was exactly the right place to be. Or it would have been, if the cat had found it easier to get down. Molly could relate.

Using a piece of chicken, she had to coax him along the branch which overhung her property. She certainly wasn't going to ask Nick for help.

So she welcomed the distraction when Amanda called a few days later to tell her that Jim was working on the plans. "He's doing the wall first, he says, and then he'll get to the other stuff."

"What other stuff?"

"You know, making the best use of the joint space."

"Sounds interesting, but I'd better warn him that we may not have enough money to do any of that. I can't let him take too much time over it."

"I'll pass it on, but I think he's enjoying himself. In any case, it's only sketches at the moment."

Molly allowed herself a second or two to visualize a renovated shop. But she mustn't indulge in daydreams. Nothing was certain yet. "Were you calling about anything else?"

"Oh, right. You haven't forgotten we're going to the gallery opening in New Haven on Wednesday, have you?"

"Of course not," Molly lied. She'd been so preoccupied with Nick, Renzo, and Simon, that her scheduled outing with her friends had already slipped her mind. "I'm looking forward to it," she added, to make amends.

"I'll pick you up at five, okay? You know what traffic is like in the evening, and we'll need to find a place to park."

"Should I dress up, Amanda? I'll be at work, but I can bring the wrap dress to change into if it's a fancy event."

"Well, I'm not going to wear anything special, just my usual."

Amanda's "usual" consisted of expensive casuals with coordinating shoes, purse, and accessories. She always looked chic. Molly had only ever seen her in heels, unless she was on her way to tennis or the gym. Apparently, unlike Molly's, her friend's feet never hurt at the end of the day.

Amanda was still talking. "Besides, you always look appropriate, and no one will notice you anyway—they'll all be focusing on the artist."

Unsure what to make of that remark, Molly concluded that Amanda had the best intentions. "What about Rosie? How's she getting there?"

"She's arranged her appointments so she can leave early. I'll pick her up first and then come for you. It'll be fun, you'll see. The three of us together."

"Sounds perfect." She meant it. She felt a tingle of anticipation at the thought of a night out. The drive would be relaxing. Plus, it wouldn't be dark until seven, so she'd have a chance to enjoy the countryside as they drove the twisty lanes leading out of Brentford.

When Wednesday finally rolled around, Molly was ready for an evening free of worries. She'd been busy all day, logging in the latest deliveries and dealing with a flurry of customers who'd walked in at four, looking for something for their book club.

Usually, she loved helping people find the perfect book.

Sometimes, though, when she had to suggest something for a group of women with differing tastes, it could be challenging, especially when she was short of time. Still, she talked them through several books she thought might suit them, pointing out that a little controversy made for a lively discussion. Her efforts were rewarded with an order for ten copies of *The Sun Never Rises*, a historical novel set in medieval Italy.

When Rosie rushed in to announce that Amanda was waiting outside in the car, Molly glanced at her watch in horror.

"So sorry, I lost track of the time. I'll be there in two minutes." She ran through to the back to fetch her things and found her friend close on her heels.

"You can't go like that. Look at your hair," Rosie moaned, rummaging in her huge handbag. She pulled out a small collapsible hairbrush. "Now hold still for a second. It's clean," she went on, evidently noticing Molly's startled expression. "I always carry a spare. You never know when a friend might require emergency attention." She grinned, and with a few deft strokes, stood back, satisfied. "There. All you need now is to touch up your lipstick, and you'll do."

Molly remembered her mother fussing over her when she was little and could only be grateful Rosie hadn't found a handkerchief, asked her to spit on it, and wiped her face. She let Luke know that he'd have to close up the shop tonight and was soon ensconced in the back seat of Amanda's Range Rover. During a lull in the conversation, a thought occurred to her.

"I know you've already told me, Amanda, but my mind is a sieve these days. Tell me again, how do you know the owner?"

Her friend glanced into the rearview mirror and smiled. "Katherine and I were in high school together and we kept in touch. She and her husband owned a gallery in Brooklyn, but when they divorced, she took her half of the money and moved up here to start again."

"Like me," added Rosie.

So, Connecticut was turning into a magnet for broken-hearted New Yorkers. Interesting.

"Well, good for her," Molly said. "It can't have been easy. She must be quite a businesswoman."

"I guess so. The place is small, but she's hoping this will help put her on the map. I'm looking forward to introducing you to each other. I think you'll like her."

Rosie chimed in. "Do you know anything about the show? Or the painter who's exhibiting? I'm not so keen on the modern stuff where you don't know what's what."

Molly smiled. One of the things she appreciated about Rosie was that she never pretended to be anyone other than who she was. She knew what she liked and said so.

"I can't remember precisely what it's about," said Amanda. "It's called *Flutter*, which is kind of weird. In any case, we don't have to stay long if we don't like it. We just need to put in an appearance to show support, right?"

"Absolutely. We women stick together," said Rosie. "So, if the paintings are horrible, we don't say so." They laughed and fell silent as Amanda navigated the one-way street system to the gallery. It wasn't easy to find, with its exterior painted black and the name printed in almost imperceptible, stylized, white letters above the door. Eventually, Amanda spotted it, and they entered, glad to escape the light drizzle that had begun to fall.

The bright lighting inside gave an air of warmth, which increased the festive atmosphere. A crowd of art lovers, drinks in hand, stood around, obscuring the pictures. Moments after the friends arrived, a waiter came up to offer them some prosecco. "Or orange juice, if you're driving?"

Amanda ignored this suggestion and took a glass of bubbly. "We're here to celebrate." She grinned. "Anyway, it will have worn off before I have to drive. Cheers."

They were clinking glasses as a short, energetic woman pushed her way through the guests in their direction.

"Amanda!" she called and clasped her friend in a hug. She wore a flowing black garment cut on some sort of bias. Her purple platform sandals gave her a couple more inches. Without them, she would be all of five feet tall, Molly guessed. The woman's long gray hair was braided and decorated with red, pink, and orange beads.

Amanda extricated herself. "It's wonderful to see you, Katherine. You haven't changed a bit. Molly, this is Katherine McIntyre, art dealer *extraordinaire*."

Their host smiled and extended a hand be-ringed with chunky jewelry that might have been plastic but delivered an arty vibe.

"And this is our friend, Rosie," Amanda announced.

Rosie had been staring intently at Katherine's head. Her next words explained why.

"I love the way those beads are woven into your braids. Who does them for you? I have clients who might be interested."

"Rosie's a hairdresser—" Amanda began, but Rosie interrupted her.

"Business owner and hairstylist, if you don't mind."

Katherine smiled. "I found a wonderful woman here in town. She gets busy, but I can let you have her name and number, if you like."

"Perfect," Rosie said. "I don't expect she'd come out to Brentford, but at least I can give her referrals." She sipped at her glass, wrinkled her nose, and giggled. "It's the bubbles. They always do this to me."

"Never mind, come and meet Sonya. She's fantastic. I know you'll love her."

Katherine took Amanda's hand and led her back through the crush. Molly and Rosie followed. As they approached the edge of the crowd, the artwork became visible. Along the walls hung a series of large watercolors featuring brilliant butterflies.

Rosie pointed out one in particular—a stunning sapphire-hued specimen. "These paintings are so exquisite. I can easily imagine having one on my wall, can't you?" They pressed forward to look. "And seems like they're popular too. A whole lot of them have red stickers, which means they're sold, right?"

Molly experienced a sudden sinking feeling. Butterflies? Wasn't this Nick's specialty? Coincidence, surely.

A second later, the women broke through to a less-cluttered part of the gallery, and Molly stopped dead. If this was the painter, she had seen her before. The tall, stylish woman talking animatedly to a smartly dressed gentleman in a navy blazer and khaki pants was Nick's mysterious girlfriend. As Molly's mouth opened in astonishment, the man moved, and his gaze fell on her. His eyes widened in surprise.

Oh, god. Nick.

How would she deal with this? Her friends hadn't yet cottoned to the state of Nick and Molly's relationship. A tidal wave of embarrassment surged up her neck and into her face. Her mouth was dry as day-old pizza. She should close it. She pressed her lips together.

"Excuse me for a minute. I'll be right back." She turned away before giving the first explanation that came to mind. "Wardrobe malfunction," she hissed desperately into Rosie's ear, hoping that would explain a prolonged absence. "I'll see you later."

Rosie stared from her to Nick and back. "But isn't that...?"

Molly didn't stay to answer.

So, this was the moment. Time to admit to herself that she'd expected to be safe from her emotions in a city like New Haven, where the chances of running into someone she knew were slim. But not zero.

The frantic knocking of another guest forced her out of the tiny bathroom where she'd lingered as long as possible. She stood for a second, uncertain as to where to go. Before she could decide, Rosie materialized in front of her.

"Oh, there you are. What happened? Your clothes look fine to me."

She couldn't avoid Nick indefinitely. She'd have to speak to him at some point. It may as well be now, when they were surrounded by other people, and it couldn't become too personal.

"It wasn't too tricky, so I managed to fix it." She took a breath. "I should go and say hello to the artist, shouldn't I?"

"I think so. She's called Sonya something, and she's real nice."

"Great." So, not only successful, good-looking, and talented, but nice too. Surprisingly, the thought didn't hurt as much as she'd anticipated it might. Nick deserved someone like Sonya.

"Lead on." She followed Rosie back to the exhibition.

Confused, that's how she felt, when it came right down to it. The man before her resembled Nick but didn't *feel* like him, somehow.

Katherine had abandoned the group and was busy talking to a guest about the painting of a rose-and-rust-colored specimen with navy circles on its wings. Amanda gave Molly a small frown. "Everything okay?" she asked.

Molly nodded and tried to relax her shoulders. Amanda, taller than her friends, scanned the crowd and finally located the artist again. "There she is. Come and meet the woman behind these wonderful works, Sonya Morten. Katherine introduced us to her while you were in the bathroom. And she's here with your next-door neighbor. Isn't that a coincidence?"

Molly followed Amanda, not at all sure she wanted to meet this woman but aware she had no plausible reason for avoiding it.

"Delighted." Sonya fixed Molly with a smile so genuine that she felt ashamed for ever having harbored such negative thoughts about her.

Nick's face, meanwhile, gave nothing away as he stood next to Sonya. Molly arranged her features into a reciprocal smile.

"Amanda tells me you and Nick are neighbors." Sonya paused, and Molly realized she should say something.

She took a deep breath. "Why, yes, we are," she said. "Good to see you, Nick."

"Hi, Molly."

If Nick's reply seemed a little flat, no one appeared to pay attention. Gradually, Amanda and Sonya contrived to make the conversation less stilted. Rosie, possibly intuiting the undercurrents beneath the idle chat, rescued the situation by remarking that they needed to see the remainder of the exhibit before leaving for the restaurant.

Forcing herself to focus on the paintings, Molly walked around, trying to ignore the sensation of something burning the back of her neck, as if someone was staring at her. She checked behind. There was no sign of Nick. Half relieved, she turned her attention back to the art.

***

"That was weird, wasn't it?" said Amanda, as the waiter brought them their warm sake. They were sitting in the new Asian fusion restaurant near the gallery, which Katherine had recommended.

Molly picked up a menu and pretended to study it. "What do you mean?" So much had been weird this evening.

"You know. Small-world stuff. Nick being there, for one."

"And looking so cool too," Rosie chimed in.

"And him knowing the artist." Amanda finished her thought. "Do you think she's his girlfriend? They seem on very familiar terms."

Molly had never raised the subject of Nick's love life with her friends. She let the comment pass. "Who knows?" she said mildly.

"Never mind that, Amanda. How about you knowing Katherine? And us all coming here on the same evening. Synchronicity, right?" Rosie's face reflected her curiosity.

Molly stayed silent. Synchronicity? Possibly.

"Don't you think so, Molly?" Rosie seemed determined to have an answer.

"Actually, I did know they were friends. But I had no idea she'd be exhibiting here."

Amanda glanced at her curiously. "You hadn't met her in

person before tonight?"

"Nope. I saw them having dinner at the Black Horse. I was with Renzo, discussing business." She didn't want to admit to watching Sonya from her bedroom window, as she went in and out of the house next door. She'd keep it vague. "I think she's been keeping Nick pretty busy lately."

Her friends looked at her with what Molly interpreted as sympathy.

"Well, she is kind of gorgeous, right, Amanda?" said Rosie.

"Sure. But more important, he hasn't been able to hang out with you." Amanda gave Molly a shrewd glance. "Which must be annoying."

"Hmm." Molly would not give any of her tumultuous feelings away. What Nick did held no interest for her.

"Shame. I thought you two were getting along so well. You know, there's a new dating website called PlentyMorePebbles. com—or something like that." Rosie gave her an encouraging smile.

Plenty more? Was Rosie serious? Molly wanted to scream at her clueless friend. But Rosie's earnest and well-meaning face stopped her. And then something shifted inside. The situation wasn't tragic—ridiculous, more like.

Molly couldn't stop herself. One look at her friends' faces and she started to laugh. After a startled moment, they joined in.

"Plenty more?" she gasped, and laughed again. "Heaven help us."

So *that* was the problem. Heaven, in the person of Simon, had tried to do just that and messed up royally. Only when the other diners in the place began to stare at them did the women subside.

Molly needed to catch her breath. "Wow. That felt good. Haven't laughed so much for a while." At least running into Nick had moved their relationship from a cool climate to a slightly warmer, if still distant, one. A step in the right direction. And the world was still spinning, after all.

CHAPTER FORTY-SIX

Someone had to chase Channing, and it was Molly's turn. She longed to wriggle out of it, but it was time she faced him again. No procrastinating.

The man himself walked into the Book Boutique before she could call him, accompanied by his mother. More accurately, *he* was accompanying *her.* His set expression told her all she needed to know about their relationship at that moment. He was a little boy whose mother was taking him to the neighbors to apologize for hitting a baseball through their window.

She smiled at Acacia, but kept her face blank as she turned to face her tormentor. "Good morning. May I help you?" Best to remain polite.

"Channing has something to say to you, don't you, dear?"

If anything, he looked even more embarrassed. His cheeks had taken on a mottled crimson tint. He cleared his throat.

"Having considered your suggestion." He ran a finger around his collar as if it were choking him. "We have decided to make the alterations required at these premises. However, we would prefer not to take down the entire wall, just to put back the linking archway that was there before."

At this point, he appeared to run out of steam. His plan actually might work better than their original idea. It would leave more room for bookcases. And with the money they were going to save, she could add extra shelves upstairs. She wouldn't give him the satisfaction of seeing how much she liked it, though.

"I believe that will be satisfactory."

"We thought it might be a good compromise," added Acacia with enthusiasm. "After Luke asked about when we'd bought the property, I wanted to find out all about it." She smiled sweetly at her son. "So, I went to Channing, and he told me there'd been a...what did you call it, dear? A misunderstanding?"

Channing raised his eyes skyward before closing them and nodding.

Acacia paid no attention to this. "I think it's an excellent idea—making the two shops back into what they were."

Behind her, Luke gave Molly a quick thumbs-up.

Molly, failing to disguise her delight, beamed. "Thank you, Channing. And Acacia. Renzo will be pleased to hear of your solution."

She waited for a "You're welcome," but it never came. Still, she would meet him halfway on this. "We can let you have our architect's drawings, which will save you some time and money. I don't think he'll have a problem modifying them."

Channing's eyebrows lifted in surprise. "You have plans already?"

What? Had he not credited her with acting like a competent businesswoman? Of *course* she had preliminary plans.

"Naturally. But I'll check with Mr. Perreira—Renzo—and if he agrees, they're yours."

"That's very generous of you, Molly." Acacia's warm brown eyes took on a slightly harder shine as she turned to face Channing. "Isn't it, dear?"

Molly almost expected her to ask, "And what do you say, son?" the way mothers did when teaching toddlers to say, "thank you." Probably best not to wait for thanks from this man.

"You might do worse than use Cavelli Construction to handle the demolition for you. They're efficient and competitive," Molly said. The company Simon had worked for deserved to have some of the business. After all, they'd likely built the wall.

Acacia patted Channing's arm. "You see, dear? I told you this would all work out well."

"Yes, Mother, you did." His voice was grudging, as though emerging from between gritted teeth, but he squared his shoulders and lifted his double chin. "Delighted to be working with you both."

He stuck out his hand and she took it. This time it was dry and warm, not clammy. She had no time to ponder the difference before he continued.

"Once I've decided on the builders, I'll ask them to contact you about the schedule, so you have time to make preparations."

Still too pompous, but he was being cooperative. Which she hadn't expected, but she'd take it.

"Thank you, Channing. We appreciate your helpfulness with the project." Always better to praise something a person hadn't done, but might, than to blame them for their lack of effort. Frequently, she found, they stepped up and became what one told them they were.

He gave her what came across as a genuine—if rueful—smile. He ought to do that more often. He was not unattractive when he put his mind to it.

"Shall we go next door and tell Renzo?" she suggested. "I'm sure he'd be happy to offer you both some coffee."

"I appreciate the invitation, but I don't have time for coffee when I'm working," said Channing. "Perhaps mother would…"

Was this a reference to their aborted "date" in Starbucks? She would ignore it, if so.

Acacia beamed at Molly. "That would be delightful, dear."

"It's the least we can do."

***

A few minutes later, Acacia sat in one of the more comfortable armchairs in the café, nursing a cup of Earl Grey tea. Renzo settled into the chair next to her and offered a slice of lemon and the sugar.

"We are so grateful for your help in fixing this difficult situation," he began, giving her a sincere smile that conveyed genuine charm.

Acacia returned his gaze with the mesmerized air of an audience member on stage in front of a hypnotist.

"I'd like to participate too," she said, unexpectedly.

"Sorry?"

"I was talking to Luke about your problem and decided to help. I would like to give you the fifteen thousand dollars you need toward making everything as beautiful as it can be."

Molly caught Renzo's eye and gave her head a small shake. There was no way Acacia could afford such an act of generosity. Her dated clothes and ten-year-old car testified to that.

"Mrs. Todd, you have done more than enough already." Renzo picked up her hand and raised it to his lips.

She positively radiated delight. "That's as may be, but I consider the shop my community. Molly and Luke are my friends, and I would like you to be too."

"The money is not necessary. You can count on my friendship."

"You see? So, what is to stop a friend from helping a friend?"

Could she be batting her eyelashes at Renzo? Molly was unable to hide a grin at the incongruity of the sight. Meanwhile, her new partner appeared oblivious to his effect on women. "Acacia, we're touched, but—" she said.

The older woman interrupted her. "Now, dear. I won't be told no."

"In that case, we thank you very much." Molly turned to Renzo to confirm this.

He nodded.

They could always return it if they didn't use it all.

***

Molly had always liked Mick Cavelli. Simon's old boss had given him the opportunity to rise in the company, and provided her with a pension when she became a widow.

"Hey, Molly," he said when she called. "I understand you've got big plans to expand. Good for you."

She needn't explain that the merger had been Renzo's idea, nor that it had been more or less forced upon them by a rent increase.

"I guess Pilgrim Properties already contacted you. What do you think? It's only a small job, but I know you're the best."

Mick laughed. "A lot smaller than anything I've handled for years. But for you, I'll do it."

"And you'll give them a fair estimate?"

"Sure. We can handle the teardown and renovation in a week. Might be less if everything slots into place and there are no nasty surprises. And I'll give you a discount on the price."

"But…"

"Let me do that for you—"

Molly had to put him straight. "Actually, you're doing it for Channing Madison. He's the one paying."

"In that case, we'll keep the discount down to ten percent," Mick said with a grin.

"Mick, you're terrific. Thank you so much."

She asked after Angie and the rest of the family, and ended the conversation with the feeling that everything seemed to be going well. Almost too well.

She felt a lot more confident when she picked up the phone to call her landlord. It never hurt to take the high road.

"Channing? I've managed to negotiate a discount with Cavelli Construction for taking down the wall. If you plan to use them, that is."

"You what?"

"And I'm happy to pass the savings along to you, if you're willing to cut us some slack on the rent, that is."

A choking noise came from the phone and Molly held it

away from her ear for a moment. "Channing?"

"Sorry about that. Well, Mrs. Stevenson. Molly. You're turning into quite a businesswoman. I'll think about it."

Typical of him to patronize her, but she recognized the comment as a concession on his part.

"Thank you. And you're turning into a model landlord."

A different sound emanated from him. Could he be laughing?

"Touché, Molly."

***

"I thought we should wait until after the Blossom Festival, since it brings so much business to town." Channing had dropped by the Java Jive to give Molly and Renzo an update on how his plans were progressing.

The festival took place the last weekend of April. Boy Scouts were already cleaning the war memorial and adding new wooden slats to the public benches that needed them. Cherry trees on the Common bloomed and the streets filled with visitors eager to photograph the clouds of pink that hung over the grass.

"That is an excellent idea." Renzo nodded. "Visitor numbers will be up that week, and parking is always terrible. You will ask the builders to stay in touch with us regarding the specific dates, so we can plan ahead?"

Channing made a note in a small book he withdrew from an inside pocket. "Anything else?"

Was he being snarky? Hard to tell. He'd been a lot less aggressive recently. There had been no reason for him to visit them—he could have handled the conversation over the phone. Molly wondered if the man was lonely. If she was right, perhaps taking a more benign interest in his tenants had shown him that he could choose another way to do things. One that might yield friends rather than adversaries.

Or possibly Acacia had ordered him to be nicer to them. Either way, the results were what counted.

Molly was relieved that work wouldn't begin until July at the earliest. Before Channing had agreed to pay for the changes, she'd seen the whole project as more of a concept than a reality. Something she loved to imagine in its finished state. Of course, there would be a vast amount to do before anything went ahead. The dust involved in tearing down a wall would be impossible to remove from her stock if she didn't prepare carefully.

Also, the shelves along the connecting wall contained the romance and thriller sections. They constituted two of her best-selling genres and had to be available for customers.

She would need someone to give her a helping hand. Funny. Without realizing it, she'd become accustomed to asking for help. People were almost always willing to do something for her. A warm glow spread through her at the thought.

But now, she and Renzo had one more major ask. Would they be able to keep the money they'd raised for the demolition to refurbish the place? That would ensure the new business started off on the right foot.

CHAPTER FORTY-SEVEN

It was pouring outside the day Nick showed up at the bookstore. Molly hadn't spoken to him since the art show. They were bound to meet sometime, but inexplicably, she hadn't imagined the scenario, so was unprepared.

After a mild April, the weather became unexpectedly erratic in mid-May, veering from sixty to eighty degrees in the course of a day, with wild storms and strong winds. Molly, forgetting to check the forecast each morning, was taken unawares every time.

She arrived at work that day just as the torrent started, holding her purse over her head, a little out of breath as she unlocked the front door. It would likely be another slow day. Business dropped off when rain threatened—people preferred to shop in the local mall where they could stay dry. So, a sensible day to do an inventory.

She shook out her jacket and hung it up in the office, behind the door. More conscious of her appearance these days, she raked a comb through her hair and checked her lipstick before heading onto the main floor. She switched on the computer and decided on some classic jazz. Soon, Billie Holiday's plaintive voice was floating through the store.

Meanwhile, she weeded out the stock in the back corner that hadn't moved in the last month. She ran her eye over *Time to Bloom Girl*, *Accept You for You*, and *Dating Can be Fun*. She might get rid of that one—clearly written by someone who hadn't tried it recently. Surely *Car Mechanics for Dummies* should be with the how-to books? She took it down and was about to return it to the right shelf when she heard the doorbell jangle as a very soggy customer entered.

She walked around the stack and promptly wished she hadn't.

In the doorway, water streaming from his hair, stood Nick, shaking his head and spraying the surrounding area with rain-drops. He reminded her of a wet dog—maybe he'd learned how to do that from Hadley. If she moved fast, she could disappear into the back room and pretend she wasn't there. But that was a ridiculous way for an adult to behave.

Taking a deep breath, she lifted her chin and walked toward the table of bestsellers near the front door, where he'd stopped, blinking. He took off his glasses to wipe them dry and stared at Molly. When his eyes refocused, his smile faltered.

He looked like he was thinking of what to say. All he came up with was, "Boy, it's raining cats and dogs out there."

Did he sound nervous? She couldn't tell. She fought an urge to leave him and hide in the back room. A silence ensued.

She wasn't sure exactly where they stood. Friends, right? Yet she hadn't spoken to him for a while. Not since the evening in the art gallery. And you couldn't call that a conversation.

Hadley hadn't run into her yard to give her an excuse to knock on Nick's door. Nothing needed fixing in her house. The light bulbs continued to shine, unlike this day's sun.

His eyes were fixed on the book in Molly's hand. He grinned. This time the smile reached his eyes. "*Car Mechanics?* Thinking of a new career?"

"What? No. I mean... Oh, right. This book." She abandoned the attempt to repress a smile. No one had teased her for a long time, and she liked the sensation. "No, just re-shelving stuff." She would act as if everything were normal. "Can I help you with something?"

"I guess not. I just stopped in to get out of the rain." Perhaps feeling this might not be enough, he added, "and to say hi to Luke."

"He should be here soon."

"Actually, I came in to ask if the book he ordered for me had come in."

Molly didn't recall anything with his name on it. "I'll check back here where we keep special orders."

He followed her to where they were arranged behind the counter, waiting to be picked up. She scanned the names on the bookmarks.

"It ought to be simple to find, if it's arrived. It's a coffee-table book. By Sonya Morten." Nick kept his tone airy. "Same title as her exhibit. *Flutter.*"

Molly tried not to let any reaction show, but inside she felt…what? Irritated? Disappointed? Or a little envious that he appeared so completely obsessed with the artist? Ah, there it stood. One book taller than the others, with a glossy white dust jacket, and an order slip with the name Nick H. sticking out of the top. How had she not noticed something so large? She must have been more distracted by thoughts of the business merger than she'd realized. She pulled it off the shelf, surprised by its heft.

"This is lovely," she murmured, opening the decorative cover and looking at the flyleaf.

He nodded. "It's even better inside."

Molly began to leaf through the pages. The colored illustrations were all of butterflies—undeniably beautiful—like the ones in the art gallery. "She's so talented," was all she could think to say.

"That's why she's my illustrator."

What had he said? She transferred her attention from the book to Nick. "Sorry. I missed that."

"Didn't Luke tell you? I'm putting together a popular guide to butterflies—one for the general reader. The idea is to explain, in layman's terms, why they're so important to the environment. Sonya's doing the illustrations."

Nick was writing a book. She'd been so preoccupied with the concept of merging the bookstore and café that she'd been paying no heed to other people's lives. His girlfriend was illustrating it. Well, Molly must rise above any niggle of disappointment and be happy for him. That's what a real friend would do.

If they never went to a concert again, so be it. He'd be attending cultural events with Sonya from now on. She lifted her eyes to his face. He seemed to be waiting for her to answer. If she wanted them to get along, she needed to be supportive.

"It sounds wonderful. I'll buy copies for all my friends." She meant it too.

He laughed. "No need to go crazy."

They stood looking at each other. Then they spoke simultaneously.

"Look…"

"Listen…"

"You first."

"No, you," said Nick.

Molly placed the butterfly book on the counter. She must get this right, so she chose her words carefully. "I want to say I'm sorry…for the way I overreacted to your remark. About me being married. No, hear me out," she said, as he raised a hand to stop her. "It's just—I liked having you as a friend. I appreciated having someone around who enjoyed the same things I did, got my sense of humor, and was so easy to be with. I didn't realize how important our friendship was to me until—"

"Me, too," Nick interrupted, but she plowed ahead.

"So, when I saw that you had a life of your own that I hadn't bothered to ask you about, I felt embarrassed. I could have taken more of an interest. When I saw you with Sonya, I realized I was clueless about men—particularly after all those horrible dates I told you about. And there I was, making assumptions again, about you."

Nick's puzzled look stopped her for a moment, but only for a moment.

She needed him to understand. To forgive her self-absorption, her reaction, everything. He said nothing. She cast around for something else to say. "You've been such a good friend to me."

He smiled at her. "I thought I was, climbing up on your roof and all."

"Oh, you were. Very helpful, in fact. Until you fell off." She glanced at him to determine how he was taking this mild attempt at teasing. To her relief, he laughed.

"I guess you'll be hiring someone else from now on. Because I won't be volunteering again. Though I can still handle light bulbs and other small repairs—for people I like."

"There's one more thing." She took a breath. "Deep down, I thought you might be right. Simon was the love of my life. I find it hard to let that go."

Nick's sympathetic eyes held hers for a moment. "I know. It's not easy. It takes as long as it takes."

"Well, if it's okay with you, I'd like to go back to where we were before, and not only for the handyman services." She laughed, sudden cheerfulness springing up. She would be friends with him *and* his girlfriend. "Would you and Sonya come over for dinner one night? Would that be all right?"

Nick frowned. "Me and Sonya? Why Sonya?"

Now it was Molly's turn to be puzzled. "She's your girlfriend, so naturally, I don't want to—"

She was interrupted by a bark of laughter from Nick. "My girlfriend? I think her husband would have something to say about it if she were."

"Her what?"

"I told you, Sonya's my illustrator. You saw some of her paintings at the art show. She's happily married."

So, not his girlfriend? Would she ever manage to read the signs when people were in a relationship? She made mistake after mistake because she never bothered to verify her assumptions. From now on, she would check her speculations before deciding she knew the answer.

"You mean she's not...?"

"Not. Just a friend. We see each other fairly frequently, of course, so she can show me her work, and I can ensure she has the details in the illustrations correct. They're better than her paintings, I think."

A weight fell from Molly's shoulders, and she suddenly felt light and free.

He was still speaking. "As for anything else..."

She wished he weren't looking at her in such an understanding way. What made things worse was, she didn't understand herself. The ensuing silence stretched awkwardly between them.

Nick broke it. "In any case, she's not my type." He smiled.

She wasn't about to ask what kind of woman that might be. That would be pushing her luck.

"So, what night should I come over?"

Come over? Oh, right. She'd asked him, so she could hardly backtrack now.

"Um...I mean, yes. Do come. When the book's done..." She was babbling and knew it, but was unable to stop. "You know, after it's finished and everything, and you have time—"

"Perhaps we ought to do this before you change your mind. How's Friday evening? Seven?"

Molly didn't even pretend to consult her calendar. "Sure. That's to say, perfect."

"Am I invited too?" Luke walked in from the back and stood twinkling at them benignly. "I'm kidding," he said, smiling as he glanced from one stricken face to the other. "But I'm glad you've buried the hatchet. Although even friends," he pointed out, "have to pay for their orders, don't they, Boss?"

"I was about to..." She made a show of searching for the code reader so she could ring up the sale.

Nick pulled out his wallet. "Absolutely." A pink tinge spread across his lightly tanned cheeks.

As he signed the sales slip, she checked the weather through the window. The Book Boutique only used paper bags, and she didn't want *Flutter* to become wet, though the rain had stopped, and a watery sun was breaking through. She slid the heavy volume into the largest bag they had and handed the package to her on-again friend.

"Thanks." He beamed at her and Luke before turning and walking out. Molly watched him as he headed toward home. She could feel herself blush when he smiled at her through the glass. He gave a small wave and kept going.

A flash of unease ran through her. How would Simon react to the fact that she and Nick were on a friendly footing again?

Well, too bad. She'd see Nick on Friday. Would Simon be watching? A shiver of something accompanied the thought. Butterflies.

CHAPTER FORTY-EIGHT

"Any plans after work?" Luke said when he returned from the Java Jive the following afternoon with a fresh cappuccino for Molly. She could get used to this kind of service. Luke rarely bought coffee from Renzo's place before the suggestion of the merger came up. Now it seemed he planned to help the café's bottom line by buying there two or three times a day.

She took a sip. "Perfect. Though we need to start using refillable cups to save on the paper ones, don't you think?"

"Indeed. I believe Renzo is planning to order some branded travel mugs when we open the bookstore/café."

Good to hear him embracing the project.

"To answer your question, I'm getting together with Renzo and Amanda later to talk about how we organize the interior of the new space, once the wall is gone."

Luke removed his glasses and blinked as he cleaned them with the initialed handkerchief he always carried. "Any chance I can join you?"

Molly was caught off-guard, not sure how Renzo would react. Luke was a major investor, and Renzo's boyfriend too. His faultless taste would ensure they ended up with something beautiful. Then again, she didn't want Amanda to feel they didn't trust her judgment completely.

"I'll only offer suggestions if you like," Luke went on. "But I have some ideas. After all, I have more experience in the bookshop than you do."

This was undeniable. He'd owned the bookstore much longer than she had. She would ask Renzo to decide, so if Luke's presence turned out to be a mistake, it wouldn't be her fault.

"If Renzo agrees, it's fine with me." She felt something like a mother whose offspring wants to do something, isn't sure she should allow it, and sends him off to "ask your father." She still wasn't accustomed to having a partner she needed to consult when making decisions. Apart from Simon, now and again.

Luke coughed. "Actually, he mentioned the meeting and when I asked if I could be there, he suggested I run it by you first."

Molly, relieved they'd cleared this hurdle, smiled at Luke.

"I guess that means you're coming. Some of it will be boring, you know. Figuring out how long things will take, especially. I don't want to close the store for more days than necessary."

"I know. But since we're planning changes, we may as well get it all done this time round, rather than in dribs and drabs."

"Agreed. I think Renzo wants us to meet in his apartment. He lives over the café, did you know?" She enjoyed a chance to tease her old boss.

Luke's cheeks glowed above his pink shirt. "I think I knew there were living quarters up there."

She smiled at Luke. "Should be easy to find, right?"

***

Molly turned the "open" sign to "closed" at six o'clock on the dot. Amanda had arrived five minutes before, carrying a sheaf of rolled-up papers under her arm.

"Ready?"

The samba music which had replaced the sad fado songs in the Java Jive gave it a more cheerful air these days. Renzo showed them the outdoor stairway, explaining that the inside staircase led into his office and storage area, which he liked to keep separate from his living space.

The windows were small, but at least they existed up here, and everywhere white painted walls reflected light. Molly's upper floor had none, which provided more room for shelving, but made everything appear lifeless, even with the lights turned on.

Renzo ushered them into the main room. "Welcome. Please sit." A table big enough for four people had been laid with a rust-red cloth. Three chairs the burnt-orange color of a monarch butterfly stood around it. Their host pulled up a fourth, this one a brilliant turquoise. Teal and burnt-orange throw cushions enlivened the white sofa against one wall. Molly noticed Amanda scanning the decor.

Renzo offered them each a *caipirinha*, which was now one of Molly's favorite cocktails. Once they had taken their places, Amanda unfurled the first of her rolls of paper and spread it out on the table.

"This is the floor plan of the combined store." She secured the curling corners with some mugs supplied by her host. "I think we should tackle first things first, which means repainting the floors and walls throughout."

Molly looked at Renzo for his reaction, and he nodded.

"I'm going to suggest a dark stain for the floor, possibly black if you like that look," Amanda continued. "The café walls are already a pale coffee, and a deeper shade—maybe coffee with cream—on the same spectrum would help define the bookshop."

"Won't that make it look gloomy?" Luke frowned as he stared at the paint samples.

Amanda carried on, unfazed. "Think about it—books provide a lot of color when they're displayed. If you keep the backdrop darker, they'll stand out more."

Renzo handed round a plate of tiny rolls. "*Pão de queijo*. Like cheese bread."

This didn't adequately convey the deliciousness that spread

over Molly's tongue as she bit into the delectable warm dough. Oh, well. Screw the waistline. She took another.

Renzo raised a question. "To paint, this will take some time, no? We shall have to close for a few days."

"We'll need to check with a builder. I reckon they could probably get it done in about ten days if the store is closed." Amanda sounded so confident that no one contradicted her. She went on to outline the new layout.

"I like it, but I have a problem," Luke said. "Doesn't this mean fewer shelves for books?"

Amanda didn't answer. Instead, she was busy unrolling the next sheet.

"I think you've forgotten about your upper floor. That area is at least the same size as this charming flat." Here she waved a hand in the general direction of the sofa.

"What are you saying?" asked Renzo.

"I think this has always been an apartment, probably for the owners originally. There's no record of the wall being built here, although there was likely a connecting door from the store once. The point is, this place has windows. I believe Molly's side does too. So, if we can uncover them, her space would be considerably brighter. People would be more inclined to browse."

Molly considered this for a moment. "I never thought about it before, but when you look up from the outside, you can see window frames."

"Aha." Amanda might have been Sherlock Holmes uncovering a valuable clue. "So, I'm thinking we can expose a couple of them to give you more natural light." She unfurled the last sheet of paper. "Assuming we can do that, here are my suggestions for that space."

Luke leaned forward, adjusting his glasses as he stared at the floor plan. "I wish I'd thought of this." His tone was rueful. "Though I don't suppose I'd have gotten round to it. I hate a mess."

Renzo looked at him. "Then you will have to avoid this

place while the building work goes on. There will be dust and bits of broken wall everywhere until they finish."

"No problem. I can find something else to do. How about selling some books on the sidewalk? What do you think, Molly?"

Amanda tsk-tsked. "Order, please, gentlemen. Let's stay on track." Her self-assured voice had been honed by years on the town zoning commission. She pointed at her plan. "As you can see, I've left the middle more or less open, so that it can house two rolling bookshelves. I'm thinking of making them low ones, for children, but that's up to you."

"I like it." Molly beamed. "Small children would be able to reach the upper shelf to find what they want. We can roll the shelves aside when we host events. Like author readings, and book clubs—"

"Also, some music evenings," broke in Renzo.

"Wonderful idea." The vision of a classical trio came to Molly's mind. Followed by a folk guitarist. A delighted audience applauding and smiling.

"I am thinking we will want more room if we plan to turn this into an arts center." Renzo's eyes reflected Molly's excitement at the prospect.

"It's a shame you live up here. We could use this side of the building too." Molly laughed, to let Renzo know she was kidding. Although...

"You think so, eh?" he said with a smile. "Maybe one day."

"Perhaps Renzo will settle down and won't need his bachelor pad anymore," offered Amanda. "Then you'll really be able to expand."

An awkward silence followed, until Amanda asked whether they'd decided on who should do the work of the painting and refurbishment.

"I want to ask Rocco Montefiore for an estimate," Molly volunteered.

"He is a nice man. He comes into the café for sandwiches

when he's working nearby. Turkey with cranberry sauce and lettuce." Renzo grinned at them. "Sorry. I have this bad habit—to identify people by what they order."

"I don't suppose he'll mind," Luke commented dryly.

"He's handled projects for me." Amanda seemed determined to keep them focused. "They've always come out well. His costs are reasonable and he leaves everything in perfect condition. He might take a little longer than some others, because he's detail-oriented where work is concerned."

"Nothing wrong with someone who wants to get it right." Luke wrinkled his brow, like a man trying to remember where he'd left his keys. "He's Rosie's friend, isn't he? Shortish guy. Broad shoulders. Handsome in a craggy way."

"Yes, and he's taken, if that's what you're getting at," said Amanda crisply.

Luke took off his glasses and began polishing them with unnecessary energy.

Renzo laughed. "Perhaps we shouldn't hire him if he's going to be a distraction."

"I was merely making an observation." Luke's tone of hauteur would have been envied by any aging aristocrat.

"Come on, you two. Back to work." Molly needed this to be settled. "The point is, I know Rocco will do a good job. In the meantime, we need to be ready for whenever Pilgrim Properties decides to take down the wall."

CHAPTER FORTY-NINE

As though she'd conjured him up, Simon, his voice clearer than his appearance, found her in the kitchen on Thursday, the evening before she expected Nick to come for dinner. She'd picked up some raspberries at Jackson's Pantry and planned to have those with some ice cream and a cookie for dessert. Now she was leafing through her favorite cookbook as she considered what the main dish should be.

She screwed up her eyes—she was having trouble making out Simon's misty form. Must be the humidity in the kitchen.

"*Darling, we need to talk,*" he said, without preamble.

She heard something, when he spoke, that made her put down the book and pay attention.

Simon leaned against the door frame. "*I miss raspberries.*"

An inexplicable shiver ran down Molly's back. Such an innocuous statement. Yet it underlined the fact that he would never taste one again.

He began to pace the kitchen floor. "*But that's not it. Honey, it's been over three years now, since—you know—I left, and...*" He hesitated. "*I think the time has come for you to let someone love you again.*"

Her heart stopped. Then started again. "I have people who love me." She counted them off on her fingers. "Heather, Jackie, Amanda, Rosie, Dad—"

Simon took a breath. He seemed to be finding this hard. "*Come on. You know that isn't what I mean. They're wonderful—no doubt about it. But it's not the same."*

He paused in his pacing to face her.

Molly considered his words. Of *course* she knew what he was getting at. "It's scary—the thought of someone completely new."

He continued to scrutinize her face. *"I can see how it might be. People leave. Sometimes forever. The love remains, though."*

Molly looked away, not wanting him to see the sadness in her eyes.

"Perhaps, to increase the odds next time," Simon said, brightening, *"don't choose a runner."* He smiled at her, and she tried to smile back. *"In which case, I think Nick might be suitable."*

She dropped the paring knife, and it clattered to the cutting board. That word again—*suitable.* And why had he landed on Nick? "What do you mean?"

"You know. Not an athlete. Husband material."

This again. "Don't be ridiculous. I'm not looking for a husband."

"You're still allowed to love a new person, even if you don't want the wedding ring."

She twisted the plain gold band she'd exchanged with him so long ago around her ring finger, a habit when anxiety overcame her. What was he suggesting? "Simon…" Words failed her.

"I know you're worried about loving someone and losing them. I know the way you think, sweetheart—if you don't love anyone, you can't have regrets. Right?"

Right. She gave a slight nod.

"You know, people generally regret the things they didn't do, not what they did. I never got to see the Pyramids, for instance. Anyway…"

"But—"

"No buts. You can do this."

"I can't." Her heart was beating fast. Too fast. This must be what it felt like to be stalked by a tiger. "I can't," she repeated, tears pricking her eyelids.

He ignored her. "*Yes, you can. You're such a loving person, and you shouldn't allow that to go to waste.*" He fell silent for a moment. "*But you'll only fall in love again if you can let me go.*"

The room tilted slightly, as if the world had spun off its axis without any warning. Let Simon go? Never.

"I won't. I can't." She was having trouble keeping her voice steady.

"*You can. You must.*" Simon's voice took on a husky tone as he said this, and he cleared his throat. His almost transparent face looked at her with so much tenderness that Molly, who'd been leaning against the counter, sank to the chair by her desk. She couldn't give this up. Knowing Simon would be there when she needed him.

"*I'll always be with you,*" said Simon, as if reading her mind. "*But I don't want to get in the way of your happiness.*"

He wasn't getting in the way. Though what had Nick said— he hadn't made a pass at her because she was still married to Simon?

"*Molly?*"

"Yes?"

"*I've been thinking about us. About me. I thought my job was to find you another husband. I realize I was mistaken. Just as well, since I never learned the knack of that, as it turned out.*"

Too true.

Simon hadn't finished. "*I think I'm here to help you move on—to be happy without me.*"

"But I am doing that—because of you. The shop is going to be great. I have new friends, and more confidence—all because you helped me."

"*That wasn't me. You already had that. It's just that you didn't let it shine through. Maybe talking to me helped a little. Either way, I know you can handle things on your own now.*"

The words sent a chill through Molly. She swallowed hard.

"But if I let you go…you might disappear." She couldn't begin to contemplate what would happen if she did.

Simon was whispering now. *"I'm certain you won't forget me. And you'll always have the love we shared. That doesn't mean you can't have more love in your life. It's the opposite. I want you to have more, much more. Enough to last you a lifetime. So, when you do find the right man, I'll be cheering you on."*

As Molly watched, emotionally drained, Simon faded away.

This was unbearable. How had Simon become so wise? And why did this hurt so much? She opened her mouth and began to howl, relieved the house was empty so she could cry herself out.

***

When Nick arrived for dinner the next day, he was carrying a modest bunch of yellow rosebuds, which he handed her without preamble.

"Just a few flowers."

"How lovely, thank you." Something stirred in Molly's memory. "Someone sent me yellow roses on Valentine's Day." She eyed him, checking for a reaction. Nick's face registered only polite interest.

"I never did find out who they were from. Was it you?" She'd be mortified if it wasn't. Embarrassed if it were.

"I thought they might cheer you up. From a friend to a friend."

"I ought to have figured that out. Thanked you then. But if you'll accept my thanks now…"

"No need. I'm happy you liked them."

"I did, but I like these even more." Rosebuds seemed a better fit for their current relationship. "Let me put them in water until I can arrange them properly."

While she filled a canning jar and stuck the flowers into it, Nick sniffed the air like a dog catching the scent of a well-grilled steak.

"Orange chocolate chip?" he guessed, after an expert sniff.

"Yup. I'm baking a few for the shop. I thought hazelnuts might be an interesting addition, but not this time, because of customer allergies."

"Well, if you want someone to test them for you, I'm available."

Molly smiled. "Okay. They'll be ready in time for dessert. Would you mind opening the wine? The glasses are over there. I need to check on dinner."

"No problem. And after I've poured, do you have anything that needs fixing?" he asked, smiling back at her.

She did. Her love life, if Simon was right. "I appreciate the offer, but everything's working—touch wood." Except my heart, she added silently. Because now she was almost certain Simon had gone for good.

"Nick, can we talk?" She busied herself arranging some vegetables on a baking sheet and putting them in the oven so she wouldn't have to look at him. The cookies needed a few more minutes.

"Sure. What's on your mind?"

Molly finally turned to face him and swallowed a mouthful of the pinot grigio Nick handed her, before speaking.

"Remember you told me I was still married to Simon?"

Nick's expression changed from relaxed to wary. Great. He was raising barriers already. Perhaps she ought to stop.

She took a breath. She could do this. If she didn't, nothing would change. "I guess you were right—then."

He nodded and waited.

"You also said friends have to be honest with each other."

"I did. Should I be worried?"

"No. Only I need to tell you..." Molly struggled to find the right words. What did she want to say? The timer pinged on the oven, and she opened the door to a blast of hot, orange-scented air. She lifted out the cookies and straightened up. She mustn't become distracted. "I believe...I'm not married anymore. Or at least, I'm trying not to be."

Nick contemplated her. She found the silence intolerable. The tray began to weigh heavy, and she placed it on the counter with a clatter. "I'm so pleased we're friends again." Was she making sense?

Evidently, Nick thought so. "Me, too. I had my work to distract me—and the book." He hesitated, as if deciding whether to continue. "But I missed us. The way we had fun with no emotional strings attached."

In spite of the heat, a shiver crossed the back of Molly's neck. "Oh, right. Exactly. No emotional strings. That's just how I feel."

He hadn't made a pass at her because she was still married—that's what he'd said. Now she'd told him she wasn't, almost thrown herself at him, and here she was, emotionally sprawling on the floor.

"I'm glad we're returning to what we had before," he said. "Going out. Dinner. Talking."

He couldn't make his feelings any clearer. All she'd done was make a fool of herself. And she blushed so easily. Well, she would have to act like an adult about this, though she felt the way she had at seven years old when she'd tried to kiss Bob Whatsisname in the school gym, and he'd pushed her away. Humiliated and confused. Determined not to try ever again.

"Sure." That was as adult as she could manage.

Nick grinned. "I'm looking forward to falling off roofs. To having you take care of Hadley when I do."

"No more falling off anything," She insisted on this. "But if you'd help me change a light bulb when I can't reach it, I'd be happy."

Happy wasn't the same as blissful. Still, having a friend was more important than looking for love, no matter what Simon said.

"Of course—and you might pay me in these—with the hazelnuts. If you want to." He helped himself to a still-warm cookie. "I like them even better than the forest-floor ones."

One more tiny thing to make it easier to let go of Simon. Not obliged to make his favorite cookies—because Nick preferred the new recipe. This was good.

"Don't eat any more of them." She smiled as she batted his hand away from the cooling rack. "Dinner's almost ready."

CHAPTER FIFTY

Molly sat in Shear Madness, having her hair cut. Rosie, snipping expertly, wanted to know how things were going.

"They're moving along, but I may be short-staffed soon, with so much to get done before the building work begins."

Rosie paused. "So, what will you do?"

"The girls are back from school, of course, but they have projects of their own. Jackie's found an internship in New York, which would mean she'd be commuting a couple of hours every day. So, she's going to live in the city with some of her friends."

"That's one of them fixed up, then. What about Heather?"

"I was hoping she'd be home and able to give me a hand in the shop, but she's interning at a place on the coast that does educational cruises for kids and adults. It's just up her alley. That's an eight-week gig, so I won't see much of her, either."

"Sounds like you need someone to help out at the store."

Molly, who'd been imagining the coming weeks as just a long empty stretch of time without her daughters, blinked and refocused. "I expect I can find someone."

"How about Kyle? He's seventeen now, and pretty responsible."

Molly turned her thoughts to Rosie's son. "I thought he was planning to join the army."

"He was, but when he heard that they'd give him a buzz cut, he changed his mind. I think girls have been paying more attention to him recently, which might have something to do with it." She caught Molly's eye in the mirror. "He's started reading, too."

Molly laughed, then noticed Rosie's expression. "I'm laughing because I'm delighted. It's not every young person who bothers to read a book if they don't have to. So, yes, please. Have him come in to see me, if he's interested."

Kyle had grown a couple of inches since Molly had last seen him, but she was careful not to mention this. She'd always hated people remarking on changes in her appearance when she was a teenager. His hair was the same black as his mother's and carefully styled—shaved at the sides but long on top. She wondered if Rosie had done it. Probably not. There must surely come a time when a boy rebelled.

He was trying to grow a beard, to judge by the wispy hairs around his mouth and chin. A small silver earring with a turquoise bead on it, finally gave her the clue. He looked like the pirate captain, Jack Sparrow.

He turned out to be strong and willing, two major assets. She hired him to work on Saturdays, to begin with, and then four more days a week. The store needed to be prepared for the big change, which meant temporarily reducing the stock.

She asked Rocco to build her a bookshelf on wheels that she had Kyle roll outside every day the weather was good. On it, she placed specially priced books, which attracted the attention of passers-by. And she began to ponder what she and Renzo could do for their grand opening as a bookshop/café.

She longed to launch Nick and Sonya's book, due to come out in the early fall. That would be a great way to make up for her past mistakes and maybe pay off part of the debt of gratitude she owed him for all his help.

***

"I wish we didn't have to close while they break through," said Renzo, his expression that of a man sunk in gloom, as he and

Molly stood by the travel section in the Book Boutique.

She could relate. "I know. It's tough. At least, after seven or eight days, Mick Cavelli tells me your place should be able to start up again. Mine might take a little longer, because of painting and such. But we'll certainly lose some business during the renovations."

"We could put the new bookshelves Amanda talked about in the café area if you're still closed."

"Thanks, Renzo. I'm hoping our core customers are loyal, so the impact shouldn't be too bad. Maybe it won't take as long as we expected if we're only rebuilding the arch, and not taking down the whole wall. We'll run specials when we reopen, to get people back into the store. How about you? Don't things slow up for you in the summer, once people begin to leave town on vacation?"

"Not necessarily. That's when the tourists start coming."

"What about putting a coffee truck out front? It won't have your usual elegant ambiance, but it may tide you over."

"Good idea, Molly. I will go to the town hall today." She could see his forehead smoothing out as he spoke. "This makes me feel better—I can still take care of my patrons while the building work is done."

Molly had canceled new deliveries for the next two weeks. Rocco was prepared to uncover the upstairs windows while Cavelli Construction was working in the store.

"Might as well make all the mess at the same time," he said with a grin.

***

A couple of days later, Nick showed up at the Book Boutique, tied Hadley up outside, and walked in.

"Wow. This does look different." His eyes scanned the space where shelving had been dismantled to allow the wall to come down. "How are the preparations going? Have you heard from your landlord about the date for construction?"

"It's becoming something of a nightmare," said Molly. "We just got word that Pilgrim has decided to go ahead right after July 4th. We'll need all hands on deck while we empty the place and refill it afterwards." The project, as her father had hinted, was turning out to involve more steps than she'd bargained for. Somehow emptying the store hadn't seemed like such a big deal in her imagination.

"I'm on vacation, you know, so I can give you a hand. When are you planning to do this?"

"As you can see, we've started already. We've only got a couple of weeks before the renovations start." Her brow furrowed.

"What?" he said.

She sighed. "Ten days seems like a long time to stay closed, but I guess it can't be helped."

"Tell me when you need me to move stuff. You should be able to get everything out fairly quickly, don't you think?"

"We will, with your help. So, thank you, Nick. That would be amazing."

Her debt to him was growing larger and larger.

"If you let your customers know, they can stock up before you close. Maybe Bill Hawley would put something in the *Bee*."

"I didn't think of that, but thanks for the suggestion." She made a note to call Bill. A small ad in the local paper wouldn't cost much, and if the editor wrote something in the "Town Updates" column, that would be a bonus. "Now, what can I do for you? Apart from setting you to work."

"I came in to find something light to read over the weekend. Now you've told me you'll be closed, I'll buy a couple more books."

Molly gazed at him. Such a kind man.

Nick chose two new thrillers and a spy novel from the stack near Molly. Other books sat around in what looked like haphazard piles. In fact, Molly knew exactly where everything was. Kyle had labeled each section as he removed the inventory from the shelves and stacked them on the floor.

"Thanks, Nick. I appreciate the business. I believe Luke put some more of those behind the desk." She pointed. "Let's see." She walked him back to the books labeled in Luke's unmistakable hand. Thrillers and suspense. She handed him another one to look at and he inspected the back cover before raising his head.

"Let me know when you need me to help out. Talking of taking time off, will you be able to relax while the store is closed?" He quirked a questioning eyebrow at her.

"In theory, yes. Though I'll still be dealing with things from home. Did you have a reason for asking?" He returned the James Patterson book to the stack and picked up something else.

"I've been meaning to ask you whether you'd like to come and see the Butterfly Encounter."

She'd never heard of the place. "What is it?"

"It's part of the Science Center in Hartford," Nick went on. "They have all kinds of live tropical butterflies, all under cover."

She pictured a vast conservatory, full of fluttering gem-like creatures, their colors winking in the sunlight. "Sounds lovely."

"It does, doesn't it? I know the man who runs it, and I think he'll give us free tickets. So, pick a day when the shop is closed, and we'll do it. It strikes me you need a break from all this."

Her back was beginning to ache after reaching and stooping to move books around. The invitation was becoming more appealing by the minute. "If we go, I know a little wine bar where we can get some lunch," she said. "My treat this time."

"So it is. Don't worry, I'll remind you. Now, let me pay for these…"

CHAPTER FIFTY-ONE

The Book Boutique and the Java Jive shut their doors for several days to allow the construction company time to do the demolition and build the connecting archway. Nothing, though, prepared Molly for the sinking feeling she experienced as she stood on the sidewalk and looked at the "Closed During Construction" sign she'd put up in the windows. Her customers would remain loyal, wouldn't they? Of *course* they would.

The workforce from Cavelli Construction arrived to prep the area they'd be working in. Mick Cavelli had promised to have crews in the shop around the clock to ensure the project came in on time. As soon as they finished their part of the job, Rocco would begin painting.

With nothing more Molly could do except worry, she and Nick drove to Hartford on the following Wednesday. As his car meandered through the smaller roads toward the state capital, she gave him an overly detailed rundown of everything that was happening with the Book Boutique, before eventually falling silent.

"So, not much going on, then?" Nick glanced sideways at her, as if checking to see how she was taking his gentle ribbing.

"Well, yes. Of course," Molly began. Then, realizing, she laughed. "You're right. This is supposed to be my day off. Even so, it's hard to forget the business stuff—worrying that something will go wrong when the work starts—"

"Okay," Nick raised a hand off the steering wheel and held it up, palm out, in her direction. "We need a time out. For the next three hours, you're not allowed to mention the shop, or the business, or the construction. After that, you can tell me all about it again. Deal?"

"Can I answer the phone if the builders call?"

"If you must. Just not in the butterfly pavilion."

"Deal. Your turn. Tell me what we're going to see."

He described it as best he could, but nothing prepared her for the extraordinary sight that greeted them as they entered the glass-ceilinged conservatory. The wave of heat and humidity struck her face, and she blinked before opening her eyes. Tropical planting in various beds contrasted with the brilliant colors of equatorial butterflies.

Molly grabbed at Nick's sleeve. "What's that one? It's huge."

The dazzling azure specimen had just landed on a toddler's head and perched there, like a wide-brimmed hat. While the child remained unaware of it, its parents pulled out their phones and were taking pictures as fast as they could before it flew away.

"Blue morpho." His voice was low, almost reverent. "Some of them get to be as wide as my hand or even larger."

As they strolled through the exhibit, Molly forgot all about business. A lime-green-and-black butterfly came to rest on the sleeve of her lemon-colored T-shirt.

"Keep still," he whispered. "It's a malachite. Gorgeous, isn't it?"

Molly turned her head to answer and found her face within inches of his. The faint scent of his aftershave filled her nostrils. She closed her eyes for a second. Suddenly, the heat became almost too much to take. "Beautiful," she said, and returned to her study of the insect.

But something in the air had changed.

She kept a foot or so of space between them as they continued to stroll among the flowers. He had an eye for pointing out tiny, hard-to-see black butterflies with an orange stripe, and the ones with transparent wings, like spun glass.

Only half her thoughts were on the butterflies flitting around them. The remainder were focused on those inside her chest. She hadn't felt this way for a long time. Stealing a look at his profile only confirmed her instinct—he was unmoved by their proximity.

After, as they walked the ten minutes or so to the wine bar, Molly kept the conversation on what they'd seen and her gaze straight ahead. But sitting across the small table from him, she found it impossible not to try and read his thoughts. Yet though he listened and talked, smiled and laughed, he revealed nothing of any feelings he might have for her.

"I like the menu," he said, studying it. "Perfect for lunch. See anything you like?"

Oh, yes. She did. Molly hastily switched her attention to the card and picked something she'd had before. "I'll have the crab cake, please," she told the waiter. "And the antipasto of the day, if you'll share, Nick."

"Great. But I don't think that'll be enough for me. I'll have a panini. The meatball one sounds good."

"Excellent choice, sir."

They ordered a glass of Malbec each, and then there was nothing to do but wait for their meal to appear.

Nick broke the silence. "How are you doing with not thinking about work? It's been almost three hours now."

Thank goodness. A reprieve from talking about anything too personal. She gave him a wry smile. "Thanks for asking. I turned the sound off on my phone, so I don't know if anyone's tried to reach me."

"You can check now, if it's bugging you."

The offer was tempting. The chance to hang out with him won out. "You know, I think I'll wait until we're on our way home, if you don't mind. Switching off for a while has been good for me."

They talked about their plans for the rest of the summer. Nick explained that he would be busy preparing for his book launch. "The publisher would like us to do some additional signings too."

"I'm glad you brought that up. I've been meaning to ask you, can I organize a launch party for your book at our grand opening? I realize it's very short notice, but I wanted to be sure we had everything finished before I suggested it. It's on…sorry, I need to check the date." She consulted the calendar on her phone. "It's the second Saturday in September."

The celebration was set for the weekend after Labor Day, when most people would be back from vacation and in the mood to start anew.

Nick flashed a glance her way and beamed. "I think that could work. I'll have to tell my publisher, because they'll want to organize the publicity and the shipping of books and so on, but sure. I'd love it."

"Wonderful."

"One thing. Strictly speaking, the book isn't out until the Tuesday after your grand opening, so they'll have to agree to an advance launch, so to speak."

Molly understood immediately. He'd have to put pressure on his publisher to let him do this signing.

"And I have to coordinate with Sonya because I'd like her to be there. Not always easy, since they have a weekend place they go to."

"Look, Nick, don't feel you have to do this. If it works, it would be wonderful, but if it causes problems, I can probably find a local author who'd like to do something."

"I'll let you know. What was the date again?"

Looking at her appointments reminded her that she had another invitation coming up. "Listen, Rosie's invited me over for a barbecue Sunday evening. Would you like to come?"

Good grief. Where had that come from? She hadn't intended to invite him. Rosie would be okay with it, wouldn't she?

But what if he came and didn't enjoy it? She stared out of the window so he wouldn't be able to read the anxiety that must surely be visible on her face.

"Is she expecting you to bring someone?"

Molly took a breath and returned her gaze to the road. "Not exactly, but I know she won't mind. She usually has about ten or twelve people, so another one won't make any difference."

Nick was silent, and Molly kept her eyes on the trees that were throwing dappled sunlight onto the road in front of them.

He seemed to come to a conclusion. "How about you check with her and let me know? I'd hate to crash the party."

"Her parties are always quite informal. And there won't be any work to do in the shop, because Rocco will only just have finished by then and everything will be drying out."

Nick grinned. "Oh, I get it. You're trying to sweeten me up, so I'll help you replace all the books afterward?"

She recognized his teasing and relaxed. "Certainly not. I wouldn't think of asking you. To help, I mean. You've already done enough."

Nick's face was thoughtful as he turned briefly to look at her. "So, you're inviting me purely because I'm ornamental?"

Molly felt certain that her cheeks were scarlet. She put a hand up to check. Yup. Burning. How to respond? May as well go for something lighthearted and hope he would think her funny.

"Well, Rocco's Mediterranean charm needs something a bit more Nordic to balance it."

"I knew having a Finnish grandfather would come in handy one day," he deadpanned, but his eyes told her he was laughing at her. With her.

"So, that's a yes?"

He nodded. "Why not?"

She would have preferred a little more enthusiasm. But he was coming.

***

As Molly cleaned off her eye makeup before bed that night, her mind raced. She had been so aware of his warmth as he stood next to her at the butterfly pavilion. His breath when he whispered into her ear. It meant nothing, of course. She was unaccustomed to it, that was all.

Only as her eyes finally closed around one-thirty in the morning did it occur to her that Simon hadn't checked in to find out how she was doing.

"Simon?" she murmured. She heard no reply, but she felt her muscles relax as she drifted off to sleep.

CHAPTER FIFTY-TWO

The builders had completed the structural transformation by early July. Molly looked through the arch and saw how much light flooded the shop, despite the polyethylene draped across the space—it benefited from Renzo's plate-glass windows. After the sheeting came down, she and Luke stepped into the café and surveyed the handiwork. It was amazing what a different vantage point did for a person.

Renzo came to stand next to his friend, flinging an arm around his shoulder. "What do you think, Luke? Do you like it?" he asked.

They waited. Afraid Luke was regretting the changes, Molly was about to reassure him that they would only be for the better, when he spoke up. "You were right. It's going to be wonderful."

Now that the store was larger, she needed to add another salesperson. Trey had asked if he could work the vacations, but he was leaving for college any day now. So, Molly ran a small ad in the *Brentford Bee*.

The first person to respond was Jenny Donovan, the young mother with twins, the one who'd been looking for a book club.

"The boys are beginning second grade soon," she said, "and I was wondering if you might need any help. Frankly, I'm pining for some adult conversation about books."

"Who are your favorite authors?"

"Well, you know I like historical fiction."

Molly did. Jenny was often one of the first to inquire about new titles and had mentioned starting a historical fiction book club.

"And I love Liv Constantine and Tana French."

Okay. Psychological crime with strong female protagonists. Some of them sociopaths.

"Oh, and I'm partial to a well-written dystopian novel once in a while too." Apparently feeling this needed clarification, she elaborated, "Like *The Hunger Games*, or Ben Winters' books, or Hugh Howey's *Silo* series."

"Perfect. I'm not as familiar with those authors as I ought to be, so your expertise will be welcome. How do you feel about three half days to start?"

***

On the day of the grand opening, Molly and Renzo stood surveying their domain.

"So, here we are," he said. "We've made it this far."

"Nervous?"

"A little. I know we have been open for a while, but in a way, today will make it all real."

Molly reminded herself it would all be over soon, and life would go on as normal. "Do you have your speech ready?"

"Kind of. How about you?"

"I have mine written down. I don't want to forget anything. Plus, I hate public speaking, so I've kept it as short as I can."

There were two things to cover this evening: the new name for the store, which they would unveil at six o'clock. Followed by Nick's launch.

Luke interrupted them. "Well, that's the upstairs arranged. Come and see."

"I have to check it out later," said Renzo. "We have customers already."

On the upper floor, small vases of flowers decorated a few

café tables, most of which had been pushed to the edge of the room, partially obscuring the newly located romance and children's sections.

Luke's suggestion that they buy tangerine folding seats to brighten the place up had taken Molly by surprise. Though they didn't cost much more than the black ones, they added a striking touch. Today, they were arranged to accommodate the audience for their first major event—Nick and Sonya's book launch. Some thirty copies of *An Everyday Guide to the World's Butterflies* lay stacked on two tables at the far end. Everything was ready.

Sonya and her husband were driving up from New York. Katherine from the art gallery in New Haven had hung some of Sonya's illustrations in the café, and they were for sale.

Molly sensed her mouth go dry. What if no one came?

"It'll be great," came Luke's voice somewhere nearby. "Don't worry."

"How did you guess what I was thinking?"

"I've known you a long time, my dear. You're good at this. You'll be fine."

She turned to smile at him gratefully. "I'm sure I will." If she acted optimistic, she'd become optimistic.

The flow of customers increased steadily all day. A two-sided chalkboard on the sidewalk proclaimed, "Grab a Coffee. Grab a Book," on one side, and "Special Book Signing Today," on the other. Two eye-catching, burnt-orange planters, with tall grasses, rust-colored chrysanthemums, and some ornamental kale stood by each door, making the shop easier to spot. Several visitors from further afield expressed their pleasure in finding such an interesting destination in this traditional town.

"See?" said Molly to Luke. "It's important to attract tourists. We should keep a supply of picture postcards here, and we could make a display of local guidebooks somewhere."

"It couldn't hurt. How about on one of the shelves in the café? Then anyone who stops in for coffee can find them."

Molly stared at Luke. "You're becoming a marketing maestro," she said in admiration. "For someone who almost expected books to sell themselves once upon a time, I'm impressed."

"You may not realize it, but there was a method to my madness back then. I had everything arranged in such a way as to draw people deeper into the store."

"So you did. I learned a lot from you—thank you." She felt a little moistening behind her eyes. There was nothing to cry about, for heaven's sake. This was a happy day. Only, she wished Simon could be here to witness it. Recently, though, he'd left her to get on with the business without comment.

She shook her head briskly, as if to reset her thoughts.

"Right. Where's my…"

Silently, Luke handed her a piece of paper covered in her handwriting. "I found this on the desk and thought you might need it. Funny how you abandon high tech when it's something important," he teased.

"Touché." She smiled and scanned the list. "Food—done. Drinks—done? "

"Prosecco, orange juice, club soda, and cola." He wrinkled his nose. "You think we really have to have that?"

"I'm afraid so. People expect a soft drink, and that's the easiest. Is Renzo going to have coffee available?"

"Yes. At least, so he told me. He's going to set up coffee urns in the café so that people can help themselves. He'll have someone monitoring it to make sure things don't get too messy, and to keep the supplies coming."

For the evening events, Amanda appointed herself head of catering and recruited Trey and Kyle to hand around hors d'oeuvres and beverages.

"You can't have a celebration without champagne," Amanda insisted, when Molly suggested they might offer some less expensive wine. "Besides, it's prosecco, so it won't break the bank."

"I'll drink to that. One of Rosie's trainee beauticians will be face painting in the children's department from two to four. Then, to celebrate Nick's book, she'll switch to doing butterflies for anyone who wants one, until the event begins. Have we got the butterfly gewgaws on display upstairs?"

Luke laughed. "Glad to hear you using the correct vocabulary. And yes, we have."

She'd managed to find all kinds of tchotchkes—magnets, cards, jewelry—to echo the book. Journals and kaleidoscopes decorated with butterflies, or lovely jigsaw puzzles made for great gifts. They had seed packets for butterfly gardens, which would be good till next spring at least. People had been buying those since before the book was available.

Molly checked her to-do list again.

"Nick should be here soon, and Sonya and her husband are supposed to be here sometime after five." She frowned, concentrating. "We must remember to check the microphone. And the video for our web page."

Molly wondered how many people would show up for Nick's signing. She'd emailed the customers on the mailing list, put it on their website, and Bill Hawley listed it in the *Bee*. Too late to do more now.

As the day wore on, her nerves subsided. Bonnie read the younger children a story before they left the store with bees, pirate eye patches, and rainbows decorating their cheeks. Their parents carried the books they'd bought.

There was a run on the LGBTQ books as Luke's friends showed up to cheer them on. He was going to host a party at his house after they closed, and she planned on going if she was still functioning by then.

Nick arrived half an hour later. "I just couldn't stand the waiting anymore, so I came to see if you needed a hand with anything."

"I think we're okay." She checked the last few items left on the sheet of paper, which she'd folded and refolded so many times that it seemed in danger of coming apart. "Although—

could you help Trey check the audiovisual equipment?"

"Happy to. Before that, though, have you eaten lunch?"

She glanced at her watch. "Wow. Two-thirty already. I haven't had time today, but thanks for asking."

"I didn't expect you to take time out—I made you a sandwich. Ham and swiss. Light on the mayo and mustard so it doesn't drip anywhere."

He'd made it? Her eyes met his for a fraction too long. "That sounds perfect, thank you."

Nick pulled a package wrapped in foil from the tote he was carrying.

"Sure thing. Why don't you eat it in the kitchen? I can keep an eye out for customers. I used to work here, you know." He winked.

Even if he was just a friend, the man was special, no doubt about it.

The afternoon passed in a blur. By half past five, the shop began to fill as people came to check out what was going on. The café did a brisk business all day.

Acacia turned up to share the honors of revealing the new name with Luke. They stood below the hidden sign, ready to pull the cord and release the cover.

Trey had installed a microphone on the sidewalk so that Molly and Renzo could make their brief speeches. Standing in front of it at one minute to six, she glanced up from the index card that contained her remarks and spotted a familiar face at the back of the crowd.

Channing. His presence might put a damper on their event. To her surprise, he smiled and raised a hand in a small salute. She waved back and pointed him out to Acacia, who beamed.

Time to begin. She stepped up to the microphone.

"Ladies and Gentlemen, thank you for being here today. First, I want to give special thanks to everyone who has made this possible. It's a very long list, but I'll try to be quick. I know this isn't the Oscars."

A low chuckle came from the audience.

"First of all, the people who've been with us from the start: Luke Bauer, whom you all know, Mrs. Acacia Todd, and Amanda Shaughnessy, who helped design the new shop. My dad, Tom Beresford…" She paused to point him out. "And his friend, Bonnie, who reads storybooks to our smallest customers." A smattering of applause greeted these last two names. It came from their smiling neighbors from Maple Corners.

"And, finally…"

Renzo stared at her in surprise. They'd agreed on the list of people just this morning, and Molly hadn't forgotten anyone.

"Finally—Mr. Channing Madison, without whose support none of this would have been possible."

The man in question gave an awkward smile and turned a rosy color as people craned their necks to identify him. He pulled at his collar with his forefinger, as though it were strangling him.

"And now we come to the main reason we're standing out here today. It's time to let you know the name of our new bookstore café."

She handed the microphone to Renzo. He cleared his throat and looked at Luke and Acacia, as if wishing they'd just release the banner and have done with it. Luke nodded his encouragement.

"I give you—Brentford Books and Beans."

CHAPTER FIFTY-THREE

Nick and Molly were the last to arrive at Luke's party. After the long and successful day, she'd been oddly reluctant to leave the shop—something like the way she'd felt when her baby daughter had been spirited away by a kind nurse so that she could catch up on her sleep. Grateful, but loath to let the day go.

Nick had stayed behind to help her tidy up and drove her over when they were done. He didn't say much as they tidied and moved things back to where they needed to be, for which she was thankful. Until finally, after signing the last few unsold copies of his book for future customers, he'd glanced up from the table and cleared his throat.

"I think it's time we joined the others, don't you? They'll be waiting for the star of the show."

"You, right?" Molly grinned at him.

Nick grinned back. "Not me, you."

"This isn't my show, it's for everyone. Me and Renzo, all the investors, and Luke too."

"Luke?"

"As the former owner, you know. He's watched his baby change into a handsome adult. And he invested too." Seeing the confusion on Nick's face, she added, "You know what I mean. It's a brand-new beginning for all of us."

Twilight was settling over the town as they reached Luke's house and searched for somewhere to park. The front door stood open, and a low murmur of voices wafted out to greet them. Nick indicated that she should enter before him. As they walked inside, he whispered, "This is where we first met, re-member?"

She twisted around to look at him. "So it is. It seems like ages ago, now."

Thanksgiving—almost a year before. In some ways, it seemed longer, in others, only yesterday.

"Ten months, two weeks, and four days," said Nick.

Molly stared at him. "What? You're very precise." She hadn't kept tabs on time that way since she'd been dating in high school. And none of those dates had racked up anything close to ten months.

"Well, it was Thanksgiving, and I'm good at dates. Profes-sor, you know."

Was he laughing at her? What kind of dates did he mean? A seedling of hope came poking through the cracks of Molly's façade. Perhaps he was interested in her after all. She still found him hard to read.

One thing she was sure of. She loved the way he took his work seriously, but not himself—so refreshing. So different from those men she'd met online. Not that there was any com-parison, obviously.

A careless guest bumped into her from behind, knocking her off-balance, and Nick grasped her arm to steady her, caus-ing a warm tide to spread through her.

She was about to thank him when he put a finger to his lips. "I think someone wants to say something."

Molly turned her attention to the fireplace, where Luke and Renzo were standing, each holding a glass of champagne. Someone clinked a knife against a bottle to silence the crowd. The few people still whispering and laughing, fell silent. Luke smiled at Renzo before turning toward the room.

"Ladies and gentlemen," Luke began. "Welcome to my home. And thank you for coming to the unveiling of the new store, Brentford Books and Beans." He lifted his glass. The audience applauded. "It's been an exciting day, and I think I speak for all of us when I say we're looking forward to a wonderful future."

More clapping and a smattering of "Hear, hears!"

"But that's not the only thing we're celebrating today."

Molly, staring at Luke in surprise, was struck by the sparkle in his eye. She glanced at Renzo, whose eyes were fixed on their host.

"I don't want to steal the thunder from Books and Beans, but I know Molly has guessed what I'm going to say, and I hope she doesn't mind."

Molly couldn't imagine what he might have to add to the celebratory remarks. Something about his future at the bookshop, perhaps. She nodded encouragingly at him. He grinned back.

"As you know, for a long time Renzo and I were business neighbors, but over the last few months, we have formed a closer relationship."

Why was Luke repeating what people already knew? She thought everyone had figured out that they were seeing each other. No matter. His advice and quite a bit of his money had made this venture possible. He was entitled to milk it a little. And there was no harm in declaring his feelings to the world.

"We..." Luke paused—for dramatic effect, she guessed. "We are planning to become life partners."

A moment of quiet followed, while some of the guests, including Molly, digested this information. She hadn't seen this coming. Not yet at any rate. Were they getting married? She tried to assume the expression of someone who'd known about this for ages. She'd never thought of Luke as the marrying type, but he'd continued to surprise her recently.

She turned to Nick. "Wonderful news, isn't it?"

His reply was drowned out by a chorus of congratulations,

whistles, and cheers that filled the room. But he nodded, and she saw his lips form the word yes. He gave her a thumbs-up.

Renzo raised a hand to silence them. "We hope to be married soon." He couldn't contain his happiness as he gazed at Luke, plainly in love. The applause began again.

Acacia sat bolt upright and leaned forward, her mouth open. Molly tugged at Nick's sleeve. "I have a feeling her hopes have just been blighted," she murmured.

"Maybe we should suggest she try that PlentyMorePebbles website you told me about."

A giggle erupted from Molly. "Shhh. Don't. She might find Channing on the same site."

His answering chuckle made some of the guests turn to look at them.

Across the room, Bill Hawley was helping Acacia, her face now more composed, to her feet. He took her arm and steered her over to Luke and Renzo. She talked to them for a minute and they kissed her on the cheek.

Passing Molly on her way out, she leaned down and confided, "They've invited me for dinner one night. Won't that be lovely?" Her smile might have been a little wobbly.

Molly put a comforting hand on Acacia's arm. "Indeed, it will. A regular treat."

"Wow. That was cool." Nick indicated the happy couple with a tilt of his head. "Did you expect them to announce anything here?"

"No. But it doesn't matter. I'm delighted for them." She smiled at the couple.

"Me too." Nick looked at her kindly. "I guess partnerships are happening all over the place."

Molly felt those butterflies again. Yet she had no reason to. Surely there was no hidden meaning in his words? She was hopeless at subtext if it wasn't in a book. Or might she be anxious because now that the business was settled, nothing barred her from focusing on her social life? Not a question to be answered now. This was Renzo and Luke's night.

"Come on," she said. "Let's go and congratulate them."

***

As the party wound down, Molly sank back into Luke's dark-blue sofa and took a sip of her gin and elderflower tonic. "Well, thank heavens that's over." She hoped her shoes were still under the seat, where she'd kicked them off when they began to feel a little tight.

"Fantastic, wasn't it?" Sonya, who'd remarked earlier that her wrist ached from signing so many books, had clearly forgotten about her discomfort. She raised her glass. "Here's to success."

The half dozen people left in the room echoed her toast. Most of the New York friends had departed. Amanda and Rosie had gone to spend the evening with their families.

Molly might have been content never to leave the sofa again, as she surveyed the room through almost closed eyelids. Every so often someone would say something to her, and she'd answer, if only to prove she was awake. The next statement startled her back to full awareness.

"And here's to love." Nick lifted his glass in a nod to their hosts. While their friends echoed him, most were looking at the happy couple. But Nick's eyes were fixed on her.

Molly had the sudden sensation that every nerve ending in her body was tingling. She was vibrating with something surely everyone could see. She imagined she was giving off sparks, the electricity level was so high. The excitement of the day, her exhaustion, the champagne, Luke's engagement to Renzo—they must be responsible.

No one in the room appeared to have noticed anything different about her. They weren't paying her any attention. They chatted amiably with each other and carried on as though nothing had changed.

And yet.

"Are you okay?" Nick's quiet voice brought her back. "You look a little…"

Molly inhaled to steady herself. "Just tired."

"We'd better get you home. Come on."

He stood and offered her a hand. She wasn't going to fall for that, in case it led to another electric shock. Ignoring it, she pulled herself up, encouraged to find that she was able to stand without any trouble. She struggled into her shoes. Inexplicably, her feet had grown by at least a size since she'd taken her heels off.

She walked over to Luke and hugged him. "Congratulations again. I'm very happy for you both." She gave Renzo a hug, too. "I can't believe it took me so long to notice you two were falling in love. I admit I did wonder about the quantity of coffee Luke was consuming."

Luke took his fiancé's hand. "In my defense, it is excellent coffee. Though not the main attraction, of course."

"I will be living here from now on. I mean full-time." Renzo smiled, and Molly saw why Luke found him irresistible.

Affecting an air of innocence, she murmured, "So your apartment will be available?"

"Hey, we talk business on Monday. Tonight, we celebrate."

"I'm only teasing. Thank you for organizing a lovely party. We've certainly launched the store and your engagement with a bang."

"Best wishes to the two of you." Nick hadn't had the chance to say anything until now. "One of your most successful parties, Luke. I'm glad you began inviting me all those years ago."

"My pleasure. I like bringing people together."

Molly sensed the conversation heading into murky waters. "I must get some sleep—I've been up since dawn."

"Your carriage awaits." Nick offered her his arm, and they headed home.

CHAPTER FIFTY-FOUR

Molly sat in the passenger seat of Nick's car, inhaling the scent of him, which seemed to permeate the interior. Light-headed had taken on a whole new meaning this evening, and she tried to talk herself out of these unfamiliar sensations as she sat there, stealing surreptitious glances at his profile.

She no longer saw his nose as beaky, the way she had when they first met. It was strong, like his faintly stubbled jaw. The wrinkles around his eyes were clearly caused by amusement—laugh lines. It occurred to her to wonder whether he'd been seeing someone else all this while. Just because he hadn't had anyone over didn't mean that there was no woman in his life.

A tear began pricking the back of her right eye. It must be the let-down after a huge success like the opening. Her mother, once a stalwart of the local amateur dramatics company, called it post-performance blues. That was it. She fumbled in her handbag and then her jacket pocket for a tissue, and, unable to find one, gave a loud sniff.

"You okay?" Nick shot a look her way and then focused on the road again. They were almost home.

"Of course. It's been a great day. Though the party may have been a celebration too far."

He didn't answer. They pulled up in his driveway and Molly continued to sit there, staring absently through the windshield. Here they were again. Back at the status quo.

Nick opened the door for her, and she stepped out of the car and winced, nearly missing her footing in the painful heels.

"Steady there." Nick took her arm. "Let me see you to your door."

"I'll be fine, don't worry."

Ignoring her protest, he walked her over to the house. Her head swam as she found the key. When she thanked him for the ride home, he moved toward her and she closed her eyes, because now, surely, he would...

"Get a good night's sleep, Molly," he said, leaning in for a hug. "You'll feel better in the morning."

He was almost brotherly. She shut the door behind her and sighed.

Nick. So caring, so appropriate, so gentlemanly. But she didn't want caring. Or appropriate. And definitely not gentlemanly. Not at this moment.

She wanted something more. Skin. A little stubble rubbing against her cheek. The feel of auburn curls in her fingers. She exhaled. The little tear gave up the struggle and trickled down the cheek where his stubble should have been.

Hemingway must have been lying in wait for her, and he purred loudly as he twined himself between and around her legs. No wonder unmarried women kept cats. Cats were so much easier than men.

***

The next morning, Molly sat in the little kitchen at the back of the store, waiting for the kettle to boil. Overcome by exhaustion, both physical and emotional, she'd slept as if drugged, and rose as Nick had predicted, feeling more like successful businesswoman Molly Stevenson. Last evening had been an aberration. She was in full command of herself now.

She began to make a list. Lists kept her organized. This one would help her contemplate the things she had to be thankful for.

Item one. Her friends, always willing to call her out, and then to support her decisions. Amanda and Rosie, of course. And Nick too. Better a friend than not there at all.

Item two. Her father and Bonnie, who made a point of inviting her when they planned visits to gardens or museums.

Item three. Her daughters and their ability to inspire uncomplicated love while giving it back.

Item four. The bookshop. She was grateful for that. No question.

Surely, that should be enough. She had no business wanting more. Look what happened to people who asked for more. She had a fleeting vision of Oliver Twist being thrown out of the workhouse and into a life of child labor. She blinked and snapped her attention back to the present.

The kettle switched itself off, and she rose to pour boiling water over her English Breakfast tea bag. A splash of milk and it was ready. Her *Keep Calm and Read On* mug reminded her that books never let her down. She squared her shoulders and carried her tea back to her desk.

Molly unlocked the front door to let in Miss Johansen, who'd been waiting outside, clutching her eggs and beaming. She must be freezing in that tiny, leopard-print skirt, even with the little fake fur jacket. A stiff autumn breeze was making its presence felt out there.

"I'm sorry I couldn't stay all day yesterday, but I had to get back to my sister. I'm sure it was a big success. I've brought you some eggs."

"Well, thank you, Elaine. And are you looking for something to read this morning?"

"Heavens, no. These are by way of a gift for your grand opening. I've got a couple of Lucinda Parks books from the library. They'll keep us going for a while. But thank you."

"I should thank you. You've been a loyal…" What was the word? Customers paid for things, didn't they? "…patron over the years."

Miss Johansen lowered her eyes and blushed like an ingénue. "Always happy to support a worthy endeavor like this one. And the place looks even better than it did in my day."

Molly couldn't subdue a grin. Worthy endeavor? Well, why not? She'd take it.

"I must go. I've got errands to run. See you soon."

As her oldest customer left, Molly held the front door open for her. She turned and surveyed the books and other book-related items with satisfaction. The shop was making money—enough to pay her and her employees. Even if some of the income was in the form of eggs.

Luke would be in any minute. He liked working part-time, and being so close to his fiancé all day was a bonus. He posted book reviews on the shelves, ensured the café always displayed the latest cookbooks and the store presented its best face. A new collection of LGBTQ literature now had its own section. A self-explanatory rainbow showed people where to look.

He enjoyed his continuing rapport with older customers, too. They included Acacia, the uncontested doyenne of the newly established Outrageous Book Club, whose mission was to introduce readers to books they might not otherwise try. This had been surprisingly successful, according to some of the regulars. Among them Miss Johansen, who usually turned up with a library copy, and Bill Hawley of the *Brentford Bee*. The latter became involved when he came to confirm a few details for the events page in the paper and fell under the spell of Acacia, who had stopped by.

"Of *course* you'll enjoy it, Bill. You need to expand your horizons. Get out of your journalistic rut," Acacia prodded him. "We're reading a memoir by the young woman who ran away to join a cult and then left to become a nun before eloping with the bishop's nephew. I'm enjoying it so far."

His startled expression evoked a chuckle from Acacia. "Don't be such a stick-in-the-mud. Covering neighborhood activities like our club is practically obligatory for a local paper."

With the air of a rabbit hypnotized by a particularly so-phisticated weasel, Bill agreed to come to the first meeting and promised to show up at the second one too. Molly wondered idly what the age difference was between them. One never knew.

Channing helped too—and made a point of ordering books to be sent out to his many business associates. He wanted Brentford Books and Beans to take care of the mailing, and when Molly saw the title he'd chosen, she almost turned him down. In the interests of good relations, though, she agreed. She drew the line when she spotted her own name on the list, and quietly crossed it off, reducing sales by one.

Her father came in once a week to say hello and often stayed to chat with customers. His expertise lay in sport and golf—subjects she never had any interest in mastering. Bonnie sometimes accompanied him to read to the toddlers. When storytime was over, she sat upstairs with her computer and worked on her novel. She told Molly she was writing a mystery story about a murder in an art gallery that would be solved by a silver-haired docent with a handsome boyfriend. And why not?

***

The weather had qualified as an Indian summer recently, and on occasional days off, Molly's father, Bonnie, and she would drive to a museum or park, stopping for lunch on the way. Bonnie proved to be knowledgeable about art—she volunteered at a small museum dedicated to nineteenth-century painters.

Molly enjoyed becoming acquainted with her father's girl-friend—and still smiled when he used the term. Her father seemed unaware that his "girl" had the face of a well-preserved woman in her mid-seventies. Although he hadn't said anything directly, she expected he and Bonnie would announce their en-gagement soon.

One Sunday afternoon, as they wandered around an exhibit at the Yale Art Gallery, Tom drew his daughter aside while his girlfriend was studying an Impressionist painting. "You know what I like about Bonnie?" He kept his voice low.

"Sure. She's attractive, she's smart, and she clearly adores you."

Tom's face turned pink, making him resemble one of Bonnie's accessories. "Yes, of course. But what I meant was—she keeps me interested."

Molly wasn't sure how to take this. "How do you mean?"

"Well, I never used to take much interest in art or music or cultural stuff. You know me. Always content with a book, or messing about in the garden, or having a drink with friends."

"Nothing wrong with that."

"No. But Bonnie encourages me to get out and try different things. I'm finally beginning to understand why people like paintings and sculptures. She's always asking me to do something new, and she makes it fun." Tom beamed at her.

"I'm delighted for you, Dad." She loved the way Bonnie brought out this unsuspected side of her father. It gave them all one more thing in common.

"And you know what? Memories of your mother aren't holding me back anymore." He blinked as if to get rid of a stray eyelash.

Molly hugged him. "That's good, Dad. You deserve to be happy again. You're the best."

Tom looked self-conscious, but not displeased at this compliment.

"Thank you, sweetheart. I'm going to remind myself of that anytime I have doubts."

"By the way, Dad." She caught his eye. "Any thoughts about making it official?"

The furrow between Tom's brows disappeared as if he'd shed ten years, and he smiled. "Well, I don't want to say anything right now, but I'd like that."

He glanced at Molly with an unspoken question. "But only if you approve. Because I haven't proposed yet, and I won't, if you think it's a bad idea."

She hastened to reassure him. "Oh, Dad. I'm all for it." Simon's observation sprang to her mind. "People's biggest regrets are the things they don't do. You don't need my blessing, but you have it anyway. Be sure to tell me when you fix the date, and I'll be there helping you two plan it."

As he finished speaking, the woman under discussion turned her head toward them and smiled. Her eyes sparkled like a young girl's. Tom guided Molly over, and the three stood in front of the Degas, enjoying each other's company.

Molly's thought drifted. What kind of wedding might they like? What on earth would constitute an appropriate gift? And what must it be like to take the plunge again at their age?

Fine, if appearances were anything to go by.

CHAPTER FIFTY-FIVE

The social life on Molly's gratitude list consisted largely of hanging out with her two best friends.

Amanda and she would find time to meet for lunch every couple of weeks, and Rosie would join them after work now and then for a drink and some gossip. This evening, they were standing in Rosie's compact kitchen, where Amanda was mixing *caipirinhas* for them.

"Renzo's cocktail is a definite winner," she announced as she muddled lime wedges and brown sugar in a glass pitcher. She topped it up with *cachaça* and poured the contents over the ice nestling in the bottom of Rosie's best tumblers.

"I agree," said Molly. "Can't wait to take a sip. It's been a long day."

"Owning your own business is always hard work, but it's so worth it, don't you think?" Amanda was an independent Realtor, though her life was so well organized that she always seemed to have free time when she needed it.

Rosie laughed. "You're right. And we deserve to kick back with this yummy drink. Although I think I will always associate it with summer—it's so refreshing."

"Nick makes them with chunks of pineapple, which is delicious too."

A moment's silence greeted this, before Rosie said, "Talking of summer, why don't we make the most of the last of it and go sit on the porch."

They picked up their drinks and wandered out. Rosie offered them tiny pastry pockets, which she'd made herself. "These are vegetarian empanadillas, in case anyone doesn't like beef."

"Scrumptious," mumbled Molly, savoring the spicy vegetables inside. "Thank you. I'd love the recipe. I might make these for…my dad." They couldn't tell that she'd been about to say Nick, could they?

Her girlfriends had stopped harping on about her love life, and hadn't raised the subject of online dating since the fiasco with Andy, the over-optimistic married swinger. Whenever she mentioned Nick, though, they'd glance at each other knowingly.

"It occurs to me," said Rosie. "You talk about Nick quite a lot."

"I do not." She didn't, surely. "Do I?"

Something about this made her friends burst out laughing.

"Only about once every ten minutes." Amanda held her hands out toward the fire that Rocco had lit for them in the pit before leaving them to chat in peace.

"Oh." Molly, not sure what constituted a crest, was certain hers had fallen.

She was finding it harder to lie to herself these days. She and Nick still went to concerts and the theater and other cultural events, but sitting next to him in the warm darkness of an auditorium only made her long for something more. Yet Nick never so much as hinted that his interest in her was anything other than friendly. At the end of a "date," he would kiss her cheek but never go further. It was better than nothing. Just. "Only, we hang out together all the time, but things aren't going anywhere."

As often happened, Amanda and Rosie spoke simultaneously.

"And you want something more?"

"When did you change your mind?"

Molly flushed, hoping her friends would think it was only the firelight. "I can't say exactly." Though she could. The shift had come about after Simon left her for the last time. She still heard his voice—a whisper in her head, frequently saying something to make her smile. She supposed she always would, which was comforting. He would continue to be on her side, no matter what. And he thought Nick was "suitable." Not that his opinion made any difference to her now.

"Nick's a kind man—" Amanda began.

"And good-looking too," put in Rosie.

"Yes, he is. I know he likes me, but something is holding him back."

"He's interested. I know he is." Amanda glanced at Molly who was biting her lower lip. "Maybe he's just shy or thinks you'll reject him. Why don't you make the first move?"

"I couldn't possibly—I would never have the nerve."

"Sure you could. You pulled off a great business deal, which took some doing. Now all you need is to show a little moxie and take a risk with Nick."

"What's the worst that can happen?" Rosie added.

Molly considered this scenario. Nick's breakup with Sam had hurt him badly. At least, she assumed so, since he never talked about her. He might not be ready to contemplate a new relationship. What if she told Nick how she felt, and he ran for the hills?

"I might lose him—as a friend." She heard her voice catch, but succeeded in controlling the threatening tears.

"That is the risk you take. But it might be better to know than to speculate."

"Amanda's right. And I'm certain Nick doesn't want to stop seeing you either, given the number of times you guys get together."

"I guess we'll just have to see what happens." This was chickening out, but Molly couldn't commit to anything at this point. She took another sip of her drink, but it had lost its sweetness somehow.

***

Molly rarely asked Nick to fix things for her these days—she was determined to attempt minor repairs herself. She'd even succeeded in repairing a running toilet not long ago, after watching a video.

But when he offered to help clear the leaves, she accepted without hesitation.

"That would be wonderful. I love my trees, but all the leaves tend to fall at once, and it all gets a bit overwhelming." They stood outside, one on each side of the hedge that divided the properties, scanning her back yard, where a moving tide of red and gold below her maple was undulating in the breeze.

"Happy to do it. And maybe we could get mine done another day."

"Of course."

Nick had a much smaller garden and only one tree, so she was definitely getting the better deal.

Molly sat in her sunny kitchen on the following Sunday morning, eating a slice of buttered toast spread with some of the homemade blueberry jam that Rosie had given her. She surveyed the back yard, where huge numbers of fallen leaves were lying in drifts, waiting for her and Nick to clear them away before they turned to mulch.

When Jackie and Heather were little, she'd enjoyed helping Simon rake the crunchy leaves into piles on top of a bright blue tarpaulin. Until the girls were seven and nine, when they decided they were too grown up to do so, they'd throw themselves into the pile to roll around, shrieking and giggling, all but drowning out the crackle of the leaves. Afterward, Simon and her dad, if he was over, would barbecue hot dogs and hamburgers.

Molly smiled at the memory and went to find her Wellington

boots. Tucking her faded jeans into them, she pulled a quilted vest over her old red sweater and headed outside to begin work.

She inhaled a faint whiff of smoke and picked up a rake. She enjoyed the smell of autumn. The illegal bonfires that some stubborn neighbor would insist on lighting, the loamy aroma of the ground after rain, and later, inside the house, warm apple cider, fragrant with cinnamon, steaming on the stove—these aromas signaled the beginning of the cozy season.

"Good morning." Nick's cheerful greeting broke into her thoughts.

"Oh, hi. Thanks for coming over."

"This is a great day for doing the leaves. I found a rake in the basement, so I'm ready to go."

Soon they were working side by side in the October sunshine, raking, and tidying her flowerbeds. She and Nick were putting the garden to bed for the winter. She shouldn't be thinking about Nick and bed in the same sentence. Focus. She pulled up the remains of some wilting bee balm, one of his recommendations. The butterfly garden–the one he'd helped her plan—had been wonderful that summer. A few dahlias and the Montauk daisy were still blooming.

"Thanks for helping me with the leaves," said Molly, as they sat in the kitchen a couple of hours later. They'd kicked off their shoes, and she'd made them a sandwich each.

Nick prized open a bottle of local hard cider and poured it into two glasses. "You're very welcome. I like some outdoor exercise."

"Let's take all this into the living room and relax. You've earned it."

She picked up a plate of sandwiches and nodded at the cider. Nick followed her through and arranged himself in an armchair before accepting a sandwich and taking an appreciative bite. She'd filled the crusty baguette with ham, tomato, and lettuce and added a touch of English mustard too, to jazz up the flavor.

"This is great, thanks," he said, his mouth still half full, as he held the sandwich in both hands.

"It's the least I could do."

Minutes later, she settled into the sofa across from him, with the rest of her cider, and a sense of satisfaction at a job well done. Nick was such a good neighbor. Which was lovely. And the problem.

She couldn't see a way to turn them into more than neighbors. Amanda wanted her to make the first move. But how could she, when she'd never done anything so brazen in her life? She caught herself. Now she was being ridiculous. *Brazen* was one of her mother's words, for sure, usually followed by *hussy*. Her mother was so last century.

But the thought of starting something, throwing herself at him, offering herself to him—they all sounded wrong.

Their empty plates with a few final crumbs littered the coffee table. Molly raised her glass of cider and took a sip. "You ever think about the future?"

Nick straightened up in the armchair opposite, where he was sprawling. His expression changed from relaxed to wary, like a contestant in a game show anticipating a trick question. Hadley, who'd been snoozing in front of the fire, with Hemingway snuggled against her chest, lifted her head as if she sensed something in the air.

"How do you mean? Like the future of the planet? Old age? What?"

Oh. This wasn't promising. But, fortified by the cider, she carried on. "You know, personally—relationships and so on. Don't you ever feel lonely?"

She was being way too obvious. She felt the blood rising in her cheeks. How mortifying.

"Not really. After all, you and I…" Nick was staring at her, his face quizzical.

Too late to quit now. "I wasn't thinking of friends. I meant, you know, lonely for something more than friendship."

Nick looked away, and she thought she saw his jaw harden, as though he were trying to control his emotions. "I guess I'm like you," he said. "I can be happy living on my own."

"Living on your own is one thing. Living without love is another." Where was all this coming from? Was she talking about him, or herself? She couldn't back off now.

Nick stared at her, his expression that of a man who's been asked to explain his philosophical worldview in a sentence. "Love is a minefield. And people get hurt."

She understood that. She felt the same way sometimes. "I know." So how was it possible for her to feel this way, if what he said was true? A flicker of something—a moment of insight—brought results. "It isn't love that hurts you. It's not having someone to give it to."

Nick said nothing for a while. He looked down at his hands, then raised his head. "And is that what you're looking for? Because after your experience, that's courageous."

Maybe it was. All she knew was that she was compelled somehow to take this chance. "I can't not try. It's time for me to fall in love again." She gulped and went on. "People have been telling me so for ages. And I think I'm ready now."

The silence stretched on and on. Well, so much for making the first move. She'd frightened him away, and no wonder.

"Oh?" When he finally spoke, Nick's voice remained neutral. His eyes were hard to read, because he sat with the light from the window behind him.

So, falling for someone might be fine for her, but not for him. An unbidden tear slid down her cheek. Oh, god. So many tears prepared to give her away.

Nick stood and came to sit next to her. He lifted a hand to her cheek and rubbed the tear away with his thumb.

"What is it, Molly? Something I said?"

Was he being deliberately obtuse? She wished she knew what he wanted.

"No, nothing you said. I'm happy, I think. A little sad too.

There will always be moments, probably."

He leaned forward and took her face in his hands. "Well, let me be here for those times." His sea-green eyes stared into hers as he kissed her lightly on the lips. "And you can be there for mine, if you want to."

Molly barely caught the drift of what he said next, and afterward, could never remember his exact words. An intense wave of energy and desire was surging through her body. She didn't question it. She bent toward him, parted her lips, and kissed him, her hands reaching for the back of his head to hold him closer. His heart beat against hers. A strong, living heart.

When they finally broke apart, he was still looking at her. "Molly…"

"I'm sorry. I don't know what came over me. I suddenly felt…"

"I don't care what came over you," he said. "I like it—very much."

He put his arms around her and kissed her again. Molly closed her eyes and gave herself to the kiss and the ones that followed. Her mind had fallen silent. All commentary drowned out by one certainty—no matter what came next, she and Nick could be happy.

She still had a month until her big birthday.

***

After Nick left to take Hadley for a walk, she sat, considering what had just happened.

An unexpected flash of scarlet caught her attention. Molly glanced out the window. A male cardinal was perched high in the leafless maple that stood in the corner of the yard, from which vantage, she supposed, he could survey his kingdom. She must remember to fill the feeder.

Molly scanned the garden for his less showy mate and spotted her on the hedge that separated her property from Nick's.

As she watched, the olive-green female took off and soared into Nick's yard.

The crimson bird flew closer, landing on the statue of Saint Francis that her mother, a staunch atheist, had given her years ago. He cocked his head to one side as if he could see Molly through the glass, in spite of the wavy effect created by being hand-rolled a century before. Molly stared back at the cardinal, which slowly closed one eye before opening it again.

Was it the window? Or had that cardinal really winked at her?

She smiled involuntarily.

The bird nodded. Then he opened his beak and let out a string of notes that sounded as though he were celebrating the day.

She grabbed her coat and set off to meet Nick on his way home.

* THE END *

ACKNOWLEDGMENTS

If you're the kind of person who reads the acknowledgments at the back of the book, you probably know that no book is written by the author alone. Not even the best-sellers. Especially not the bestsellers. So I want to thank the people who helped me realize my dream of publishing my debut novel (hopefully to be followed by another!).

First, thanks to my critique group, who as ever, gave me helpful suggestions, as well as all the encouragement a writer needs. Liz Morten, C. Lee McKenzie, Gillian Foster, and Lori Stewart believed in Molly from the start, and made me produce new pages every week until I was done.

The women writers at the Women's Fiction Writers Association were a godsend. Their daily write-in sessions, beginning at the start of the pandemic lockdown, finally made me sit and write every day. Without them and their humor, support, and encouragement, I might not even have a first draft yet.

Among them are Carla Damron, Lita Harris, Pamela Stockwell, Marie Watts, Joan Fernandez, and Stephanie Claypool, who read it and liked it enough to review it before it was published. Thank you!

Kim Caldwell Steffen was my first editor and improved the book immeasurably. Kelly Hartog suggested making Molly the owner of the bookstore, not an employee, which inspired me to revise it to what you see here.

The team of people at Atmosphere Press includes editors, artists and designers, formatters, proofreaders, and production and distribution experts. Any typos should probably be laid at my door, since I signed off on the final version! Thanks in particular to Megan Turner, Alex Kale, and Ronaldo Alves, Erin Larson-Burnett, Cameron Finch, Cassandra Felten, and David Wojciechowski for delivering the book, and always being there to answer any concerns I might have had.

I have to thank my social media expert and marketing assistant Kiana Stockwell, who has made sure that readers, including you, know about the book.

And thank you to my family and friends, who encouraged me and believed I could do it, even when I had doubts.

ABOUT ATMOSPHERE PRESS

Atmosphere Press is an independent, full-service publisher for excellent books in all genres and for all audiences. Learn more about what we do at atmospherepress.com.

We encourage you to check out some of Atmosphere's latest releases, which are available at Amazon.com and via order from your local bookstore:

Icarus Never Flew 'Round Here, by Matt Edwards

COMFREY, WYOMING: Maiden Voyage, by Daphne Birkmeyer

The Chimera Wolf, by P.A. Power

Umbilical, by Jane Kay

The Two-Blood Lion, by Nick Westfield

Shogun of the Heavens: The Fall of Immortals, by I.D.G. Curry

Hot Air Rising, by Matthew Taylor

30 Summers, by A.S. Randall

Delilah Recovered, by Amelia Estelle Dellos

A Prophecy in Ash, by Julie Zantopoulos

The Killer Half, by JB Blake

Ocean Lessons, by Karen Lethlean

Unrealized Fantasies, by Marilyn Whitehorse

The Mayari Chronicles: Initium, by Karen McClain

Squeeze Plays, by Jeffrey Marshall

JADA: Just Another Dead Animal, by James Morris

Hart Street and Main: Metamorphosis, by Tabitha Sprunger

Karma One, by Colleen Hollis

Ndalla's World, by Beth Franz

Adonai, by Arman Isayan

ABOUT THE AUTHOR

photo credit: Amy Dolego-Winton Studios

Gabi Coatsworth was born in Britain but has spent most of her life trying to figure out how America works by living there. So if you find a British flavor in her books, don't be surprised. Her memoir, *Love's Journey Home*, was published in May 2022, by Atmosphere Press.

Unlike many writers, she can't write in coffee shops because they're too distracting, and she only drinks coffee as a last resort. She lives in Connecticut in a cottage that's American on the outside, and English inside. If she's not reading, writing, or traveling, you'll find her in her flower garden, and holding a cup of her preferred beverage, strong English tea – she believes Earl Grey is for the weak.

You can find her all over the internet. And to learn more, or to sign up for special bonus materials, start here: https://linktr.ee/gabicoatsworth or on her website www.GabiCoatsworth.com.

MORE FROM
GABI COATSWORTH

If you've enjoyed this book, you'll like *Love's Journey Home*, Gabi's memoir of romance, reality, and redemption. Part romance, part medical memoir, all heart, it's for everyone who needs to know that they can make it through life's hardships and find happiness again.

Described as 'captivating from the first page," "touching and beautifully written," and "a page-turner" by reviewers, its average Goodreads rating is 4.75.

Available from your favorite retailers.

CPSIA information can be obtained
at www.ICGtesting.com
Printed in the USA
LVHW092138260723
753599LV00032B/435